ORIGIN

A LUX NOVEL

BOOK FOUR

Other books by Jennifer L. Armentrout

The Lux Series:

Obsidian: A Lux Novel, Book One
Onyx: A Lux Novel, Book Two
Opal: A Lux Novel, Book Three
Shadows: A Lux Novella

The Covenant Series:

Daimon
Half-Blood
Pure
Deity
Apollyon

Single Titles:

Obsession: An Arum Novel
Cursed

ORIGIN

A LUX NOVEL
BOOK FOUR

JENNIFER L. ARMENTROUT

This book is a work of fiction. Names, characters, places, and incidents are the product of the author's imagination or are used fictitiously. Any resemblance to actual events, locales, or persons, living or dead, is coincidental.

Entangled Publishing, LLC
2614 South Timberline Road
Suite 109
Fort Collins, CO 80525
Visit our website at www.entangledpublishing.com.

Edited by Liz Pelletier and Karen Grove
Cover design by Liz Pelletier

Ebook ISBN 978-1-62266-076-6
Print ISBN 978-1-62266-075-9

Manufactured in the United States of America

First Edition September 2013

The author acknowledges the copyrighted or trademarked status and trademark owners of the following wordmarks mentioned in this work of fiction: Lite-Brite, Netflix, Whopper Jr., *The Hunger Games*, *Terminator*, Kool-Aid, G.I. Joe, NFL, Eurocup, Mogwai, Gizmo, *Gremlins*, Disneyland, *Cloverfield*, Magneto, *The Omen*, Match.com, Applebee's, Outback Steakhouse, Rambo, Freddy Krueger, Michael Myers, *Halloween*, Jedi, X-Men, *Jurassic Park*, Rainbow Brite, Electric Slide, Olive Garden, Taser, Humvee, Frisbee, Gumby, Lysol, Ritz-Carlton, Hummer, Flamingo, Treasure Island, Bellagio, Caesar's Palace, Paris, Converse, *Sweet Evil*, Jaguar, Volkswagen, A Little White Wedding Chapel, *The Hangover*, Charlie Brown, "Don't Cha," Godzilla, BMW, the Venetian, YouTube, Frogger, Mercedes, the Mirage, Slinky, Dodge Journey, Funyuns, He-Man, ET

For my mother, who was my biggest fan and supporter. You will be missed but never forgotten.

Chapter 1

Katy

I was on fire again. Worse than when I got sick from the mutation or when onyx was sprayed in my face. The mutated cells in my body bounced around as if they were trying to claw their way through my skin. Maybe they were. It felt like I was splayed wide open. There was a wetness gathering on my cheeks.

They were tears, I realized slowly.

Tears of pain and anger—a fury so potent it tasted like blood in the back of my throat. Or maybe it really was blood. Maybe I was drowning in my own blood.

My memories after the doors had sealed shut were hazy. Daemon's parting words haunted every waking moment. *I love you, Kat. Always have. Always will.* There had been a hissing sound as the doors closed, and I'd been left alone with the Arum.

I think they tried to eat me.

Everything had gone black, and I'd woken up in this world where it hurt to breathe. Remembering his voice, his words, soothed some of the torment. But then I remembered Blake's parting smile as he held the opal necklace—my opal necklace; the one Daemon had given me just before the sirens went off and the doors started coming down—and my anger flared. I'd been captured, and I didn't know if Daemon had made it out along with the rest of them.

I didn't know anything.

Forcing my eyes open, I blinked at the harsh lights shining down on me. For a moment, I couldn't see around their bright glow. Everything had an aura. But finally it cleared, and I saw a white ceiling behind the lights.

"Good. You're awake."

In spite of the pulsating burning, my body locked up at the sound of the unfamiliar male voice. I tried to look toward the source, but pain shot down my body, curling my toes. I couldn't move my neck, my arms, or my legs.

Icy horror drenched my veins. Onyx bands were around my neck, my wrists, my ankles, holding me down. Panic erupted, seizing the air in my lungs. I thought about the bruises Dawson had seen around Beth's neck. A shudder of revulsion and fear rocked through me.

The sound of footsteps neared, and a face, cocked sideways, came into view, blocking the light. It was an older man, maybe in his late forties, with dark hair sprinkled with gray buzzed close to the scalp. He wore a military uniform in dark green. There were three rows of colorful buttons above the left breast and a winged eagle on the right. Even in my pain-clouded mind and confusion, I knew this guy was important.

"How are you feeling?" he asked in a level voice.

I blinked slowly, wondering if this man was being serious. "Everything…everything hurts," I croaked.

"It's the bands, but I think you know that." He motioned to something or someone behind him. "We had to take certain precautions when we transported you."

Transported me? My heart rate kicked up as I stared at him. Where in the hell was I? Was I still at Mount Weather?

"My name is Sergeant Jason Dasher. I'm going to release you so we can talk and you can be looked over. Do you see the dark dots in the ceiling?" he asked. My gaze followed his, and then I saw the almost invisible blotches. "It's a blend of onyx and diamond. You know what the onyx does, and if you fight us, this room will fill up with it. Whatever resistance you've built won't help you here."

The whole room? At Mount Weather, it had just been a puff in the face. Not an endless stream of it.

"Did you know diamonds have the highest index of light refraction? While it does not have the same painful effects of onyx, in large enough quantities, and when onyx is in use, it has the ability to drain Luxen, leaving them unable to draw from the Source. It will have the same effect on you."

Good to know.

"The room is outfitted with onyx as a security precaution," he continued, his dark brown eyes focused on mine again. "In case you somehow are able to tap into the Source or attack any member of my staff. With hybrids, we never know the extent of your abilities."

Right now I didn't think I'd be able to sit up without assistance, let alone go ninja on anyone.

"Do you understand?" His chin lifted as he waited. "We don't want to hurt you, but we will neutralize you if you pose a threat. Do you understand, Katy?"

I didn't want to answer, but I also wanted out of the damn onyx bands. "Yes."

"Good." He smiled, but it was practiced and not very friendly. "We don't want you to be in pain. That is not what Daedalus is about. And it is far from what we are. You may not believe that right now, but we hope you will come to understand what we are about. The truth behind who we are and who the Luxen are."

"Kind of hard to…believe right now."

Sergeant Dasher seemed to take that for what it was worth, and then he reached down somewhere under the cold table. There was a loud *click*, and the bands lifted on their own, sliding off my neck and ankles.

Letting out a shaky breath, I slowly lifted my trembling arm. Entire parts of my body felt either numb or hypersensitive.

He placed a hand on my arm, and I flinched. "I'm not going to hurt you," he said. "I'm just going to help you sit up."

Given that I didn't have much control over my shaking limbs, I wasn't in any condition to protest. The sergeant had me upright in a few seconds. I clutched the edges of the table to keep myself steady as I took in several breaths. My head hung from my neck like a wet noodle, and my hair slid over my shoulders, shielding the room for a moment.

"You'll probably be a little dizzy. That should pass."

When I lifted my head, I saw a short, balding man dressed in a white lab coat standing by a door that was such a shiny black it reflected the room. He held a paper cup in his hand and what looked like a manual pressure cuff in the other.

Slowly, my eyes traveled over the room. It reminded me of a weird doctor's office, outfitted with tiny tables with instruments on them, cabinets, and black hoses hooked to the wall.

When motioned forward by the sergeant, the man in the lab coat approached the table and carefully held the cup to my mouth. I drank greedily. The coolness soothed the rawness in my throat, but I drank too fast and ended up with a coughing fit that was both loud and painful.

"I'm Dr. Roth, one of the physicians at the base." He put the cup aside and reached into his jacket, pulling out a stethoscope. "I'm just going to listen to your heart, okay? And then I'm going to take your blood pressure."

I jumped a little when he pressed the cold chest piece against my skin.

He then placed it on my back. "Take a nice deep breath." When I did, he repeated his instructions. "Good. Extend your arm out."

I did and immediately noticed the red welt circling my wrist. There was another above my other hand. Swallowing hard, I looked away, seconds from slipping into full freak-out mode, especially when my eyes met the sergeant's. They weren't hostile, but the eyes belonged to a stranger. I was utterly alone—with strangers who knew what I was and had captured me for a purpose.

My blood pressure had to be through the roof, because my pulse was pounding, and the tightening in my chest couldn't be a good thing. As the pressure cuff squeezed down, I inhaled several deep breaths, then asked, "Where am I?"

Sergeant Dasher clasped his hands behind his back. "You're in Nevada."

I stared at him, and the walls—all white with the exception of those shiny black dots—crowded in. "Nevada? That's…that's clear across the country. A different time zone."

Silence.

Then it struck me. A strangled laugh escaped. "Area 51?"

There was more silence, as if they couldn't confirm the existence of such a place. Area mother-freaking 51. I didn't know if I should laugh or cry.

Dr. Roth released the cuff. "Her blood pressure is a little high, but that's expected. I would like to do a more intensive examination."

Visions of probes and all kinds of nasty things lit up my brain. I slid off the table quickly, backing away from the men, on legs that barely held my weight. "No. You can't do this. You can't—"

"We can," Sergeant Dasher interrupted. "Under the Patriot Act, we are able to apprehend, relocate, and detain anyone, human or nonhuman, who poses a risk to the Nation's security."

"What?" My back hit the wall. "I'm not a terrorist."

"But you are a risk," he responded. "We hope to change that, but as you can see, your right to freedom was relinquished the moment you were mutated."

Legs giving out, I slid down the wall and sat down hard. "I can't…" My brain didn't want to process any of this. "My mom…"

The sergeant said nothing.

My mom…oh my God, my mom had to be going insane. She would be panicked and devastated. She would never get over this.

Pressing my palms against my forehead, I squeezed my eyes shut. "This isn't right."

"What did you think would happen?" Dasher asked.

I opened my eyes, my breath coming out in short bursts.

"When you infiltrated a government facility, did you think you would just walk out and everything would be fine? That there'd be no consequences for such actions?" He bent down in front of me. "Or that a group of kids, alien or hybrid, would be able to get as far as you did without us allowing it?"

Coldness radiated over my body. Good question. What *had* we thought? We had suspected it could be a trap. I had practically prepared myself for it, but we couldn't walk away and let Beth rot in there. None of us could've done that.

I stared up at the man. "What happened to…to the others?"

"They've escaped."

Relief coursed through me. At least Daemon wasn't locked up somewhere. That gave me some sort of comfort.

"We only needed to catch one of you, to be honest. Either you or the one who mutated you. Having one of you will draw the other out." He paused. "Right now, Daemon Black has disappeared off our radar, but we imagine it won't stay that way for long. We have learned through our studies that the bond between a Luxen and the one he or she mutates is quite intense, especially between a male and female. And from our observations, you two are extremely… close."

Yeah, my relief crashed and burned in fiery glory, and fear seized me. There was no point in pretending I had no idea what he was talking about, but I would never confirm it was Daemon. *Never*.

"I know you're afraid and angry."

"Yeah, I'm feeling both of those things strongly."

"That is understandable. We are not as bad as you think we are, Katy. We had every right to use lethal methods when we caught you. We could've taken out your friends. We didn't." He stood, clasping his hands again. "You will see we are not the enemy here."

Not the enemy? They *were* the enemy—a greater threat than a whole flock of Arum—because they had the *entire government* behind them. Because they could just snap up people and take them away from everything—their family, their friends, their entire life—and get away with it.

I was so screwed.

As the situation really sank in, my tenacious grip on keeping it together slipped, and then completely fell away. Stark terror whipped through me, turning into panic, creating an ugly mess of emotions powered by adrenaline. Instinct took over—the kind I hadn't been born with but had been shaped by what I'd become when Daemon had healed me.

I sprang to my feet. Aching muscles screamed in protest, and my head swam from the sudden movement, but I remained standing. The doctor moved to the side, his face paling as he reached for the wall. The sergeant didn't so much as blink an eye. He was not afraid of my badassery.

Calling upon the Source should've been easy, considering all the violent emotions rolling within me, but there wasn't a rush—like the kind you get when you're poised atop a high roller coaster—or even a building of static over my skin.

There was nothing.

Through the fog of horror and panic clouding my thoughts, a bit of reality seeped in, and I remembered I couldn't use the Source in here.

"Doctor?" said the sergeant.

In need of a weapon, I darted around him, heading for the table with the tiny instruments. I didn't know what I would do if I managed to get out of this room. The door could've been locked. I wasn't thinking beyond that very second. I just needed to get out of there. Now.

Before I could reach the tray, the doctor slapped his hand against the wall. A horrific, familiar sound of air releasing in a series of small puffs followed. There was no other warning. No smell. No change in the consistency of the air.

But those little dots in the ceiling and walls had released weaponized onyx, and there was no escaping it. Horror drowned me. The breath I took cut off as red-hot pain started at my scalp and coursed down my body. Like I was being doused with gasoline and set ablaze, a fire swept over my skin. My legs gave out, and my knees cracked off the tile floor. The onyx-filled air scratched my throat and scorched my lungs.

I curled into a ball, fingers clawing at the floor as my mouth opened in a silent scream. My body spasmed uncontrollably as the onyx invaded every cell. There was no end. No hope that the fire would be extinguished by Daemon's quick thinking, and I silently called out his name, over and over again, but there was no answer.

There was and would be nothing but pain.

• • •

DAEMON

Thirty-one hours, forty-two minutes, and twenty seconds had passed since the doors had closed, separating Kat from me. Thirty-one hours, forty-two minutes, and ten seconds since I last saw her. For thirty-one hours and forty-one minutes Kat had been in the hands of Daedalus.

Each second, every minute and hour that ticked by had driven me fucking insane.

They had locked me up in a one-room cabin, which was really a cell decked out in everything that would piss off a Luxen, but it hadn't stopped me. I'd blown that door and the Luxen guarding me into another damn galaxy. Bitter anger surged through me, coating my insides with acid as I picked up speed, flying past the row of cabins, avoiding the cluster of homes, and heading straight for the trees surrounding the Luxen community hidden under the shadows of Seneca Rocks. Not even halfway there, I saw a blur of white streaking straight for me.

They were going to try to stop me? Yeah, not going to happen.

I skidded to a halt, and the light zoomed past and then whirled around. Shaped like a human, it stood directly in front of me, so bright that the Luxen lit up the dark trees behind him.

We are only trying to protect you, Daemon.

Just like Dawson and Matthew had thought knocking me out at Mount Weather and then locking me up would protect me. Oh, I had a nuclear-size bone to pick with those two.

We don't want to hurt you.

"That's a shame." I cracked my neck. Behind me, several more were gathering. "I have no problem hurting you."

The Luxen in front of me extended his arms. *It doesn't have to be this way.*

There was no other way. Letting my human form fade was like shedding too-tight clothing. A reddish tint spread over the grass like blood. *Let's get this over with.*

None of them hesitated.

Neither did I.

The Luxen shot forward, a blur of brilliant limbs. I dipped under his arms, springing up behind him. Catching his arms, I slammed my foot into his bowed back. No sooner had that Luxen gone down than another took his place.

Launching to the side, I clotheslined the one racing at me and then dipped, narrowly missing a foot with my name on it. I welcomed this—the physicality of fighting. I poured every bit of fury and frustration into each punch and kick, tearing through three more of them.

A pulse of light cut through the shadows, aiming straight for me. Bending down, I slammed a fist into the ground. Soil flew into the sky as a shockwave rippled outward, catching the Luxen and tossing him into the air. I sprang up, grabbing him as intense, bright light blew off me, turning night into day for the briefest moment.

I spun, tossing him like a disk.

He smacked into a tree and hit the ground, but he quickly shot to his feet. Charging forward, white light tinged in blue trailed behind him like a tail on a comet. Lobbing at me what amounted to a nuclear power–strength ball of energy, he let out an inhuman battle roar.

Oh, so he wanted to play that way?

I leaned to the side; the bolt fizzled out as it zoomed past. Pulling on the Source, I reared back, letting the power soar. I slammed my foot down, creating a crater and another ripple, knocking the Luxen off balance. Throwing my arm out, I let the Source go. It flew from my hand like a bullet, hitting him squarely in the chest.

He went down, alive but all kinds of twitchy.

"What do you think you're doing, Daemon?"

At the sound of Ethan Smith's level voice, I turned. The Elder, in his human form, stood several yards back among the fallen. My body shook with unspent power. *They shouldn't have tried to stop me. None of you should have tried to stop me.*

Ethan clasped his hands in front of him. "You shouldn't be willing to risk your community for a human girl."

There was a good chance I was going to zap him into next week. *She is not something I'm ever going to discuss with you.*

"We are your kind, Daemon." He took a step forward. "You need to stay with us. Going after this human will only—"

I threw my hand out, grabbing by the neck the Luxen who was sneaking up on me. Turning to him, we both slipped into human form. His eyes filled with terror. "For real?" I growled.

"Crap," he muttered.

Lifting him into the air, I choke-slammed the stupid SOB into the ground. Soil and rock flew into the air as I straightened, returning my gaze to Ethan.

The Elder paled. "You're fighting your own kind, Daemon. That is unforgiveable."

"I'm not asking for your forgiveness. I'm not asking for shit."

"You'll be cast out," he threatened.

"Guess what?" I backed away, keeping an eye on the Luxen on the ground who had started to stir. "I don't care."

Anger rolled off Ethan, and the calm, almost docile expression vanished. "You think I don't know what you did to that girl? What your brother did to the other one? Both of you have brought this onto yourselves. This is why we don't mix with them. Humans bring nothing but trouble. You are going to cause trouble, cause them to look too closely at us. We don't need that, Daemon. You're risking a lot for a human."

"This is their planet," I said, surprising myself with that statement, but it was true. Kat had said it before, and I repeated her words. "We are the guests here, buddy."

Ethan's eyes narrowed. "For now."

My head cocked to the side at those two words. Didn't take a genius to figure out that was a warning, but right now, it wasn't my priority. Kat was. "Don't follow me."

"Daemon—"

"I mean it, Ethan. If you or anyone else comes after me, I won't go easy like I just did."

The Elder sneered. "Is she truly worth this?"

A cold wind moved down my spine. Without the support of the Luxen community, I'd be on my own, not welcomed in any of their colonies. Word traveled fast; Ethan would make sure of it. But there wasn't a moment of hesitation.

"Yes," I said. "She is worth *everything*."

Ethan sucked in a sharp breath. "You're done here."

"So be it."

Pivoting, I took off through the trees, racing toward my house. My brain was churning. I didn't have much of a plan. Nothing concrete, but I knew I was going to need a few things. Money was one of them. A car. Running the whole way to Mount Weather wasn't an option. Going back to the house was going to be difficult, because I knew Dee and Dawson would be there—and they would try to stop me.

At this point, I'd like to see them try.

But as I crested the rocky hill and picked up speed, what Ethan had said overshadowed my plotting. *Both of you have brought this onto yourselves.* Had we? The answer was simple and right in my face. Both Dawson and I had put the girls in danger simply by being interested in them. Neither of us had planned on them getting hurt, or that healing them would mutate them into something not quite human or Luxen, but we knew the risks.

I especially knew the risks.

It was why I had pushed Katy away in the beginning, had gone to extremes to keep her away from Dee and me. Partly due to what had happened to Dawson, but also because there were so many risks. And yet I had brought Kat deep into this world. Held her hand and practically escorted her right into it. Look at what that got her.

It wasn't supposed to happen this way.

If anyone was to be caught, if things went down badly in Mount Weather, it should've been me. Not Kat. Never her.

Cursing under my breath, I hit a patch of ground lit by silvery moonlight seconds before breaking clear of the forest and slowed down without intending to.

My eyes went straight to Kat's house, and pressure clamped down on my chest.

The house was dark and still, as if it had been the years before she had moved in. No life, an empty, dark shell of a home.

I stopped beside her mother's car and let out a ragged breath that did nothing to relieve the pressure building in my chest. In the darkness, I knew I wasn't seen, and if the DOD or Daedalus were watching for me, they could take me in. It would make it easier for me.

If I closed my eyes, I could see Kat coming out the front door, wearing that damn shirt that said MY BLOG IS BETTER THAN YOUR VLOG, and those shorts…those legs…

Man, I had been such an ass to her, but she hadn't backed down from me. Not for one second.

A light flipped on in my house. A second later, the front door opened, and Dawson stood there. The breeze carried his soft curse.

I had to say Dawson looked a thousand times better since I'd last seen him. The dark shadows that had been under his eyes were mostly gone. Some of the weight had returned. Like before the DOD and Daedalus had captured him, it would be nearly impossible to tell us apart with the exception of his longer, shaggier hair. Yeah, he looked like a million bucks. He had Bethany back.

I knew I sounded bitter, but I didn't care.

The moment my feet touched the stairs, a shockwave erupted from me, cracking the cement of the steps and rattling the floorboards.

Blood drained from my brother's face as he took a step back. A sick sense of satisfaction swelled in me. "Weren't expecting me so soon?"

"Daemon." Dawson's back hit the front door. "I know you're pissed."

Another burst of energy left me, hitting the ceiling of the roof. Wood cracked. A fissure appeared, splitting down the center. My vision tinted as the Source filled me, turning the world white. "You have no idea, brother."

"We wanted to keep you safe until we knew what to do—how to get Kat back. That's all."

I took a deep breath as I stepped up to Dawson, going eye to eye with him. "Did you think that locking me up in the community was the best answer?"

"We—"

"Did you think you could stop me?" Power shot from me, smacking into the door behind Dawson, blowing it off the hinges and into the house. "I'll burn the world down to save her."

Chapter 2

Katy

Soaking wet and chilled to the bone, I pulled myself off the floor. I had no idea how much time had passed since the first dose of onyx had been released and the last blast of icy water had knocked me flat on my back.

Giving in and letting them do what they wanted hadn't seemed like an option in the beginning. At first the pain was worth it, because I'd be damned if I was going to make this easy for them. Once the onyx had been washed from my skin and I could move again, I rushed the door. I wasn't making any progress, and by the fourth cycle of being doused with onyx and then drowned, I was done.

I was really, truly done.

Once I was able to stand without collapsing, I shuffled toward the cold table in slow, achy steps. I was pretty sure the table had a very thin layer of diamonds over the surface. The kind of money it must've taken to outfit a room, let alone a whole building, in diamonds had to be astronomical—and further explained the nation's debt problem. And really, out of everything to be thinking about, that shouldn't even make the list, but I think the onyx had shorted out my brain.

Sergeant Dasher had come and gone during the whole process, replaced by men in army fatigues. The berets they wore hid most of their faces, but from what I could see, they didn't seem much older than me, maybe in their early twenties.

Two of them were in the room now, both with pistols strapped to their thighs. Part of me was surprised they hadn't broken out the tranqs, but the onyx served its purpose. The one wearing a dark green beret stood near the controls, watching me, one hand on his pistol and the other on the button of pain. The other, face hidden by a khaki beret, guarded the door.

I placed my hands on the table. Through the wet ropes of my soaked hair, my fingers looked too white and pasty. I was cold and shivering so badly I wondered if I was actually experiencing a seizure. "I'm…I'm done," I rasped out.

A muscle popped on Khaki Beret's face.

I tried to lift myself onto the table, because I knew if I didn't sit, I was going to fall, but the deep tremor in my muscles caused me to wobble to the side. The room whirled for a second. There just might be some permanent damage. I almost laughed, because what good would I be to Daedalus if they broke me?

Dr. Roth had remained the whole time, sitting in the corner of the room, looking weary, but now he stood, pressure cuff in hand. "Help her onto the table."

Khaki Beret came toward me, determination locking his jaw. I backpedaled in a feeble attempt to put some distance between us. My heart pounded insanely fast. I didn't want him touching me. I didn't want any of them touching me.

Legs shaking, I took another step back, and my muscles just stopped working. I hit the floor hard on my butt, but I was so numb, the pain really didn't register.

Khaki Beret stared down at me, and from my vantage point, I could see his entire face. He had the most startling blue eyes, and while he looked like he was so over this routine, there seemed to be some level of compassion to his stare.

Without saying a word, he bent down and scooped me up. He smelled of fresh detergent, the same kind my mom used, and tears welled in my eyes. Before I could put up a fight, which would've been pointless, he deposited me on the table. When he backed away, I gripped the edges of the table, feeling like I'd been here before.

And I had.

Another cup of water was given to me, which I accepted. The doctor sighed loudly. "Is fighting this out of your system now?"

I dropped the paper cup on the table and forced my tongue to move. It felt swollen and difficult to control. "I don't want to be here."

"Of course you don't." He placed the chest piece under my shirt, like he had done before. "No one in this room, or even in this building, expects that from you, but fighting us, before you even know what we're about, is only going to hurt you in the end. Now breathe in deeply."

I breathed in, but the air got stuck. The line of white cabinets across the room blurred. I would not cry. I would not cry.

The doctor went through the motions, checking my breathing and blood pressure before he spoke again. "Katy—may I call you Katy?"

A short, hoarse laugh escaped me. So polite. "Sure."

He smiled as he placed the pressure cuff on the table and then stepped back, folding his arms. "I need to do a full exam, Katy. I promise it will not hurt. It will be like any other physical exam you've had before."

Fear balled in my core. I folded my arms around my waist, shivering. "I don't want that."

"We can postpone it for a little bit, but it must be done." Turning, he walked over to one of the cabinets and retrieved a dark brown blanket. Returning to the table, he draped it over my bent shoulders. "Once you regain your strength, we're going to move you to your quarters. There you will be able to wash up and get into fresh, clean clothes. There's also a TV if you want to watch, or you can rest. It's pretty late, and you have a big day tomorrow."

I held the blanket close, shaking. He made it sound like I was at a hotel. "Big day tomorrow?"

He nodded. "There is a lot we need to show you. Hopefully, then you'll understand what Daedalus is truly about."

I fought the urge to laugh again. "I know what you guys are about. I know what—"

"You know *only* what you've been told," the doctor interrupted. "And what you do know is only half true." He cocked his head to the side. "I know you're thinking of Dawson and Bethany. You don't know the whole story behind them."

My eyes narrowed, and the answering rush of anger warmed my insides. How dare he put what Daedalus did to Bethany and Dawson back on them? "I know enough."

Dr. Roth glanced at Green Beret by the controls, and then he nodded. Green Beret quietly exited the room, leaving the doctor and Khaki Beret behind. "Katy—"

"I know you basically tortured them," I cut in, growing more furious by the second. "I know you brought people in here and forced Dawson to heal them, and when that didn't work, those humans died. I know you kept them away from each other and used Beth to get Dawson to do what you wanted. You're worse than evil."

"You don't know the whole story," he repeated evenly, completely unfazed by my accusations. He looked at Khaki Beret. "Archer, you were here when Bethany and Dawson were brought in?"

I turned to Archer, and he nodded. "When the subjects were brought in, both were understandably difficult to deal with, but after the female had gone through the mutation, she was even more violent. They were allowed to stay together until it became obvious there was a safety issue. That was why they were separated and eventually moved to different locations."

I shook my head as I pulled the blanket closer. I wanted to yell at them at the top of my lungs. "I'm not stupid."

"I don't think you are," the doctor answered. "Hybrids are notoriously unbalanced, even the ones who have mutated successfully. Beth was and is unstable."

Knots formed in my belly. I could easily remember how crazy Beth had been at Vaughn's house. She had seemed fine when we found her at Mount Weather, but she hadn't always been that way. Were Dawson and everyone in danger? Could I even believe anything these people were telling me?

"That's why I need to do a full exam, Katy."

I looked at the doctor. "Are you saying I'm unstable?"

He didn't respond immediately, and it felt like the table had dropped out from underneath me.

"There is a chance," he said. "Even with successful mutations, there is an instability issue that arises when the hybrid uses the Source."

Clenching the blanket until the feeling came back in my knuckles, I willed my heart to slow down. It wasn't working. "I don't believe you. I don't believe anything you're saying. Dawson was—"

"Dawson was a sad case," he said, cutting me off. "And you will come to understand that. What happened with Dawson was unintentional. He would've been released eventually, once we were sure he could assimilate again. And Beth—"

"Just stop," I snarled, and my own voice surprised me. "I don't want to hear any more of your lies."

"You have no idea, Miss Swartz, how dangerous the Luxen are and the threat those who have been mutated by them pose."

"The Luxen aren't dangerous! And the hybrids wouldn't be,

either, if you left us alone. We haven't done anything to you. We wouldn't have. We weren't doing anything until you—"

"Do you know why the Luxen came to Earth?" he asked.

"Yes." My knuckles ached. "The Arum destroyed their planet."

"Do you know why their planet was destroyed? Or the origins of the Arum?"

"They were at war. The Arum were trying to take their abilities and kill them." I was totally up to date on my Alien 101. The Arum were the opposite of the Luxen, more shadow than light, and they *fed* off the Luxen. "And you're working with those monsters."

Dr. Roth shook his head. "Like with any great war, the Arum and Luxen have been fighting for so long that I doubt many of them even know what sparked the battle."

"So are you trying to say that the Arum and the Luxen are like the intergalactic Gaza Strip?"

Archer snorted at that.

"I don't even know why we're talking about this," I said, suddenly so tired I wasn't sure I could think straight. "None of that matters."

"It *does* matter," the doctor said. "It goes to show how very little you truly know about any of this."

"Well, I guess you're going to educate me?"

He smiled, and I wanted to knock the condescending look off his face. Too bad that would require my letting go of the blanket and mustering up the energy to do so. "During their prime, the Luxen were the most powerful and intelligent life-form in the entire universe. Just like in any set of species, evolution evolved in response, creating a natural predator—the Arum."

I stared at the man. "What are you saying?"

He met my gaze. "The Luxen weren't the victims in their war. They were the cause of it."

• • •

Daemon

"How did you get out?" Dawson asked.

It had taken everything for me not to slam my fist into his face. I had calmed down enough that bringing the house down on its foundation was unlikely to occur. Still a possibility, though.

"Better question is how many did I lay out to get here?" I tensed, waiting. Dawson blocked the doorway. "Don't fight me on any of this, brother. You won't be able to stop me, and you know it."

He held my gaze for a moment, then swore as he stepped aside. I slid past him, my eyes going to the staircase.

"Dee's asleep," he said, running a hand through his hair. "Daemon—"

"Where's Beth?"

"Here," came a soft voice from the dining room.

I turned around and, hell, it was like the girl materialized out of smoke and shadows. I'd forgotten how much of a tiny thing she was. Slim and elfin, with lots of brown hair and a pointy, stubborn little chin. She was a lot paler than I remembered.

"Hey there." My beef wasn't with her. I glanced back at my brother. "You think it's wise to have her here?"

He went to her side, draping his arm over her shoulders. "We planned on leaving. Matthew was going to set us up in Pennsylvania, near South Mountain."

I nodded. The mountain was rocking a decent amount of quartzite but no Luxen community that we knew of.

"But we didn't want to leave right now," Beth added quietly, her eyes darting around the room, not settling on anything in particular. She was dressed in one of Dawson's T-shirts and a pair of Dee's sweats.

Both swallowed her whole. "It didn't seem right. Someone should be here with Dee."

"But it's not really safe for you two," I pointed out. "Matthew could stay with Dee."

"We're fine." Dawson bent his head, pressing a kiss against Beth's forehead before pinning me with a serious look. "You shouldn't be out of the colony. We had you there to keep you safe. If the police see you or the—"

"The police aren't going to see me." That concern made sense. Since Kat and I were both presumed missing, or that we'd run away, my reappearance would raise a lot of questions. "Neither will Kat's mom."

He didn't look convinced. "You're not worried about the DOD?"

I said nothing.

He shook his head. "Shit."

Beside him, Beth shifted her slight weight from one foot to the next. "You're going after her, aren't you?"

"The hell he is," my brother cut in, and when I said nothing, he strung together so many curse words I was actually impressed. "Dammit, Daemon, out of everyone, I know what you're feeling, but what you're doing is insane. And seriously, how did you get out of the cabin?"

Striding forward, I brushed past him and headed for the kitchen. It was strange being back in here. Everything was the same—gray granite countertops, white appliances, the god-awful country decorations Dee had thrown up on the walls, and the heavy oak kitchen table.

I stared at the table. Like a mirage, Kat appeared, sitting on the edge. Deep pain sliced across my chest. God, I missed her, and it killed me not knowing what was really happening to her or what they were doing.

Then again, I had a good idea. I knew enough from what they'd done to Dawson and Beth, and that made me physically ill.

"Daemon?" He had followed me.

I turned from the table. "We don't need to have this conversation, and I'm not in the mood to state the obvious. You know what I'm doing. It's why you put me in the colony."

"I don't even understand how you got out. There was onyx all over that place."

Each colony had cabins meant to keep Luxen who'd become dangerous to our kind or to humans and that the Elders didn't want to take them to the human police.

"If there's a will, there's a way." I smiled when his eyes narrowed.

"Daemon…"

"I'm here to get a few things, and then I'm gone." I opened up the fridge and grabbed a bottle of water. Taking a swig, I faced him. We were the same height, so we met eye to eye. "I mean it. Don't push me on this."

He flinched, but his green eyes met mine. "There's nothing I can say that's going to change your mind?"

"Nope."

He stepped back, rubbing his hand down his jaw. Behind him, Beth sat in the chair, her arms wrapped around her waist, her gaze going everywhere except toward us.

Dawson leaned against the counter. "You going to make me beat you into submission?"

Beth's head jerked up, and I laughed. "I'd like to see you try, little brother."

"Little brother," he scoffed, but a faint smile pulled at his lips. Relief was evident on Beth's face. "By how many seconds?" he asked.

"Enough." I tossed the water bottle in the garbage.

Several moments passed, and then he said, "I'll help you."

"Hell no." I folded my arms. "I don't want your help. I don't want any of you taking part in this."

Determination set his jaw. "Bull. You helped us. It's too dangerous to do it on your own. So if you're going to be stubborn and ignore the fact that you kept me on a leash, which you are, I'm not going to let you do this by yourself."

"I'm sorry I held you back. Now, knowing exactly how you felt, I would've stormed that damn place the very same night you came home. But I'm not going to let you help. Look at what happened when we were in this all together. I can't be worried about you guys. I want you and Dee as far away as possible from this."

"But—"

"I'm not going to argue with you." I placed my hands on his shoulders and squeezed. "I know you want to help. I appreciate that. But if you really want to help, don't try to stop me."

Dawson closed his eyes, his features pinching as his chest rose sharply. "Letting you do this by yourself isn't right. You wouldn't let me."

"I know. I'm going to be okay. I'm always okay." I leaned in, resting my forehead against his. As I clasped the sides of his face, I kept my voice low. "You just got Beth back, and running off with me isn't right. She needs you. You need her, and I need..."

"You need Katy." He opened his eyes, and for the first time since the shit went down at Mount Weather, there was understanding in his gaze. "I get that. I do."

"She needs you, too," Beth whispered.

Dawson and I broke apart. He turned to her. She was still sitting at the table, her hands opening and closing in her lap in quick, repetitive movements.

"What did you say, babe?" he asked.

"Kat needs him." Her lashes lifted, and although her gaze was fixed on us, she wasn't looking at us, not really. "They'll tell her things at first. They'll trick her, but the things they'll do..."

It felt like all the oxygen was sucked out of the room.

Dawson was by her side immediately, kneeling so that she had to look at him. He took her hand in his and brought it to his lips. "It's okay, Beth."

She followed his movements almost obsessively, but there was a strange sheen gathering in her eyes, as if she were slipping further away. The hair on the back of my neck rose, and I stepped forward.

"She won't be at Mount Weather," Beth said, her stare drifting over Dawson's shoulder. "They'll take her far away and make her do things."

"Do what?" The words were out of my mouth before I could stop them.

Dawson shot me a look over his shoulder, but I ignored it. "You don't have to talk about this, babe. All right?"

A long moment passed before she said anything. "When I saw him with you, I knew, but you all seemed like you knew, too. He's bad news. He was there, too, with me."

My hands curled into fists as I remembered Beth's reaction to seeing him, but we had shut her up. "Blake?"

She nodded slowly. "All of them are bad. They don't mean to be." Her focus drifted to Dawson, and she whispered, "I don't mean to be."

"Oh, baby, you're not bad." He placed a hand on her cheek. "You're not bad at all."

Her lower lip trembled. "I've done terrible things. You have no idea. I've ki—"

"It doesn't matter." He went down on his knees. "None of that matters."

A shudder rolled through her, and then she looked up, her eyes locking on mine. "Don't let them do those things to Katy. They'll change her."

I couldn't move or breathe.

Her face crumpled. "They've changed me. I close my eyes, and I see their faces—all of them. I can't get them out no matter what I do. They're *inside* of me."

Good God…

"Look at me, Beth." Dawson guided her face back to his. "You're here with me. You're not there anymore. You know that, right? Keep looking at me. Nothing's inside of you."

She shook her head vigorously. "No. You don't understand. You—"

Backing off, I let my brother handle this. He talked to her in low, soothing tones, but when she quieted, she stared forward, shaking her head side-to-side slowly, her eyes wide and mouth open. She didn't blink, didn't even seem to acknowledge him or me.

Nobody's home, I realized.

As Dawson talked her through whatever was afflicting her, horror—real, true horror—turned my insides cold. The pain that was in my brother's eyes as he smoothed her hair back from her pale face ate me up. At that moment, he looked like he wanted nothing more than to trade places with her.

I gripped the counter behind me, unable to look away.

I could easily see myself doing the same thing. Except it wouldn't be Beth I'd be holding in my arms and coaxing back to reality—it would be Kat.

I was only in my bedroom long enough to change into fresh clothing. Being in there was a blessing and a curse. For some reason it made me feel closer to Kat. Maybe it was because of what we'd shared in my bed and all the moments before then. It also tore me up, because she wasn't in my arms and she wasn't safe.

I didn't know if she'd ever truly be safe again.

As I pulled the clean shirt over my head, I sensed my sister before she spoke. Blowing out a low breath, I turned and found her standing in my doorway, dressed in bubblegum pink pajamas I'd given her for Christmas last year.

She looked as shitty as I felt. "Daemon—"

"If you're going to start in on how I need to wait and think this through, you can save it." I sat down on the bed, dragging a hand through my hair. "It's not going to change what I want."

"I know what you want, and I don't blame you." She cautiously stepped into my room. "No one wants to see you get hurt…or worse."

"Worse is what Kat is going through right this moment. She's your friend. Or was. And you're okay with waiting? Knowing what they could be doing to her?"

She flinched, and her eyes shone like emeralds in the low light. "That's not fair," she whispered.

Maybe not, and any other time I would've felt like an ass for the low blow, but I couldn't muster the empathy.

"We can't lose you," she said after a few moments of awkward-as-hell silence. "You have to understand that we did what we did because we love you."

"But I love her," I said without hesitation.

Her eyes widened, probably since it was the first time she'd heard me say it out loud—well, about anyone other than my family. I wished I had said it more often, especially to Kat. Funny how that kind of shit always turns out in the end. While you're deep in something, you never say or do what you need to. It's always after the fact, when it's too late, that you realize what you should've said or done.

It couldn't be too late. The fact that I was still alive was testament to that.

Tears filled my sister's eyes as she said in a quiet voice, "She loves you, too."

The burn in my chest expanded and crawled up my throat.

"You know, I always knew she liked you before she admitted it to me or herself."

I smiled slightly. "Yeah, same here."

Dee twisted the length of her hair in her hands. "I knew she'd be…she'd be perfect for you. She'd never put up with your crap." Dee sighed. "I know Kat and I had our problems over…Adam, but I love Kat, too."

I couldn't do this—sit here and talk about her like we were at some kind of wake or memorial. This shit was too much.

She took a little breath, a sure sign she was about to unload. "I wish I hadn't been so hard on her. I mean, she totally needed to know that she should've trusted me and all of that, but if I could've let go of it sooner, then…well, you know what I mean. It would've been better for everyone. I hate the idea that I might never—" She cut herself off quickly, but I knew what she was getting at. She might never see Kat again. "Anyway, I had asked her before prom if she was scared about going back to Mount Weather."

My chest seized like someone had grabbed me in a bear hug. "What did she say?"

Dee let go of her hair. "She said she was, but, Daemon, she was so brave. She even laughed, and I told her…" She stared at her hands, her expression pinched. "I told her to be careful and to keep you and Dawson safe. And you know, she said she would, and she did, in a way."

Christ.

I rubbed my palm over my chest where it felt like a fist-sized hole had opened up.

"But before I had asked her that, she had been trying to talk to me about Adam and everything, and I had cut her off with that question. She kept trying to make amends, and I kept pushing her back. She probably hated me—"

"That's not the case." I looked Dee dead-on. "She didn't hate you. Kat understood. She knew you needed time, and she…" I stood, suddenly needing to get out of this room and this house and onto the road.

"We haven't run out of time," she said quietly, almost like she was begging…and damn if that didn't hurt. "We *haven't*."

Anger flashed through me, and it took everything for me not to lash out. Because keeping me in that damn cabin had been nothing but a waste of time. Taking several deep breaths, I asked a question I wasn't sure I wanted an answer to. "Have you seen her mom?"

Her lower lip trembled. "I have."

I caught my sister's stare and held it. "Tell me."

Her expression said that was the last thing she wanted to do. "The police were at her house all day after…we got back. I talked to them, and then to her mom. The police think you two ran away. Or at least that's what they told her mom, but I think one of them is an implant. He was way too adamant about it."

"Of course," I muttered.

"Her mom doesn't believe it, though. She knows Katy. And Dawson has been keeping a low profile with Beth and all. It would seem suspicious to anyone with two brain cells." She plopped back down, arms falling in her lap. "It was really hard. Her mom was so upset. I could tell she thinks the worst, especially after Will and Carissa 'disappearing,'" Dee said, using air quotes. "She's really bad off."

Guilt exploded like buckshot, leaving dozens of holes in me. Kat's mom shouldn't be going through this—worrying about her daughter, missing her, and fearing the worst.

"Daemon? Don't leave us. We'll find a way to get her, but please don't leave us. Please."

I stared at her in silence. I couldn't make a promise I had no intention of keeping and she already knew that. "I have to go. You know that. I have to get her back."

Her lower lip trembled. "But what if you don't get her back? What if you are put in there with her?"

"Then at least I'm with her. I'm there for her." I walked up to my sister and clasped her cheeks. Tears rolled down, pooling along my fingers. I hated to see her cry, but I hated what was happening to Kat more. “Don’t worry, Dee. This is me we’re talking about. You know damn well I can get myself out of any situation. And you know I will get her out of there.”

And nothing in this world would stop me.

Chapter 3

Katy

I was amazed that with all the reeling my brain was doing, I'd be able to do something normal like change into fresh clothes—a pair of black jogging pants and a gray cotton shirt. The clothing fit on a disturbing level, even the undergarments.

Like they knew I'd be coming.

Like they had snooped around in my undie drawer and got my size.

I wanted to hurl.

Instead of dwelling on that, which would most definitely lead to me flipping out and getting a face full of onyx and icy water again, I focused on my cell. Oh, excuse me. My *quarters*, as Dr. Roth reminded me.

It was about the size of a hotel room, a good three hundred square feet or so. Tile covered the floors, cold under my bare feet. I had no idea where my shoes were. There was a double bed tucked up against the wall, a tiny end table beside it, a dresser, and a TV mounted on the wall at the foot of the bed. In the ceiling were the fearsome black dots of pain, but there were no water hoses in the room.

And there was a door across from the bed.

Padding to it, I placed the tips of my fingers on the door and cautiously pushed it open, half expecting a net made of onyx to drop on me.

It didn't.

Inside was a small bathroom with another door at the end. That one was locked.

I wheeled around and went back into the bedroom.

The trip to my cell hadn't been scenic. We'd walked straight out of the room I'd woken up in and into an elevator that had opened straight across from where I was now. I hadn't really even gotten a chance to look down the hallway to see how many rooms there were like the one I was in now.

I bet there were a lot.

Having no idea what time it was, if it were night or day, I shuffled over to the bed and pulled down the brown blanket. I sat and pressed my back against the wall, tucking my legs against my chest. I tugged the blanket to my chin and sat facing the door.

I was tired—weary to my very core. My eyes were heavy, and my body ached from the effort to sit up, but the idea of falling asleep scared the ever-loving crap out of me. What if someone came into the room while I slept? That was a very real concern. The door locked from the outside, meaning I was completely at their whim.

To keep myself from dozing off, I focused on the one thousand questions circling in my head. Dr. Roth had made that cloak-and-dagger statement about the Luxen being behind the war that had started God knew how long ago. Even if they had been, did it matter now? I didn't think it did. Not when this generation of Luxen was so far removed from what their ancestors might've plotted. I honestly didn't even understand why he had brought it up. To show how little I knew? Or was there something more? And what about Bethany? Was she really dangerous?

I shook my head. Even if the Luxen started a war hundreds, if not thousands, of years ago, that didn't mean they were evil. And if Bethany was dangerous, it probably had something to do with what they had done to her. I wasn't going to let them pull me into their lies, but I had to admit, what they had said unnerved me.

My brain mulled over more questions. How long were they planning to keep me here? What about school? My mom? I thought of Carissa. Had she been brought to a place like this? I still had no idea how she'd ended up mutated, or why. Luc, the ridiculously intelligent and even a bit scary teen hybrid, had helped us get into Mount Weather and had warned that I may never know what happened to Carissa. I wasn't sure I could live with that. Never knowing why she ended up in my bedroom and self-destructed wasn't right. And if I ended up like her, or like the countless other hybrids the government kidnapped, what would happen to my mom?

With no answers to any of those questions, I finally let my mind go where it wanted, where I'd been desperately trying to prevent it from going.

Daemon.

My eyes fell shut as I exhaled. I didn't even have to try to see him. His face pieced together perfectly.

His broad cheekbones, lips that were full and almost always expressive, and those eyes—those beautiful green eyes that were like two polished emeralds, abnormally bright. I knew my memory really didn't do him justice. He had this masculine beauty I'd never seen before in real life, had only read about in the books I loved.

Man, I missed books already.

In his true form, Daemon was extraordinary. All of the Luxen were breathtakingly beautiful; being made of pure light, they were mesmerizing to look upon, like seeing a star up close.

Daemon Black could be as prickly as a hedgehog having a really bad day, but underneath all that spindly armor, he was sweet, protective, and incredibly selfless. He'd dedicated most of his life to keeping his family and his kind safe, continually facing danger with little thought to his own safety. I was in constant awe of him. Though it hadn't always been like that.

A tear dripped down my cheek unbidden.

Resting my chin against my knees, I swiped at the wetness. I prayed that he was okay—as okay as he could be. That Matthew, Dawson, and Andrew were keeping a tight leash on him. That they wouldn't let him do what I knew he wanted to: the same thing I'd do if the situation were flipped.

Although I wanted him—needed him—to hold me, this was the last place I wanted him to be. The very last place.

Heart aching, I tried thinking about the good things—better things—but the memories weren't enough. There was a strong chance I might never see him again.

The tears slipped out of my tightly squeezed eyes.

Crying solved nothing, but it was hard to hold it in when exhaustion dogged me. I kept my eyes closed, slowly counting until the knot of messy, raw emotions climbed back down my throat.

The next thing I knew, I jolted awake, my heart pounding and mouth dry. I hadn't remembered falling asleep, but I must've. A weird tingle moved over my skin as I dragged in a deep breath. Did I have a nightmare? I couldn't remember, but something felt off. Disoriented, I threw the blanket back and looked around the dark cell.

Every muscle in my body seized as my eyes picked out a darker, thicker shadow in the corner by the door. Tiny hairs on my body rose. Air halted in my lungs, and fear sunk its icy claws into my stomach, freezing me in place.

I wasn't alone.

The shadow pulled away from the wall, moving forward quickly.

My first instinct screamed Arum, and I reached blindly for the opal necklace, realizing too late I didn't have it anymore.

"You're still having nightmares," the shadow said.

At the sound of the familiar voice, fear gave way to rage so potent that it tasted like battery acid. I was on my feet before I knew it.

"Blake," I spat.

Chapter 4

Katy

My brain clicked off and something a hell of a lot more primitive and aggressive took over. I felt the horrible, sinking sense of betrayal. Swinging out, my fist connected with what felt like Blake's cheekbone. It wasn't a girlie hit, either. Every bit of anger and pent-up hatred I felt toward him was packed into that punch.

He let out a startled groan as white-hot pain danced across my hand. "Katy—"

"You bastard!" I swung again, my knuckles slamming into his jaw this time.

He let out another grunt of pain as he staggered back. "Jesus."

I spun, grabbing for a tiny lamp beside the bed, and without warning, the overhead light came on. I wasn't sure how it did. If my abilities didn't work in here, then Blake's shouldn't, either. The sudden glare caught me off guard, and Blake took advantage.

He sprang forward, forcing me to back away from the lamp. "I wouldn't do that if I were you," he warned.

"Go screw yourself." I swung at him again.

He caught my fist and twisted. Sharp pain shot up my arm, and I let out a surprised gasp. He spun me around, and I kicked out. Letting go of my arm, he narrowly avoided the thrust of my knee. "This is ridiculous," he said, hazel eyes narrowed. Anger churned the green flecks.

"You betrayed us."

Blake sort of shrugged, and, well, I sort of lost my shit again.

I launched myself at him like some kind of ninja—a really lame ninja, because he easily dodged my attack. My left leg banged into the bed, and the very next second, he slammed into my back. Air punched out of my lungs as I toppled forward, hitting the bed on my side, bouncing it against the wall.

His knees went down on the mattress as he grabbed hold of my shoulders, rolling me onto my back. I slapped at his arms, and he let out a curse. Rearing up, I swung at him once more.

"Stop it," he growled, grabbing my wrist. The next moment he had hold of my other one. Stretching my arms above my head, he leaned over me, bringing his face within inches of mine, and spoke low. "Stop it, Katy. There are cameras everywhere. You can't see them, but they are there. They are watching right now. How do you think the lights just came on? It's not magic, and they *will* flood this whole room with onyx. I don't know about you, but I don't find that very appealing."

I struggled to push him off, and he shifted his weight so that his knees pressed into my legs, trapping them. Panic was a slow crawl inside me, causing my pulse to jump. I didn't like his weight on me. It reminded me of how he had snuck into my house at night and slept beside me. How he'd watched me sleep. Nausea rose swiftly, and the panic grew. "Get off me!"

"I don't know. You're likely to hit me again."

"I will!" I bucked my hips, but he didn't move, and my heart was racing so fast, I was sure I was going to have a heart attack.

Blake gave me a little shake. "You need to calm down. I'm not going to hurt you. Okay? You can trust me."

Eyes wide, I let out a strangled laugh. "Trust you? Are you insane?"

"You really don't have a choice." Bronze-colored hair fell over his forehead. Usually it was styled in that artfully messy way, but it looked like he'd run out of hair gel today.

I wanted to hit him again, and I strained against his hold, getting nowhere. "I'm going to break your face!"

"Understandable." He pushed down, eyes narrowing. "I know we don't have the most stable relationship—"

"We don't have *any* relationship. We have nothing!" Breathing heavily, I willed my muscles to stop trembling. Several moments passed as he stared down at me, nostrils flared and mouth set in a hard, grim line. I wanted to look away, but to do so was a weakness, and that was the worst thing I could show. "I hate you." It seemed pointless to say that, but it made me feel better.

He flinched, and when he spoke, his voice was barely above a whisper. "I hated lying to you, but I had no choice. Whatever I would've told you, you would've told Daemon and the other Luxen. And I couldn't let that happen. Neither could Daedalus. But we aren't the bad guys here."

I shook my head, dumbfounded and pissed beyond belief. "You *are* the bad guys! You set us up! From the very beginning. It was all leading to this. And you helped them. How could you?"

"We needed to."

"This is *my* life." Tears of anger swelled in my eyes because I had no control over my life now, partly thanks to him, and I struggled to keep my voice level. "Was any of it true? Chris? You wanting to get him out of here?"

Blake didn't say anything for a long moment. "They would've let Chris go at any time. The story of them holding him against his will was just that—a story to make you sympathize with me."

"Son. Of. A. Bitch," I hissed.

"I *was* sent to make sure the mutation held. They didn't know what my uncle and Dr. Michaels were planning, but once they knew that the mutation had held, they needed to know who mutated you and how strong it was. That's why I came back after the night…the night you and Daemon let me go."

Our compassion that night had been the final nail in our coffins. It was so ironically sad. I wanted to claw his eyes out.

He let out a ragged breath. "We needed to make sure you were powerful enough for this. They knew Dawson would come back for Beth, but they wanted to see how far you'd get."

"This?" I whispered. "What is *this*?"

"The truth, Katy, the real truth."

"Like you're capable of telling the truth." I rolled my body, trying to throw him off. Muttering another curse, he lifted up, still holding my wrists, and hauled me off the bed. My bare feet slid over the tile as he dragged me toward the bathroom. "What are you doing?"

"I think you need to cool off," he replied, jaw set.

Digging in, all I managed to do was rub the bottoms of my feet raw. Once inside the bathroom, I threw my weight to the side, and he slammed into the sink. Before I could start whaling on him again, he thrust me backward.

Arms spinning like wheels, I toppled over the short rim of the shower stall and landed inside on my butt. A sharp slice of pain shot up my spine.

Blake bolted forward, one hand clamping down on my shoulder, the other reaching blindly to the side. An instant later, freezing water surged out of the showerhead.

Shrieking, I clamored to stand up, but his other hand landed on my shoulder, holding me still as the icy water drenched me. I sputtered, arms flailing against the cold. "Let me out of here!"

"Not until you're ready to listen to me."

"There's nothing you can say!" Soaked clothing clung to my skin. The steady stream of water plastered my hair to my face. Fearing he was trying to drown me, I went for his face, but he smacked my hands away.

"Listen to me." He grasped my chin, his fingers digging into my cheeks, forcing me to meet his eyes. "Blame me all you want, but do you think you wouldn't be here even if you never met me? If so, you're insane. The moment Daemon mutated you, your fate was sealed. If you want to get pissed at anyone, you need to get pissed at him. *He* put you in this situation."

Blake had stunned me into immobility. "You're freaking nuts. You're blaming Daemon for this? He saved my life. I would've—"

"He mutated you, knowing that he was being watched. He's not stupid. He had to know that the DOD would find out."

Actually, he and his family hadn't known about hybrids until I turned into one. "It's so typical of you, Blake. Everything is everyone else's fault."

His eyes narrowed, and the green flecks deepened. "You don't get it."

"You're right." I knocked his hands off my face. "I'll *never* get it."

Backing off, he shook his head as I climbed out of the shower stall. He reached over, turned off the water, and grabbed a towel, tossing it toward me. "Don't try to hit me again."

"Don't tell me what to do." Using the towel, I tried to dry off as best I could.

He clenched his fists. "Look, I get it. You're pissed at me. Great. Get over it, because there are more important things to focus on."

"Get over it?" I was going to choke him with this towel.

"Yes." He leaned against the closed door, eyeing me warily. "You really have no idea what's going on, Kat."

"Don't call me that." I dabbed at my clothing angrily and uselessly.

"Are you calmed down enough? I need to talk, and you need to listen. Things are not what you think. And I wish I could've told you the truth earlier. I couldn't, but I am now."

A strangled laugh escaped me as I shook my head in disbelief.

His eyes narrowed, and he stepped forward. My back straightened in warning, and he didn't come any closer. "Let's get one thing clear. If Daemon was locked up somewhere, you would've thrown everyone and baby Jesus under the bus to free him. That's what you think I did. So don't act like you're better than me."

Would I? Yes, I would, but the difference between us was that Blake was looking for acceptance and forgiveness after he told more lies than truths. And to me, that was bat-shit crazy.

"You think you can justify this? Well, you're wrong. You can't. You're a monster, Blake. A real living and breathing monster. Nothing, no matter what your intentions are or what the real truth is, will ever change that."

A tiny flicker of unrest shone in his steady gaze.

It took everything in me not to rip the towel rod off the wall and shove it through his eye. I tossed the towel aside, shaking more from anger than the wet coldness seeping through my clothes.

He pushed off the door, and I took a step back, on guard. He frowned. "Daedalus aren't the bad guys here." Opening the bathroom door, he headed out. "That's reality."

I followed him. "How can you even say that with a straight face?"

He sat on my bed. "I know what you're thinking. You want to fight them. I get that. I do. And I know I've lied to you about almost everything, but you wouldn't believe the truth without seeing it. And once you do, things will be different."

There was nothing in this world that they could show me that would change my mind, but I also recognized the futility of fighting him on this. "I need to get dry clothes on."

"I'll wait."

I stared at him. "You're not staying in here while I get dressed."

He glared in annoyance. "Get changed in the bathroom. Close the door. Your virtue is safe from me." And then he winked. "Unless you want that to change, and I'm so down for that. It does get boring around here."

My palm itched to wrap around a very unladylike place and twist. The words that came out of my mouth were my own. I felt them. I *believed* them.

"I'm going to kill you one day," I promised.

A wry smile appeared on his face as he met my stare. "You've killed, Katy. You know how it feels to take a life, but you aren't a murderer. You aren't a killer." He caught my sharp inhale with a knowing look. "Not yet, at least."

I turned away, curling my hands into fists.

"Like I said, we aren't the bad guys. The Luxen are, and you will see that I'm not lying. We are here to stop them from taking over."

Chapter 5

Katy

The moment Blake and I stepped out of my cell, two military guys surrounded us. One of them was Archer. Seeing his familiar face didn't bring the warm fuzzies. He and the other guy were heavily armed.

They ushered Blake and me toward the elevator, and I craned my neck, trying to see around them to get a grasp on my surroundings. There were several doors like mine, and it looked just like the corridor at Mount Weather. A heavy hand landed on the small of my back, startling me.

It was Archer.

He sent me a look I couldn't decipher, and then I was in the elevator, squeezed between him and Blake. I couldn't even lift my hand to brush away the damp, cold hair that clung to the back of my neck without knocking into them.

Archer leaned forward, pushing a button I couldn't see because of his mammoth body. I frowned, realizing I didn't even know how many floors this place had.

As if he were reading my mind, Blake looked down at me. "We're underground right now. Most of the base is, with the exception of the two upper levels. You're on the seventh floor. Floor seven and six are housing for…well, visitors."

I wondered why he was even telling me this. The layout had to be important information. It was like…like he trusted me with the knowledge, like I was already one of *them*. I shook the ridiculous notion out of my head. "You mean the prisoners?"

Archer stiffened beside me.

Blake ignored that. "The fifth floor houses Luxen who are being assimilated."

Since the last of the Luxen arrived when Daemon and his family did, more than eighteen years ago, I couldn't imagine how they were still assimilating any of them. My educated guess was that these were Luxen who they believed didn't "fit" with the humans for one reason or another. I shuddered.

And underground? I hated the idea of being underground. It was too much like being dead and buried.

I wiggled my way out from between them, stepping back as I dragged in a deep breath. Blake eyed me curiously, but it was Archer who planted a hand on my shoulder, guiding me forward so I wasn't behind them, like I was going to ninja-stab them in their backs with my invisible knife.

The elevator came to a stop, and the doors slid open. Immediately I caught the scent of food—fresh bread and cooked meat. My stomach roared to life, grumbling like a troll.

Archer's brow went up.

Blake laughed.

My cheeks flamed. Good to know my sense of pride and embarrassment was still intact.

"When was the last time you ate?" Archer asked. It was the first time he'd spoken since I'd been with him and Dr. Roth.

I hesitated. "I…I don't know."

He frowned, and I looked away as we stepped out into the wide, brightly lit hallway. I honestly had no idea what day it was or how many days I had been out of it. Up until when I smelled food, I hadn't even been hungry.

"You're meeting with Dr. Roth," Blake said, starting toward the left.

The hand on my shoulder tightened, and even though I wanted to shove it off, I became very still. Archer looked like he knew how to break a neck in six seconds flat. Blake's gaze went from Archer's hand to the man's face.

"She's going to get something to eat first," Archer said.

Blake protested. "The doctor is waiting. So is—"

"They can wait a couple more minutes so the girl can eat something."

"Whatever." Blake lifted his hand in a way that said, *It's your problem, not mine*. "I'll let him know."

Archer steered me toward the right. Only then did I realize the other military guy had gone with Blake. For a second, everything spun as we started forward. He walked liked Daemon, taking long, quick strides. I struggled to keep up while trying to absorb every detail of where I was. Which wasn't much. Everything was white and lit by bright track lighting. Identical doors lined both sides of the endless hallway. The low hum of conversation behind closed doors was barely discernible.

The scent of food grew stronger, and then we came upon double glass doors. He opened them with his free hand. I felt like I was being escorted into the principal's office instead of into the rather normal-looking cafeteria.

Clean square tables were spaced in three rows. Most of the ones up front were occupied. Archer led me to the first vacant table and pushed me down into a seat. Not a big fan of being manhandled, I shot him a glare.

"Stay here," he said, then spun on his heel.

Where in the hell did he think I would go? I watched him walk toward the front where a short line of people was waiting.

I could still make a run for it and take the risk of not knowing where to go, but my stomach tumbled at the prospect. I knew how many floors were above. I scanned the room, and my heart sank. Little black dots of doom were everywhere, and the cameras weren't so hidden. Someone was probably watching me right now.

Men and women in lab coats and fatigues milled around, none of them giving me more than a cursory glance as they passed by. I sat uncomfortably straight, wondering how commonplace it was for them to see a kidnapped teenager scared out of her mind.

Probably more than I cared to know.

We are here to stop them.

Blake's words came back to me, and I sucked in a breath. Stop who? How could the Luxen be the bad guys? My mind raced, caught between wanting to figure out what he meant and not trusting anything he said.

Archer returned with a plate of eggs and bacon in one hand and a little carton of milk in the other. He sat them down in front of me wordlessly, then produced a plastic fork.

I stared at the plate as he sat across from me. A lump formed in my throat as I reached out slowly, my hand hovering over the fork. I suddenly thought of what Blake had said about his stay here—about how everything had been covered in onyx. Had that been true? The fork was obviously harmless, and I had no idea what to believe anymore.

"It's okay," Archer said.

My fingers wrapped around the plastic fork, and when nothing hurt, I breathed a sigh of relief. "Thank you."

He watched me, his expression telling me he had no idea what I was thanking him for, and I kind of wondered, too. I was surprised by his kindness. Or at least I saw this as kindness. He could've been like Blake and the other guy and not given a damn about my starving.

I ate my food quickly. The whole thing was awkward on a painful level. He didn't speak, and he didn't take his eyes off me once, like he was on alert for shenanigans. I wasn't sure what he expected me to do with a plastic plate and fork. Once, his gaze seemed drawn to my left cheek, and I wasn't sure what he was staring at. I hadn't looked in the mirror when I got ready.

The food tasted like sawdust in my mouth, and my jaw ached from the chewing, but I cleared the plate, figuring I needed the energy.

When I finished, the plate and utensil were left behind on the table. Archer's hand was on my shoulder again. Our trip back was silent and the hall a bit more crowded. We stopped outside a closed room. Without knocking, he opened the door.

Another medical room.

White walls. Cabinets. Trays with medical instruments. A table with…*stirrups*.

I backpedaled, shaking my head. My heart pounded crazy fast as my gaze bounced from Dr. Roth to Blake, who was sitting in a plastic chair. The other guy who'd gone with Blake earlier was nowhere to be found.

Archer's hand tightened, and before I could get completely out the door, he stopped me. "Don't," he said softly, loud enough for only me to hear. "No one wants a repeat of yesterday."

My head jerked toward him, and my eyes locked with his blue ones. "I don't want to do this."

He didn't blink. "You don't have a choice."

Tears rushed my eyes as his words sunk in. I glanced at the doctor, then at Blake. The latter looked away, a muscle popping in his jaw. The hopelessness of it all hit me. Up until that moment, I don't know what I was really thinking. That I still had some say in what was going to happen around me and *to* me.

Dr. Roth cleared his throat. "How are you feeling today, Katy?"

I wanted to laugh, but my voice came out a croak. "What do you think?"

"It'll get easier." He stepped to the side, motioning me toward the table. "Especially once we get this done."

Pressure clamped down on my chest, and my hands opened and closed at my sides. I'd never had a panic attack before, but I was pretty sure I was seconds away from one. "I don't want them in the room." The words came out quick and raspy.

Blake glanced around and then stood, rolling his eyes. "I'll wait outside."

I wanted to kick him as he strolled by, but Archer was still there. I turned to him, my eyes feeling like they were bulging out of my head.

"No," he said, moving to stand in front of the door. He clasped his hands. "I'm not leaving."

I wanted to cry. There would be no fighting back. The room, like the hallway and cafeteria, had shiny walls. No doubt it was the mixture of onyx and diamond.

The doctor handed me one of those god-awful hospital gowns, then pointed toward a curtain. "You can get changed behind there."

In a numb haze, I headed behind the curtain. My fingers fumbled over my clothing and then the gown. Stepping out from behind the curtain, my body was hot and cold, legs weak as I walked forward. Everything was too bright, and my arms shook as I hoisted myself onto the padded table. I clutched the little ties on the gown, unable to look up.

"I'm going to take some blood first," the doctor said.

Everything that happened next I was either hyperaware of or completely detached from. The sharpness of the needle as it slid into my vein, I felt all the way to my toes, then the slight tug of a tube being replaced atop the needle. The doctor was talking to me, but I didn't really hear him.

When it was all done, and I was in my clothes again, I sat on the table, staring down at the white sneakers he had given me. They were my size—a perfect match. My chest rose and fell in deep, slow breaths.

I was numb.

Dr. Roth explained that blood work would be done. Something about checking out the level of mutation, a workup of my DNA so it could be studied. He told me I wasn't pregnant, which was something I already knew; I almost laughed at that but felt too sick, really, to do anything other than breathe.

After that was all said and done, Archer stepped forward and led me out of the room. He'd said nothing the entire time. When he placed his hand on my shoulder, I shrugged it off, not wanting to be touched by anyone. He didn't place his hand on my shoulder again.

Blake was leaning against the wall outside the office, his eyes sliding open when the door shut behind us. "Finally. We're running late."

I kept my lips sealed, because if I opened my mouth to say anything, I was going to cry. And I didn't want to cry. Not in front of Blake or Archer or any of them.

"Okay." Blake drew the word out as we started down the hall. "This should be fun."

"Don't talk," Archer said.

Blake made a face but remained quiet until we stopped in front of closed double doors like the kind you see in hospitals. He smacked a black button on the wall, and the doors opened, revealing Sergeant Dasher.

He was dressed as he had been before, in full military uniform. "Glad you could finally join us."

That nervous, crazy-sounding laugh bubbled up my throat again. "Sorry." A giggle escaped.

All three guys sent me a look, Blake's the most curious, but I shook my head and took another deep breath. I knew I needed to keep it together. I had to pay attention and keep my wits about me. I was way beyond enemy lines. Freaking out and getting pummeled with onyx wasn't going to help me. Neither was breaking down in hysterics and finding a corner to rock in.

It was hard—probably the hardest thing I'd ever done—but I pulled it together.

Sergeant Dasher pivoted on his heel. "There's something I would like to show you, Katy. I hope this will make things easier for you."

Doubtful, but I followed him. The corridor split into two halls, and we headed down the right one. This place had to be massive—a massive maze of halls and rooms.

The sergeant stopped in front of a door. There was a control panel on the wall with a blinking red light at eye level. He stepped in front of it. The light went green, there was a soft sucking noise, and the door opened, revealing a large square room full of doctors. It was a lab and waiting room in one. I stepped through, immediately wincing at the smell of antiseptic. The sight and smell brought a wave of memories back.

I recognized rooms like this—I'd been in rooms like this before.

With my dad when he was sick. He'd spent time in a room very much like this one when he was receiving treatment for cancer. It paralyzed me.

There were several U-shaped stations in the middle of the space; each one displayed ten recliners that I knew would be comfy. Many were occupied with people—humans—in every stage of sickness. From the optimistic, bright-eyed newly diagnosed to the frail, barely even aware of where they were, and all of them were hooked up to fluid bags and something that looked nothing like chemo. It was clear liquid, but it shimmered under the light, like Dee used to when she faded in and out.

Doctors roamed, checking bags and chatting with the patients. Toward the back were several long tables where people peered into microscopes and measured out medicine. Some were at computers, their white lab coats billowing around the chairs.

Sergeant Dasher stopped beside me. "This is familiar to you, isn't it?"

I looked at him sharply, only vaguely aware that Archer was glued to my other side and Blake had stepped back. Obviously he wasn't as talkative around the sergeant. "Yes. How do you know?"

A small smile appeared. "We've done our research. What kind of cancer did your father have?"

I flinched. The words *cancer* and *father* still carried a powerful punch. "He had brain cancer."

Sergeant Dasher's gaze moved toward the station nearest us. "I would like you to meet someone."

Before I could say anything, he stepped forward, stopping at one of the recliners that had its back to us. Archer nodded, and I reluctantly shifted so that I could see what the sergeant was looking at.

It was a kid. Maybe nine or ten, and with the sallow skin tone and bald head, I couldn't tell if it was a boy or girl, but the child's eyes were a bright blue.

"This is Lori. She's a patient of ours." He winked at the young girl. "Lori, this is Katy."

Lori turned those big, friendly eyes on me as she extended a small, terribly pale hand. "Hi, Katy."

I took her cold hand and shook it, not sure what else to do. "Hi."

Her smile spread. "Are you sick, too?"

I didn't know what to say at first. "No."

"Katy's here to help us," Sergeant Dasher said as the little girl pulled her hand back, tucking it under the pale gray blanket. "Lori has grade four, primary CNS lymphoma."

I wanted to look away, because I was a coward and I *knew*. That was the same kind of cancer my father had. Most likely terminal. It didn't seem fair. Lori was way too young for something like this.

He smiled at the girl. "It's an aggressive disease, but Lori is very strong."

She nodded fervently. "I'm stronger than most girls my age!"

I forced a smile I didn't feel as he stepped to the side, allowing a doctor to check the bags. Her bright baby blues bounced among the three of us. "They're giving me medicine that'll make me get better," she said, biting down on her lower lip. "And this medicine doesn't make me feel as bad."

I didn't know what to say, and I couldn't speak until we stepped back from the girl and moved to a corner where we weren't in anyone's way. "Why are you showing this to me?" I asked.

"You understand the severity of disease," he said, turning his gaze to the floor of the lab. "How cancer, autoimmune diseases, staph infections, and so many more things can rob a person of his or her life, sometimes before it really gets started. Decades have been spent on finding the cure to cancer or to Alzheimer's to no avail. Every year, a new disease arises, capable of destroying life."

All of that was true.

"But here," he said, spreading his arms wide, "we take a stand against disease with your help. Your DNA is invaluable to us, just like the Luxen chemical makeup is. We could inject you with the AIDS virus, and you wouldn't get sick. We've tried. Whatever is in the Luxen DNA, it makes both them and the hybrids resilient to all known human diseases. It is the same for the Arum."

A shudder rolled down my spine. "You're really injecting hybrids and Luxen with diseases?"

He nodded. "We have. It enables us to study how the hybrid's, or the Luxen's, body fights off the disease. We hope to be able to replicate it, and in some cases we have had success, especially with LH-11."

"LH-11?" I asked, watching Blake now. He was talking to another young kid—a boy who was having fluid administered. They were laughing. It seemed…normal.

"Gene replication," the sergeant explained. "It slows the growth of inoperable tumors. Lori has responded well to it. LH-11 is a product of years of research. We are hoping it's the answer."

I didn't know what to say as my gaze moved across the room. "The cure to cancer?"

"And many, many more diseases, Katy. This is what Daedalus is about, and you can help make this possible."

Leaning against the wall, I flattened my palms. Part of me wanted to believe what I was hearing and seeing—that Daedalus was only trying to find the cure for diseases—but I knew better. Believing that was like believing in Santa. "And that's all? You're just trying to make the world a better place?"

"Yes. But there are different ways, outside of the scope of medicine, to make the world a better place. Ways that *you* can help make the world a better place."

I felt like I was getting a sales pitch, but even in the position I was in, I could recognize how powerful a cure for such deadly diseases could be, how much it would change the world for the better. Closing my eyes, I drew in a deep breath. "How so?"

"Come." Dasher cupped my elbow, not giving me much of a choice. He led me to the opposite end of the lab, where a section of the wall appeared to be a shuttered window. He knocked on the wall. The shutters rolled up, making a series of mechanical *click*s. "What do you see?"

The air went out of my lungs. "Luxen," I whispered.

There was no doubt in my mind that the people sitting in matching recliners on the other side of the window, letting doctors take their blood, were not from around here. Their beauty was a dead giveaway. So was the fact that a lot of them were in their true form. Their soft glow filled the room.

"Do any of them look like they don't want to be here?" he asked quietly.

Placing my hands on the window, I leaned in. The ones who didn't look like a human lightbulb were smiling and laughing. Some were snacking on food, and others were chatting. Most of them were older, in their twenties or thirties, I guessed.

None of them looked like hostages.

"Do they, Katy?" he prodded.

I shook my head, thoroughly confused. Were they here of their own volition? I couldn't understand how.

"They want to help. No one is forcing them."

"But you're forcing me," I told him, aware that Archer was now behind us. "You forced Bethany and Dawson."

Sergeant Dasher cocked his head to the side. "It doesn't have to be that way."

"So you don't deny it?"

"There are three kinds of Luxen, Miss Swartz. There are those who are like the ones on the other side of this window, Luxen who understand how their biology can greatly improve our lives. Then there are those who have assimilated into society and who pose little to no risk."

"And the third group?"

He was silent for a moment. "The third group is the one that generations before us had feared upon the arrival of the Luxen. There are those who wish to take control of Earth and subjugate mankind."

My head swung toward him. "What the what?"

His eyes met mine. "How many Luxen do you think there are, Miss Swartz?"

I shook my head. "I don't know." Daemon had once mentioned how many he thought were here, but I couldn't recall the amount. "Thousands?"

Dasher spoke with authority. "There are roughly forty-five thousand inhabiting Earth."

Whoa, that was a lot.

"About seventy percent of that forty-five thousand have been assimilated. Another ten percent can be trusted completely, like those in the other room. And the last twenty percent? There are nine thousand Luxen who want to see mankind under their thumbs—nine thousand beings who can wield as much destruction as a small warhead. We barely keep them under control as it is, and all it would take for a complete upheaval of our society is for them to sway more Luxen to their side. But want to know another startling number?"

Staring at him, I had no idea what to say.

"Let me ask you a question, Ms. Swartz. Where exactly do you think Daemon Black, his family, and his friends fall?"

"They aren't interested in subjugating a house fly!" I barked out a harsh laugh. "Insinuating that is just ridiculous."

"Is it?" He paused. "You can never really, truly know someone. And I am sure when you first met Daemon and his family, you never would've assumed what they are, correct?"

He had me there.

"You have to admit that if they were so good at hiding the fact they weren't even human, how good they must be at hiding something as invisible as their allegiance," he said. "You forget that they are not human, and they are not, I can assure you, a part of the ten percent that we trust."

I opened my mouth, but no words came out. I didn't—couldn't—believe what he said, but he had said all of this without an ounce of scorn. As if he were just stating facts, like a doctor would when telling a patient he had terminal cancer.

He turned back to the window, lifting his chin. "It is speculated that there are hundreds of thousands of Luxen out there, in space, who traveled to other points in the universe. What do you think would happen if they came here? Remember, these are Luxen who have had little to no contact with mankind."

"I…" A shiver of unease traveled up my spine and across my shoulders. Turning my attention to the window, I watched a Luxen flicker into his true form. When I spoke, I didn't recognize my own voice. "I don't know."

"They would obliterate us."

I sucked in a sharp breath, still not wanting to believe what he was saying. "That sounds a little extreme."

"Does it?" He paused, sounding curious. "Look at our own history. One stronger nation takes over another. The Luxen's and even the Arum's mentalities are no different from ours. Basic Darwinism."

"Survival of the fittest," I murmured, and for a moment I could almost see it. An invasion of Hollywood proportions, and I knew enough about the Luxen to know that if that many came here, and they wanted to take over, they would.

Closing my eyes, I shook my head again. He was mind-screwing me. There wasn't an army of Luxen about to invade. "What does any of this have to do with me?"

"Besides the fact that you are strong, as is the Luxen who mutated you, and your blood could possibly help us come one step closer to a successful batch of LH-11? We would love to study the connection between you and the one who mutated you. Very few have been able to do it successfully, and it would be a great achievement to have another Luxen who could successfully mutate other humans and create hybrids who are stable."

I thought of all those humans Dawson had been forced to mutate and watch die. I couldn't bear it if Daemon had to go through that, creating humans that would only…

I took a deep breath. "Is that what happened to Carissa?"

"Who?"

"You know who," I said tiredly. "She was mutated, but she was unstable. She came after me and self-destructed. She was a…" Good person. But I stopped, because I realized that if the sergeant knew anything about Carissa, he either wasn't talking or he simply didn't care.

A few moments passed before he continued. "But that's not the only thing Daedalus is concerned with. Having the Luxen here who mutated you would be great, but that's not what we're focused on."

I looked at him sharply, and my heart rate picked up. Surprise shuttled through me. They weren't focused on luring Daemon in?

"We wanted you," Sergeant Dasher said.

It felt like the floor moved under my feet. "What?"

His expression was neither cold nor warm. "See, Miss Swartz, there're those nine thousand Luxen we need help dealing with. And when the rest of the Luxen come to Earth—and they will—we will need everything in our arsenal to save mankind. That means hybrids like you, and hopefully many more, who can fight."

What the…? I was sure I'd slipped into an alternate universe. My brain pretty much imploded.

Dasher regarded me closely. "So, the question is, will you be with us, or will you stand against your own kind? Because you will have to make a choice, Miss Swartz. Between your own people or those of the one who mutated you."

Chapter 6

Daemon

After saying good-bye to Dawson and Bethany, I left the house just as dawn broke. What had happened with Beth haunted my every step. She seemed a little better, but I didn't know. I had no doubt that Dawson would take care of her, though.

I looked back at the house. A cold, distant part of me acknowledged that I might not see this place, or my brother and sister, ever again. That knowledge didn't lessen my resolve.

I headed in the opposite direction of the colony, picking up speed. Although I stayed in my human form, I moved faster than I could be tracked.

Dawson had told me earlier that my car had been stowed away at Matthew's, which helped detour local law enforcement that weren't bought out by the DOD and were actually concerned about another set of missing teenagers.

It took me less than five minutes to make the trek to Matthew's cabin in the middle of nowhere. I slowed as I reached his driveway, spying his SUV.

I smirked.

I needed to get out of state, at least into Virginia. I could travel the entire way in my true form. Hell, it probably would even be quicker, but I'd wear myself out, and I was pretty sure the little meet and greet I was going to do at Mount Weather would be exhausting.

Considering how ticked off I was at Matthew right at the moment, I was going to enjoy "borrowing" his car, since mine would draw attention from those I didn't have time to deal with. I slid into the driver's seat, reached down, and yanked on the manifold hiding the wires.

When Dawson and I were little, we used to hotwire cars with our fingers for shits and giggles at the mall in Cumberland. Took us a couple of tries until we discovered the exact charge needed to do a jump-start and not fry the computers or the whole wiring system. We'd then move them into different parking spots and watch the owners come out, dumbfounded by how their cars had moved.

We'd bored easily as kids.

I wrapped my fingers around the wires and sent a little charge through them. The car sputtered, and the engine turned over.

Still had the magic touch.

Not wasting any time, I got the hell out of Matthew's driveway and headed for the highway. There was no way he'd be as understanding as Dawson, at least not at the moment.

My brother was set to take care of a few things for me. He'd move enough money to get Kat and me by for a couple of years to an account I'd meticulously kept off the radar just in case shit went downhill one day.

And shit definitely had gone downhill.

Dawson and Dee also had strategically hidden "oh-crap" accounts, just as the Thompsons did. Matthew had gotten us doing that. I used to think it was paranoia, but, damn, he'd been smart. There was no way I could come back, and neither could Kat. We'd have to find a way for her to see her mom, but neither of us could stay here when I got her out of there. It would be too dangerous.

But before I headed to Mount Weather, I had a little visit to make.

Blake couldn't have been the only one to screw us.

There was a teen hybrid who had a lot of explaining to do.

A little bit after noon, I stashed Matthew's car behind the rundown gas station on the same road as Luc's club. Not that the potholed dirt pathway was really a road. The last thing I wanted was for them to know I was coming. Something about Luc was off, and in a big way. The fact that he was barely a teenager and running a club was a big clue. And he was out here, with other Luxen, and unprotected from the Arum?

Yeah, something was off about the kid.

Staying in my human form, I took off through the weeds and into the wooded area behind the gas station. Bright sunlight filtered through the branches, and warm May air rushed me as I flew over the uneven ground. Seconds later, I cleared the stand of trees and hit the overgrown field.

Last time I'd been here with Kat, the field was nothing more than a frozen patch of grass. Now the reeds whipped at my jeans and dandelions carpeted the grass. Kat had a thing for dandelions. She couldn't keep her fingers off them when we'd been training with the onyx. From the moment those yellow weeds started poking through the ground, she'd snap them up and pop their heads off.

A wry grin tugged at my lips as I skidded to a stop in front of the windowless door. *Demented Kitten*.

I placed my hands on the steel door, sliding them down the center, feeling for gaps or locks to manipulate. There was no way this door was unlocking anytime soon.

Backing up, I scanned the front of the building. Squat and no windows, more like a warehouse than a club. I stalked around the side, knocking empty cardboard boxes out of the way. In the back was a loading dock.

Score.

Pressing my hands on the thin gap between the doors, I heard the wonderful sound of locks unclicking. I quickly eased the door open and stepped into a dark storage area. Slipping through the shadows, I hugged the wall, my gaze flitting over white containers and piles of papers. There was a distinct smell of alcohol in the air. Another door loomed ahead, and I opened it. The minute I stepped into the narrow corridor lined with dry erase boards with stick figures—*what the hell?*—drawn all over them, the hair on the back of my neck rose, and a cold shiver snaked its way down my spine.

Arum.

I barreled out of the corridor, seconds from flipping into my true form. Instead I ground to a halt, face-to-face with the business end of a sawed-off shotgun.

That would sting.

The proud owner of the redneck killer was Big Boy the Bouncer, still rocking overalls. "Hands up, and don't even think about going Lite-Brite on my ass, pretty boy."

Jaw clenched tightly, I raised my hands. "There's an Arum here."

"No shit," the bouncer said.

I cocked a brow. "So Luc is working with Arum, too?"

"Luc ain't workin' for no one." The bouncer stepped forward, eyes narrowed. "Where's that girl who's normally with ya? She be sneakin' around here, too?"

He glanced behind me, and I took advantage of the momentary distraction. My hand shot out faster than he could react. I snatched the shotgun from his grip and flipped it around. "How does it feel to have this pointed at your head?" I asked.

Big Boy's nostrils flared. "Ain't feelin' real good."

"Didn't think so." My finger itched on the trigger. "I'd like to keep my pretty face intact."

The bouncer chortled. "And you do have a pretty face."

Banjos started playing in my head.

"Oh, look," said a new voice. "A love connection is made."

"Not quite," I said, wrapping my free hand around the barrel.

"Did you think I didn't know you were here?"

Without taking my eyes off Big Boy, I smirked. "Does it matter?"

"Yeah, if you were trying to sneak up on me, I guess it does." Luc ambled out of the shadows and into my line of sight. He was dressed in black running pants and a T-shirt that read, ZOMBIES NEED LOVE, TOO. Nice. "You can put the gun down, Daemon."

Smiling coldly, I let heat encompass my hand. Warmth flared, and the smell of burning metal wafted into the air. When the barrel was made useless, I handed it back to Big Boy.

The bouncer looked down at the gun and sighed. "I hate when this happens."

I watched Luc hop up on the bar and swing his legs like a petulant child. Under the dim bar lighting, the ring around his oddly colored eyes seemed to be blurred. "You and I need to—"

Whipping around, I let out a roar as my human form faded. I shot across the empty dance floor, heading straight for the mass of shadows forming under the cage.

The Arum turned, and the second before we slammed into each other like two boulders rolling down a hill, I saw him in his true form—dark as midnight oil and shiny as glass. The impact shook the walls and rattled the cages hanging from the ceilings.

"Oh, jeez," Luc said. "Can't we all just get along?"

The Arum swept his arms around my waist as I threw him back into the wall. Plaster cracked and plumed into the air. He didn't let go. The SOB was strong.

Spinning around, he broke my hold and his smoky arm snaked out, aiming for my chest. I darted to the side, throwing up my arm to blast the annoying bastard into next year.

"Boys. *Boys!* No fighting in my club," Luc called, sounding irritated.

We ignored him.

Energy crackled over my palms, spitting white fire into the air.

You don't know who you're messsing with, the Arum hissed, sending his words straight into my skull, which just pissed me off. I let go of the ball of energy.

It smacked into his shoulder.

He jerked away and then turned his head back to me, cocking it to the side. His form became more solid.

Static crackled down my arms. Light pulsed throughout the room. This guy was really starting to get on my nerves.

"I wouldn't do that if I were you," Luc said. "Hunter is very, very hungry."

I was about to show Luc just what I thought about his advice when a form stepped out of the hallway leading to his office. It was a woman—a pretty, blond-haired woman who was oh-so human. Her eyes were wide. "Hunter?"

What. The. Hell.

Distracted, the Arum glanced back at the woman around the same time the Source fizzled out of me. He must've communicated with her, because she frowned and said, "But he's one of *them*."

Hunter's head swung back to me, and his chest rose as he took a step back. A second later, a man stood before me, coming in at my height. Dark brown hair and those damn pale Arum eyes were fixed on me.

"Serena," he said. "Go back to Luc's office."

The woman's frown grew into a scowl, reminding me so much of Kat that my chest ached. "Excuse me?"

His head snapped toward her, eyes narrowing. An instant later, Big Boy strode across the dance floor, wrapping an arm around the woman's shoulders. "This really ain't where ya need to be right now."

"But—"

"Come on, I got some stuff to show ya," Big Boy said.

Hunter glared. "What stuff?"

Big Boy winked over his shoulder. "Stuff."

As they disappeared down the hallway, the Arum's lip curled. "I do not like this."

Luc chuckled. "She's not his type."

Wait—what in the hell was going on? An Arum with a human?

"You want to tone down the light?" the asshole said. "You're blinding me."

Power rippled through me, and I wanted to slam my fist through his face, but he wasn't attacking, which was strange. And he was with a human woman he appeared to be *really* with, which was even more bizarre.

I took my human form. "I don't like your tone."

He smirked.

My eyes narrowed.

"You two should play nice." Luc clapped his hands together. "You never know when you'll need such an unlikely ally."

Hunter and I looked at each other. Both of us snorted. Doubtful.

The boy shrugged. "Okay. So, this is a very exciting day for me. I have Hunter, who needs no last name and only shows up when he wants something or someone to feed off, and I have Daemon Black, who looks like he wants to do me physical harm."

"That's about right," I snarled.

"Care to tell me why?" he asked.

My hands curled into fists. "Like you don't know."

He shook his head. "I really don't, but I'll hazard a guess. I don't see Katy, and I don't feel her. So I'm assuming your little break-in at Mount Weather didn't go smoothly."

I took a step forward, rage swirling inside me.

"You broke into Mount Weather?" Hunter choked out a laugh. "Are you insane?"

"Shut up," I said, keeping my eyes on Luc.

Hunter made a deep noise. "Our little mutual white flag of friendship is going to come to a halt if you tell me to shut up again."

I spared him a brief glance. "Shut. Up."

Dark shadows drifted over the Arum's shoulder, and I faced him fully. "What?" I said, throwing my hands up in a universal come-get-some gesture. "I have a lot of pent-up violence I'd love to take out on someone."

"Guys." Luc sighed, sliding off the bar. "Seriously? Can't you two bromance it out?"

Hunter ignored him, taking a step forward. "You think you can take me?"

"Think?" I scoffed, going toe-to-toe with the alien. "I know."

The Arum laughed as he took one long finger and poked me in the chest—*poked me in the chest*! "Well, let's find out."

I grabbed his wrist, my fingers circling his cool skin. "Man, you really are—"

"Enough!" Luc shouted.

The next second I was pinned against one side of the club, and Hunter was on the other, several feet off the ground. The Arum's expression most likely mirrored mine. Both of us struggled against the invisible hold, but neither of us could do a damn thing to get down.

Luc moved to the center of the floor. "I don't have all day, guys. I have things to do. A nap I want to take this afternoon. There's a new movie out on Netflix I want to watch, and a goddamn coupon for a free Whopper Jr. that's calling my name."

"Uh…" I said.

"Look." Luc turned to me, his expression clouded. In that moment, he looked way older than I knew he was. "I'm guessing you think I was somehow a part of Katy being captured. You're wrong."

I sneered. "And I should believe you?"

"Do I look like I give a flying rainbow if you believe me? You broke into Mount Weather, a government stronghold. It takes no stretch of imagination to guess that something went wrong. I did what I promised."

"Blake betrayed us. Daedalus has Kat."

"And I told you to not trust anyone who had something to gain or lose." Luc exhaled roughly. "Blake is…well, he's Blake. But before you cast judgment, ask yourself how many people you'd crucify to get Katy back?"

The hold on me let go, and I slid down the wall, hitting my feet. As I stared at the teen, I believed him. "I have to get her back."

"If Daedalus has your girl, you can kiss her good-bye," Hunter said from across the room. "They are some fuc—"

"And you?" Luc cut in. "I told you to stay in my office. Not listening to me is not how to get something from me."

Hunter gave an awkward shrug, and a second later, he was standing on the floor, looking as cuddly as a pit bull.

Luc cast both of us dark looks. "I get that you two have problems—big problems—but guess what? You're not the only aliens out there who are butt sore. There are bigger problems than what you guys have. Yeah, I know, hard to believe."

I glanced over at Hunter, who shrugged again and said, "Someone didn't get his warm milk this morning."

I snickered.

Luc's head swung toward him, and damn if I couldn't believe I was standing in a room with an Arum and not killing him—but he was also not trying to kill me. "You need to be glad that I like you," Luc said in a low voice. "Look, I need to talk to Daemon. Can you go do something? If not, then maybe you can be helpful?"

The Arum rolled his eyes. "Yeah, I have my own problems." He started back toward the hall and then stopped, glancing at me. "See you on the flip side."

I gave him the middle finger good-bye.

When he disappeared down the corridor, Luc turned toward me and folded his arms. "What happened?"

Seeing that I had nothing to lose, I told him what went down at Mount Weather. Luc gave a low whistle and shook his head. "Man, I'm sorry. Truly I am. If Daedalus has her, then I don't—"

"Don't say it," I growled. "She's not lost to me. We got Bethany out. *You* got out."

Luc blinked. "Yeah, you got Bethany out, but Katy got caught in the process. And I'm…I'm not like Katy."

I didn't know what the hell that meant. Turning from him, I thrust my fingers through my hair. "Did you know that Blake would betray us?"

There was a pause. "And if I did, what would you do?"

A bitter laugh snuck out. "I'd kill you."

"Understandable," he replied evenly. "Let me ask you a question. Would you have still helped your brother rescue Bethany if you knew Blake would betray you?"

Facing Luc, I slowly shook my head as the truth hit me square in the chest. If I'd known that Kat wouldn't be coming home, I don't think I could say yes, and I couldn't put to words the fact that I would choose her over my brother.

He tipped his head to the side. "I didn't know. That doesn't mean I trusted Blake. I don't trust anyone."

"Anyone?"

He ignored the question. "What do you want from me, since you obviously aren't going to try to kill me? Do you want me to take down the security again? I can do that. It'll be a freebie for you, but it'll also be a suicide mission. They'll be expecting you."

"I don't want you to take anything down."

He looked at me, confused. "But you're going after her?"

"Yes."

"You'll get caught."

"I know."

Luc stared at me so long I thought the kid might've had a seizure. "So you really were coming here to kick my ass?"

My lips twitched. "Yeah, I was."

The kid shook his head. "Do you have any idea what you're getting yourself into?"

"I know." I folded my arms. "And I know once they have me, they are going to want me to make hybrids."

"Have you ever had to watch people die, over and over again? No? Ask your brother."

I didn't hesitate. "She's worth whatever I have to go through."

"There are worse things," he said quietly. "If you and Hunter could put away your differences for two seconds, he'd probably tell you himself. There are things that they are doing there that will blow your mind."

"Even more reason for me to get Kat out."

"And what's your plan? How are you going to get her out?" he asked, curious.

Good question. "I haven't gotten that far yet."

Luc watched me a moment, then busted into laughter. "Good plan. I like it. Only a few things could go wrong with that."

"How did you get out, Luc?"

He tilted his head to the side. "You don't want to know what I did. And you won't do what I did."

A cold shiver crawled over my skin. I believed the kid.

Luc stepped back. "I got to take care of this other issue, so..."

My gaze slid to the hallway. "Working with Arum, huh?"

His mouth twitched. "Arum and Luxen aren't that different. They're just as screwed as you guys are."

Funny. I didn't see it that way.

Luc tipped his chin down and swore. Looking up at me, he said, "Daedalus's biggest weakness is their arrogance. Their need to create what should never be created. Their need to control what can never be controlled. They're tinkering with evolution, my friend. That never ends well in the movies, does it?"

"No. It doesn't." I started to turn away.

"Wait," he called out, stopping me. "I can help you."

I faced him, head tilted to the side. "What do you mean?"

Luc's amethyst eyes, so like Ethan's that it was disturbing, latched onto mine. There was something a little off about his, though, with the line around the pupils. "Their biggest defense is that the world doesn't know they exist. They don't know *we* exist."

I couldn't look away, and I decided that this Luc kid was kind of creepy.

He smiled then. "They have something that I want, and I bet it's where they're keeping Katy."

My eyes narrowed. Tit for tat never sat well with me. "What do you want?"

"They have something called LH-11. I want that."

"LH-11?" I frowned. "What the hell is that?"

"The beginning of everything and the end of the beginning," he said mysteriously, and a strange gleam filled his purplish eyes. "You'll know it when you see it. Get it for me, and I'll make sure you get out of wherever it is you're at."

I stared at him. "I don't doubt your awesomeness, but how can you get Kat and me out of a place if you don't even know where it is?"

He arched a brow. "You must doubt my awesomeness if you're asking, and you shouldn't. I have people everywhere, Daemon. I'll check around with them, and they'll let me know when you show up."

Laughing softly, I shook my head. "Why should I trust you?"

"I've never asked you to trust me. You also have no other choice." He paused, and hell if he didn't have a point. "Get me the LH-11, and I'll make sure you and your *Kitten* get out of whatever hellhole they have you in. It's a promise."

Chapter 7

Katy

It felt like forever since I was given a lunch of mashed potatoes and Salisbury steak. I was too amped up to check out the TV. Waiting in the silence drove me to pace the length of my cell. My nerves were stretched to the point that every time I heard footsteps outside the room, my heart leapt into my throat and I moved back from the door.

I was skittish, reacting to every sound. Having no concept of the amount of time that was passing or even what day it was, I felt like I was trapped in an airless bubble.

Making my hundredth pass in front of the bed, I mulled over what I did know. There were people here who wanted to be here—humans and Luxen, probably even a few hybrids. They were testing LH-11 on cancer patients, and God knew what LH-11 really was. A part of me could get behind that—if the Luxen really were here because they wanted to help. Finding the cure to deadly diseases was important. If Daedalus had simply asked me and hadn't wanted to keep me in a cell, I would've gladly given up my blood.

I couldn't shake what Sergeant Dasher had told me. Were there really nine thousand or so Luxen out there plotting against humans? Hundreds of thousands who could come to Earth at any time? Daemon had mentioned others before, but never once had he said anything about his kind, even a small enclave, wanting to take over.

What if that were true?

It couldn't be.

The Luxen weren't the bad guys here. The Arum and Daedalus were. The organization might have pretty packaging, but it was rotten inside.

Footsteps sounded outside the room, and I jumped a good couple of inches into the air. The door opened. It was Archer.

"What's going on?" I asked, immediately wary.

The beret that seemed permanently attached to his head hid his eyes, but his jaw was tight. "I'm to take you to the training rooms."

He did the hand-on-the-shoulder thing, and I wondered if he really thought I'd try to run. I wanted to, but I wasn't that stupid. Yet. "What goes on in the training rooms?" I asked when we were in the elevator.

He didn't answer, which wasn't very reassuring, and it ticked me off. The least these people could do was tell me what was going on. I tried to shrug off his hand, but it was glued to my shoulder the whole way.

Archer was a man of few words, and that made me even more nervous and jumpy, but it was more than that. There seemed to be something different about him. I couldn't put my fingers on it, but it was there.

By the time we hit the training floor, my stomach was churning. The hallway was identical to the medical floor, except there were a lot of double doors. We stopped at one and, when he keyed in a code, the doors slid open.

Blake and Sergeant Dasher were in the room. Dasher turned to us, smiling tightly. There was something different in his expression. A hint of desperation in his dark brown eyes unnerved me. I couldn't help but think of those blood work results.

"Hello, Miss Swartz," he said. "I hope you took the time to rest up."

Well, that didn't sound good.

Two men in lab coats sat in front of an array of monitors. The rooms on the screen looked padded to me. My fingers felt numb from clenching them so hard.

"We're ready," one of the men said.

"What's going on?" I asked, hating how my voice broke halfway through the question.

Blake's expression was blank, while Archer took up his position as sentry by the door.

"We need to see the extent of your abilities," Sergeant Dasher explained, moving to stand behind the two men. "Inside of this controlled room, you'll be able to use the Source. We know from our previous investigations that you do have some control, but what we don't know is the extent of your abilities. Hybrids who have successfully mutated can react just as quickly as a Luxen. They can control the Source just as well."

My heart skipped. "What purpose does this serve? Why do you need to know? I'm obviously a successful mutation."

"Wc don't truly know that, Katy."

I frowned. "I don't get it. Earlier you said I was strong—"

"You *are* strong, but you've never consistently used your abilities or done so without the hybrid who mutated you. It's possible that you've been feeding off his ability. And a hybrid may appear to have successfully mutated, but we've discovered that the more one taps into the Source, the more evident the instability in his or her mutation becomes. We need to test for any type of unpredictability in your mutation."

As his words sank in and made sense, I wanted to run from the room, but I was rooted to the floor. "So you want to see if I basically self-destruct like…" Like Carissa, but I couldn't say her name out loud. When he neither confirmed nor denied it, I took a step back. A whole new horror rose to the surface. "What happens if I do? I mean, I know what happens to me, but what about…?"

"The one who mutated you?" he asked, and I nodded. "You can say it, Miss Swartz. We know it was Daemon Black. There is no need to try to protect him."

I still wouldn't say his name. "What happens?"

"We know that the Luxen and the human he mutates are joined on a biological level if the mutation holds. It's not something we understand completely." He paused, clearing his throat. "But for those who turn unstable, the connection is voided out."

"Voided out?"

He nodded. "The biological link between the two is broken. Possibly due to the fact that, in those cases, the mutation wasn't as strong as suspected. We really just don't know everything yet."

A shudder of relief rolled through me. It wasn't like I didn't have a sense of self-preservation, but at least I knew if I blew up, Daemon would still be alive. But I stalled, not wanting to go into that room. "Is that the only thing that breaks the link?"

The sergeant didn't respond.

My eyes narrowed. "Don't you think I have a right to know?"

"All in good time," he replied. "Now is just not the time."

"I think it's a damn good time."

His eyebrows shot up in surprise, further angering me.

"What?" I said, throwing up my hands. Archer stepped closer to me, but I ignored him. "I think I have a right to know everything."

His surprise faded, replaced with a cool expression. "This is not the time."

I held my ground, hands curling into fists. "I don't see there being any better time."

"Katy…" Archer's soft warning was ignored, and he moved

closer, his chest almost against my back.

"No. I want to know what else can break the link. Obviously something can. I also want to know how long you really think you can keep me here." Once the lid came off my mouth, there was no shutting it. "What about school? You want an uneducated hybrid running amuck? What about my mom? My friends? What about my life? My blog?" Okay, my blog was seriously the least of my worries, but dammit, it was important to me. "You've stolen my life and think that I should just stand here and take it? That I shouldn't demand answers? You know what? You can kiss my ass."

Whatever warmth had been in Sergeant Dasher's expression seeped away. He stared back at me, and in that moment, I realized I probably should've kept my mouth shut. I had needed to say those words, but the hard look he gave me was frightening.

"I don't tolerate foul language. And I don't tolerate smart-mouthed little girls who don't understand what is going on. We have tried to make this as comfortable as we can for you, but we all have limits, Miss Swartz. You will not question me or any of my staff. We will let you know things when we feel it's the appropriate time and not before. Do you understand?"

I could feel every breath Archer took, and it seemed like he stopped, waiting for me. "Yes," I spat. "I understand."

Archer took a breath.

"Good," the sergeant said. "Since that's now settled, let's move on."

One of the men at the monitors pressed a button and a small door opened to the training room. Archer didn't let me go until I was inside the room. Then he did.

I spun around as he backed toward the door, my eyes going wide. I started to ask him not to leave me, but he looked away quickly. And then he was gone, closing the door behind him.

Heart pounding, I darted my eyes around the room. It was about twenty feet by twenty, with a cement floor and another door on the opposite side, and the walls weren't padded. Nope. I wouldn't get that lucky. The walls were white with scuffs of red. Was that…dried blood?

Oh God.

But that fear trickled away as awareness kicked in. The rush of power was tiny at first, a rush that felt like tips of fingers were trailing down my arms, but it grew quickly, spreading to my core.

It was like taking a breath of fresh air for the first time. Numbness and exhaustion eked away, replaced with a low buzz of energy that was in the back of my skull, thrumming through my veins and filling the coldness in my soul.

My eyes fluttered shut, and I saw Daemon in my head. Not because I could *really* see him, but because feeling this reminded me of him. As the Source wrapped its way around me, I imagined being in Daemon's embrace.

An intercom clicked on overhead, and Sergeant Dasher's voice filled the room, causing my head to jerk up. "We need to test your ability, Katy."

I didn't want to talk to the ass-hat, but I wanted to get this over with more. "Okay. So you want me to call on the Source or what?"

"You will do that, but we need your ability tested under stress."

"Under stress?" I whispered, glancing around the room. Unease unfurled in my belly, spreading like a noxious weed, threatening to choke me. "I'm feeling pretty stressed right now."

The intercom clicked on again. "That's not the kind of stress we're talking about."

Before his words had a chance to sink in, there was a loud thumping noise that reverberated through the small room. I whipped around.

Across from me, the other door was sliding open, inch by inch. The first thing I noticed was a pair of black sweatpants like the pair I had on, and then a white shirt covering narrow hips. My gaze crawled up, and I let out a surprised gasp.

Standing before me was a girl I had met before. It felt like a lifetime ago, but I recognized her immediately. Her blond hair was pulled back in a neat ponytail, revealing a pretty face offset by bruises and scratches.

"Mo," I said, taking a step forward.

The girl who had been in the cage next to mine when Will had held me captive stared back at me. I'd wondered many times what had happened to her, and I guessed now I knew. A heartbeat passed, I said her name again, and then it hit me with startling clarity. She was showing the same vast emptiness that Carissa had when she'd been in my bedroom.

My heart sank. I doubted there was anything I could do that would remind the girl of me.

She stepped into the room and waited. A moment later, the intercom buzzed and Sergeant Dasher's voice came through. "Mo will assist in the first round of the stress tests."

First round? There was more than one? "What is she—?"

Mo flung her hand out, and the Source crackled over her knuckles. Shock held me immobile until the last possible moment. I darted to the side, but the blast of whitish light tinged in blue smacked into my shoulder. Pain burst and rushed down my arm. The impact spun me around, and I barely kept my balance.

Confusion swirled as I clutched my shoulder, not surprised to find the material singed. "What the hell?" I demanded. "Why—?"

Another blast sent me dropping to my knees as it whizzed by right where I'd been standing. It hit the wall behind me, fizzling out. In the blink of an eye, Mo was right in front of me. I started to stand, but her knee came up, catching me in the chin and snapping my head back. Starbursts blinded me as I fell back on my butt, stunned.

Reaching down, Mo grabbed ahold of my ponytail and lifted me to my feet with surprising ease. Her hand swung out, the blow catching me right below the eye. That burst of pain caused my ears to ring, and it did something else.

It knocked the stupor right out of me.

Suddenly I understood this stress test, and it sickened and horrified me. I had to believe that if Daedalus knew everything, then they had to have known that I'd met Mo. That seeing her here, in better physical shape than she had been in that cage, would not only knock me off guard but would confirm the futility of fighting against them.

But they did want me to fight—they wanted me to fight Mo, using the Source. Because what else, other than getting your ass handed to you on a silver platter, would cause such major stress?

Another punch caught me right under the eye. She put a hell of a lot of *oomph* behind it. A metallic taste sprang into my mouth as I called on the Source, just like the sergeant wanted.

But Mo…she was so much faster than me, so much better.

As the ass-kicking of a lifetime picked up, I held on to the small sliver of hope I had: Daemon wouldn't be subjected to this.

• • •

DAEMON

Stashing Matthew's SUV several miles from the access road leading to Mount Weather, I hoped whoever found his car got it back to him in one piece. It was a pretty sweet ride. Not as good as Dolly, but not many cars were.

I traveled the last couple of miles in my true form, rushing through the heavy thicket. I reached the access road within minutes, and seconds later I was at the cusp of the forest, staring at the all-too-familiar fence that surrounded the grounds.

There were definitely more guards on duty—at least three of them by the gate, and I bet there were more inside. Cameras and security systems weren't going to go down this time. I didn't want them to.

I wanted to get caught.

Dawson probably thought I hadn't given this much consideration. A lot was on the line—not only my future but my family's and Kat's. Once the DOD realized I was here, things were going to get rough. Getting in wouldn't be the problem, and if I got whatever it was that Luc wanted, he would get us out—if he wasn't lying. And if he was, I would find another way.

Part of me hoped that Kat was still here, that Daedalus hadn't moved her to another location. Probably foolish to hope for that, because I had a feeling a big ol' dose of disappointment was heading my way.

So, yeah, I wanted to get caught, but I wasn't going to make this easy for them.

Stepping out from under the cover of the trees, I let my human form take hold under a strong beam of sunlight. The guards were oblivious to my presence at first, and as I took another step forward, the conversation I had with Kat the night she finally admitted her feelings for me came to mind.

I'd told her that we made the good kind of crazy together, and I hadn't known how true that really was until this very moment, because what I was about to do was really, truly, 100 percent certifiable.

The first guard, who was pulling something—a cell phone?—out of his black cargo pants, turned, his eyes drifting through the trees. His gaze moved over me and then darted back. The cell phone fell from his fingers, and he shouted, one hand going for the gun on his thigh and the other for the microphone on his shoulder. The two guards behind him whipped around, drawing their weapons.

Time to get this show on the road.

Summoning the Source, I stayed in my human form, but I knew the moment they became sure of what I was. It was probably my eyes. The world was tinted in a brilliant sheen.

A series of popping sounds followed, telling me that the guards weren't messing around.

I raised my hand, and the bullets appeared to hit an invisible wall. In reality, it was the energy reflecting the bullets. I could've sent them back at the guards, but all I did was stop them. They fell to the ground harmlessly.

"I wouldn't suggest you try that again," I said, lowering my hand.

Of course they didn't listen. Why? That would be too easy.

The guard in the front unloaded his weapon, and I repelled all the bullets. After a few seconds, I was so done with this. Turning around, I extended an arm back toward the trees. They began to tremble. Branches shook, sending a waterfall of green needles whirling into the air. Pulling them forward, I spun around.

Thousands of needles shot through the air, speeding forward. They split around me, heading straight for the dumbstruck guards.

The needles slammed into the men, turning them into human pincushions. Not killing them, but if their grunts of pain and surprise were any indication, it had to sting like a bitch. The guards were on their knees, guns forgotten on the ground beside them. Waving my hand, I sent their weapons flying into the woods, never to be seen again.

I prowled forward, passing them with a smirk. Summoning the Source once more, I let the energy crackle down my arm. A bolt of light hit the gate on the electric fence. A burst of white exploded, dancing across the chain-link, frying out the power to the fence and leaving a nice, comfy hole to walk right through.

Stalking over the neatly trimmed landscape that we had previously run across, I took a deep breath as the doors to Mount Weather slid open.

A freaking army of officers emptied out, dressed like they were ready for Armageddon or a guest spot on a SWAT team. Their faces were covered with shields, like that would help them. Going down on one knee, they leveled a dozen or so semiautomatic rifles on me. Stopping so many bullets would prove tricky.

People were going to die.

That sucked, but it wouldn't stop me.

Then a tall, slender form came into view, walking out of the dimly lit tunnel. The men donned in black uniforms parted, never taking their rifles off me while allowing the primly dressed woman to easily navigate her way to the front.

"Nancy Husher," I snarled, my hands curling into fists. I'd known the woman for years. Never liked her, which was compounded by the fact that I knew she worked within Daedalus and had known what really happened to Dawson.

Her mouth spread into the tight-lipped smile she was famous for, the one that said she was about to shove a wicked dagger into your back while kissing your cheek. She was just who I was hoping to find.

"Daemon Black," she said, clasping her hands together. "We've been expecting you."

Chapter 8

Katy

After the disastrous training session, I knew the taste of true fear each time someone neared my door. My heart hammered painfully until the sound of footsteps faded, and when the door finally opened, revealing Archer with my evening meal, I almost vomited.

I had no appetite.

I couldn't sleep that night.

Every time I closed my eyes, all I could picture was Mo standing before me, more than ready to kick my ass every which way from Sunday. The vast emptiness that had clouded her eyes had quickly blossomed into determination. My beating may not have been as severe if I had fought back, but I hadn't. Fighting her would have been wrong.

When the door opened the following morning, I was only running on a few hours of sleep. It was Archer, and in his quiet way, he motioned me to follow him.

Sick to my stomach, I had no other choice but to go wherever he was leading me. The nausea grew as we rode the elevator to the floor that housed the training rooms. It took everything in me to step off the elevator and not grab onto one of the bars for dear life.

But he led me behind the room we'd gone to before, through double doors, and then farther down a hall, where we passed through another set of doors.

"Where are we going?"

He didn't respond until we stopped outside a steel door that glinted from an overabundance of onyx and diamonds. "There is something Sergeant Dasher wants you to see."

I could only imagine what rested beyond the door.

He placed his forefinger against the security pad, and the light flipped from red to green. Mechanical *clicks* followed. I held my breath as he opened the door.

The room inside was lit only by one dim bulb in the ceiling. There were no chairs or tables. To the right was a large mirror that ran the length of the wall.

"What is this?" I asked.

"Something you must see," Sergeant Dasher said from behind us, causing me to jump and spin around. Where in the hell had he come from? "Something I hope will ensure that we won't have a repeat of our last training session."

I crossed my arms and lifted my chin. "There's nothing you can show me that will change that. I am not going to fight other hybrids."

Dasher's expression remained the same. "As I explained, we must make sure you are stable. That is the purpose of these training sessions. And the reason why we must make sure you are strong and able to harness the Source lies beyond this mirror."

Confused, I glanced back at Archer. He stood near the door, face shadowed by the beret. "What's on the other side?"

"The truth," responded Dasher.

I coughed out a laugh that caused the scraped skin on my face to sting. "Then you have a room full of delusional military officers on the other side?"

His look was as dry as sand as he reached over, flipping a switch along the wall.

Sudden light exploded, but it came from behind the mirror. It was a one-way mirror, like in police stations, and the room was not empty.

My heart kicked in my chest as I stepped forward. "What…?"

There was a man on the other side sitting in a chair, and not willingly. Onyx bands covered his wrists and ankles, locking him down. A shock of white-blond hair covered his forehead, but he slowly lifted his head.

He was a Luxen.

The angular beauty gave him away, and so did the vibrant green eyes—eyes that reminded me so much of Daemon that an ache pierced my chest and sent a ball of emotion straight into my throat.

"Can…can he see us?" I asked. It seemed that way. The Luxen's eyes were fixed on where I stood.

"No." Dasher moved forward, leaning against the mirror. A small intercom box was within arm's reach.

Pain etched the man's beautiful face. Veins bulged along his neck as his chest rose on a ragged breath. "I know you're there."

I looked at Dasher sharply. "You sure he can't see us?"

He nodded.

Reluctantly I returned my attention to the other room. The Luxen was sweating and trembling. "He's…he's in pain. This is so wrong. It's a complete—"

"You do not know who sits on the other side of this glass, Miss Swartz." He flicked a button on the intercom. "Hello, Shawn."

The Luxen's lips twisted up on one side. "My name is not Shawn."

"That has been your given name for many years." Dasher shook his head. "He prefers to go by his true name. As you know, that is something we cannot speak."

"Who are you talking to?" Shawn demanded, his gaze unnervingly landing on where I stood. "Another human? Or even better? An abomination—a fucking hybrid?"

I gasped before I could stop myself. It wasn't what he said but the distaste and hatred that bled into each word.

"Shawn is what you would call a terrorist," the sergeant said, and the Luxen in the other room sneered. "He belonged to a cell that we'd been monitoring for a couple of years. They planned to take out the Golden Gate Bridge during rush hour. Hundreds of lives—"

"Thousands of lives," Shawn interrupted, his green eyes glowing luminous. "We would've killed *thousands*. And then we would've—"

"But you didn't." Dasher smiled then, and my stomach dropped. It was probably the first real smile I'd seen from the man. "We stopped you." He glanced over his shoulder at me. "He was the only one we could bring in alive."

Shawn laughed harshly. "You might have stopped me, but you haven't accomplished anything, you simpleminded *ape*. We are superior. Mankind is *nothing* compared to us. You will see. You have dug your own graves, and you cannot stop what is coming. All of you will—"

Dasher flipped off the intercom, bringing the tirade to a halt. "I have heard this many times over." He turned to me, head tilted to the side. "This is what we are dealing with. The Luxen in that room wants to kill humans. There are many like him. That is why we are doing what we are doing."

Wordless, I stared at the Luxen as my brain slowly turned over what I had just witnessed. The intercom was off, but the man's mouth was still moving, raw hatred seeping from his lips. The kind of blind animosity shown by all terrorists, no matter who or *what* they were, was carved into his face.

"Do you understand?" the sergeant asked, drawing my attention.

Wrapping my arms around my waist, I shook my head slowly.

"You can't judge an entire race based on a few individuals." The words sounded empty to me.

"True," Dasher agreed quietly. "But that would only be the case if we were dealing with humans. We cannot hold these beings to the same moral standard. And believe me when I tell you, they do not hold us to theirs."

Hours turned into days. Days possibly into weeks, but I really couldn't be sure. I understood now how Dawson couldn't keep track of time. Everything blended here, and I couldn't remember the last time I'd seen the sun or the night sky. I wasn't served breakfast like I had the first day I'd been awake, which threw off the time of day for me, and the only way I knew when a full forty-eight hours had passed was when I was taken to Dr. Roth for blood work. I'd seen him around five times, maybe more.

I'd lost count.

I'd lost a lot of things. Or it felt that way. Weight. The ability to smile or laugh. Tears. The only thing I retained was anger, and each time I squared off with Mo or another hybrid I didn't know—didn't even care to get to know because of what we had to do—my anger and frustration went up a notch. It surprised me that I could still feel so much.

But I hadn't given in yet. I hadn't fought back during any of the stress tests. It was my only means of control.

I refused to fight them—to beat up on them or potentially kill them if things got out of hand. It was like being in a real, albeit messed-up, version of *The Hunger Games*.

The Hunger Games for alien hybrids.

I started to grin but winced as the motion pulled my torn lip. I might have refused to go all *Terminator* on them, but the other hybrids were *so* on board. So much so that some of them talked while they kicked my ass. They told me that I needed to fight, that I needed to prepare for the day the other Luxen came and for those who were already here. It was obvious they sincerely believed that the true villains were the Luxen. They may have been drinking the Kool-Aid, but I was not. Even so, there was a tiny part of me that wondered how Daedalus could control so many if there wasn't some truth in what they were saying?

And then there was Shawn, the Luxen who wanted to kill thousands of humans. If I were to believe Dasher, there were a hell of lot more like him out there—just waiting to take over Earth. But to even think that Daemon or Dee, or even Ash, was a part of something like that…I couldn't even consider it.

Forcing my eyes open, I saw the same thing I always saw after being hauled out of the training rooms and deposited—mostly unconscious—in my cell. The white ceiling with little black dots—a mixture of onyx and diamond.

God, I hated those dots.

I took a deep breath and cried out, immediately wishing I hadn't. Sharp pain radiated across my ribs from a Mo-size kick. My entire body throbbed. There wasn't one part of me that didn't ache.

Movement from the farthest corner of my cell, by the door, drew my attention. Slowly and quite painfully, I turned my head.

Archer stood there, bundling a cloth in his hand. "I was beginning to worry."

I cleared my throat and then opened my jaw, wincing. "Why?"

He came forward, the beret forever hiding his eyes. "You were out for a while this time, the longest yet."

I turned my head back to the ceiling. I hadn't realized that he was keeping track of my ass-kickings. He hadn't been here other times when I awoke. Neither had Blake. I hadn't seen that ass-hat in a while, and I wasn't sure he was even here anymore.

I drew in a slower, longer breath. As sad as it was, when I was awake, I missed the moments of oblivion. It wasn't always just a black, vast nothingness. Sometimes I dreamed of Daemon, and when I was awake I clung to those faint images that seemed to blur and fade the minute I opened my eyes.

Archer sat on the edge of the bed, and my eyes snapped open. The aching muscles tensed. Although he proved to be not so bad, all things considered, I trusted no one.

He held up the bundle. "It's just ice. Looks like you could use it."

I watched him warily. "I don't…I don't know what it looks like."

"*It* being your face?" he asked, palming the bundle. "It doesn't look pretty."

It didn't feel pretty. Ignoring the throbbing in my shoulder, I tried to pull my arm out from under the blanket. "I can do it."

"You don't look like you can lift a finger. Just stay still. And don't talk."

I wasn't sure if I should be offended by the whole *don't talk* part, but then he pressed the icy bundle against my cheek, causing me to suck in a sharp breath.

"They could have gotten one of the Luxen to heal you, but your refusing to fight back isn't going to make it easy on you." He pressed the ice bag down, and I drew back. "Try to keep that in mind when you go to the training room next time."

I started to scowl, but it hurt. "Oh. Like this is my fault."

He shook his head. "I didn't say that."

"Fighting them is wrong," I said after a few seconds. "I'm not going to self-destruct." Or at least I hoped I wasn't. "Making them do that is…is inhumane. And I won't—"

"You will," he said simply. "You're no different than them."

"No different." I started to sit up, but he pinned me with a look that had me settling back down. "Mo doesn't even seem human anymore. None of them do. They're like robots."

"They're trained."

"T-Trained?" I sputtered as he moved the ice to my chin. "They're mindless—"

"It doesn't matter what they are. You keep doing this? Not fighting back, not giving Sergeant Dasher what he wants, you're going to keep being a human punching bag. And what does that solve? One of these days, one of the hybrids will kill you." He lowered his voice, so low that I wondered if the microphones could even pick it up. "And what happens to the one who mutated you? He will die, Katy."

Pressure clamped down on my chest and a whole different kind of pain surfaced. At once, I saw Daemon in my head—that ever-present, infuriating smirk on his expressive face—and I missed him so badly a burning crawled up my throat. My hands curled under the blanket as a hole opened up in my chest.

Several minutes passed in silence, and while I lay there, staring at his brown-and-white-camouflaged shoulder, I searched for something to say, anything to drive the emptiness out of me, and I finally came up with something.

"Can I ask you a question?"

"You probably shouldn't talk anymore." He switched the bag of ice to his other hand.

I ignored that, because I was pretty sure I'd go crazy if I kept silent. "Are there really Luxen out there who want to take over? Others like Shawn?"

He didn't respond.

Closing my eyes, I let out a weary sigh. "Will it kill you to just answer the question?"

Another moment passed. "The fact that you're even asking is answer enough."

Was it?

"Are there good humans and bad humans, Katy?"

I thought it was weird how he said *humans*. "Yes, but that's different."

"Is it?"

When the icy bundle landed on my cheek again, it didn't feel so bad. "I think so."

"Because humans are weaker? Keep in mind that humans have access to weapons of mass destruction, just like the Luxen do. And do you really think that the Luxen don't know what happens here?" he asked quietly, and I stilled. "That there are some who, for their own reasons, support what Daedalus does, while others fear losing what life they have built here? Do you really want an answer to that question?"

"Yes," I whispered, but I was lying. A part of me didn't want to know.

Archer moved the bag of ice again. "There are Luxen who want to take over, Katy. There is a threat, and if that day comes when the Luxen have to choose sides, which side will they stand on? Where will you stand?"

• • •

DAEMON

I was about ten seconds from snapping someone's neck.

Who knew how many days had passed since Nancy did the little meet and greet at Mount Weather? A couple? A week or more? Hell if I knew. I had no idea what time of day it was or how much time had passed. Once they had escorted me inside, Nancy had disappeared, and a whole slew of stupid shit proceeded to take place—an exam, blood work, physical, and the lamest interrogation this side of the Blue Ridge Mountains. I went along with everything to just speed up the process, but then absolutely freaking nothing happened.

I was stashed in a room—probably the same kind of room Dawson's ass had been held in once upon a time—growing more furious by the second. I couldn't tap into the Source. I could, however,

take my true form, but the only good that did was lighting up the room when it was dark. Not exactly helpful.

Pacing the length of the cell, I couldn't help but wonder for the thousandth time if Kat was doing the same thing some other place. I didn't feel her, but the weird link between us only seemed to work if we were nearby. There was still a chance, a small sliver of hope, that she was at Mount Weather.

Who knew what time it was when the door to my room opened and three G.I. Joe wannabes motioned me out. I brushed past them, grinning when the one I knocked shoulders with muttered a curse.

"What?" I challenged, facing the guard, ready for a fight. "You got a problem?"

The guy sneered. "Move it along."

One of them, a very brave soul, prodded me in the shoulder. I turned my glare on him, and he wilted back. "Yeah, I didn't think so."

And with that, the three commandos guided me down the hallway that was nearly identical to the one that led to the room we'd found Beth in. Once in the elevator, we descended a couple of floors, and then walked out and into another corridor populated with various military personnel, some of them in uniform and others in suits. All of them gave our little happy group a wide berth.

My already nonexistent patience was stretched thin by the time we stopped in front of two dark, shiny double doors. My spidey senses were telling me the thing was rigged with onyx.

The commandos did some secret squirrel shit with the control panel, and the doors slid open, revealing a long rectangular table. The room wasn't empty. Oh no. Inside was my favorite person.

Nancy Husher sat at the head of the table, hands folded in front of her and hair pulled back in a tight ponytail. "Hello, Daemon."

I so wasn't in the mood for bullshit. "Oh. You're still around after all this time? Here I thought you just dumped me."

"I'd never dump you, Daemon. You're too valuable."

"*That* I know." I sat down without being told and leaned back, folding my arms. The soldiers shut the doors and took up guard in front of them. I shot them a dismissive glance before turning to Nancy. "What? No blood tests or exams today? No endless stream of stupid questions?"

Nancy was clearly struggling to maintain her cool facade. I hoped to whatever God was out there that I pushed every button the woman had. "No. There's no need for any more of that. We've gotten what we need."

"And what is that?"

One of her fingers moved up and then stilled. "You think you know what Daedalus is trying to do. Or at least you have your assumptions."

"I honestly don't give two shits what your little freak group is doing."

"You don't?" One thin brow rose.

"Nope," I said.

Her smile spread. "You know what I think, Daemon? You're a whole lot of bluster. A smart mouth with the muscles to back it up, but in reality you have no control in this situation, and deep down you know that. So keep running your mouth. I find it amusing."

My jaw clenched. "I live to entertain you."

"Well, that's good to know, and since that is now cleared up, may we move on?" When I nodded, her shrewd gaze sharpened. "First I want to make it clear that if at any time you pose a threat to me or to anyone else, we have weapons here that I would loathe to use on you but will."

"I'm sure you would loathe to do that."

"I would. There are PEP weapons, Daemon. Do you know what that stands for? Pulse Energy Projectile. It disrupts electronic and light wavelengths on a catastrophic level. One shot and it is fatal to your kind. I would hate to lose you. Or Katy. Get what I'm saying?"

My hand closed into a fist. "I get it."

"I know you have your assumptions when it comes to Daedalus, but we hope to change that during the course of your stay with us."

"Hmm, my assumptions? Oh, are you referencing that time when you and your minions led me to believe that my brother was dead?"

Nancy didn't even blink. "Your brother and his girlfriend were held by Daedalus because of what Dawson did to Bethany—for their safety. I know you don't believe that, and that isn't a concern of mine. There is a reason why Luxen are forbidden to heal humans. The consequences of such actions are vast, and in most cases result in unstable DNA changes within the human body, especially outside of controlled environments."

I cocked my head at that, remembering what happened to Carissa. "What is that supposed to mean?"

"Even if humans survive the mutation with our help, there is still a chance that the mutations are unstable."

"With your help?" I laughed coldly. "Shooting people up with God knows what is helping them?"

She nodded. "It was that or let Katy die. That is what would have happened."

I stilled, but my heart rate picked up.

"Sometimes the mutations fade. Sometimes they kill them. Sometimes they hold, and then people combust under stress. And sometimes they hold perfectly. We have to determine that, because we cannot allow unstable hybrids into society."

Anger whirled through me like a freight train. "You make it sound like you're doing the world a favor."

"We are." She leaned back, sliding her hands off the table. "We are studying Luxen and hybrids, trying to cure disease. We are stopping potentially dangerous hybrids from hurting innocent people."

"Kat's not dangerous," I ground out.

Nancy tilted her head to the side. "That's yet to be seen. The truth is she's never been tested, and that's what we're doing now."

I leaned forward very slowly, and the room started to carry a white sheen to it. "And what does that mean?"

Nancy held up her hand, warding off the three stooges by the door. "Kat has proven to show signs of extreme anger, a hallmark of instability in a hybrid."

"Really? Kat's angry? Could it be because you're holding her captive?" The words tasted like acid.

"She attacked several members of my team."

A smile spread across my face. *That's my girl.* "So sorry to hear that."

"So was I. We have so much hope when it comes to you two. The way you've worked together? It's a perfect symbiotic relationship. Very few Luxen and humans have reached that. Mostly the mutation acts as a parasite to the human." She folded her arms, stretching the drab brown of her suit jacket. "You could mean so much to what we're trying to accomplish."

"Which is curing disease and saving innocent people?" I snorted. "And that's it? Really, do you think I'm stupid?"

"No. I think you're very much the opposite of stupid." Nancy exhaled through her nose as she leaned forward, placing her hands on the dark gray table. "Daedalus's goal is to change the landscape of human evolution. Doing so requires drastic methods at times, but the end results are worth every fleck of blood, trickle of sweat, and teardrop."

"As long as it's not your blood, sweat, and tears?"

"Oh, I have given this everything, Daemon." She beamed. "What if I could tell you that we could not only eradicate some of the most virulent diseases, but we could stop wars before they even started?"

And there it was, I realized. "How would you do that?"

"Do you think any country would want to fight an army of hybrids?" She cocked her head. "Knowing what a successfully mutated one is capable of?"

Part of me was disgusted at the implications. The other half was just plain old pissed off. "Creating hybrids so they can fight stupid wars and die? You tortured my brother for this?"

"You say tortured; I say motivated."

All right, this was one of the moments in my life when I really wanted to knock someone through a wall. And I think she knew that.

"Let's get to the point, Daemon. We need your help—your willingness. If things go smoothly for us, they will go smoothly for you. What will it take to come to an agreement?"

Nothing in this world should have made me consider this. It went against nature; that was how wrong this was. But I was a bartering man, and when it came down to it, no matter what Daedalus wanted, what Luc wanted, there was one thing that mattered. "There's only one thing I want."

"And that is?"

"I want to see Kat."

Nancy's smile didn't fade. "And what are you willing to do to accomplish that?"

"Anything," I said without hesitation, and I meant it. "I will do *anything*, but I want to see Kat first, and I want to see her now."

Calculating light filled her dark eyes. "Then I am sure we can work something out."

CHAPTER 9

KATY

My legs ached as I trailed behind Archer, limping our way to the training room. Who would I fight today? Mo? The guy with a Mohawk? Or would it be the girl with the really pretty red hair? It didn't matter. I'd be getting my butt kicked. The only thing I did know was that they wouldn't let any of the other hybrids kill me. I was too *valuable*.

Archer slowed his step, allowing me to gimp my way up to him. He hadn't said anything since he left my cell yesterday, but I was used to his silence. I couldn't figure him out, though. It didn't seem like he supported any of this, but he never said it outright. Maybe it was just a job to him.

We stopped in front of the doors I'd come to loathe. Taking a deep breath, I stepped through when they opened. No point in delaying the inevitable.

Sergeant Dasher waited inside, dressed in the same uniform he'd been wearing since the first time I saw him. I wondered if he had an endless supply of them. If not, he had to have one hell of a dry-cleaning bill.

These were the stupid things I thought of before I was pummeled into one giant bruise.

Dasher gave me a once-over. From the brief glimpse of my reflection in the foggy mirror in the bathroom, I knew I looked like a hot mess. On the right side of my face, my cheek and eye were an ugly shade of purple and swollen. My lower lip was split. The rest of my body looked like a smorgasbord of bruises.

He shook his head and stepped aside, allowing Dr. Roth to check me over. The doctor took my blood pressure, listened to me breathe, and then shined a light in my eyes.

"She looks a little worse for wear," he said, tucking his stethoscope under his lab coat. "But she can participate in the stress test."

"It would be nice if she actually participated," grumbled one of the guys at the control panels. "And not just stand there."

I shot him a glare, but before I could open my mouth, Sergeant Dasher cut in. "Today will be different," he said.

Folding my arms, I fixed my eyes on him. "No. It won't. I'm not fighting them."

His chin went up a notch. "Perhaps we've introduced you to the stress test incorrectly."

"Gee," I said, smiling inwardly at the way his eyes narrowed. "What part of this whole thing is incorrect?"

"We do not want you to fight to just fight, Katy. We want to make sure your mutation is viable. I can see that you are unwilling to hurt just another hybrid."

A tiny smidgen of hope flared inside me, like a fragile seedling poking through the ground. Maybe making a stand, accumulating all these bruises, had meant something. It was a small step that probably meant nothing to them but everything to me.

"But we must see your abilities under high stress." He motioned to the guys at the panels, and my hope crashed and burned. The door opened. "I think you will be more accepting of this test."

Oh God, I didn't want to walk through those doors, but I forced one foot in front of the other, refusing to show an ounce of weakness.

The door closed behind me, and I faced the other door, waiting while knots formed in my stomach. How in the world could they make this acceptable? There was nothing they could—

In that instant, the other door opened, and Blake stepped through.

I choked out a dry, bitter laugh as he swaggered into the room, barely paying heed to the door closing behind him. Suddenly Dasher's words about being more acceptable made sense.

Blake frowned as he stopped in front of me. "You look like crap."

The simmering anger sparked. "And you're surprised? You know what they're doing in here."

He thrust his fingers through his hair as his eyes moved over my face. "Katy, all you had to do was tap into the Source. You're making this harder on yourself."

"*I'm* making this—?" I cut myself off as the anger heated up in me. The Source stirred in my belly, and I felt the tiny hairs on my body rise. "You're insane."

"Look at yourself." He waved a hand at me. "All you had to do was do what they asked, and you could've avoided all of this."

I stepped forward, glaring at him. "If you hadn't betrayed us, I would've avoided all of this in the first place."

"No." A look of sadness crept across his face. "You would've ended up here no matter what."

"I don't agree."

"You don't want to agree."

I sucked in a deep breath, but the anger was getting the better of me. Blake moved to put his hand on my shoulder, but I knocked his arm away. "Don't touch me."

He stared at me a moment, and then his eyes narrowed. "Like I told you before, if you want to be mad at anyone, get mad at Daemon. He did this to you. Not me."

That did it.

All the pent-up anger and frustration whipped through me like a category-five hurricane. My brain clicked off, and I swung without thinking. My fist just grazed his jaw, but the Source had reared its head at the same time. A bolt of light shot from my hand and spun him around.

He caught himself on the wall, letting out a surprised laugh. "Damn, Katy. That hurt."

Energy crackled down my spine, fusing with my bones. "How dare you blame *him* for this? This isn't his fault!"

Blake turned around and leaned against the wall. Blood trickled from his lip, and he wiped at it with the back of his hand. A strange gleam entered his eyes, and then he pushed off the wall. "This is completely his fault."

I flung my arm out and another bolt of energy shot forward, but he dodged it, laughing as he spun around, his arms out at his sides. "Is that the best you got?" he goaded me. "Come on. I promise I'll go easy on you, *Kitten*."

At the use of the pet name—Daemon's pet name—I lost it.Blake was on me in a second. I darted to the side, ignoring the painful protest of my muscles. His arm came out in a wide sweep, and whitish-red light crackled. I spun at the last second, narrowly avoiding taking a direct hit.

Letting the rush of energy swell through me once more, I sent another blast arcing across the room, hitting him in the shoulder.

He stumbled back, hands dropping to his knees as he doubled over. "I think you can do better than that, *Kitten*."

Fiery hot rage slipped over my eyes like a veil. Launching myself forward, I tackled him like an NFL linebacker on speed. We went down in a mess of tangled legs and arms. I landed on top of him, swinging my arm back and bringing it down repeatedly. I wasn't really seeing where I was hitting, only feeling the flare of pain across my knuckles as they connected with flesh.

Blake shoved his arms between mine and swept them out, knocking me off balance. I teetered for a second, and then he raised his hips and rolled. I slammed onto my back, knocking the air out of my lungs. I aimed for his face, hell-bent on clawing his eyes out.

He caught my wrists and pinned them above my head as he leaned down. A cut had opened under his left eye, and his cheek was starting to swell. A vicious amount of satisfaction rushed through me.

"Can I ask you a question?" Blake grinned, turning the flecks of green in his eyes brighter. "Did you ever tell Daemon that you kissed me? I bet you haven't."

Each breath I took I felt in every part of my body. My skin became hypersensitive to his weight and proximity. The power built inside, and the room seemed to be tinted in a brilliant sheen of white. Fury consumed me, riding every breath and latching onto every cell.

His grin spread. "Just like you never told him how we liked to cuddle—"

The power burst from me, and suddenly I was off the floor—*we* were off the floor—levitating several feet in the air. My hair streamed down behind me, and his hair fell forward into his eyes.

"Shit," Blake whispered.

Flipping upward, I tore my wrists free from his grip and slammed my hands into his chest. Shock rippled across his pale face a second before he flew backward, crashing into the wall. The cement cracked, and a fissure spread out like a wicked spiderweb. The whole room seemed to shake with the impact as Blake's head snapped back, and then he slumped forward. Part of me expected him to catch himself before he smacked into the floor, but he didn't. He hit with a fleshy splat that knocked the anger right out of me.

As if I'd been held up by invisible strings that had now been cut, I landed on the balls of my feet and rocked forward a step.

"Blake?" I croaked out.

He didn't move.

Oh no…

Arms shaking, I started to kneel down, but something dark and thick spread out from under his body. My gaze flicked up to the wall. A Blake-size imprint was clearly visible, a form reaching through at least three feet of cement.

Oh God, no…

Slowly, I looked down. Blood pooled out from under his motionless body and seeped across the gray cement floor, stretching toward my sneakers.

Stumbling back, I opened my mouth, but there was no sound. Blake didn't move. He didn't roll over with a groan. He didn't move at all. And the visible skin on his hands and forearms was paling already, turning a ghastly shade of white that stood out with such stark contrast against the deep red of the blood.

Blake was dead.

Oh my God.

Time slowed and then sped up. If he was dead, then that meant the Luxen who had mutated him was, too, because that was how it worked. They were joined together, like Daemon and I, and if one died…the other died, too.

Blake had it coming in more ways than one. I'd even promised to kill him, but words…words were one thing. Actions were a totally different ballpark. And Blake, even with all the terrible things he'd done, was a product of circumstance. He was only goading me. He'd killed not really meaning to. He'd betrayed to save another.

Just like I did—and would.

My hand shook as I pressed it against my mouth. Everything I'd said to him came back in a rush. And in that tiny second when I'd caved to the fury—nothing in a span of millions—I had changed, become something I wasn't sure I could ever come back from. My chest rose rapidly at the same time my lungs compressed painfully.

The intercom clicked on, the initial buzz startling me in the dead silence. Sergeant Dasher's voice filled the room, but I couldn't take my eyes off Blake's lifeless form. "Perfect," he said. "You've passed this stress test."

It was too much—ending up here, so far away from my mom and Daemon and everything that I knew, then the exam and the subsequent showdowns with the hybrids. And now this? It was too much.

Letting my head fall back, I opened my mouth to scream, but there was no sound. Nothing as Archer entered and gently placed his hand on my shoulder, steering me out of the room. Dasher said something, sounding very much like an approving father, and then I was taken out of the training room and into an office, where Dr. Roth waited to take more blood. They brought in a female Luxen to heal me. Minutes turned into hours, and still, I said nothing and felt nothing.

• • •

DAEMON

Being handcuffed with metal coated in onyx, blindfolded for five hours, and then put on some flight wasn't my idea of a fun time. I guess they were afraid that I'd bring the plane down, which was stupid. It was getting me to where I wanted to go. I didn't know the location, but I knew it had to be where they were keeping Kat.

And if she wasn't there, I was going to go postal.

Once the plane landed, I was hustled to a waiting car. From underneath the blindfold, I could make out bright light, and the smell was really dry and acidic, vaguely familiar. The desert? It hit me during the two-hour drive that I was going back to the place I'd last been to damn near thirteen years ago.

Area 51.

I smirked. Keeping me blindfolded was pointless. I knew where we were. All Luxen, once discovered, were processed through the remote detachment of Edwards Air Force Base. I'd been young, but I'd never forget the dryness to the air or the remote, barren landscape of Groom Lake.

When the vehicle rolled to a stop, I sighed and waited for the door beside me to be opened. Hands landed on my shoulders, and I was dragged out of the car, thinking whoever had their hands on me was real lucky that mine were handcuffed behind my back, or someone was going to be leaving work today with a broken jaw.

The dry heat of the Nevada desert beat down as I was led several yards, and then a wave of cool air hit me, raising the strands of hair off my forehead. We were in an elevator before the blindfold was removed.

Nancy Husher smiled up at me. "Sorry for that, but we must take precaution."

I met her eyes. "I know where we are. I've been here before."

A single thin brow went up. "Many things have changed since you were a child, Daemon."

"Can I get these off yet?" I wiggled my fingers.

She glanced at one of the soldiers in camouflage. He was young from what I could tell, but the khaki-colored beret hid most of his upper face. "Unlock the handcuffs. He's not going to give us any trouble." She looked back at me. "I do believe Daemon knows this place is outfitted with an onyx defense system."

The guard stepped forward, fishing out a key. The set of his jaw said he wasn't too sure if he should believe her, but he unlocked the cuffs. They scraped along the raw skin of my wrists as they slipped off. I shook my shoulders out, relieving the cramped muscles. Red marks circled my wrists, but it wasn't too bad.

"I'll behave," I said, cracking my neck. "But I want to see Kat now."

The elevator slid to a stop and the doors opened. Nancy stepped out, and the soldier motioned me forward. "There's something you need to see first."

I ground to a halt. "That's not a part of the deal, Nancy. You want me to go along with this, I want to see Kat now."

She glanced over her shoulder. "What I'm about to show you has to do with Katy. Then you will see her."

"I want—" I whipped around, eyeballing the guard breathing down my neck. "Seriously, dude, you need to back the hell up."

The guy was half a head shorter than me and nowhere in my league of extraordinary ass-kicking abilities, but he didn't back down. "Keep. Walking."

I stiffened. "And if I don't?"

"Daemon," Nancy called, her voice laced with impatience. "All you're doing is delaying what you want."

As much as I hated to admit it, she had a point. Sending the punk one last promising look, I turned and followed the woman down the hall. Everything was white with the exception of the black dots in the wall and ceilings.

I didn't recall much about the inside of the buildings from when I'd been here as a kid, but I did remember there were very few places we'd been able to go. Most of the time we'd been kept to a community floor until we had assimilated and been set free.

Being back here didn't sit well with me for a multitude of reasons.

Nancy stepped in front of a door and leaned down. A red light clicked on and shone in her right eye. The light on the panel turned green and the door unlocked. That was going to prove tricky, and I wondered whether, if I took on Nancy's form, the systems had been prepped to recognize that. Then again, I felt as drained as the desert floor from whatever this building was outfitted with, so I wasn't sure what I could actually pull off.

Inside the small circular room, there were several monitors manned by men in uniform. Each of the screens showed a different room, hall, or floor.

"Leave us," she announced.

The men stood up from their stations and hastily exited the room, leaving Nancy and me with the tool who had come in with us.

"What did you want to show me?" I asked. "EuroCup?"

Her lips pursed. "This is one of many security control rooms stationed throughout the buildings. From here, we can monitor everything in Paradise Ranch."

"Paradise Ranch?" I laughed bitterly. "Is that what you're calling it now?"

She shrugged and then turned to one of the stations, her fingers flying over the keyboard. "All of the rooms are recorded. That helps us monitor activity for various reasons."

I ran a hand over the scruff growing on my cheek. "Okay."

"One of our concerns whenever we bring in new hybrids is to make sure they are not a danger to themselves or others," she began, folding her arms. "It's a process we take very seriously, and we go through several rounds of testing to ensure that they are viable."

I really did not like where this was heading if it had anything to do with Kat.

"Katy has proven to have some issues and can become very dangerous."

I ground down on my teeth so hard I was surprised they didn't crack. "If she's done anything, it's because she was provoked."

"Really?" Nancy punched a button on the keyboard, and the screen above her to the left flickered on.

Kat.

All the air went out of my lungs. My heart stopped and then sped up.

Kat was on the screen, sitting down with her back pressed against a wall. The image was grainy, but it was her—*it was her*. She was in the clothes she'd worn the night she was captured at Mount Weather, and that had to be weeks ago. Confusion rose swiftly. When was this taken? It couldn't be a live feed.

Her hair hung down on the sides, shielding her beautiful face. I started to tell her to look up but realized at the last minute that would make me look like an imbecile.

"As you can see, no one is near her," Nancy said. "That is Sergeant Dasher in the room with her. He is doing the initial interview."

Suddenly, Kat's chin jerked up, and she sprang to her feet, racing around a tall man in a military uniform. The next second, she hit the floor. I stared in open horror as Kat withered, and then one of the men unhooked a water hose from the wall.

Nancy flicked a button, and there was a different image. It took me a second to recover from the last scene and get what was going on now, but when I did, pure, red-hot rage lit me up.

On the screen were Kat and freaking Blake, squaring off. She whirled, grabbing for a lamp, but he darted in front, blocking her. When she swung on him, pride swelled in me. That was *my* Kitten, claws and all.

But the next thing had me searching for a way out of the room. Blake had intercepted her punch, twisted her arm, and swung her around. Pain registered on Kat's face, and then he had her down on her back, pinned to the bed.

I saw red.

"This isn't happening now," Nancy said calmly. "This was a while ago, when she first arrived. It's muted."

Breathing heavily, I turned back to the TV. They were struggling, and Blake had obviously overpowered her. She was still fighting, though, her back bowing and her body twisting under his. Violence rose in me, powered by potent rage and a level of helplessness I'd never felt before, and it tasted like Blake's blood. My hands formed fists, and I wanted to smash them in the monitor, since his face wasn't in front of me.

When he had pulled her off the bed, and I saw him dragging her across the floor and off the screen, I spun toward Nancy. "What happened? Where did he take her?"

"Into the bathroom, where there are no cameras. We do believe in some sort of privacy." She clicked something and the video fast-forwarded a couple of minutes, and Blake entered from the right. He sat on the bed—*her* bed—and Kat appeared a few seconds later, absolutely soaked.

I stepped forward, exhaling out of my nose. Words were exchanged between them, and then Kat whirled, opened a dresser, and grabbed clothes. She disappeared back into the bathroom.

Blake dropped his head into his hands.

"I'm going to fucking kill him," I promised to no one in particular, but it was one I was going to keep. He would pay for this—all of this—one way or another.

The soldier cleared his throat. "Blake isn't an issue anymore."

I faced him, breathing raggedly. "Care to tell me why?"

He pressed his lips together. "Blake's dead."

"What?"

"He's dead," the guy repeated. "Katy killed him two days ago."

The floor felt like it dropped out from underneath me. My first response was to deny it, because I didn't want to believe that Kat would have had to do something like that—that she had to go through it.

The monitor was turned off, and Nancy watched me. "The reason I'm showing you this isn't to upset you or to make you mad. You need to see with your own eyes that Katy has proven to be dangerous."

"I have no doubt in my mind that if Kat really did do that, she had a reason." My heart thudded in my chest. I *needed* to see her. If she had done this… I couldn't bear to think about what she had to be going through. "And I would've done it, too, if I were in her shoes."

Nancy *tsk*ed softly, and I added her to my Going to Die Painfully list. "I hate to think of you as being unstable, too," she said.

"Kat isn't unstable. All these videos show is her defending herself, or that she was scared."

Nancy made a sound of disagreement. "Hybrids can be so unpredictable."

I met her gaze and held it. "So can Luxen."

Chapter 10

Daemon

They let me clean up in an empty communal area. At first I didn't want to waste the time. I needed to get to Kat, but they weren't giving me much of a choice, which turned out to be a good thing because I looked like something straight out of the mountains. The growth on my face was out of control. After a shave and a quick shower, I put on the black sweats and white shirt that had been left behind. Same standard uniform they had used years ago. Nothing like dressing everyone the same to make them feel like a nameless face in a crowd of nameless faces.

It was all about control and keeping everyone in line when I'd been here before. To me it looked like Daedalus was no different.

I almost laughed when realization kicked in. It probably had always been Daedalus running the show, even when I'd been assimilated here so many years ago.

When the guard returned, it was the tool from earlier, and the first thing he did was check the plastic razor for the blade.

I cocked an eyebrow at him. "I'm not that stupid."

"Good to know," was the reply. "Ready?"

"Been."

He stepped aside, allowing me back into the hallway. As we headed to another elevator, he was glued to my hip. "As close as you're riding me, man, I feel like I need to take you out to dinner or something. At least I should get your name."

He punched in a floor. "People call me Archer."

My eyes narrowed. There was something about him that reminded me of Luc, and hell if that boded well. "Is that your name?"

"That's what I was born with."

The dude was as charming as…well, as me on a bad day. Flipping my gaze to the red number on the elevator, I watched it steadily go down. My gut twisted. If Nancy was screwing with me and Kat wasn't here, I was about to find out.

I didn't know what I'd do if she wasn't. Probably go insane.

I couldn't stop what came out of my mouth next. "Have you seen her—Kat?"

A muscle flexed in Archer's jaw, and my imagination ran wild until he answered. "Yes. I've been assigned to her. I'm sure that pleases you to no end."

"Is she okay?" I asked, ignoring the jab.

He turned to me, and surprise crossed his features. Trading insults and barbs wasn't on my to-do list right now. "She can…she can be as expected."

I didn't like the way that sounded. Taking a deep breath, I ran a hand through my damp hair. The image of Beth freaking out popped into my head. A tremor ran down the muscles in my arm. There was no doubt in my mind that no matter what condition Kat was in, I could handle it. I would help her get better. Nothing in this world could stop that, but I didn't want her to have experienced anything that would've damaged her.

Like killing Blake surely would have.

"She was asleep the last time I checked in," he said as the elevator came to a stop. "She hasn't been sleeping well since they brought her in, but she seems to be making up for it today."

I nodded slowly and followed him out into the hallway. It struck me then how brave they were in only giving me one guard, but then again, they knew what I wanted, and I knew what was at risk if I acted a fool.

My heart was tripping out, my hands opening and closing sporadically at my sides. Anxious energy rolled through me, and as we neared the middle of the wide hall, I felt something I hadn't felt in way too long.

A warm tingle shimmied along the back of my neck.

"She's here." My voice sounded hoarse.

He glanced back at me. "Yes. She's here."

I didn't need to tell him that I'd had my doubts, that a part of me had held on to the cold possibility that they'd played to my weakness. It must've been written all over my face, and I didn't care to even hide it.

Kat was *here*.

Archer stopped before a door and punched in a code after doing the eye-reading bit. There was a soft sound of locks clicking out of place. He glanced at me, hand on the doorknob. "I'm not sure how long they'll give you."

Then he opened the door.

Like walking through quicksand or in a dream, I moved forward without feeling the floor beneath me. The air seemed to thicken, slowing my progress, but in reality I was rushing that damn door and still not moving quickly enough.

Senses on high alert, I stepped into the cell, vaguely aware of the door closing behind me. My gaze shot right to the bed pressed up against the wall.

My heart stopped. My entire world came to a halt.

I walked forward, and my step faltered. Only at the last possible second, I caught myself from hitting the floor on my knees. The back of my throat and eyes burned.

Kat was curled on her side, facing the door, appearing terribly small on the bed. The chocolate-colored length of her hair fell across her cheek, covering the sleeve of her exposed arm. She was asleep, but her features pinched as if even in rest she wasn't wholly comfortable. Her small hands were tucked under her rounded chin, lips slightly parted.

Her beauty struck me hard, like a bolt of lightning right in the chest. I froze there, for how long I don't know, unable to take my eyes off her, and then I took two long strides that brought me to the edge of the bed.

Peering down at her, I opened my mouth to say something, but there were no words. I was struck speechless, and I swear Kat was the only one who could do this to me.

I sat beside her, my heart pounding as she stirred but didn't wake. Part of me hated the idea of waking her. Up close, I could see the dark shadows blooming under her thick lashes like faint ink smudges. And honestly, I was happy—no, *thrilled*—to just be in her presence, even if it meant that I wasted the entire time soaking her up.

But I couldn't stop myself from touching her.

Slowly, I reached out and carefully brushed the silky strands of hair back from her cheek, fanning the long length over the stark white pillow. Now I could see the faint bruises across her cheekbone, a faded shade of yellow. There was a thin cut on her lower lip, too. Anger punched its way through me. I inhaled deeply, letting my breath eke its way out.

Placing one hand on the other side of her, I lowered my head and pressed a soft kiss to the cut on her lip, silently promising that I'd make whoever was responsible for the bruises and pain she'd faced pay dearly. Instinctively, I let the healing warmth flow from me to her, erasing the bruises from sight.

A soft, warm sigh blew across my mouth, and I lifted my gaze, unwilling to pull too far away. Kat's lashes fluttered and her shoulders hitched as she dragged in a deeper breath. I waited with my heart in my throat.

She slowly opened her eyes, and her gray stare was unfocused as it moved over my face. "Daemon?"

The sound of her voice, husky with sleep, was like coming home. The burning turned into a ball in my throat. Leaning back, I placed the tips of my fingers on her chin. "Hey, Kitten," I said, my own voice hoarse as hell.

She stared at me as the cloudiness in her gaze cleared. "Am I dreaming?"

My laugh came out strangled. "No, Kitten, you're not dreaming. I'm really here."

A heartbeat passed, and then she rose up on her elbows. A single strand of hair fell across her face. I straightened, giving her more room. My heart rate kicked into supersonic speed, matching hers. Then she was sitting up fully, her hands on my face. My eyes closed as I felt the gentle touch all the way to my soul.

Kat slid her hands over my cheeks, as if she were trying to convince herself that I was real. I placed mine over her hands and opened my eyes. Hers were wide and wet, shining with tears. "It's okay," I told her. "Everything's going to be okay, Kitten."

"How…how are you here?" She swallowed. "I don't understand."

"You're going to be mad." I pressed a kiss to her open palm. I reveled in the shudder that rolled through her. "I turned myself in."

She jerked back, but I held onto her hands, not letting her get away. And yeah, I was selfish. I wasn't ready to go without her touch. "Daemon, what…? What were you thinking? You shouldn't—"

"I wasn't going to let you go through this by yourself." I slid my hands down her arms, cupping her elbows. "There was no way I could do that. I know that's not what you wanted, but *this* wasn't want I wanted."

She gave a little shake of her head, and her voice was barely a whisper. "But your family, Daemon? Your—"

"You're more important." The moment those words came out of my mouth, I knew they were true. Family had always come first for me, and Kat was a part of my family—a bigger part. She was my future.

"But the things they're going to make you do..." The wetness in her eyes swelled, and a single tear escaped, racing down her cheek. "I don't want you to go through—"

I caught the tear with a kiss. "And I'm not going to let you do this by yourself. You're my—you're my everything, Kat." At the sound of her soft inhale, I smiled again. "Come on, Kitten, did you really expect anything less from me? I love you."

Her hands fell to my shoulders, flexing until her fingers dug through the cotton of my shirt, and she stared at me for so long I started to worry. Then she sprang forward, wrapping her arms around my neck and practically tackling me.

Laughing against the top of her head, I caught myself before I toppled over. One second she was beside me, and then she was in my lap, wrapping her arms and legs around me. This—*this* was the Kat I knew.

"You're crazy," she whispered against my neck. "You're absolutely crazy, but I love you. I love you so much. I don't want you here, but I love you."

I slid my hand down her spine, curling my fingers against her lower back. "I'll never grow tired of hearing you say that."

She pressed against me, her fingers burying in the hair at the nape of my neck. "I missed you so much, Daemon."

"You have no idea..." I ran out of words at that point. Her being this close after so long was the sweetest kind of torture. Each breath she took, I felt in *every* part of my body, in some areas more than others. Really inappropriate, but she always had a powerful hold over me. Common sense jumped out the window.

She pulled back, her eyes searching mine, and then she reclaimed the distance, and, damn, the kiss was half innocent, half desperate, and wholly perfect. My grip on her back tightened as she tilted her head, and even though the kiss started out as something sweet, I totally took it there. I deepened the kiss, throwing every fear into it, every minute that had passed that we'd been separated, and everything I felt for her. Her breathy moan shook me, and when she wiggled it nearly undid me.

I gripped her hips and pushed her back. It was the last thing I wanted to do. "Cameras, remember?"

Color crawled up her neck and splashed across her cheeks. "Oh, yeah, everywhere except— "

"The bathroom," I supplied, catching the flash of surprise across her face. "They've filled me in."

"Everything?" When I nodded, the rosy color in her cheeks disappeared, and she quickly scuttled out of my lap. She settled beside me, her gaze straight ahead. Several moments passed, and she took a deep breath. "I'm…glad you're here, but I wish you weren't."

"I know." I didn't take offense to that statement.

She tucked her hair back. "Daemon, I…"

I placed two fingers under her chin and tilted her face back to mine. *"I know,"* I said again, searching her eyes. "I saw some of the stuff, and they told me about— "

"I don't want to talk about that," she said quickly, sliding her hands over her bent knees.

Concern rose inside me, but I forced a smile. "Okay. That's okay." I slid my arm back around her shoulders, tugging her closer. There was no resistance. She melted into my side, curling her fingers into my shirt. I kissed her forehead. I kept my voice low. "I'm going to get us out of this."

Her hand balled around my shirt as she lifted her head. "How?" she whispered.

I leaned over, pressing close to her ear. "Trust me. I'm sure they're watching us, and I don't want to give them any reason to separate us right now."

She nodded in understanding, but her mouth grew tense. "Have you seen what they've been doing here?"

I shook my head, and she took a deep breath. In hushed tones, she told me about the sick humans they were treating, the Luxen and the hybrids. As we talked, we stretched out on the bed, facing each other. I could tell she was skating over a lot of stuff. For one thing, she didn't talk about anything she'd been doing or how she got those bruises. I figured it had to do with Blake and that was why she was mum on the topic, but she did mention a little girl named Lori who was dying from cancer. A pinched look appeared when she talked about her. Kat hadn't smiled once. The knowledge nagged at me, threatening to ruin the reunion.

"They said that there are bad Luxen out there," she said. "That it's why they have me here, to learn how to fight against them."

"What?"

She tensed. "They said that there were thousands of Luxen who wanted to harm humans and that more would be coming. I'm guessing they didn't say anything like that to you?"

"No." I almost laughed, but then I remembered what Ethan had said. There was no way that could've had anything to do with what she was saying. Or could it? "They told me they want more hybrids." A troubled look crossed her face, and I wished I hadn't said that. "What kind of cancer does Lori have?" I asked, running my hand up her arm. I hadn't stopped touching her. Not once since I'd entered the room.

The tips of her fingers were resting on my chin, and we were as close as we could be that would seem appropriate, considering we had eyes on us. "Same kind of cancer my dad had."

I squeezed her hand. "I'm sorry."

Her fingers followed the curve of my jaw. "I only saw her once, but she's not doing too well. They're giving her some kind of treatment they're getting from the Luxen and hybrids. They call it LH-11."

"LH-11?"

She nodded and then frowned. "What?"

Holy crap, that was what Luc wanted. Which begged the question, what the hell did Luc want with a serum that Daedalus was using on sick humans? Her frown deepened, and I bridged the insignificant space between us, keeping my voice low. "I'll tell you later."

Understanding flared, and she brought her leg up a little so it rested against mine. My breath caught, and a different kind of awareness crept into Kat's eyes. She bit down on her lower lip, and I fought back a groan.

That pretty color edged into her cheeks again, so not helping the situation. I brought my hand up her arm, senses flaring as she shivered. "You know what I'd give for some privacy right about now?"

Her lashes lowered. "You're terrible."

"I am."

Her expression clouded over. "I feel like there's a big clock hanging over us right now, like we're running out of time."

We probably were. "Don't think about it."

"It's kind of hard not to."

There was a pause, and I cupped her cheek, smoothing my thumb over the delicate bone. Several moments passed.

"Did you see my mom at all?"

"No." I wanted to tell her why, and tell her more, but divulging any information at this point was a risk. I had an idea, though. I could take my true form and talk to her that way, but I doubted the powers that be would appreciate that. I wasn't willing to risk it at this moment. "But Dee has been keeping an eye on her."

Kat kept her eyes closed. "I miss my mom," she whispered, and my heart cracked. "I really miss her."

I didn't know what to say, and what could I say? *I'm sorry* wouldn't cut it. So as I searched for a distraction, I let myself get reacquainted with the angles of her face, the graceful column of her neck, and the slope of her shoulders. "Tell me something I don't know."

Several moments passed before she spoke. "I've always wanted a Mogwai."

"What?"

Kat's lashes still fanned her cheeks, but she was finally smiling, and some of the pressure eased off my chest. "You've seen *Gremlins*, right? Remember Gizmo?" When I nodded, she laughed. The sound was hoarse, as if she hadn't laughed in a while. Which I figured she hadn't. "Mom let me watch it when I was a kid, and I was obsessed with Gizmo. I wanted one more than I wanted anything in the world. I even promised Mom that I wouldn't feed it after midnight or get it wet."

I rested my chin atop her head and grinned at the image of the little brown and white furball-sprouting pods. "I don't know."

"What?" She burrowed closer, tucking her fingers against the collar of my shirt.

Throwing my arm around her waist, I took what felt like the first real breath in weeks. "If I had a Mogwai, I'd totally feed it after midnight. That Mohawk gremlin was a badass."

She laughed again, the sound tinkling inside me, and I felt about a thousand pounds lighter. "Why doesn't that surprise me?" she said. "You'd totally bond with the gremlin."

"What can I say? It's my sparkling personality."

Chapter 11

Katy

Part of me still believed I was dreaming. I would wake up and Daemon would be gone. I'd be alone with my thoughts, haunted by what I had done. Fear and shame kept me from telling him about Blake. Killing Will had been one thing. An act of self-defense, and the bastard had still managed to shoot me, but Blake? That had been an act of anger and nothing else.

How could Daemon look at me the same, knowing I was a murderer? Because that was what I had done—I had murdered Blake.

"You with me?" he asked.

"Yes." Pushing away the troubling thoughts, I touched him. Honestly, I kept touching him, reminding myself that he was really there. I thought he was doing the same thing, but he had always been the touchy type, something I loved about him. I wanted more. There was a desperate urge to lose myself in him, in a way I'd only ever been able to do with Daemon.

I traced his lower lip with the pad of my finger. A muscle flexed in his jaw, and his eyes brightened. My heart did a funny little cartwheel, and he closed those beautiful eyes, face tensing. I started to pull my hand back.

He caught my wrist. "Don't."

"I'm sorry. It's just that you…" I trailed off, not sure of how to explain it.

A lopsided grin appeared on his face. "I can deal. Can you?"

"Yes." *Not really*, I admitted to myself. I wanted to climb into him. I wanted nothing between us. I wanted *him*. But shenanigans of the fun and naughty kind weren't appropriate given the situation, and exhibitionism wasn't something I wanted to indulge in. So I settled for the next best thing. I threaded my fingers through his. "I feel bad that I'm happy you're here."

"Don't be." His eyes opened, and the pupils shone like diamonds. "I honestly don't want to be anyplace else."

I snorted. "Really?"

"Really." He kissed me softly and quickly pulled back. "Sounds crazy but it's true."

I wanted to ask him how he planned on getting us out of here. There had to be a plan. Hopefully. I couldn't imagine that he busted up in Daedalus and hadn't thought about a way out. It wasn't like I hadn't been thinking about how to escape. There was just no foreseeable escape route. I licked my lips. Daemon's eyes flared.

"What if…?" I swallowed, keeping my voice low. "What if this is our future?"

"No." The arm around my waist drew me forward, and an instant later I was pressed against his front. His mouth moved against the sensitive spot under my ear as he spoke in a low whisper. "This isn't our future, Kitten. I promise you."

I sucked in a sharp breath. Memories of being this close to him hadn't done the real thing any justice. The hardness of his chest against mine scrambled my thoughts, but it was his words that flooded my body with warmth. Daemon never promised something he didn't hold to.

Fitting my head in the space between his neck and shoulder, I inhaled the smell of soap and the outdoorsy scent that was uniquely his. “Say it,” I whispered.

His hand slid up my spine, leaving a wake of shivers. “Say what, Kitten?”

“You know.”

He rubbed his chin in my hair. “I love…my car, Dolly.”

My lips cracked into a tiny grimace. “That’s not it.”

“Oh.” His voice dripped innocence. “I know. I love *Ghost Investigators*.”

“You’re such a douche.”

He laughed softly. “But you love me.”

“I do.” I pressed a kiss against his shoulder.

There was a pause, and I felt his heart rate kick up. Mine quickly matched his. “I love you,” he said, voice gruff. “I love you more than anything.”

I let myself rest against him, probably relaxing for the first time since I’d gotten there. It wasn’t that I felt stronger because he was there, though in a way I was. But it was because I now had someone on my side, someone who had my back. I wasn’t alone in this, and if it had been the other way around, I would’ve done the same thing he’d done. I doubted—

The door to the cell opened suddenly, and Daemon stiffened just like I did. Over his shoulder I saw Sergeant Dasher and Nancy Husher. Behind the incredibly douchetastic duo was Archer and another guard.

“Are we interrupting?” Nancy asked.

Daemon snorted. “No. We were just saying how sad we were that you guys weren’t visiting us.”

Nancy clasped her hands. In her black pantsuit, she looked like a walking ad for women who hate color. “For some reason I doubt that.”

My grip on the front of Daemon's shirt tightened as my eyes bounced to the sergeant. His gaze wasn't outright hostile, but then again, that didn't tell me much.

The sergeant cleared his throat. "We have work to do."

Insanely fast, Daemon was sitting up, and somehow he'd maneuvered his body so that I was behind him. "Work on what?" he asked, threading his fingers together between his knees. "And I don't believe I've had the honor of meeting you."

"That's Sergeant Dasher," I explained, trying to move so I wasn't behind him. He shifted, blocking me once more.

"Is that so?" Daemon's voice became low and dangerous, and my stomach sank. "I think I've seen you before."

"I don't think you have," Dasher responded evenly.

"Oh, he has." Nancy gestured at me. "I showed him the video of the first day Katy was here and your meeting with her."

I closed my eyes and muttered a curse. Daemon was so gonna kill him.

"Yeah, I've seen that." Each word was punctuated with what I knew was a death glare. I pried an eye open. Dasher didn't look completely unfazed. The lines around his mouth were tense. "I've tucked those images away in a very special place," Daemon finished.

I placed a hand on his back. "What work do we have to do?"

"We need to run some joint tests, and then we'll go from there," answered Dasher.

My muscles locked up, an action duly noted by Daemon. More stress tests? I couldn't foresee that going well with Daemon involved.

"It's nothing too complicated or intensive." Nancy stepped aside, motioning to the door. "Please. The sooner we get started, the quicker it is over."

Daemon didn't move.

Nancy eyed us calmly. "Do I need to remind you of what you promised, Daemon?"

I shot him a sharp look. "Promised what?"

Before he could respond, Nancy did. "He promised to do whatever we asked *without* causing trouble if we brought him to you."

"What?" I stared at him. When he didn't say anything, I almost wanted to hit him. God only knew what they'd make him do. Taking a deep breath, I scooted around him and stood. A second later, he was on his feet and in front of me. Tucking my hair back, I slid my sneakers on.

We didn't say anything as we stepped out into the hall. I glanced at Archer, but he was closely watching Daemon. I must not have been the DEFCON threat anymore. When we stopped in front of the elevator, I felt Daemon's hand wrap around mine, and a little of the tautness eased out of my shoulders. How many times had I stepped into these elevators? I'd lost count, but this time was different.

Daemon was here.

They led us to the med floor and took us into a room that accommodated two patients. Dr. Roth was waiting for us, his expression eager as he hooked both of us up to a blood pressure meter.

"I've been waiting a long time to run tests on someone like you," he said to Daemon, voice high-pitched.

Daemon arched a brow. "Another fanboy. I have them everywhere."

I muttered, "Only you would see that as a good thing."

He shot me a grin.

Color heightened the doctor's cheeks. "It's not often we get a powerful Luxen like you. We had thought that Dawson would be the one, but…"

Daemon's face turned dark. "You *worked* with my brother?"

Uh oh.

Eyes widening, Dr. Roth glanced at where Nancy and Sergeant Dasher stood. He cleared his throat as he unwrapped the cuffs. "Their blood pressure is identical. Perfect. One-twenty over eighty."

Nancy scribbled it down on a clipboard that I swore just appeared in her hands. I shifted in the chair, bringing my focus back to Daemon. He was eyeballing the doctor like he wanted to beat information out of him.

Dr. Roth checked our pulses next. Resting pulse was in the fifties, which was apparently a good thing, because Roth was practically humming. "Katy's rate was in the high sixties each time before, blood pressure well into the high levels. It appears that with his presence, her rates are optimizing, matching his. This is good."

"Why is it good?" I asked.

He pulled out a stethoscope. "It's a good indication that the mutation is on a perfect, cellular level."

"Or an indication that I'm pretty damn awesome," Daemon suggested coolly.

That earned a small smile from the doctor, and my anxiety notched up. One would think that Daemon being his normal cocky, arrogant self was a good thing, but I'd learned that his smartass responses could mean he was seconds from exploding.

"Hearts beating in perfect sync. Very good," Roth murmured, turning to Dasher. "She passed the stress test, correct? No outward signs of destabilization?"

"She did perfectly, as we'd hoped."

I sucked in a sharp breath, pressing my hand to my stomach. I'd done as they expected? Did that mean they expected me to kill Blake? I couldn't even consider that.

Daemon glanced at me. His eyes narrowed. "What exactly are these stress tests?"

My mouth opened, but I didn't know what to say. I didn't want him to know what had happened—what I'd done. I turned to Dasher, and his expression was guarded. I prayed that the man had common sense. If he told Daemon about the fighting, it was likely that Daemon would go postal.

"The stress testing is run of the mill," he explained. "I'm sure Katy can tell you that."

Yeah, totally run of the mill, if getting your ass kicked and murder were ordinary things; but in a twisted way, I appreciated the lie. "Yeah, completely run of the mill."

Doubt crossed Daemon's features as he turned back to the doctor. "Were these stress tests the same kind of things Dawson did?"

No one answered, which was answer enough. Daemon was very still, but his stare was sharp, and his mouth pressed into a hard line. He then reached over and took my hand in his, the gentle grasp so at odds with his demeanor.

"So we can move on to the more important phase of our work today." Dr. Roth walked over to a cart full of utensils. "One of the most remarkable things about our extraterrestrial friends is their ability to heal not only themselves but others. We believe that unlocking that ability will provide us with the necessary information to replicate the function to heal others suffering from various diseases."

The doctor picked up something, but his hand hid it as he turned back to us. "The whole purpose of this next exercise, Daemon, is to see how fast you can heal. We need to be able to see this before we can move on."

The anxiety that had been riding me exploded like a cannonball. This could only be leading to one thing.

"Do tell?" Daemon asked in a low voice.

Roth visibly swallowed as he approached us, and I noticed that Archer and another guard were also closing ranks. "We need you to heal Katy," he said.

The hand around mine tightened, and Daemon leaned forward. "Heal her from what exactly? Because I'm a little confused. I've already taken care of those bruises—which, by the way, I would *love* to know how she got them."

My pulse kicked up as I took in my surroundings. The black

dots were everywhere, and I had a feeling we were about to get reacquainted with the loving embrace of onyx.

"It won't be anything serious," the doctor explained gently. "Just a minor scratch that she will barely feel. Then I'm going to do some blood work and monitor your vitals. That is all."

Suddenly all I could think about was Dawson and Bethany, of all the things they had done to Bethany to force Dawson to heal others. Nausea rolled, and I felt dizzy. Dasher hadn't acted like getting Daemon here was a priority, but now that he was, we were going to see all the sides of Daedalus. And how could they start rolling in other people to heal until they knew the true extent of his abilities?

"No." Daemon was seething. "You're not going to hurt her."

"You promised," Nancy said. "Do I need to continuously remind you of that?"

"I didn't agree to you hurting her," he replied, the pupils of his eyes starting to glow.

Archer moved in closer. The other guard moved to the wall, near a very unfriendly looking button. Stuff was about to hit the fan, and when Dr. Roth showed what was in his hand, Daemon shot to his feet, letting go of mine and moving in front of me.

"Not going to happen, buddy," he said, hands closing into fists.

Light glinted off the steel scalpel Roth held. The good doctor took a wise step back. "I promise she will barely feel it. I'm a doctor. I know how to make a clean cut."

The muscles in Daemon's back locked up. "No."

Nancy made a sound of impatience as she lowered the clipboard. "This can be easy or this can become very difficult."

His head swung in her direction. "Difficult for you or me?"

"For you and for Katy." She took a step forward, either very brave or very stupid. "We could always restrain you. Or we could do this and get it over with. The choice is yours."

Daemon looked like he was going to call their bluff, and I knew that they would go through with it. If he or I put up a fight, they'd fill this room with onyx, restrain him until they did whatever they wanted to me, and then release him. Either way, this was going to happen. The decision was ours—to go the clean or messy route.

I stood on legs that felt weak. "Daemon."

He looked over his shoulder at me. *"No."*

Forcing a smile that felt weird, I shrugged. "It's going to happen either way. Trust me." Pain flickered across his face at the last two words. "If we do this, then it's over. You agreed to this."

"I did *not* agree to this."

"I know…but you're here, and…" And this was why I didn't want him here. Turning to the doctor, I held out my hand. "He's not going to let anyone do this. I'm going to have to do it myself."

Daemon stared at me incredulously. The doctor turned to Nancy, who nodded. It was obvious that her position, whatever it was, usurped the sergeant's.

"Go ahead," Nancy said. "I trust that Katy knows what will happen if she decides to use that knife in a very bad manner."

I shot the woman a hateful look as the cool instrument landed in my palm. Mustering up my courage, I turned to Daemon. He was still staring at me like I was insane. "Ready?"

"No." His chest rose in a deep breath, and a very rare thing happened. Helplessness had crept into his eyes, turning them a mossy shade of green. "Kat…"

"We have to."

Our eyes locked, and then he extended his hand. "I'll do it."

I stiffened. "No way."

"Give it to me, Kat."

There were several reasons why I wasn't giving him the scalpel. Mainly because I didn't want him to feel guilty about it, and I was also afraid he'd turn it into a projectile. I shifted slightly, opening my left hand. I'd never cut myself before, at least on purpose. My heart was pounding crazy fast and my stomach was jumping. The edge of the scalpel was wicked sharp, so I assumed it wouldn't take much pressure to do the deed.

I poised it over my open palm, squeezing my eyes shut.

"Wait!" Daemon shouted, causing me to jerk. When I looked up, his pupils were completely white. "I need to be in my true form."

Now I was staring at him like he was nuts. There had been many times when he did quick patch-up work in his human form. He only turned into a glow stick when things were serious. I had no idea what he was up to.

He turned to Nancy and the sergeant, who wore mirror looks of suspicion. "I want to make sure I do this quick and fast. I don't want her to be in pain, and I don't want it to scar."

They seemed to believe that, because Nancy nodded her approval. Daemon took a deep breath, and then his body started to shimmer. He was changing. The outline of his form began to fade out, clothes and all. For a second, I forgot that we were in this room, that I was holding a scalpel about to slice open my own flesh, and that we were basically prisoners of Daedalus.

Watching him take on his true form was nothing short of awe-inspiring.

Just before he'd completely faded out, he started to take shape again. Arms. Legs. Torso. Head. For a brief second, I could see him, *really* see him. The skin was translucent, like a jellyfish, and the network of veins was filled with a pearlescent glow. The features were Daemon, but sharper and more defined, and then he was shining as bright as the sun. A human-shaped light tinged in red that was so beautiful to look upon that tears filled my eyes.

I really don't want you to do this.

Like always, hearing his voice in my head came as a shock. I didn't think I'd ever get used to it. I started to respond vocally but caught myself. *You shouldn't have come here, Daemon. This is what they want.*

The luminous head cocked to the side. *Coming here for you was the only thing I could do. Doesn't mean I have to be okay with everything. Now do this before I change my mind and see if I really can't tap into the Source and kill someone.*

My gaze fell to the scalpel, and I cringed. Getting a good grip on the handle, I could feel several eyes on me. Being the coward that I am, I squeezed my eyes shut, brought the blade down on my palm, and sliced.

I hissed at the flare of pain and dropped the scalpel, watching the thin cut immediately bubble with blood. It was like a paper cut times a million.

Jesus H. Mary mother of Christ in crutches, came Daemon's voice.

I'm not sure that's how it goes, I told him, squeezing my palm shut against the burn.

I was vaguely aware of the doctor stooping down and grabbing the blade as I looked up. The light from Daemon surrounded me as his hand outstretched, fingers becoming more visible as they circled my injured hand.

Open up, he said.

I shook my head, and his phantom sigh bounced around my head. He gently pried my hand open, his touch as warm as clothes freshly removed from the dryer. *Man, that hurt more than I thought.*

There was a low growl that replaced the sigh. *Did you really think it wasn't going to hurt, Kitten?*

Whatever. I let him guide me over to the chair, and I sat, watching as he knelt before me, his head bowed. Heat flared over my palm as he started to do his thing.

"Amazing," Dr. Roth whispered.

My eyes were trained on Daemon's glowing, bent head. The warmth that blew off him filled the room. I reached out and placed my uninjured hand on his shoulder. His light pulsed, and the red at the edges bled inward an inch or so. Interesting.

You know how I like it when you touch me in this form. His voice sent a shiver down my spine.

Why do you have to make everything sound so dirty? But I didn't pull my hand back.

His chuckle rolled through me, and by then, the pain in my palm had stopped. *I'm not the one with the dirty mind, Kitten.*

I rolled my eyes.

Both of his hands circled mine, and I was sure at that point my hand was already healed. *Now stop distracting me.*

I snorted. *Me? You're such a douche canoe.*

"Fascinating," Dr. Roth murmured. "They're communicating. It never fails to amaze me when I see it."

Daemon ignored him. *I took this form to tell you that I spoke with Luc before I went to Mount Weather.*

I sat up straight, all ears. *Did he have anything to do with this?*

No. And I believe him. He's going to help us get out. I need—

"Show us your hand, Katy." Nancy's voice intruded.

I wanted to ignore her, but when I glanced up, I saw the other guard moving closer to Daemon with what looked like a stun gun in his hand. I jerked my hand from Daemon's and showed them. "Happy?"

"Daemon, take your human form," Nancy ordered, voice clipped.

A heartbeat passed, and then Daemon stood. In his true form, he seemed taller and was a hell of a lot more intimidating. His light pulsed once, more red than white, and then it dimmed out.

He stood there, minus the glowworm thing. Only his eyes burned with white light. "I don't know if you've realized this or not, but I don't like to be ordered to do things."

Nancy cocked her head to the side. "I don't know if you've realized this or not, but I'm used to people taking my orders."

A smirk graced his face. "Ever hear of the saying you catch more lions with honey than vinegar?"

"I think it's 'catch more bees' and not lions," I mumbled.

"Whatever."

Dr. Roth examined my hand. "Remarkable. Only a faint pink line. It will probably be completely gone within the hour." He turned to Nancy and Dasher, practically thrumming with excitement. "Other Luxen have healed in this amount of time, but not to where the cut is completely sealed."

Like Daemon needed help feeling special.

The doctor shook his head as he stared up at him. "Truly amazing."

I wondered if the good doctor was going to kiss him.

Before he could start drooling on Daemon, the door burst open and an out-of-breath officer appeared, cheeks ruddy with the color of his buzzed hair. "We have a problem," he announced, taking several deep breaths.

Nancy gave him an arch look, and I couldn't help but think the guy in the doorway would probably get yelled at later for barging in here.

Dasher cleared his throat. "What is the problem, Collins?"

The officer's eyes bounced across the room, moving over Daemon and me before darting back to us and then finally settling on the sergeant. "It's a problem in building B, sir, from the *ninth* floor. It requires your immediate attention."

Chapter 12

Katy

Building B? I vaguely remembered hearing someone mention another building attached to this one underground but had no idea what or who was housed there. I was 100 percent ready to find out, though. Whatever it was, it appeared dire, because Sergeant Dasher left the room without further word.

Nancy was right on his heels. "Take them back to their rooms. Doctor?" She paused. "You will probably want to join us." And then they were gone.

I turned to Archer. "What's going on?"

He gave me a look that said I was dumb for asking. I scowled. "What's in building B?"

The other soldier stepped forward. "You ask too many questions and need to learn when to shut up."

I blinked. That was all it took, and Daemon had the stocky guard by the neck and pinned to the wall. My eyes popped.

"And you need to learn to speak to the ladies with a little bit of manners," he snarled.

"Daemon!" I screeched, preparing myself for the onyx.

But it never came.

Daemon pried his fingers off the gasping soldier's throat, one by one, and stepped back. The soldier slumped against the wall. Archer had done nothing.

"You let him do that?" the guard accused, pointing at Archer. "What the hell, man?"

Archer shrugged. "He had a point. You need to learn manners."

I squelched the urge to laugh because Daemon was eyeballing the soldier like he wanted to snap his neck. Hurrying to Daemon's side, I wrapped my hand around his and squeezed.

He looked down, not seeing me at first. Then he lowered his head, brushing his lips across my forehead. My shoulders slumped in relief. I doubted Archer would've allowed a round two.

"Whatever," the man spat, then spun on his heel, exiting the room and leaving Archer to fend for himself with the two of us.

He didn't look concerned.

The trip back to our cells was uneventful up until the moment Archer said, "Nope. You two are not going in one of them together."

I whirled on him. "Why not?"

"My orders are to put you two in your rooms—plural." He punched in the code. "Don't make this hard. If you do, all they're going to do is keep you apart longer."

I started to protest, but the hard set to his mouth told me that he wouldn't be convinced. I took a ragged breath. "Will you at least tell us what's in building B?"

Archer looked at Daemon and then me. Finally he muttered a curse and stepped forward, chin lowered. Beside me Daemon stiffened, and Archer shot him a warning glare. Voice low, he said, "I'm sure they'll show you eventually, and you'll probably wish they hadn't. Origins are kept in that building."

"Origins?" Daemon repeated, brows furrowing. "What the hell is that?"

Archer shrugged. "That's all I can tell you. Now please, Katy, go into your room."

Daemon's hand tightened around mine, and then he swooped down, catching my chin in his other hand and tilting my head back. His mouth was on mine, and the kiss…the kiss was fierce, hard and branding, curling my toes inside my sneakers and stealing my breath. My free hand fell to his chest as the touch of our mouths rearranged my insides. In spite of the audience, luscious heat rose as he angled the kiss, pulling me hard against him.

Archer exhaled loudly.

Lifting his head, Daemon winked at me. "It'll be okay."

I nodded and barely remembered walking into my room, but there I was, staring at the bed Daemon had been sitting on earlier, as the door closed and locked behind me.

I smacked my hands over my face, stunned for a minute or two. When I'd fallen asleep the day before, I had been physically exhausted from using the Source and emotionally devastated from what I'd done. As I'd lain on that damn bed, staring at the ceiling, hopelessness had crept in, and even now it still had a hold on me.

But things were different. I had to keep telling myself that, to stop the bleakness from taking complete control. Pushing down what I'd done probably wasn't something therapists across the nation would suggest as a healthy practice, but I had to. Those hours before I'd fallen asleep…

I shook my head.

Things *were* different now. Daemon was here. Speaking of which, I had this feeling that he was still nearby. The tingling had died off, but I just knew that he was still close; I felt it on a cellular level.

I turned, eyeing the wall. Then I remembered the door in the bathroom. Spinning around, I hurried into the bathroom and tried the knob on the door. Locked. Hoping my suspicions were correct, I knocked. "Daemon?"

Nothing.

I pressed my cheek against the cool wood, closing my eyes as I flattened my palms on the door. Did I really believe that they'd put us in two cells joined by a bathroom? Then again, they had kept Dawson and Bethany together in the beginning—hadn't that been what Dawson had said? But my luck wasn't that—

The door opened, and I tumbled forward. Strong arms and a hard chest caught me before I toppled right over.

"Whoa, Kitten..."

I looked up, heart pounding. "We share a bathroom!"

"I see." A small grin appeared, his eyes sparkling.

Grabbing fistfuls of his shirt, I rocked back on the heels of my sneakers. "I can't believe it. You're in the cell beside me! All we—"

Daemon's hands landed on my hips, his grip tight and sure, and then his mouth was on mine, picking up that soul-shattering kiss we'd started in the hallway. He was moving me backward at the same time. Somehow, and I really didn't know how other than that he had skills, he managed to shut the door behind us without taking his hands off me.

Those lips of his...they moved over mine, tantalizingly slow and deep, as if we were kissing for the very first time. His hands slid around, and when my back hit the sink, he lifted me so that I perched on the edge, and he kept pressing forward, pushing my knees apart with his hips. The smoldering heat was back, a flame that burned brighter at the slow, thorough kiss.

My chest rose and fell rapidly as I clutched his shoulders, almost completely lost in him. I'd read enough romance novels in my day to know that a bathroom and Daemon were things fantasies were made of, but...

I managed to break contact—though not much. Our lips brushed when I spoke. "Wait. We need to—"

"I know," he cut in.

"Good." I placed my trembling hands on his chest. "We're on the same page—"

Daemon kissed me again, spinning my senses. He was leisurely in his exploration of the kiss, pulling back and nipping at my lip until a breathy moan that would've embarrassed me any other time escaped me.

"Daemon—"

He caught whatever else I was going to say with his mouth. His hands slid up my waist, stopping when the tips of his fingers brushed the underside of my chest. My whole body jerked, and I knew right then that if I didn't stop this, we were going to waste very valuable time.

I pulled back, dragging in air that tasted of Daemon. "We really should be talking."

"I know." That half grin appeared. "That's what I've been trying to tell you."

My mouth dropped open. "What? You haven't been talking! You've been—"

"Kissing you senseless?" he asked innocently. "Sorry. It's all I want to do while you're here. Well, not *all* I want to do, but pretty close to everything else I—"

"I get it." I groaned, wanting to fan my face. Leaning back against the plastic mirror, I dropped my hands into my lap. Touching him wasn't helping, either. Neither was that smug half grin of his. "Wow."

With his hands exactly where they stopped under my chest, he leaned in and pressed his forehead against mine. In a low voice he said, "I want to make sure your hand is okay."

I frowned. "It is."

"I need to make sure." He leaned back a little, his eyes meeting mine meaningfully, and then I got it. When he saw the understanding cross my face, he grinned. A second later, he was in his true form—so bright in the small room, I had to close my eyes. *They say there are no cameras in here, but I know the room has to be bugged,* he said. *Besides, I also don't trust the fact that they're letting us have access to each other. They have to know we'll do this, so there's probably a reason.*

I shuddered. *I know, but they did let Dawson and Bethany stay together until…* I forced that thought out of my head. We were wasting time. *What did Luc tell you?*

He said he can help us get out of here, but he really didn't go into detail. He apparently has people on the payroll here and said they'd find me once I get something for him—something you've mentioned. LH-11.

Shock rippled through me. *Why would he want that?*

Don't know. Daemon's hands moved back to my hips, and then he tugged me off the sink. Moving too fast for me to comprehend, he sat on the closed lid of the toilet and settled me in his lap. His hand came up my back, pressing down on the nape of my neck until my cheek rested against his shoulder. The heat from him in his true form wasn't overwhelming like it had been the first time. *And it doesn't really matter, right?*

I savored his embrace. *Does it? That stuff is being given to humans who are sick. Why would Luc want that?*

Honestly, it can't be any worse than what Daedalus is doing with it, no matter how many good things they claim to be using it for.

Very true. I sighed. I didn't dare be hopeful about this. If Luc really was on our side and he could help us, there were still a lot of obstacles in our way. Almost impossible ones. *I've seen it before. Maybe we'll be close to it again.*

We need to be. A couple of moments passed, and then he said, *We can't stay in here forever. I have a feeling they are allowing this, and if we abuse it, then they'll separate us.*

I nodded. What I didn't understand was why they would allow this unsupervised visit? Something that we could do whenever we wanted. Were they trying to show us that they weren't going to keep us apart? After all, they'd claimed they weren't the enemies here, but there was so much about Daedalus I didn't understand, like with Blake…

Shuddering, I turned my head in to his shoulder and breathed deeply. I wanted to force the memory of Blake out of my head, make as if he never existed.

"Kat?"

Lifting my head, I opened my eyes and realized he was no longer in his true form. "Daemon?"

His eyes drifted over my face. "What have they been doing to you in here?"

I froze, our gazes locking for an instant, and then I pushed off him, retreating a couple of steps. "Nothing really. Just tests."

He dropped his hands to his bent knees and softly said, "I know it's more than that, Kat. How did you get those bruises on your face?"

I glanced at the mirror. My complexion was pale, but there wasn't a trace left from the fights. "We shouldn't talk about this."

"I don't think they care that we're talking about this. The bruises are gone now, from when I healed you, but they were there before—faint but there." He stood, though he didn't come any closer. "You can talk to me. You should know that by now."

My eyes swung back to him. God, I did know that. I'd learned the hard way over the past winter. If I had trusted him with my secrets, Adam would still be alive and neither of us would probably be in this situation.

Guilt soured my stomach, but this was different. Telling him about the exams and the stress tests would only upset him, and he'd act upon it. Plus, admitting that I had killed Blake—and not so much in self-defense—was horrifying to even consider. I didn't want to think about it, let alone talk about it.

Daemon sighed. "Don't you trust me?"

"I do." My eyes went wide. "I trust you with my life, but I just… There's nothing to say about what has been going on in here."

"I think there's a lot to say."

I shook my head. "I don't want to argue about this."

"We're not arguing." He crossed the distance, placing his hands on my shoulders. "You're just being stubborn as hell, as usual."

"Look who's talking."

"Great movie," he replied. "I watched a lot of old movies in my spare time."

I rolled my eyes but cracked a grin.

He cupped my cheek as he lowered his chin, peering at me through thick lashes. "I'm worried about you, Kitten."

Pressure clamped down on my chest. Rarely did he admit to being worried about anything, and that was the last thing I wanted him to be doing. "I'm okay. I promise."

He continued to stare, as if he could see right through me, right through my lies.

• • •

Daemon

Hours had passed since Kat and I parted ways and some poor excuse for dinner had been brought to my room. I tried to watch TV and even tried to sleep, but it was damn hard when I knew she was right next door, or when I heard her moving around in the bathroom. Once, in what might have been the middle of the night, I'd heard her footsteps at the door, and I knew she had been standing there, fighting the same need I was. But we had to be careful. Whatever reason they had for putting us in a space we could share couldn't be a good thing, and I didn't want to risk them relocating us, forcing us apart.

But I was worried about her. I knew she was hiding stuff, keeping whatever had gone on there before I arrived to herself. So like an idiot with no self-control whatsoever, I had gotten up and opened the bathroom door.

It had been dark and quiet, but I'd been correct. Kat was standing there, arms at her sides and so incredibly still. Seeing her like that punched a hole in my chest. She couldn't stand or sit still for longer than twenty seconds, but now…

I'd kissed her gently and had said, "Go to sleep, Kitten. So we both can rest."

She nodded and then said those three little words that never failed to bring me to my knees. "I love you."

And then she was back in her room, and I was in mine. Finally, I did sleep.

When morning came, so did Nancy. Nothing like seeing her prim face and plastic smile first thing to start the day off right.

I'd expected to be reunited with Kat, but I was taken to the med floor for more blood tests and then shown the hospital room Kat had spoken of.

"Where is the little girl?" I asked, scanning the chairs for the small child Kat had mentioned but not seeing one. "I think her name was Lori or something."

Nancy's expression remained blank. "Unfortunately, she didn't respond as we'd hoped. She passed a few days ago."

Shit. I hoped Kat didn't learn that. "You guys were giving her the LH-11?"

"Yes."

"And it didn't work?"

Her gaze sharpened. "You're asking a lot of questions, Daemon."

"Hey, you have me here, most likely using my DNA for this. Don't you think I'm going to be a little curious about it?"

She held my stare for a moment and then turned back to one of the patients who was having a fluid bag changed out. "You think too much, and you know what they say about curiosity."

"That it's possibly the most cliché and stupid saying ever?"

One side of her lips tipped up. "I like you, Daemon. You're a pain in the ass and a smart-mouth, but I like you."

I smiled tightly. "No one can deny my charm."

"I'm sure that's true." She paused as the sergeant entered the room, conversing quietly with one of the doctors. "Lori was given LH-11, but her reaction was not favorable."

"What?" he asked. "It didn't heal the cancer?"

Nancy didn't respond, and that was that. Somehow I figured the unfavorable reaction was due to more than the cancer not healing. "You know what I think?" I said.

She tipped her head to the side. "I can only imagine."

"Messing with human, hybrid, and alien DNA is probably asking for a world of trouble. You guys really don't know what you have."

"But we're learning."

"And making mistakes?" I asked.

She smiled. "There are no such things as mistakes, Daemon."

I wasn't so sure about that, but then my attention shifted to the window at the end of the room. My eyes narrowed. I could see other Luxen in there. Many of them looked as happy as a kid at Disneyland.

"Ah." Nancy smiled, nodding at the window. "I see you've noticed. They are here because they want to help. If only you'd be that accommodating."

I snorted. Who knew why the other Luxen were here, happy as clams, and I really didn't care. I got that there were parts of Daedalus that were actually attempting to do something good, but I also knew what they did to my brother in the process.

All around me, doctors and lab technicians milled about. Some of the bags hooked up to the patients had a strange glittering liquid in them that vaguely resembled what we bled in our true form. "Is that LH-11?" I asked, gesturing at one of the bags.

Nancy nodded. "One of the versions—the newest—but that really isn't a concern of yours. We have—"

A siren sounded, cutting off her words with an ear-piercing shrill. Lights on the ceilings flashed red. Patients and doctors looked around in alarm. Sergeant Dasher stormed out of the room.

Nancy cursed under her breath as she spun toward the door. "Washington, escort Mr. Black back to his room immediately." She pointed at another guard. "Williamson, shut this room down. No one goes in or out."

"What's going on?" I asked.

She shot me a look before stomping past. Like hell I wanted to go back to my room when things were obviously just getting fun. Out in the hall, lighting was dim and the blinking red light caused an annoying strobe effect.

The Guard of the Moment took one step, and chaos stormed into the corridor.

Soldiers poured out of rooms, locking them down and taking up guard in front of them. Another came down the hall, clutching a walkie-talkie in a knuckle-white grip. "We have activity on elevator ten, coming out of building B. Lock it down now."

Huh, the infamous building B strikes again.

Farther down the hall, another door opened, and I saw Archer first and then Kat. She had a hand pressed over the fleshy part of her elbow. Behind her was Dr. Roth. My eyes narrowed when I saw a wicked-looking syringe in his hand. He brushed past Kat and Archer, heading straight for the guy on the walkie-talkie.

Kat turned, her gaze finding me. I started forward. No way was I not going to be beside her when the shit hit the fan, which apparently was happening.

"Where do you think you're going?" Washington demanded, hand going to the weapon on his thigh. "I have orders to take you back to your room."

I turned to him slowly, then back to the three elevators across from us. All of them were stopped on different floors, the lights red. "Exactly how are we supposed to get to my room?"

His eyes narrowed. "Stairwell?"

Tool had a point, but like I cared. I turned away, but his hand clamped down on my shoulder. "You stop me, and I will end you," I warned.

Whatever Washington saw in my face must've assured him that I wasn't fooling around, because he didn't interfere when I shrugged off his grip and went to Kat, dropping an arm around her shoulders. Her body was tense.

"You okay?" I asked, eyeing Archer. He also had his hand on his weapon, but he wasn't watching us. His eyes were on the middle elevator. He was hearing something in his earpiece and, by the look on his face, he wasn't happy.

She nodded, pushing a strand of hair that had escaped her ponytail out of her face. "Any idea what's going on?"

"Something about building B." Instinct suddenly told me that maybe being in our rooms would be a good thing. "This has never happened before?"

Kat shook her head. "No. Maybe it's a drill."

Double doors at the end of the hall suddenly burst open, and a swarm of officers in SWAT gear came through, armed to the teeth with rifles, faces shielded.

Reacting immediately, I swept an arm around Kat's waist and shoved her back against the wall, shielding her with my body. "I don't think this is a drill."

"It's not," Archer said, drawing his weapon.

The light above the middle elevator blinked from floor seven to floor six and then floor five.

"I thought the elevators were locked down?" someone demanded.

The men dressed in black shuffled forward, going down on their knees in front of the elevator. Someone else said, "Locking down the elevators ain't going to stop it. You know that."

"I don't care," the man yelled into the radio. "Shut down the damn elevator before it reaches the top level. Drop cement down the shaft if you need to. Stop the damn elevator!"

"Stop what?" I glanced at Archer.

The red light blinked on the fourth floor.

"Origin," he said, a muscle popping in his chin. "There's a stairway to the right, all the way down the hall. I'd suggest getting there now."

My gaze swung back to the elevator. Part of me wanted to stay to see what the hell an origin was and why they were acting like the *Cloverfield* monster was going to come out of the elevator shaft, but Kat was here, and obviously whatever was about to rain down on us wasn't a friendly.

"What the hell is up with them recently?" one of the men in black gear muttered. "They've been acting up nonstop."

I started to turn, but Kat smacked me. "No," she said, her gray eyes wide. "I want to see this."

My muscles clenched. "Absolutely not."

A *ding* ricocheted through the floor, signaling that the elevator had arrived. I was seconds from just picking Kat up and throwing her over my shoulder. She saw it, too, and her look became challenging.

But then her gaze shot over my shoulder, and I turned my head. The elevator doors slid open slowly. Guns were clicked, safeties going off.

"Don't shoot!" Dr. Roth ordered, waving the syringe around like a white flag. "I can take care of this. Whatever you do, don't shoot. Don't—"

A small shadow fell out of the elevator, and then one leg appeared, covered in black sweats, and then a torso and tiny shoulders.

My mouth dropped open.

It was a kid—*a kid*. Probably no older than five, and he stepped out in front of all the grown men with *really* big guns trained on him.

The kid smiled.

And then the proverbial poo hit the fan.

Chapter 13

Daemon

"Uh..." I muttered.

The kid's eyes were purple—like two amethyst jewels with those weird lines around the pupils, just like Luc's. And they were cold and flat as they scanned the officers in front of him.

Dr. Roth stepped forward. "Micah, what are you doing? You know you're not supposed to be in this building. Where is your—?"

Several things happened so fast and, seriously, I wouldn't have believed it if I hadn't seen it with my own eyes.

The kid lifted a hand, and there was a succession of several pops—of bullets leaving the chambers of the rifles. Kat's horrified gasp said she was thinking the same thing I was. Were they really going to shoot a kid?

But the bullets stopped, as if the kid were a Luxen or hybrid, but he wasn't one of my kind. I would've felt that. Maybe he was a hybrid, because those bullets hit a shimmery blue wall around him. The blue light expanded, swallowing the bullets—dozens of them—lighting them up like blue fireflies. They hung in the air for a second and then popped out of existence. The kid curled his fingers inward, like he was motioning them to come play with him, and in a total Magneto way, the guns flew from the officers' hands, zinging toward the kid. They, too, stopped in midair and lit up in vibrant shades of blue. A second later the guns were dust.

Kat's hands dug into my back. "Holy…"

"Shit," I finished.

Dr. Roth was trying to push past the soldiers. "Micah, you can't—"

"I don't want to go back to that building," the kid said in a voice that was oddly high and flat at the same time.

Washington the Tool moved in, holding a pistol. Dr. Roth shouted, and Micah's head whipped around. The guard's face paled, and Micah closed his fist. Washington hit the floor on his knees, grasping his head as he doubled over. Mouth open in a silent scream, blood poured from the guy's eyes.

"Micah!" Dr. Roth shoved an officer out of the way. "That is bad! Bad, Micah!"

Bad—that was *bad*? I could come up with dozens of words better suited than *bad*.

"Holy smokes," Kat whispered. "The kid's like Damien from *The Omen*."

I would've laughed, because with the bowl-cut brown hair and slight, mischievous grin, he did look like the little Antichrist. Except it wasn't funny because Washington was face-first on the floor, and the freaky kid was now staring at me with those purple eyes.

Man, I did not like freaky kids.

"He was gonna hurt me," said Micah, never taking his eyes off me. "And you all are going to make me go back to my room. I don't wanna go back to my room."

Several of the officers shuttled backward as Micah took a step forward, but Dr. Roth remained, hiding the syringe behind his back. "Why don't you want to go back to your room, Micah?"

"A better question is why is he staring at you?" Kat whispered.

True.

Micah cautiously made his way around the officers, who were now giving him a wide berth. His steps were light and extremely catlike. "The other ones don't want to play with me."

There were more of him? Dear God…

The doctor turned, smiling at the boy. "Is it because you're not sharing your toys?"

Kat choked on what sounded like a near-hysterical laugh.

Micah's eyes slid to the doctor. "Sharing is not how you assert dominance."

What. The. Holy. Hell.

"Sharing doesn't always mean you're giving up control, Micah. We've taught you that."

The little boy shrugged as he turned his gaze back to me. "Will you play with me?"

"Uh…" I had no idea what to say.

Micah cocked his head to the side and smiled. Two dimples appeared in his round cheeks. "Can he play with me, Dr. Roth?"

If that doctor said yes, I was going to have a serious issue with this.

Dr. Roth nodded. "I'm sure he can later, Micah, but right now we need you to go back to your room."

The little boy's lower lip stuck out. "I don't wanna go back to my room!"

I half expected the kid's head to start spinning, and maybe it would have, but the doctor shot forward, syringe in hand.

Micah spun and shouted as he balled up his tiny hands. Dr. Roth dropped the syringe and went down on one knee. "Micah," he gasped, pressing his hands to his temples. "You need to stop."

Micah stomped a foot. "I don't wanna—"

Out of freaking nowhere, a dart slammed into the kid's neck. His eyes widened, and then his legs gave out. Before he fell face-first, I shot forward and caught the tyke in my arms. Kid was freaky as hell, but still, he was a kid.

I looked up and saw Sergeant Dasher standing to the right. "Good shot, Archer," the sergeant said.

Archer slid the gun back into his holster with a curt nod.

I turned back to Micah. His eyes were open, and they locked onto mine. He wasn't moving at all, but the kid was in there, fully functional. "What the hell?" I whispered.

"Someone get Washington to the med room and make sure his brains aren't completely scrambled." Dasher was giving out orders. "Roth, get the kid into an exam room immediately and find out how he was able to get out of building B, and where in the hell is his tracker?"

Roth stumbled to his feet, rubbing his temple. "Yes…yes, sir."

Dasher stepped up to him, eyes glinting and his voice low. "If he does it again, he will be terminated. Do you understand?"

Terminated? Jesus. Someone appeared at my side and grabbed for the kid. I almost didn't want to let him go, but that became a nonissue. Micah's hand caught the front of my shirt and held on as the officer picked him up.

Those strange eyes were even more bizarre up close. The circle around the pupils was irregular, as if the black had bled at the edges.

They don't know we exist.

Stunned, I jerked back, breaking the grip on my shirt. The kid's voice was in my head. Impossible, but it had happened. I watched in disbelief as the officer had him now and was turning away. Stranger yet, it was the exact same thing Luc had said.

That kid wasn't like Kat or me. That kid was something completely different.

• • •

KATY

Holy crap on a cracker…

A kid had just disarmed about fifteen men and probably would've done a hell of a lot more if Archer hadn't tranq'd the kid. To be honest, I didn't even know what I just saw or what the kid was, but Daemon looked substantially more freaked than I felt. Fear pinged inside me. Did the kid do something to him?

Pushing off the wall, I hurried to Daemon. "Are you okay?"

He ran a hand through his hair as he nodded.

"Someone needs to get these two back to their rooms," Sergeant Dasher said, taking a deep breath and then barking out more orders. Archer moved toward us.

"Wait." I wrapped an arm around Daemon's, refusing to budge. "What was *that*?"

"I don't have time for this." Dasher's eyes narrowed. "Take them back to their rooms, Archer."

Anger rose inside me, bitter and powerful. "Make time for this."

Dasher's head snapped toward me, and I glared back at him. Daemon was tuning in to the conversation, fixing his attention on the sergeant. The muscles under my hand flexed. "That kid wasn't a Luxen or a hybrid," he said. "I think you guys owe us a straight-up answer."

"He is what we call an origin," Nancy answered, coming up behind the sergeant. "As in a new beginning: the origin of the perfect species."

I opened my mouth, then clamped it shut. The origin of the perfect species? I felt like I'd fallen headfirst into a really bad science-fiction movie, except this was all real.

"Go ahead, Sergeant. I have time for them." She tipped up her chin, meeting Dasher's incredulous stare. "And I want a complete write-up on how and why there have been two incidences with the origins in the matter of twenty-four hours."

Dasher exhaled loudly out his nose. "Yes, ma'am."

I was sort of stunned when he snapped his heels together and pivoted, but my suspicion about Nancy being the one who ran the show was confirmed.

She extended an arm toward one of the closed doors. "Let's sit."

Keeping an arm around Daemon's, I followed Nancy into a small room with just a round table and five chairs. Archer joined us, forever our shadow, but remained by the door while the three of us sat.

Daemon dropped an elbow on the table and a hand on my knee as he leaned in, his bright eyes fixed on Nancy. "Okay. So this kid is an origin. Or whatever. What does that mean exactly?"

Nancy leaned back in her chair, crossing one leg over the other. "We weren't ready to share this with you yet, but considering what you witnessed, we really don't have a choice. Sometimes things don't go as planned, so we must adapt."

"Sure," I said, placing my hand over Daemon's. He flipped his up, his fingers threading mine, and our joined hands rested on my knee.

"The Origin Project is Daedalus's greatest achievement," Nancy started, her gaze unwavering. "Ironically, it started as an accident more than forty years ago. It began with one and has grown to more than a hundred as of now. As I said before, sometimes what we plan for doesn't happen. So we must adapt."

I glanced at Daemon, and he looked as bewildered and as impatient as I felt, but I had this sickening, sinking feeling. On some level I knew that whatever we were about to hear was going to blow our minds.

"Forty years ago we had a Luxen male and a female hybrid who he had mutated. They, very much like you two, were young and in love." Her upper lip curled in dismissive mirth. "They were allowed to see each other, and at some point during their stay with us, the female became pregnant."

Oh, jeez.

"At first we weren't aware, not until she started to show. You see, back then, we didn't test for hormones related to pregnancy. From what we've gathered, it is very difficult for a Luxen to conceive with another, so it didn't cross our minds that one would be able to conceive with a human, hybrid or not."

"Is that true?" I asked Daemon. Baby making wasn't something we talked about. "That it's hard for Luxen to conceive?"

Daemon's jaw worked. "Yes, but we can't conceive with humans, as far as I know. It's like a dog and cat getting together."

Ew. I made a face. "Nice comparison."

Daemon smirked.

"You're right," Nancy said. "Luxen cannot conceive with humans, and for the most part, they cannot conceive with a hybrid, but when the mutation is perfect, complete on a cellular level, and if there appears to be a true *want*, they can."

For some reason, heat crawled up my neck. Talking about babies with Nancy was worse than having the sex talk with my mom, and that had been bad enough to make me want to punch myself in the stomach.

"When it was discovered that the hybrid was pregnant, the team was split on whether or not the pregnancy should be terminated. That may sound harsh," she said in response to the way Daemon stiffened, "but you must understand we had no idea what this pregnancy could do or what a child of a Luxen and hybrid would be like. We had no idea what we were dealing with, but thankfully termination was vetoed, and we were given the opportunity to study this occurrence."

"So…so they had a baby?" I asked.

Nancy nodded. "The length of pregnancy was normal by human

standards—between eight and nine months. Our hybrid was a little early."

"Luxen take about a year," Daemon said, and I winced, thinking that was a hell of a long time to be stuck carrying triplets. "But like I said, it's hard."

"When the baby was born, there was nothing remarkable in appearance, with the exception of the child's eyes. They were purplish in color, which is an extremely rare human coloring, with a wavy dark circle around the iris. Blood work showed that the baby had adopted both human and Luxen DNA, which was different from the mutated DNA of a hybrid. It wasn't until the child started to grow that we realized what that meant."

I had no idea what that meant.

A smile graced Nancy's face—a genuine one, like a kid's on Christmas morning. "Growth rate was normal, like any human child, but the child showed signs of significant intelligence from onset, learning to speak well before a normal child, and early intelligence tests put the child over two hundred in the IQ department, which is rare. Only a half of one percent of the population has an IQ over one hundred and forty. And there was more."

I remember Daemon telling me before that Luxen matured faster than humans, not in physical appearance but in intellect and social skills, which seemed doubtful considering how he acted sometimes.

He slid me a long look, as if he knew what I was thinking. I squeezed his hand. "What do you mean by more?" he asked, turning back to Nancy.

"Well, really, it's been limitless and still a learning experience. Each child—each generation—appears to have different abilities." A certain light filled her eyes as she spoke. "The first one was able to do something that no hybrid has been able to do. He could heal."

I sat back, blinking rapidly. "But…I thought only Luxen could do that?"

"We believed the same thing until Ro came along. We named him after the first documented Egyptian Pharaoh, who was believed to be a myth."

"Wait. You named him? What about his parents?" I asked.

She shrugged one shoulder, and that was all the answer we got. "Ro's ability to heal others and himself ran parallel to Luxen ability, obviously inherited from his father. Over the course of his childhood, we were able to learn that he could speak telepathically with not just Luxen and hybrids but humans, also. Onyx and diamond mixtures had no effect on him. He had the speed and strength of a Luxen but was faster and stronger. And like the Luxen, he could tap into the Source just as easily. His ability to problem solve and strategize at such a young age was off the charts. The only thing that he and any of the other origins have not been able to do is change their appearance. Ro was the perfect specimen."

It took a few moments for all of this to sink in, and when it did, one thing stood out among everything she had said. It was a small word but so powerful. "Where is Ro now?"

A little of the light went out of her eyes. "Ro is no longer with us."

Which explained the use of past tense. "What happened to him?"

"He died, simply put. But he was not the last. Several more were born, and we were able to learn how the conception was possible." Excited, her speech sped up. "The most interesting factor was that conception could happen between any Luxen male and female hybrid who had been successfully mutated."

Daemon slipped his hand free as he leaned back in the chair. His brows furrowed in awareness. "So Daedalus just happened to have a bunch of horny Luxen and hybrids who were willing to do it while they were here? Because that seems odd to me. This place isn't really the most romantic. Doesn't really set the mood."

My stomach roiled at where his questions were heading, and the air turned stagnant in the room. There was a reason Nancy was being so open with us. After all, Daemon and I were the "perfect specimens," according to Dr. Roth, mutated on a cellular level.

Nancy's gaze turned cool. "You'd be surprised what people in love do when they have a few moments of privacy. And really, it only takes a few moments."

And suddenly, the fact that we were able to share a bathroom also made sense. Was Nancy hoping that Daemon and I would cave to our wild-monkey lust and bring little Daemon babies into the world?

God, I thought I was going to hurl when she confirmed it.

"After all, we haven't stopped you from spending a few moments here and there alone, have we?" Her smile officially creeped me out. "And you two are young and so very much in love. I'm sure you'll make use of your free time sooner or later."

Sergeant Dasher hadn't mentioned any of this during his sales pitch about protecting the world against an alien invasion or curing diseases. Then again, there were many sides to Daedalus. He had said that.

Daemon opened his mouth, no doubt to say something I'd kick him for, but I cut him off. "I have a hard time believing you've had that many people who just…well, you know."

"Well, in some cases, the pregnancies were purely accidental. In other instances, we assisted the process."

Air came into my body but got stuck in my lungs. "Assisted?"

"It's not what you think." She laughed; the sound was shrill and nerve-racking. "There have been volunteers over the years, Luxen and hybrids who understand what Daedalus is truly about. In other cases, we did in vitro fertilization."

The knots moved up my throat like bile, which was a bad thing because my mouth was hanging open. Nothing there to stop it from spewing out.

A muscle in Daemon's jaw was working overtime, thumping away. "What? Is Daedalus moonlighting as Match.com for Luxen and hybrids?"

Nancy sent him a dry look, and I couldn't stop the shudder of revulsion. In vitro meant there had to be a female hybrid to carry the baby. No matter what she said, I doubted all of them were willing.

The pupils of Daemon's eyes had started to glow. "How many of them do you have?"

"Hundreds," she repeated. "The younger ones are kept here, and as they grow older, they are moved to different locations."

"How are you controlling them? From what it looked like, you barely had any control over Micah."

Her lips thinned. "We use trackers that usually keep them where they are supposed to be. However, from time to time, they find ways around them. The ones who aren't controllable are dealt with."

"Dealt with?" I whispered, horrified at where my imagination took that.

"The origins are superior in almost every way. They are remarkable, but they can become very dangerous. If they have not assimilated, then they have to be dealt with accordingly."

My imagination had been dead-on. "Oh my God…"

Daemon slammed his hand down on the table, causing Archer to move forward, hand going to his weapon. "You're basically creating a race of test-tube babies, and if they're not acceptable, you kill them?"

"I don't expect you to understand," Nancy replied evenly as she stood and moved behind her chair. She gripped the back. "The origins are the perfect species, but like with any race of being or creature, there are…duds. It happens. The positives and potential outweigh the nastier side."

I shook my head. "What exactly is so positive about this?"

"Many of our origins have grown up and have assimilated into society. We have trained them so that they will reach the height of success. Each of them has been tailored from birth to assume a certain role. They will become doctors of unequaled abilities, researchers who will unlock the unknown, senators and politicians who are able to see the bigger picture and will bring about social change." She paused and turned toward where Archer stood. "And some will become soldiers of unprecedented talent, joining the ranks of hybrids and humans, creating an army that will be unstoppable."

Tiny hairs on the back of my neck rose as I slowly twisted in my chair. My eyes met Archer's. His expression was emotionless. "Are you…?"

"Archer?" Nancy said, smiling.

Taking his hand off the handle of his gun, he reached up to his left eye with two fingers. He made a pinching motion and a colored contact lens popped out, revealing an iris that was shiny like an amethyst jewel.

I sucked in a sharp breath. "Holy crapola…"

Daemon swore under his breath, and now it made sense why it was only Archer who guarded Daemon and me. If he was anything like Micah, he could handle whatever we threw at him.

"Well, aren't you just a special snowflake," Daemon murmured.

"That I am." Archer's lips quirked into a half grin. "It's a secret. We wouldn't want the other officers or soldiers to be uncomfortable around me."

Which explained why he hadn't gone all superhuman on Micah and had shot him with a tranq gun instead. A thousand questions rushed to the tip of my tongue, but I was struck silent by the implications of what and who he was.

Daemon folded his arms as he focused on Nancy again. "Interesting reveal and all, but I have a bigger question to ask you."

She spread her arms wide in a welcoming way. "Go ahead."

"How do you determine who brings the babies into the world?"

Oh God, my stomach tensed even more, and I bent over, clutching the end of the table.

"It's simple, actually. Besides the in vitro, we look for Luxen and hybrids like you two."

Chapter 14

Daemon

We had to get out of there. Sooner, not later. That was all I could think about.

When we were escorted back to our rooms, I looked at Archer a little more differently and a hell of lot more closely. The soldier had always seemed different, but I would've never guessed that he was something other than human. I had sensed nothing unusual from him, not a damn thing other than this off vibe, but I did notice that Kat seemed comfortable around him. Other than a few smartass responses, which I of all people couldn't hold against him, he seemed like a pretty okay guy.

And frankly, I didn't care what the hell he was. Knowing that he was something different only meant I needed to watch him more carefully. What *did* matter was the fact that they were breeding children here.

That disturbed the hell out of me, and it also angered me.

The moment the door was shut behind me, I headed for the bathroom. Kat had the same idea. A second later, her door opened, and she walked in, quietly shutting the door behind her.

Her face was pale. "I want to vomit."

"Well, let me get out of the way, then."

Her brows pinched. "Daemon, they…" She shook her head, eyes wide. "There are no words for this. It's beyond anything I could've imagined."

"Same here." I leaned against the sink as she sat on the edge of the closed lid. "Dawson never mentioned anything like that to you, did he?"

She shook her head. Dawson rarely spoke about his time with Daedalus, and when he did, he usually told Kat. "No, but he said some of the things were insane. He was probably talking about this."

Before I said any more, I shifted without warning to my true form. *Sorry*, I said when she winced. *Luc had warned me that the things here would blow my mind. Speaking of which, notice anything about Archer's and Micah's eyes—and who has the same kind? Luc's got the weird, blurred line effect going on, too. Hell, I should've known that kid wasn't a normal hybrid. He's an origin.*

Kat ran her palms over her thighs. When she was nervous, she was always fidgeting. Normally I found it cute, but I hated the why behind it now. *This is beyond us*, she said. *How many kids do you think they have? How many people are out there in the world, masquerading as normal humans?*

Well, that's no different than us pretending to be normal.

We're not superhumans who can drop a person on the ground by curling our fists.

I was kind of envious of that ability. *Yeah, too bad, because that would come in handy when someone is getting on your nerves.*

Her hand shot out, smacking my leg. *And what the heck was that? She—that evil woman in a pantsuit—didn't mention anything about that.*

Pretty much all women who wear pantsuits are evil.

Kat's head tipped to the side. *Okay. I do have to agree with that, but can we focus?*

We can now that you agree. I reached over and tweaked her nose, which earned me a dirty look. *We need to get the hell out of here and quick.*

I agree. She knocked my hand away when I went for her nose again. *No offense, but I have no desire to be making any weird babies with you right now.*

I choked on my laugh. *You'd be blessed to have a child of mine. Admit it.*

Her eyes rolled. *Seriously, your ego knows no limit, no matter the situation.*

Hey. I like to be consistent.

That you are, she said, voice dry in my thoughts.

As much as I love the idea of the whole process involved in making a baby with you, it's not ever going to happen under these circumstances.

A pretty flush covered her cheeks. *Glad we're on the same page, buddy.*

I laughed.

We need to get the LH-11 and somehow get in contact with Luc. That sounds impossible to me. Kat's gaze wandered to the closed door. *We don't even know where it's kept.*

Nothing is truly impossible, I reminded her. *But I think we do need another plan.*

Any ideas? She tugged the elastic band out of her hair and untangled the mass of waves. *Maybe we could set the origins loose in the compound. I bet that would cause enough of a distraction. Or maybe you could take on the form of one of the staff here...*

They were good ideas, but there were problems: I bet Daedalus had defenses in place in case a Luxen morphed into someone else, and how would we get to the other building to let out a bunch of miniature super-soldiers?

Kat turned to me, biting on her lower lip as she reached out. Her fingers snaked through the light and touched my arm. My entire body jerked. In my true form, I was hypersensitive. *They weren't really good ideas, were they?*

They were great ideas, but…

Not easily done. She slid her hand up my arm, her head tilting to the side as her gaze wandered over me. My light reflected off her cheeks, giving her a rosy glow. She was beautiful, and I was so, so desperately in love with her.

Her chin jerked up, and she sucked in a breath, eyes widening.

Okay, I may have actually thought that last bit at her.

You did. A small smile split her lips. *I liked hearing it. A lot.*

Kneeling down so I was eye level with her, I cupped her cheek. *I promise you that this isn't going to be our future, Kitten. I will give that to you—a normal life.*

Her eyes glistened. *I don't expect a normal life. I just expect a life with you.*

Yeah, that did crazy things to my heart. Like it stopped beating for a moment, and I was dead in front of her for a second. *Sometimes I don't think I…*

What?

I gave a shake of my head. Never mind. I lowered my hand and backed up, breaking contact. *Luc said he'd know once I got ahold of LH-11. Obviously who he has in here has to be close to us. Anyone you can think of who might be a friendly?*

I don't know. The only ones I've really been around are the doctor, the sergeant, and Archer. She paused, her nose wrinkling. It did that whenever she was concentrating. *You know, I always thought Archer might be on Team Not Insane, but knowing that he's one of them—an origin—I don't know what to think of him.*

I thought about that for a moment. *He's been good to you, hasn't he?*

Some of the color leeched from her cheeks. *Yeah, he has been.*

Counting to ten before I continued, I said, *And the other ones really haven't been?*

She didn't answer immediately. *Talking about that stuff isn't going to help us get out of here.*

Most likely not, but—

"Daemon," she said out loud, eyes narrowing. *We need a plan to get out of here. That's what I need. Not a therapy session.*

I rose to my feet. *I don't know. Therapy might help that temper of yours, Kitten.*

Whatever. She folded her arms, lips pursed. *So, back to other options? Sounds like everything will be a Hail Mary. And anything we attempt, if we're busted, we're totally, irrevocably screwed.*

Holding my breath, I slipped back into my human form, then shook my shoulders out. "Sounds about right," I agreed.

• • •

KATY

Days passed, and while there weren't any more origins running amuck through the compound, and no one was trying to coerce Daemon and me into making babies like there was no tomorrow, a general sense of unease had settled over me.

My stress tests had picked back up, but they didn't involve any other hybrids. For some reason, I was kept away from the others, though I knew they were still there. During my tests, I was forced to use the Source for a really messed-up version of target practice.

Minus the guns and bullets.

It still blew my mind that they were actually training me, like I had been drafted into the army. A day or so ago, while we were in the bathroom, I had asked Daemon again about the other Luxen.

A look of surprise had flickered over his face. "What?"

Having a conversation while knowing that we were most likely being listened to was difficult. Very quickly and quietly, I had told him about Shawn and what Dasher had said.

"That's insane." He'd shaken his head. "I mean, I'm sure there are Luxen out there who hate humans, but an invasion? Thousands of Luxen turning on mankind? I don't believe that."

And I could see that he didn't. I wanted to believe that, too. I didn't think he had reason to lie to me, but Daedalus had so many sides to them. One of them had to be the truth.

All of this was so much bigger than Daemon and me. We wanted out of here, to have a future where we weren't a freak science experiment or controlled by a secret organization, but what Daedalus was doing with the origins had far-reaching implications that went beyond what either of us could understand.

I kept thinking of the *Terminator* movies, about how the computers became self-aware and then nuked the hell out of the world. Take out the computers and replace them with origins. Heck, replace them with Luxen, Arum, or hybrids, and we had an apocalyptical event on our hands. Stuff like this never ended well in the movies or books. Why would real life be any different?

We hadn't gotten any further in our escape plans, either. We sort of sucked at that, and I wanted to be mad at Daemon for exposing himself to this with no clear plan, but I couldn't, because he had done it for me.

It was sometime after lunch had been brought that Archer showed up and escorted me to the med room. I expected to see Daemon, but they had gotten him earlier. I hated not knowing what was going on with him.

"What are we doing today?" I asked, sitting on the table. We were alone in the room.

"We're waiting on the doctor."

"That much I figured." I glanced at Archer and took a deep breath. "What does it feel like? Being an origin?"

He folded his arms. "What does it feel like being a hybrid?"

"I don't know." I shrugged. "I guess I feel like I've always felt."

"Exactly," he replied. "We aren't that different."

He was completely different from anything I'd ever seen. "Do you know your parents?"

"No."

"And that doesn't bother you?"

There was a pause. "Well, it's not something I've dwelled on. I can't change the past. There's very little I can change about anything."

I hated the bland tone, as if none of this affected him at all. "So you are what you are? And that's it?"

"Yes. That is it, Katy."

Pulling my legs up, I sat cross-legged. "Were you raised here?"

"Yes. I grew up here."

"Did you ever live anyplace else?"

"I did for a short period of time. Once I got older we were moved to a different location for our training." He paused. "You're asking a lot of questions."

"So?" I popped my chin onto my fist. "I'm curious. Have you ever lived on your own, in the outside world?"

His jaw flexed, and then he shook his head.

"Have you ever wanted to?"

He opened his mouth and then closed it. He didn't answer.

"You have." I knew I was right. I couldn't see his eyes under the beret, and his expression hadn't changed, but I knew it. "But they won't let you, will they? So you've never been to a regular school? Gone to an Applebee's?"

"I've been to an Applebee's," he responded drily. "And an Outback, too."

"Well, congrats. You've seen everything."

His mouth twitched. "Your sarcasm is not needed."

"Have you ever been to a mall? Gone to a normal library? Have you fallen in love?" I shot off questions left and right, knowing I was probably getting on his nerves. "Have you dressed up for Halloween and gone trick-or-treating? Do you celebrate Christmas? Ever eaten an overcooked turkey and pretended it tasted good?"

"I'm assuming you've done all those things." When I nodded, he took a step forward, and then suddenly he was in my face, leaning down so low that the beret touched my forehead. It shocked me, because I hadn't seen him move, but I refused to back away. A small smile appeared on his lips. "I'm also assuming there's a point to these questions. That maybe you want to somehow prove to me that I haven't lived, that I haven't experienced life, all the mundane things that actually give a person reason for living. Is that what you're trying to do?"

Unable to look away from him, I swallowed. "Yes."

"You don't have to prove that or point it out to me," he said, then straightened. Without speaking out loud, I heard his next words in my thoughts. *I already know I haven't truly lived a single day, Katy. All of us know that.*

I gasped at the intrusion of his voice and at the bleak hopelessness of his words. "All of you?" I whispered.

He nodded as he took a step back. "All of us."

The door opened, silencing us. Dr. Roth came in, followed by the sergeant, Nancy, and another guard. Our conversation immediately dropped out of my thoughts. Seeing the sergeant and Nancy together didn't bring good tidings.

Roth went straight to the tray and started messing with the instruments there. Ice drenched my veins when he picked up a scalpel. "What's going on?"

Nancy sat down in a chair placed in the corner, trusty clipboard in hand. "We have more testing to complete, and we need to move forward."

Remembering the last test that involved a scalpel, I blanched. "Details?"

"Since you have proven to have undergone a stable mutation, we can now focus on the more important aspect of the Luxen abilities," Nancy explained, but I wasn't really watching her. My eyes were trained on Dr. Roth. "Daemon has proven to have remarkable control over the Source, as expected. He has passed all of his testing, and that last healing he did on you was successful, but we need to make sure he can heal more severe injuries before we can bring in subjects."

My stomach dropped, and my hands shook as I clenched the edge of the table. "What do you mean?"

"Before we can bring in humans, we must make sure he can heal a severe injury. There's no reason to subject a human to it if he cannot do it."

Oh God…

"He can heal serious injuries," I blurted out, shrinking back when the doctor stood in front of me. "How do you think I got mutated in the first place?"

"Sometimes that is a fluke, Katy." Sergeant Dasher moved to the other side of the table.

I dragged in air, but my lungs seemed to have stopped working. Daedalus could barely replicate the mutation and had subjected Beth and Dawson to horrific things, trying to get Dawson to mutate other humans. What Daedalus didn't know was that there had to be a true want, a need behind the healing. A need and want like love. That was why it was so hard to replicate.

I almost told them that to save my own skin, but then I realized it probably wouldn't make a difference. Will hadn't believed me when I told him. There was no science behind that. It made the whole healing thing almost magical.

"We've learned from the last time that having Daemon in the room during the procedure isn't a good idea. He will be brought in after we are done," Dasher continued. "Lay down on your stomach, Katy."

A little relief eked through me when I realized it would be way too hard to slit my throat with me lying on my stomach, but I still delayed. "What if he can't heal me? What if it was a fluke?"

"Then this whole experiment is over," Nancy said from her corner. "But I think you and I both know that won't be the case."

"If you know it won't be the case, then why do you need to do this?" It wasn't just the pain I was trying to avoid. I didn't want them to bring Daemon in here and make him go through this. I'd seen what that had done to Dawson, what that would do to *anyone*.

"We have to do trials," Dr. Roth said, his look sympathetic. "We would sedate you, but we have no way of knowing how that would affect the process."

My eyes swung toward Archer, but he looked away. No help there. There was no help anywhere in this room. This was going to happen, and this was going to suck donkey butt.

"Get on your stomach, Katy. The quicker you do this, the quicker it will be over." Sergeant Dasher placed his hands on the table. "Or we will put you on your stomach."

I looked up, my gaze locking with his, and my shoulders squared. Did he really think I was just going to do this willingly and make it easy for all of them? He so had another thing coming.

"Then you're going to have to put me on my stomach," I told him.

He put me on my stomach pretty quickly. It was rather embarrassing how fast he got me flipped over with the help of the other guard who had come in with them. Dasher had hold of my feet, and the guard had my palms pinned down next to my head. I flopped around like a fish for a few seconds before realizing it was doing no good.

All I could lift was my head, which put me at eye level with the guard's chest. "There's a special place in hell for you people."

No one responded—not out loud, that is.

Archer's voice filled my head. *Close your eyes, and take a deep breath when I tell you.*

Too panicked to even pay attention to what he was saying or give much thought to why he was trying to help me, I gasped for a breath.

The back of my shirt was lifted and chilly air rushed over my skin, sending a wave of goose bumps from my spine to my shoulders.

Oh God. Oh God. Oh God. My brain was shutting down, fear taking hold with razor-sharp claws.

Katy.

The cold edge of the scalpel came down on my skin, right below my shoulder blade.

Katy, take a deep breath!

I opened my mouth.

There was a quick jerk of the doctor's arm and fire lit my back, an intensely deep, burning pain that split my skin and muscle.

I didn't take a deep breath. I couldn't.

I screamed.

Chapter 15

Daemon

I didn't feel too spiffy.

About four minutes ago, my heart had started pounding like crazy. I felt sick to my stomach and could barely concentrate on putting one stupid foot in front of the other.

The feeling was vaguely familiar. So was the shortness of breath. I'd experienced this own brand of hell when Kat had been shot, but that didn't make any sense. Relatively speaking, she was sort of safe here, at least from random psychos with guns, and there was no reason anyone would hurt her. Not at this moment, that was, but I knew they had done stuff to Beth to force my brother to mutate humans.

A warm tingle exploded along the back of my neck as the guard and I headed down the hall on the med floor. Kat was nearby. Good.

But the sick feeling, the general sense of dread and pressure building in my chest only worsened the closer I got to her.

This wasn't good. Not good at all.

I stumbled, almost losing my balance, and that brought a big ol' dose of what-the-hell. I *never* stumbled. I had wonderful poise. Or balance. Whatever.

The Rambo wannabe stopped in front of one of the many windowless doors and did the eyeball thing. There was a clicking sound, and the door opened. Air punched out of my lungs the moment I got a good eyeful of the room.

My worst nightmare had come true, springing to life in horrifying clarity and detail.

No one was standing near her, but there were people in the room, even though I really didn't see them. All I saw was Kat. She was lying on her stomach, head turned to the side. Her face was ungodly pale and strained, eyes barely open. A fine sheen of sweat covered her forehead.

Dear God, there was so much blood—seeping off Kat's back, pooling on the gurney table she was lying on, and dripping into the pans below the table.

Her back…her back was a mangled mess. Muscle cut and bone exposed. It looked like Freddy Krueger had gotten hold of her. I was pretty sure her spine was…I couldn't even finish the thought.

Maybe a second had passed from when I entered the room and lurched forward, knocking the dumbass guard out of the way. I faltered when I reached her side and threw my hands out to catch myself. They landed in blood—her blood.

"Jesus," I whispered. "Kat…oh God, Kat…"

Her lashes didn't move. Nothing. A strand of hair clung to her sweat-soaked, pale cheek.

My heart was pounding erratically, struggling to keep up, and I knew it wasn't mine that was faltering. It was Kat's. I didn't know how this happened. Not that I didn't care, because I did want to know, but it wasn't what was important now.

"I got this," I told her, not paying heed to anyone in the room. "I'm going to fix this."

Still nothing, and I cursed as I turned, preparing to shed my human skin, because this…this would require everything in me to fix.

My gaze met Nancy's for a second. "You bitch."

She tapped her pen on her clipboard and made a soft *tsk*ing sound. "We need to make sure you can heal again on what is considered a catastrophic level. Those wounds were made precisely to be fatal, but to take time, unlike a stomach wound or inflictions to other various parts of the body. You will need to heal her."

I was so going to kill that lady one day.

Rage spiked, fueling me, and I shifted into my true form; the roar rose from the depths of my soul. The table shook. Utensils clamored and toppled off the tray. Cabinet doors opened.

"Jesus," someone muttered.

I placed my hands on Kat. *Kitten, I'm here. I'm here, baby. I'm going to make this go away. All of this.*

There was no answer, and the tangy taste of fear coated me. Warmth radiated out from my hands, and the white light tinged with red swallowed Kat. Vaguely I heard Nancy saying, "It's time to move on to the mutation phase."

Healing Kat had exhausted me. That made everyone in that room very lucky because I was sure I could've taken out at least two of them before they got hold of me, if I could move my legs.

They had tried to remove me from the room after I'd healed Kat. Like hell I'd leave them alone with her. Nancy and Dasher had left some time ago, but the doctor hung out, checking Kat's vitals. They were fine, he'd said. She was perfectly healed.

I wanted to murder him.

And I think he knew because he stayed far from my reach.

The doctor eventually left. Only Archer remained. He didn't speak, which was freaking fine by me. What little respect I'd gained for the man was lost the second I realized that he'd been in this room the entire time they did…did this to her. All to prove that I was strong enough to bring her back from the brink of death.

I knew what was coming next: an endless stream of half-dead humans.

Pushing that reality out of my head, I focused on Kat. I sat by the bed, on the stupid rolling chair Nancy had been in, holding her limp hand, smoothing my thumb in circles, hoping that it reached her somehow. She hadn't woken yet, and I hoped she had been passed out through the whole process.

At some point, a female nurse had come in to clean her up. I didn't want anyone near her, but I also didn't want Kat to wake up covered in her own blood. I wanted her to wake up and have no memory of this—of any of this.

"I got it," I said, standing.

The nurse shook her head. "But I—"

I took a step toward her. "I will do this."

"Let him do it," Archer said, shoulders stiff. "Leave."

The nurse looked like she would argue, but finally she left. Archer turned his head as I stripped away the blood-soaked clothing and began cleaning her back. And her back…there were scars—vicious, angry-looking red marks below her shoulder blades—reminding me of one of those books she had at home about a fallen angel whose wings had been ripped away.

I don't know why she scarred this time. The bullet had left a faint mark on her chest, but nothing like this. Maybe it was because of how long it took me to heal her. Maybe it was because the bullet hole was so small and this…this wasn't.

A low, inhuman sound crawled up my throat, startling Archer. I mustered whatever energy I had left and finished changing her. Then I settled back down and picked up her small hand. The silence was as thick as fog in the room until Archer broke it.

"We can take her back to her room."

I pressed my lips to her knuckles. "I'm not leaving her."

"I wasn't suggesting that." There was a pause. "They didn't give me any specific orders. You can stay with her."

A bed would be better for her, I imagined. Pushing myself up, I clenched my jaw as I slid my arms under her.

"Wait." Archer was beside us, and I turned, curling my lip in a snarl. He backed away, holding his hands up. "I was only going to suggest that I could carry her. You don't look like you're capable of walking right now."

"You're not touching her."

"I'm—"

"No," I growled, hoisting Kat's slight weight off the table. "Not happening."

Archer shook his head, but he turned, heading for the door. Satisfied, I turned Kat as gently as I could in my arms, worried that her back would cause her pain. When I was sure she was okay like this, I took a step forward and then another.

The trip back to the room was as easy as walking barefoot over a floor of razors. My energy level was in the pits. Laying her down on her side and crawling in the bed beside her soaked up whatever strength I had left. I wanted to pull the blanket up so she wouldn't be cold, but my arm was like stone between us.

Any other time I would've rather taken Nancy out to a romantic dinner than accept Archer's help, but I said nothing when he lifted the blanket and draped it over us.

He left the room, and finally Kat and I were alone.

I watched her until I could no longer keep my eyes open. I then counted each breath she took until I could no longer remember what the last number was. And when that happened, I repeated her name, over and over again, until it was the last thing I thought before I slipped into oblivion.

• • •

KATY

I woke with a start, gasping in air and expecting it to burn me from the inside out, for the pain to still be there, ravaging every ounce of my being.

But I felt okay. Aching and sore, but otherwise okay, considering what had happened. Oddly, I felt detached from what the doctor did, but as I lay there, I could still feel the ghost hands on my wrists and ankles, holding me down.

An ugly feeling, a mess of emotions ranging from anger to helplessness, rattled my stomach. What they had done to prove that Daemon could heal fatal injuries was horrendous, and that word felt too light, not severe or heavy enough.

Feeling icky and uncomfortable in my own skin, I forced my eyes open.

Daemon lay beside me in a deep sleep. Dark shadows fanned his cheeks. Bruised shadows were under his eyes, a purplish tint of exhaustion. His cheeks were pale and lips parted. Several locks of wavy dark brown hair tumbled over his forehead. I'd never seen him look so worn out before. His chest rose steadily and evenly, but fear trickled through my veins.

I rose up on my elbow and leaned over, placing my hand on his chest. His heart beat under my palm, slightly accelerated due to mine.

As I watched him sleep, that ugly mess of emotion took on a new form. Hatred encased it, crystallizing into a hardened shell of bitterness and rage. My hand curled into a fist against his chest.

What they had done to me was reprehensible, but what they had forced Daemon to do was beyond that. And it would only get worse from this point on. They'd start bringing in humans, and when he failed to mutate them successfully, they would hurt me to get at Daemon.

I would become Bethany, and he'd become Dawson.

Squeezing my eyes shut, I exhaled a long breath. No. I couldn't let this happen. *We* couldn't let this happen. But in reality, it was already happening. Pieces of me had gone dark by what I'd done and what had been forced upon me. And if these ugly things kept piling up—which they would—how could we be any different? How could we not turn into Bethany and Dawson?

It struck me then.

I opened my eyes, my gaze traveling over Daemon's broad cheekbones. It wasn't that I had to be stronger than Beth, because I was sure she had been strong and still was. It wasn't that Daemon had to be better than Dawson. We had to be stronger and better than *them*—Daedalus.

Lowering my head, I placed a soft kiss to Daemon's lips and swore in that moment, we would walk out of this. It wasn't just Daemon promising me. It wouldn't just be in his hands to fix.

It would be us—together.

His arm suddenly snaked around my waist, and he tugged me against him. One startling green eye opened. "Hey there," he murmured.

"I didn't mean to wake you."

The corner of his mouth tipped up. "You didn't."

"You've been awake a while?" When his smile spread, I shook my head. "So you just laid there and let me stare at you like a creeper?"

"Pretty much, Kitten. I figured I'd let you get your fill, but then you kissed me and, well, I like to be a bit more involved in that." Both eyes opened, and as always, staring into them had an exhilarating quality to it. "How are you feeling?"

"I'm okay. I feel great, actually." Settling down beside him, I wiggled my head onto his arm, and his hand curled back, tangling in my hair. "How about you? I know that had to have taken a lot out of you."

"You shouldn't be worried about me. What they—"

"I know what they did. I know why they did it." I tipped my chin down as I slid a hand between us. He stiffened as the back of my knuckles brushed over his stomach. "I'm not going to lie. It hurt like hell. When they were doing it, I wanted… You don't even want to know what I wanted, but I'm okay because of you. But I hate what they made you do."

His breath grazed my forehead, and there was a long stretch of silence. "You amaze me," was all he said.

"What?" I looked up. "Daemon, I am not amazing. You are. The things you can do? What you have done for me? You—"

He placed a finger on my lips, silencing me. "After what you went through, you're more concerned about me? Yeah, you amaze me, Kitten, you really do."

I felt a grin pulling at my lips, and it kind of felt strange to want to smile after everything. "Well, how about this? We're both amazing."

"I like that." He lowered his mouth to mine, and the kiss was sweet and tender, just as consuming as the other ones because it offered a promise—a promise of more, of a future. "You know, I haven't told you this enough, and I should tell you every chance I get, but I love you."

I sucked in a sharp gasp. Hearing him say those words never failed to affect me deeply. "I know you do, even if you don't say it all the time." I reached up and ran the tips of my fingers over the curve of his cheek. "I love you."

Daemon's eyes drifted shut, and his body tensed. He seemed to draw those words into him.

"How tired are you?" I asked after a couple of moments of staring at him like a goober.

His arm tightened around me. "Pretty tired."

"Would it help to go into your true form?"

He gave a lopsided shrug. "Probably."

"Then do it."

"Aren't you bossy?"

"Shut up and take your true form so you feel better. How about that for bossy?"

He laughed softly. "I love it."

I started to point out that he was getting mighty comfortable with that L-word, but he shifted ever so slightly and brought his lips to mine once more. This kiss was deeper, starved and urgent. Eyes closed, I could still see the white light as he started to change. I gasped in surprise, getting lost in the warmth and the intimacy of the moment. When he pulled back, I could barely open my eyes, he was so bright.

"Better?" I asked out loud, voice thick with emotion.

His hand found mine. It was strange seeing those light-encased fingers thread through mine, curling around them. *I was better the moment you woke up.*

Chapter 16

Daemon

Daedalus wasted no time once they were confident I had mad healing skills. As soon as they thought I was rested, they brought me into a room on the med floor. There was nothing in the white-walled space except two plastic chairs facing each other.

I turned to Nancy, brows raised. "Nice decorating you got going on here."

She ignored it. "Sit."

"What if I prefer to stand?"

"I really don't care." She turned to where a camera was perched in the corner and nodded. Then she faced me. "You know what is expected of you. We're starting out with one of our new recruits. He's twenty-one and in otherwise good health."

"Except for the fatal injury you're about to inflict on him?"

Nancy shot me a bland look.

"And he signed up for this?"

"That he did. You'd be surprised by how many people are willing to risk their lives to become something great."

I was more surprised by the level of stupidity of some people. To sign up for a mutation that had a success rate of less than one percent didn't seem very bright to me, but what did I know?

She handed over a wide cuff. "This is a piece of opal. I'm sure you're well aware of what it does. It will enhance in the healing and ensure that you're not going to be exhausted."

I took the silver cuff and stared at the black stone with the red marking in the center. "You're literally handing me a piece of opal, knowing it counteracts the onyx."

She gave me a pointed look. "You also know that we have soldiers armed with those nasty little weapons I told you about. That outweighs you having opal."

Slipping it around my wrist, I welcomed the jolt of energy. I glanced up at Nancy, finding her watching me like I was her prized bull. I had a feeling that even if I ran from room to room, zapping people to death, she wouldn't bring the big guns out. Not unless I did something crazy insane.

I was just too special.

And I was pissed off, too. She could've given me the piece of opal when I had needed to heal Kat. One of these days I was going to do serious harm to this woman.

The bright-eyed, bushy-tailed soldier marched into the room, and without further instructions copped a squat on one of the chairs. The kid looked on the young side of twenty-one, and while I tried to have no feelings about any of this, a niggle of guilt rose.

Not because I planned on screwing this up or anything. Why would I? If I didn't successfully bring a hybrid into this world, then eventually they'd turn their evil, sadistic eyes on Kat.

So, yeah, I was rocking the whole "there needs to be a 'true want' to heal the person," but I still had no idea if it would work. If it didn't, homeboy here would either live out the rest of his life as a boring old human being or would self-destruct in a few days.

For his sake and Kat's, I hoped he was welcomed into the world of happy hybrids.

"How are we doing this?" I asked Nancy.

She motioned for one of the two guards who'd come into the room with Patient Zero. One of them stepped forward, brandishing a nasty-looking knife, the kind that Michael Myers would run around with in *Halloween*.

"Oh jeez," I muttered, folding my arms. This was going to get messy.

Patient Too Stupid to Live handled the knife with confidence. Before he could do anything with it, the door opened and Kat walked in, Archer right on her heels.

My arms fell to my sides as unease exploded into alarm. "What is she doing here?"

Nancy smiled tightly. "We thought you could use the motivation."

Understanding lit me up like a firecracker. Their kind of motivation was a warning. They knew damn well that we were aware of what happened to Bethany when Dawson failed. I watched Kat shake off Archer's hand and stomp over to the corner. She stayed there.

I focused on Nancy, staring her down until she finally, after several moments, broke eye contact. "Get on with it, then," I said.

She nodded at Patient Most Likely to Die, who, without saying a damn word, took a deep breath and slammed that serial-killer knife right into his stomach with a wheezy grunt. He then yanked the knife out, letting it fall from his grasp. A guard shot forward, grabbing it.

"Holy shit," I said, eyes going wide. Patient Zero had balls.

Kat winced and looked away as blood spilled from the fresh wound. "That...that was disturbing."

He probably had less than two minutes to live if blood kept pounding out of his rapidly paling body like that. He was clutching his stomach, doubled over. A metallic scent filled the air.

"Do it," Nancy said, shifting her weight as eagerness filled her gaze.

Shaking my head in macabre fascination, I knelt by the guy and placed my hands on his stomach. Blood immediately covered my hands. I didn't have a light stomach, but, damn, I could see the dude's intestines. What kind of magic Kool-Aid was this kid drinking to willingly do this to himself? Christ.

I let my human form fade out, and whitish-red light swallowed the guy and most of the room. Concentrating on the wound, I pictured the jagged edges healing shut, stopping the blood loss. I honestly didn't have a freaking clue when it came to healing. It was something that sort of happened on its own. I pictured the wound, and sometimes snapshots of the energies would flicker through my head with no thought of my own. What I did focus on was the light filtering through the veins…and Kat.

I glanced up as I took a breath. An expression of rapture had settled on Nancy's face, that of a mother who caught her first glimpse of her child. I sought out Kat, and there she was. She had a look of awe on her beautiful face as she stared back at me.

My heart skipped, and I turned back to the guy I was healing. *I'm doing this for her*, I told him. *You better hope it was enough, for your sake.*

The guy's head jerked up. Color had already returned to his cheeks.

With the opal, I didn't feel a bit drained like I normally would after such a massive healing.

I let go and stood, drifting back a step. Staying in my true form long enough for the man to stand on shaky legs, I glanced over at Kat once more. One hand was pressed to her chin. Beside her, Archer looked a bit unnerved by the whole thing. Something occurred to me then.

Slipping back into my human form, I turned to Nancy, who was staring at Patient Zero with so much awe and hope it was actually sickening. "Why can't they make hybrids?" I asked. "The origins can heal. Why can't they?"

Nancy barely looked at me as she motioned at the camera. "They can heal just about any wound, but they cannot cure disease or mutate. We do not know why, but it is their only limitation." Guiding the guy back into the seat, she handled him with surprising gentleness. "How are you feeling, Largent?"

After taking several deep breaths, Largent cleared his throat. "A little sore, but otherwise I feel good—great." He smiled as he glanced between Nancy and me. "Did it work?"

"Well, you're alive," I said drily. "That's a good start."

The door opened, and Dr. Roth rushed in, stethoscope thumping over his chest. He spared me a glance. "Amazing. I was watching through the monitors. Truly remarkable."

"Yeah. Yeah." I started toward Kat, but Nancy's sharp voice rang out, like claws on a chalkboard.

"Stay there, Daemon."

I turned my head slowly, aware that the other guards had moved between Kat and me. "Why? I did what you wanted."

"We haven't seen anything yet other than the fact you healed him." Nancy moved around the chair, watching the doctor and Largent. "How are his vitals?"

"Perfect," the doctor said, standing as he wrapped the stethoscope around his neck. He reached inside his lab coat and pulled out a small black case. "We can start Prometheus."

"What is that?" I asked, watching as the doctor pulled out a syringe full of shimmery blue liquid. Out of the corner of my eye, I saw Archer cock his head to the side as he stared at the needle.

"Prometheus is Greek," Kat said. "Well, he was a Titan. In mythology, he created man."

A flash of amusement flickered in my eyes.

She shrugged. "It was in a paranormal book I read once."

I couldn't hold back a small grin. Her and her nerdy reading habits. Made me want to kiss her and do other stuff. And she picked up on it, too, because a flush stained her cheeks. Alas, wasn't going to happen.

Dr. Roth rolled up Largent's sleeve. "Prometheus should act faster, without the need to wait for the fever. It will speed up the mutation process."

Hell, I wondered if Largent really was okay with being the first guinea pig. But it didn't matter. They shot him up with the blue gunk. He slumped over—not a good sign—and Roth went into doctor mode. Vitals were through the roof. People were starting to look a tad bit nervous. No one was really paying attention to me, so I started inching toward Kat. I was halfway there when Largent shot up from the chair, knocking the doctor on his ass.

I put myself between Kat and the general area of where Largent was standing. He stumbled forward and then bent over, grasping his knees. Sweat poured off the guy's forehead, dripping onto the floor. A sickly sweet stench replaced the metallic.

"What is happening?" demanded Nancy.

The doctor started to unwind the stethoscope as he went to the soldier's side and placed a hand on his shoulder. "What are you feeling, Largent?"

The man's arms were trembling. "Cramping," he gasped. "My whole body is cramping. It feels like my insides are—" He jerked up, throwing his head back. Throat working, he opened his mouth and let out a scream.

A bluish, blackish substance spewed from his mouth, splattering the doctor's white lab coat. Largent wobbled to the side, his hoarse scream ending in a thick gurgle. The same liquid leaked from the corners of his eyes, streamed from his nose and ears.

"Oh boy," I said, backing up. "I don't think whatever you injected him with is working."

Nancy cut me a dark glare. "Largent, can you tell me what—?"

The soldier spun around and ran—and I mean he ran at full light speed—toward the door. Kat screamed and then clasped her hands over her mouth. I moved to block the grisly sight, but it was too late. Largent smacked into the door with a fleshy, wet *thud*, hitting it at the kind of speed jumping out of a fifty-story window would do.

Silence descended, and then Nancy said, "Well, that was disappointing."

• • •

KATY

As long as I lived, I'd never be able to scrape from my mind the sight of the soldier going from relatively normal to something that looked like stage one of a zombie infection to going splat against the door.

We had to wait in that room until staff came and cleaned up enough of the mess that we could leave without stepping in the… uh, stuff. They wouldn't let Daemon or me get within an inch of each other as we waited, like it was his fault somehow. He'd healed the guy—he did his part. Whatever was in Prometheus had done this. The blood wasn't on Daemon's hands.

Out in the hallway, the soldiers took Daemon down one wing, and Archer took me down another. We were halfway toward the elevators when one of the elevator doors on the right opened, and two soldiers stepped out, escorting a child.

I skidded to a complete stop.

Not just any child. It was one of them—the origins. Tiny hairs on my body rose at the sight. The boy wasn't Micah, but he had the same dark hair cut in the same style. Maybe a little bit younger, but I was never good at judging ages.

"Keep walking," Archer said, placing a hand on my back.

Forcing my legs to move, I didn't know what it was about those kids that freaked me out. Okay. There were probably a lot of things about those kids that could freak me out. The main thing was the abnormal intelligence gleaming in their oddly colored eyes and the small childlike smile that seemed to mock the adults around them.

God, Daemon and I needed to get out of this place for a whole truckload of reasons.

As we crossed paths with them, the little boy lifted his head and looked straight at me. The moment our gazes collided, a sharp tingle of awareness traveled up my spine and exploded along the back of my skull. Dizziness swept through me, and I stopped again, feeling strange. I wondered if the kid was doing some kind of weird Jedi mind trick on me.

The kid's eyes widened.

My fingers started to tingle.

Help us, and we'll help you.

My mouth dropped open. I didn't—I couldn't. My brain stopped working, and the words repeated themselves. The kid broke contact, and then they were behind us, and I was standing there, quaking with adrenaline and confusion.

Archer's face came into view, eyes narrowed. "He said something to you."

I snapped out of it and immediately went on guard. "Why would you think that?"

"Because you have a freaked-out look on your face." Dropping his hand on my shoulder, he spun me around and gave a little push toward the elevator. As the doors slid shut, he hit the stop button. "There are no cameras in the elevators, Katy. Besides the bathrooms, it's the only area in the building free from watchful eyes."

Having no idea where he was going with that and still mind-blown from everything, I took a step back, hitting the wall. "Okay."

"The origins are able to pick up thoughts. It's one thing that Nancy didn't tell you. They can read thoughts. So you better be very careful what you're thinking when you're around one of them."

I gaped. "They can read minds? Wait, that means you can do it, too!"

He gave a noncommittal shrug. "I try not to. Hearing other people's thoughts is really annoying more than anything else, but when you're young, you really don't think about it. You just do it. And they do it all the time."

"I… This is insane. They can read minds, too? What else can they do?" I felt like I'd fallen through a rabbit hole and woken up in an X-Men comic. And all of the things I've thought about around Archer? I was sure at some point I had thought about escaping here and—

"I've never told anyone anything I've picked up from you," he said.

"Oh my God…you're doing it right now." My heart pounded. "And why should I trust that?"

"Probably because I've never asked you to trust me."

I blinked. Hadn't Luc said something like that? "Why wouldn't you tell Nancy?"

He shrugged again. "That doesn't matter."

"Yes. It totally—"

"No. It doesn't. Not right now. Look, we don't have a lot of time. Be careful when you're around the origins. I picked up on what he said to you. Have you seen the movie *Jurassic Park*?"

"Uh, yeah." What an odd question.

A wry smile appeared. "Remember the raptors? Letting the origins out would be like unlocking the gates on the raptor cages. You get what I'm saying? These origins, the newest batch, are nothing like what Daedalus has had in the past. They're evolving and adapting in ways no one can control. They can do things I cannot even think of. Daedalus already has problems keeping them in line."

I struggled to process all of this. Strangely, common sense kept spewing out denials, when in reality I knew anything was possible.

I was an alien/human hybrid, after all. "Why are these origins different?"

"They were given Prometheus to help accelerate their learning and abilities." Archer snorted. "Like they needed it. But unlike poor Largent, it worked with them."

Largent's mangled body flashed before me, and I winced. "What is the Prometheus serum?"

He looked at me skeptically. "You know what Prometheus was in Greek mythology. I can't believe you haven't figured it out yet."

Gee, way to make me feel stupid.

He laughed.

I glared at him. "You're reading my thoughts, aren't you?"

"Sorry." He didn't look sorry at all. "You said it yourself. Prometheus was credited with creating mankind. Think about it. What is Daedalus doing?"

"Trying to create the perfect species, but that really doesn't tell me anything."

He shook his head as he reached over and tapped a finger along the fleshy part of my elbow. "When you first mutated, you were given a serum. It was the first serum that Daedalus created, but they want something better, something faster. Prometheus is what's being tested now, and not just on humans healed by Luxen."

"I…" I didn't get it at first, and then I thought about those bags in the room where the sick patients were receiving Daedalus's own breed of medication. "They're giving it to humans who are sick, aren't they?"

He nodded.

"Then that means Prometheus is LH-11?" When he nodded again, I forced myself not to go any further with the realization, lest Archer was being nosy. "Why are you telling me this?"

He pivoted slightly and restarted the elevator. Casting me a long look, he simply said, "We have a mutual friend, Katy."

Chapter 17

Katy

I could barely contain myself waiting for a few moments alone with Daemon. We hadn't been abusing the bathroom privileges, knowing that's what they wanted us to do. It took forever before I felt the familiar tingle along my neck. Holding off a couple of minutes, I then bum-rushed the bathroom and knocked softly on the door to his cell.

He was there within a second. "Miss me?"

"Do your Lite-Brite thing." I moved from one foot to the other. "Come on."

He looked at me strangely, but a second later he was a glowing comet. *What's up?*

In a rush, I told him everything about the creepy kid in the hallway, what Archer had said about them, what Prometheus really was, and what Archer had said about us sharing a mutual friend. *I don't trust any of this, but either Archer hasn't told anyone what he's picked up from you or me or he has, and for some reason we haven't been called out on it.*

Daemon's light pulsed. *Jesus, this just keeps getting more and more bizarre.*

You're telling me. I leaned against the sink. *If they decide to shoot someone up with it again…* I shuddered. *Maybe they'll just wait until the mutation takes hold this time.*

That, or I have a feeling they're going to have a really hefty cleanup bill.

Ew. That was really…

One light-encased arm stretched out. Warm fingers brushed my cheek. *I'm sorry you had to see that.*

I'm sorry you had to be a part of that. I took a deep breath. *But you know what happened to Largent isn't on your conscience, right?*

Yes. I know. Trust me, Kitten, I'm not going to take on any unnecessary guilt. His sigh shuttled through me. *So, about Archer…*

We talked a couple more minutes about Archer. Both of us agreed that there was a good chance he was Luc's inside guy, but it didn't make sense. Archer obviously had access to the LH-11 and could've gotten it for Luc. We couldn't trust him—we weren't going to make the mistake of trusting anyone again.

But I did have an idea. One that Daemon was also interested in. Once we got our hands on the LH-11, we had only one chance to escape. And if the origins really were like raptors, then they could become the perfect distraction, allowing us a small shot to bust out of there.

No matter what we did, it would be risky, with about a 99 percent fail rate. But both Daemon and I felt more confident relying on each other than just Luc—and possibly Archer. We'd been burned way too many times before.

Daemon took his human form and kissed me quickly before we went back into our rooms. This was always the hardest—forcing ourselves to go to our own beds—but the last thing we needed was to risk getting caught up in the moment…in each other. Because that always seemed to happen when we were together. And we also didn't fully trust that they'd allow us to come and go from each other's rooms—everything felt like a test.

I headed back to my bed. Sitting down, I pulled my knees up to my chest and rested my chin on them. Those quiet moments of doing nothing were the worst. In no time, things I didn't want to think about crept in and pushed away the stuff I needed to focus on.

I really wanted Daemon to see that I was holding it together, that none of this was messing with my head. I didn't want him to worry about me.

Closing my eyes, I shifted until my forehead was against my knees. I told myself the cheesiest thing possible: there was a light at the end of this dark tunnel. I followed that up with the ever faithful: every dark cloud had a silver lining.

I wondered how long I could keep telling myself that.

• • •

Daemon

The wondrous team behind Daedalus actually waited until the mutation took hold this time around. It was another recruit who apparently had been all kinds of gung ho. This one stabbed himself in the chest, right below the heart instead of the gut. Still messy. Kat had been there to witness it again. I had healed the idiot. Overall it was a relative success, except I couldn't get near the LH-11. A damn shame, because there had been serum left over in the syringe.

Kat and I weren't relying on Luc, but if we could get the LH-11, and if it turned out that someone, whether it was Archer or not, could help us get out, I was going to take it. Kat's plan of letting the kids loose was the best we had, but the technicalities of how we could do that remained to be seen. Not to mention we had no idea what we'd actually be unleashing. As much as I hated to admit it, there were innocent people in these buildings.

In the three days while we waited for the second guinea pig to show signs of mutation, I was asked to heal three more soldiers and one who had to be a civilian—a female who looked too nervous to have signed up for this without coercion. She didn't stab herself but was injected with a lethal dose of something.

And I hadn't been able to heal her, like, at all. I didn't know what it was, and it had been terrible. She'd started foaming at the mouth, convulsing, and I tried, but there had been nothing I could do. I couldn't *see* the injury in my head, and it just didn't work.

The woman had died right there, under Kat's horrified gaze.

Nancy hadn't been happy when they carted off the woman's motionless body. Her mood was compounded on the fourth day, when Prometheus, otherwise known as LH-11, was given to the second soldier I had healed. Later that day, he ended up face-planting a wall. I didn't know what it was with them and running into walls, but that was number two.

On the fifth day, the third subject was given LH-11. He lasted an additional twenty-four hours before bleeding out through every orifice, including the belly button. Or that was what I was told.

The deaths, well, they did stack up, one after another. Kind of hard not to take them personally. Did I blame myself? Hell to the no. Did it piss me off and make me want to douse the entire compound in gasoline and start throwing matches? Hell yes.

They kept me away from Kat most of the days, only allowing us to be in the same room when I did the healing thing, and we had a few minutes here and there in our bathroom of secrets. It wasn't enough. Kat looked as exhausted as I felt, which I'd thought would've given my hormones a rest, but oh no. Every time I heard the shower click on, I had to call upon every ounce of self-control. The bathrooms didn't have cameras, and I could be quiet, which was perfect for a little freaky deaky, but there was no way in hell I was risking the chance of baby Daemons in this hellhole.

Was I totally against the idea of having kids with Kat one day? Other than breaking out in hives at the thought of that, the idea wasn't too horrible. Of course, I wanted the white picket fence bullshit…if it occurred a good ten years from now, and the kids didn't have weird bowl haircuts and couldn't Jedi mind-screw people.

I didn't think that was asking too much.

On the sixth day, when the third soldier was given LH-11, he made it through the rest of the day and well into the seventh day. He immediately began showing signs of a successful mutation. He passed the stress test with flying colors.

Nancy was so thrilled, I thought she was going to kiss me—and I thought I was actually going to have to hit a chick.

"You deserve a reward," she said, and I thought I deserved to put my foot up her ass. "You may spend the night with Kat. No one will stop you from doing so."

I said nothing. While I wasn't going to turn that down, it was rather creepy hearing Nancy tell me I could spend the night with Kat while they watched us on video. I thought of those kids on the lower floors. Yeah, not going to happen.

Kat had been up to something, inching closer to the tray. She had stopped when Nancy made her announcement. Her nose wrinkled, and I was a bit insulted, although she was probably thinking the same thing I was.

They brought in another subject, this one another soldier, but I was distracted by whatever Kat was doing. She was way too close to the trays, practically standing in front of them.

A stabbing motion later, and I had blood on my hands and a very happy Nancy bouncing around the room.

Dr. Roth had placed the spent needle next to the unused ones. I saw Kat make grabby fingers, but something occurred to me.

"Does this mean I'm joined to them?" I asked, wiping my hands on a towel that had been all but thrown at me. "The ones who don't face-plant a wall? If I die, they die?"

Nancy laughed.

My brows rose. "I don't see how that's a funny question."

"It's a very good, self-serving question." She clasped her hands together, dark eyes glimmering. "No. The Prometheus serum that is given to the mutated subject breaks the bond."

That was a relief. I didn't like the idea of several Achilles' heels running around. "How is that possible?"

A guard opened the door as Nancy crossed the room. "We've had many years to narrow down the interworking of the mutation and the consequences, Daemon. Just as we know that there needs to be a true want behind the mutation." She turned to me, head tilted to the side. "Yes. We've known that. It's not a magical or spiritual thing, but a mixture of ability, strength, and determination."

Well, shit…

"Your brother was almost there." Nancy's voice lowered, and my body tensed. "It wasn't lack of determination or ability. And trust me, he was motivated. We made sure of that. But he simply was not strong enough."

I locked my jaw down. Anger slithered through my veins like venom.

"We don't need him. Bethany, on the other hand, well, that's yet to be seen. But you?" She placed a hand on my chest. "You're a keeper, Daemon."

Chapter 18

Katy

You're a keeper, Daemon.

Oh my God, I almost stabbed the needle through Nancy's eye. Good thing I didn't, because that would defeat the whole purpose of what I'd done.

Crossing my arms, I folded my hands around the syringe and kept it hidden under my arm. I dutifully followed Daemon and Archer out, half expecting someone to tackle me from behind.

No one did.

In the excitement of a potentially successful mutation, no one was paying attention to me. No one besides Daemon ever did during these things, except Archer, and if he was peeping into my thoughts, he sure as hell hadn't said anything.

I hadn't really thought any of this through when I grabbed the serum, but as I held it in my hand, I knew that if I did get caught, I was probably going to regret it. So would Daemon. If Archer was peeking in my thoughts right now, and he wasn't working with Luc, we were so screwed.

We went to the elevator, Nancy and the newly mutated hybrid heading in the other direction. We were alone—just the three of us—as the elevator doors slid shut. I almost couldn't believe our luck. My heart was pounding with excitement and fear, like a drummer doing a solo.

Nudging Daemon in the arm, I got his attention. He glanced at me, and I looked down at my hand, carefully opening my fingers. Just the tip of the top of the syringe was visible. His eyes flicked up and widened, meeting mine.

In that instant, both of us knew what this meant. With the LH-11 in hand, we had no time. Someone would eventually realize it was missing, or they might've even caught me on the security tapes. Either way, it was do or die time.

The elevator doors slid shut, and Archer turned to us. Daemon shifted forward, but Archer's hand shot out. My breath caught in my throat as his hand hit the control panel. The elevator didn't move.

Archer's gaze dropped to my hand, and his head tilted to the side. "You have the LH-11? Jesus. You two are… I didn't think you'd do it. Luc said you would." His eyes flicked to Daemon. "But I really didn't think either of you would pull it off."

My heart was pounding so fast my fingers tingled around the needle. "What are you going to do about it?"

"I know what you're thinking." Archer's attention was on Daemon. "Why didn't I get the serum for Luc? That's not what I was here for, and we don't have time to explain it. They're going to know it's missing very soon." There was a quick pause, and he was back to me. "And the plan in your head is crazy."

I had been thinking about the origins, but now I was thinking about Rainbow Brite doing the Electric Slide. Anything to keep Archer out of my head.

He made a face. "Seriously, guys?" he said, taking off his beret. He shoved it in his back pocket. "What exactly do you two hope to accomplish? Your plan has a hundred percent fail rate."

"You're a smart-ass," Daemon said, shoulders stiffening. "And I don't like you."

"And I don't care." Archer turned to me. "Give me the LH-11."

My fingers tightened around it. "Hell no."

His eyes narrowed. "Okay. I know what you guys are about to do. Even though I warned you not to do it, you're planning on letting the freak show out, and then what? Making a run for it? Besides the fact you don't know how to get to that building, you're going to need your hands, and you don't want to stick yourself with that needle. Trust me."

Indecision flooded me. "You don't understand. Every time we've trusted someone, we've been burned. Handing this over…"

"Luc's never betrayed you, has he?" When I shook my head, Archer grimaced. "And I would never betray Luc. Even I'm a bit scared of that little shit."

I glanced at Daemon. "What do you think?"

There was a moment of silence, and then he said, "If you screw us over, I will not think twice about killing you in front of God and everyone. You got that?"

"But we need to get the LH-11 out of the compound," I said.

"I'm going with you guys, like it or not." Archer winked. "I hear the Olive Garden is a good restaurant to try out."

I remembered our conversation about him having a normal life, and for some reason that made what I was about to do a little easier. I didn't understand why he was helping us or Luc, or why he hadn't gotten this before, but like he said, we were already in too deep. Swallowing hard, I handed over the syringe and felt like I was handing over my life, which in a way I was. He took it, grabbed his beret, and wrapped it around the syringe, then shoved the bundle in his front cargo pocket.

"Let's get this show on the road," Daemon said, eyeing Archer as he reached down and squeezed my hand briefly.

"You're wearing a piece of opal?" Archer asked.

"Yes." He flashed a daring grin. "Nancy's crush on me is useful, huh?" He waved his wrist around, and the red inside the opal seemed to flicker. "Time to be awesome."

"Turn into Nancy." Archer hit the floor button. "Quickly."

Daemon's form flickered and morphed, shortening several inches. His waves straightened into thin, dark hair pulled into a ponytail. His features blurred completely. Boobs appeared. That's about when I knew where he was going with this. A drab woman's pantsuit later, Nancy Husher stood beside me.

But it wasn't Nancy.

"That's so freaky," I murmured, eyeing him/her/whatever for a telltale sign that it was really Daemon.

She smirked.

Yep. It was still Daemon.

"Do you think this is going to work?" I asked him.

"I'm going to say the glass is half full on that."

I tucked loose strands of hair behind my ear. "That's reassuring."

"We're going to let the kids loose, and then we're going to get back on this elevator and head to ground level." He eyed Archer with every ounce of authority Nancy carried. "I'm going to give her the opal when we get outside." He glanced at me. "Don't argue with me about that. You're going to need it because we are going to run, and we'll run faster than we've ever run before. Can you do that?"

This plan did not sound good to me. There was nothing but a desert wasteland outside, probably for a hundred miles, but I nodded. "Well, we know they won't kill you. You're too awesome."

"You betcha. Ready?"

I wanted to say no, but I said yes, and then Archer hit the button for the ninth floor. As the elevator jerked into movement, my heart pounded.

It stopped on the fifth floor.

Crap. We had not planned on that.

"It's okay," Archer said. "This is how you access building B."

Terror pooled in my stomach as we stepped out into the wide hallway. All of this could be a trap or another setup, but there was no going back.

Archer placed his hand on my shoulder, like he normally would when he was escorting me around. If that made Daemon unhappy, he didn't show it. His expression remained in the cool disdain that was all Nancy.

There were people in the hall, but no one really paid any attention to us. We made it to the end of the hall and got in a wider elevator. Archer hit a button marked B, and the elevator kicked into gear. Once it stopped, we entered another hall and went straight across to yet another elevator, and then he chose the ninth floor.

Nine floors underground. Ugh.

It seemed like a long way to travel for the little origins to get out, but then again, they were like baby Einsteins on crack.

Mouth dry, I willed my heart to slow down before I had a panic attack. Within seconds, the elevator stopped, and the doors opened. Archer stepped aside, letting Daemon and me walk out first. Out of the corner of my eye, I saw him hit the stop button.

The elevator had opened into a small, windowless lobby. Two soldiers were posted in front of double doors. They straightened immediately when they saw us.

"Ms. Husher. Officer Archer," the one on the right said, nodding. "May I ask why you're bringing her down here?"

Daemon stepped forward, clasping his hands together in total Nancy fashion. "I thought it would be a good idea for her to see our greatest achievements in their own environment. Perhaps it will give her a better understanding of things here."

I had to clamp my mouth shut, because the words that came out of his mouth were so like Nancy that I wanted to laugh. Not a normal laugh, either, but that crazy, hysterical giggling kind.

The guards exchanged looks. Mr. Talkative stepped forward. "I'm not sure if that's a good idea."

"Are you questioning me?" said Daemon, in the snootiest Nancy voice ever.

I bit down on my lower lip.

"No, ma'am, but this area is closed to all personnel that don't have clearance and…and to guests." Mr. Talkative glanced at me and then Archer. "That was the order you gave."

"Then I should be able to bring who I want down here, don't you think?"

With each heartbeat, I knew we were running out of time. The hand on my shoulder tightened, and I knew even Archer was thinking that.

"Y-Yes, but this goes against protocol," Mr. Talkative stuttered. "We can't—"

"You know what?" Daemon took a step forward, glancing up. I didn't see any cameras, but that didn't mean they weren't there. "Protocol this."

Daemon/Nancy threw out his hand and a bolt of light erupted from his palm. The arc of energy split in two, one smacking into the chest of Mr. Talkative and the other into the silent guard. They went down, smoke wafting up from their bodies. The smell of burned clothing and flesh hit my nose.

"Well, that's one way of doing it," Archer said drily. "No turning back now."

Daemon/Nancy cast him a look. "Can you open these doors?"

Archer stepped forward and bent. The red light on the panel flipped green. The airtight seal popped, and the doors slid open.

Half expecting someone to jump out and point a gun at our faces as we walked into an open area of the ninth floor, I held my breath.

No one stopped us, but we did get a couple of weird looks from the staff milling about.

The floor was a different layout than the ones I'd seen, shaped like a circle with several doors and long windows. In the middle was something that reminded me of a nursing station.

Archer dropped his hand, and I felt something cool pressed into mine. I looked down, startled to find I was holding a gun. "No safety, Katy." Then he stepped up beside Daemon. In a low voice, he said, "We've got to do this fast. See the double doors there? That's where they should be at this time of day." He paused. "They already know we're here."

A chill snaked down my spine. The gun felt way too heavy in my hand.

"Well, that isn't creepy or anything." Daemon glanced at me. "Stay close."

I nodded, and then we started around the station toward the double doors with two tiny windows. Archer was right behind us.

A man stepped out. "Ms. Husher—"

Daemon threw his arm out, hitting the guy in the chest with a broad swipe. The man went up in the air, white lab coat flapping like the wings of a dove before he smashed into the window of the center station. The glass splintered but did not break as the man slid down.

Someone screamed; the sound was jarring. Another man in a lab coat rushed toward the opening to the station. Archer spun around, catching him around the neck. A second later, a blur of white shot past my face and smacked into the opposite wall.

Chaos erupted.

Archer blocked the entrance to the station, which must've had stuff we didn't want them to get access to, sending one person flying after another until the remaining staff had huddled against the door—the door we needed to get into.

Daemon stepped before them, the pupils of his eyes turning white. "If I were you guys, I would move out of the way."

Most of them ran like rats. Two stayed. "We can't let you do this. You don't understand what they're capable of—"

I raised the gun. "Move."

They moved.

Which was a good thing because I had never shot a gun before. Not like I didn't know how to use one, but pulling the trigger seemed harder than moving a finger. "Thank you," I said, and then felt stupid for saying that.

Daemon hurried to the door, still in Nancy form. I saw a panel and realized we'd need Archer. I started to turn to him, but the sound of locks turning echoed like thunder. I whipped around, my breath stalling in my chest as the doors receded into the walls.

Daemon took a step back. So did I. Neither of us had been prepared for this.

Micah met us at the door of the classroom. All the chairs were filled with little boys of different ages. Same haircuts. Same black pants. Same white shirts. All had a look of disturbingly keen intelligence, and they were turned in their seats, staring at us. At the front of the classroom, a woman lay on the floor, facedown.

"Thank you." Micah smiled, stepping out. He stopped in front of Archer and lifted his arm. A thin black bracelet circled his wrist.

Silently, Archer moved his fingers over the bracelet, and there was a soft *click*. It slipped from Micah's arm and clattered to the floor. I had no idea what that was, but I figured it was important.

Micah turned to where the remaining staff huddled together. His head tilted to the side. "All we want to do is play. None of you let us play."

That's when the screams started.

The staff started dropping like hot potatoes, hitting the floor on their knees, clutching their heads. Micah kept smiling.

"Come on," Archer said, wheeling a chair toward the door. He shoved it in place, keeping the door open.

Glancing back at the classroom, I saw that the boys were on their feet, moving toward the door. Yeah, it was definitely time to go.

The men were still unconscious in the hallway, and we hit the elevator on the right. Once inside, Archer pressed the button for the ground level.

Daemon glanced down at my hand. "You sure you're okay with that?"

I forced a smile. "This is all I have until I get out of this stupid building."

He nodded. "Just don't shoot yourself…or me."

"Or me," added Archer.

I rolled my eyes. "What faith you guys have in me."

Daemon lowered his head toward mine. "Oh, I have faith in you. There's other—"

"Don't even think about saying something dirty or trying to kiss me while you're still in Nancy's body." I put a hand on his chest, holding him back.

Daemon chuckled. "You're no fun."

"You two need to focus on the task at hand—"

A siren went off somewhere in the building. The elevator jerked to a stop on the third floor. Lights dimmed, and then a red light flicked on in the ceiling.

"Now it's really going to get fun," Archer said as the elevator door opened.

In the hall, soldiers and staff rushed about, calling out orders. Archer took out the first soldier who looked our way and shouted. Daemon did the same. A soldier pulled a gun, and I lifted mine, squeezing off a round. The kickback startled me. The bullet hit the guy in the leg.

Daemon lost his hold on Nancy's form, slipping into his own. His eyes were wide as he stared at me.

"What?" I asked. "You didn't think I'd do it?"

"Stairwell," Archer shouted.

"Didn't realize you shooting a gun would be so sexy." Daemon took my free hand. "Let's go."

We raced down the hallway a few feet behind Archer. Overhead lights went out, replaced by flashing red and yellow domes. Archer and Daemon were throwing blasts of energy balls like it was going out of style, causing most of the soldiers to stay back. We passed a set of elevators. Two of them opened and a handful of origins stepped out. We kept going, but I had to look back—I had to see what they were going to do. I had to *know*.

They were the perfect diversion.

Everyone's attention was on them. One of the little boys had stopped in the middle of the hallway. He bent and picked up a fallen handgun, and I saw that his wrist was bare of the bracelet. The gun smoked and then melted, re-forming into the shape of a small ball.

The little boy giggled.

And then he spun, throwing the twisted wreck of a gun right at a soldier creeping up on him. The gun went straight through the man's stomach.

My step faltered. Holy crap.

Had we done the right thing letting them loose? What would happen if they got out—out into the real world? The kind of damage they could render was astronomical.

Daemon's grip on my hand tightened, pulling me back to the task at hand. I'd have time to worry about them later. Hopefully.

We rounded the corner at full speed, and I was suddenly forehead-level with a pistol, so close that I could see the finger on the trigger, see the tiny spark of it firing. A scream got stuck in my throat. Daemon roared, the sound final as it bounced around my skull.

The bullet stopped, its tip singeing my forehead. It didn't go any farther. Just stopped. Air leaked out of my lungs.

Daemon snatched the bullet away, then yanked me to his chest as we spun, and there was Micah several feet behind us, one hand raised.

"That wasn't very nice," he said in that monotone child voice. "I like them."

The soldier blanched, and then he was on the floor face-first—not screaming or clutching his head—and blood pooled out from under him.

Another origin appeared behind Micah, and then another and another and another. The soldiers blocking the stairwell hit the floors. *Thump. Thump. Thump*. A path was cleared.

"Come on," Archer urged.

Turning back to Micah, my gaze locked with the child's. "Thank you."

Micah nodded.

With one last look, I turned and darted around the bodies. The thin soles of my shoes slipped on the wet floors—floors slippery with blood. It was already seeping through the bottom of my shoes. I couldn't think about that now.

Archer pushed open the stairwell door, and as it swung shut behind us, Daemon spun on me, his hands suddenly gripping my upper arms. He roughly pulled me against him and up on the tips of my toes.

"I almost lost you. Again." His lips brushed over the hot spot on my forehead, and then he kissed me, a deep and forceful kiss that tasted of residual fear, desperation, and anger. The kiss was dizzying in its intensity, and when he pulled back I felt stripped bare.

"No time for swooning," he said with a wink.

Then we were tearing up the stairs, hand in hand. Archer caught a soldier on the landing. With a brutal throw, he tossed him over the railing. A series of sickening cracks caused my stomach to lurch violently.

Soldiers spilled out onto the second-floor landing. In their hands weren't normal pistols but what looked like stun guns.

Using the railing, Daemon let go of my hand and vaulted up a level. A soldier blew past me, landing two levels down on his side. Archer was right behind Daemon. He ripped a stun gun away and tossed it down to me. Switching the pistol to my left hand, I hurried up the rest of the stairs and squeezed on the first soldier I was near.

Like I suspected, it was some kind of Taser. Two wires shot out, smacking the soldier in the neck. The man started twitching like he was having a seizure and went down. The clip disengaged, allowing me to hit the one swinging on Archer.

Once the landing was clear, Daemon dragged two of the unconscious men to the door, stacking them atop each other.

"Come on," Archer urged as he rounded the landing, shedding the long-sleeve camo top. He reached to his neck, tucking dog tags under his white shirt.

With all the onyx and diamond in the building, I was pretty useless without my gun and Taser. The muscles in my legs were starting to burn, but I ignored them and pushed on.

When we reached ground level, Archer looked over his shoulder at us. He didn't speak out loud, and the message was directed at both of us. *We don't try to take any vehicles from the hangar. Once outside, we'll be faster than anything they have. We head south toward Vegas, on Great Basin Highway. If we get separated, we meet at Ash Springs. That's about eighty miles from here.*

Eighty miles?

There's a hotel called The Springs. It's used to having weird people show up. While I wondered what kind of weird people, and realized that was a stupid thing to even be thinking about, Archer reached into his back pocket and pulled out a wallet. He shoved cash in Daemon's hand. *This should be enough.*

Daemon nodded curtly, and then Archer looked at me. "Ready?"

"Yes," I croaked, my fingers tightening around the guns.

With fear so thick I could taste its bitter tang, I took a deep breath and nodded again, mostly for my own benefit.

The door opened, and for the first time in what had to be months, I breathed in fresh air from the outside. Dry but clean air, not manufactured. Hope bubbled up, giving me the strength to power forward. I could see a slice of sky beyond the vehicles, the color of dusk, pale blue and orange-red. It was the most beautiful thing I'd ever seen. Freedom was right *there*.

But between us and freedom was a small army of soldiers. Not as many as I'd expected, but I assumed that a lot were still underground, dealing with the origins.

Daemon and Archer wasted no time engaging. Bursts of white light lit up the hangar, ricocheting off tan Humvees, tearing through canvas. Sparks flew. Punches were thrown in close combat. I did my part—Tasing anyone I could get close to.

As I darted around the fallen bodies, I spied an artillery load in the back of a flatbed truck. "Daemon!"

He twisted around and saw what I was pointing at. I took off, narrowly avoiding being tackled. I turned, squeezing off another round. Metal prongs dug into the back of the soldier. Bright white light tinged in red crackled over Daemon's shoulders, wrapping around his right arm. Energy pulsed, arcing over the space between him and the truck.

Seeing what he was about to do, several soldiers ran, taking cover behind the large Humvees. I did the same, heading for a row of vehicles as Daemon hit the back of the truck, and it went up like the Fourth of July. The explosion rocked through the hangar, a powerful wave that shook my insides and knocked me flat on my butt. Thick gray smoke billowed through the enclosure. In an instant, I lost sight of Daemon and Archer. Over the popping explosions, I thought I heard Sergeant Dasher.

I was stunned into immobility for a second, blinking out the acrid stench of burning metal and gunpowder. A second was all it took.

Out of the heavy smoke, a soldier appeared. I sat up, whipping the stun gun around.

"Oh, no you don't," he said, catching my arm in both hands, above my elbow and below, and twisting.

Pain shot up my arm and burst along my shoulders. I held on, rolling my body so that I broke the brutal hold. The soldier was trained, and even with all the work Daedalus had put into training me, I was no match. He caught my arm again, the pain sharper and more intense. I dropped the stun gun, and the soldier landed a stinging blow across my cheek.

I don't know what happened next. The other gun was in my left hand. My ears were ringing. Smoke burned my eyes. My brain had clicked into survival mode. I fired the gun. Warm liquid sprayed me across the face.

With the gun being in my left hand, my aim was slightly off. I hit him in the left side of his chest. I wasn't even sure what part of him I was aiming at, but I hit him. There was a gurgling sound that I found so strange, because I could hear it over the yelling, over the screaming, and over the shells still going off. Nausea rolled up my stomach.

A hand landed on my shoulder.

Screaming, I whirled and came within two seconds of offing Daemon. My heart almost stopped. "Dammit. You scared the crap out of me."

"You were supposed to stay with me, Kitten. That wasn't staying with me."

Sending him a look, I edged around the back of a Humvee. The encroaching night sky beckoned us like a siren. Archer was a few Humvees down. He caught sight of us, looked at the opening, and nodded.

"Wait," Daemon said.

Dasher appeared out one of the doors, surrounded by guards. His usually neat hair was a mess. His uniform was wrinkled. He was scanning the strewn debris, issuing orders I couldn't make sense of.

Daemon looked up, his gaze tracking the floodlights. A half grin appeared, and he caught my stare, winking. "Follow me."

We backtracked, creeping along the side of the Humvee. Peering out around the scorched canvas, I saw the coast was clear. Hurrying down the row of vehicles, Daemon stopped in front of a metal pole that rose to the ceiling.

When he placed his hands on the beam, the Source flared from his fingertips. A wave of light rolled up the pole and spread out across the ceiling. Lightbulbs blew, one after another, stretching the length of the hangar, plunging the room into near darkness.

"Nice," I uttered.

Daemon chuckled and grabbed my hand. We started running again, meeting up with Archer. Panicked voices rose, creating a diversion for the three of us to head toward the lower opening, in the opposite direction from Dasher's crew. But the moment we stepped out from behind the row of Humvees, the dim glow from outside cast enough light.

Dasher spotted us immediately. "Stop!" he screeched. "This isn't going to work. You can't leave!" He pushed past the guards, literally shoving them out of the way. He was absolutely frazzled, probably knowing that Nancy's golden boy was within steps of freedom. "You won't get away!"

Daemon whipped around. "You have no idea how badly I've wanted to do this."

Dasher opened his mouth, and Daemon threw his arm out. The unseen push of the Source lifted Dasher off his feet and sent him flying into the air like a rag doll. He cracked into the wall of the hangar and fell forward. Daemon started toward him.

"No!" yelled Archer. "We don't have time for this."

He was right. As much as I wanted to see Dasher taken out, one more second and we'd be overrun. Tugging on Daemon, I pulled him toward the darkening opening of the hangar. "Daemon," I pleaded. "We need to go!"

"That man's been touched by God, I swear." Daemon turned, a muscle jumping in his jaw.

The sound of boots pounding on pavement echoed like thunder around us as Archer moved to the front. "Get down."

Daemon's arms went around my waist as we bent down, and he curled his body over mine in a near-crushing embrace. Through the thin slit between his arms, I saw Archer place his hands on the back of a Humvee. I didn't know how he did it, but the six-thousand-pound vehicle lifted into the air and was thrown like a Frisbee.

"Good God," I said.

The Humvee crashed into the others. Like a hulking domino, it created a rolling chain reaction, destroying nearly the entire fleet and sending soldiers fleeing.

Daemon sprang up, bringing me with him. He tore the silver cuff off his wrist and slid it onto mine. Almost immediately, a jolt of energy went through me. Layers of exhaustion lifted off, my lungs expanded, and my muscles flexed. It was like taking several shots of pure caffeine. The Source roared to life, a warm spring bubbling through my veins.

"Don't shoot!" screamed Nancy, barreling out from the side hangar. "Don't shoot to kill! We need them alive!"

Daemon's hand tightened on mine, and then we were running with Archer. Each step took us closer to the outside. My speed picked up, as did theirs.

And then we were outside, under the deep blue sky. I looked up for a second and saw stars poking through, glimmering like a thousand diamonds, and I wanted to cry, because we were out.

We were out.

Chapter 19

Daemon

We were out.

But we weren't free yet.

Not all the vehicles were out of order. They were after us, on land and in the sky. We were moving fast, though. Wearing the opal, Kat could almost pick up my kind of speed, but with the chopping of helicopter blades quickly approaching about ten miles out, Archer broke apart from us, heading to the west.

I'll create a diversion, he said. *Remember. Ash Springs.*

Then he was off, a blur that disappeared into the horizon. There wasn't an opportunity to ask what he was doing or to stop him. A few seconds later, there was a pulse of light, and then another spaced out a mile apart. I didn't look back to see if the spotlights from the helicopter had veered off our course, taking the bait. I didn't think about what would happen to him if he were caught. I couldn't afford to think or worry about anything other than getting Kat somewhere safe, even if it was just for the night.

We raced across the desert, our feet stirring up the scent of sage.

There was nothing for miles, and then we came across a herd of free-roaming cattle. Then nothing again as we kept close to the highway.

The farther and longer we went, concern piled on top of itself. Even with the opal, I knew Kat couldn't keep up for much longer, not for eighty miles. Hybrids tired quickly, even with the enhancer. Unlike us, where it actually took more energy to slow down, she was going to crash. Hell, eighty miles would wear me out, but Kat… For her I'd run a million miles. And I knew she'd do the same for me, but she couldn't. It wasn't in her DNA.

There was no time to stop and ask her how she was doing, but her heart rate was through the roof, and each ragged breath she took expelled immediately.

The trickle of fear that had been in my veins grew with each step and each rapid beat of my heart. This could kill her, or at the least do some serious damage.

I spared a brief glance at the night sky. Nothing but stars, and no lights in the distance. We still had another thirty or so miles to go, and it would be too much of a risk for me to take my true form and speed up the process. Light streaking across the desert at night would be way too obvious and give all those UFO enthusiasts something to talk about.

Slowing down unexpectedly, I had to slip an arm around Kat's waist to keep her from falling. She was breathing heavily as she looked up at me, the skin around her mouth pale and pinched.

"Why…why are we stopping?"

"You can't go on much longer, Kitten."

She shook her head, but her hair stayed plastered to her cheeks. "I can—I can do this."

"I know you want to, but this is too much. I'll take the opal and carry you."

"No. No way—"

"Kat. Please." My voice broke on the last word, and her eyes widened. "Please let me do this."

Her hands shook as she brushed the sweat-soaked hair away from her face. That stubborn little chin raised a notch, but she took off the opal cuff. "I hate…the idea of being carried."

She handed over the cuff, and I slipped it on, getting a little zap from it. I also took the gun from her, slipping it in the waistband of my pants. "How about you get on my back? So in a way you're not being carried—you're riding me." I paused and then winked.

Kat stared.

"What?" I laughed, and her eyes immediately narrowed. "You should see yourself right now. Like a kitten—that's what I keep telling you. Your hackles are raised."

Her eyes rolled as she shuffled behind me. "You should conserve your energy and stop talking."

"Ouch."

"You'll get over it." She placed her hands on my shoulders. "Besides, you could be knocked down a peg or two."

I crouched, hooking my arms under the backs of her knees. With a little hop, she slid her arms around my neck and wrapped her legs to my sides. "Baby, I'm so far up the ladder there aren't any pegs under me to be knocked down."

"Wow," she said. "That's a new one."

"You loved it." Tightening my grip on her, I let the Source tap into the opal and blend with it. "Hold on, Kitten. I'm going to start to glow just a little, and we're going to go fast."

"I like when you glow. It's like having my own personal flashlight."

I grinned. "Glad I can be of assistance."

She patted my chest. "Giddy up."

Feeling much better about this, I kicked off the ground and picked up the kind of speed I couldn't while running alongside Kat. Her weight was nothing, which was concerning all by itself. I needed to get the girl some steak and burgers stat.

When I saw we were approaching city lights, I veered closer to the highway, searching out a sign, and there it was. Ash Springs—ten miles out.

"Almost there, Kitten."

I had slowed down enough that she was able to wiggle free. "I can run the rest of the way."

Wanting to argue but knowing that if I did, it would only delay getting somewhere to hunker down, I kept my mouth shut. I also knew it was more than that. Kat wanted to prove, not just to me but to herself, that she was an asset not a hindrance. That need to show she could stand on equal ground with me and the other Luxen had been what drove her to trust Blake. I took off the opal and handed it back to her. "Let's do this, then."

She nodded. "Thank you."

I took her smaller hand in mine, and we ran the rest of the way to Ash Springs. The whole trip took us about twenty or so minutes, but those minutes felt like a lifetime. Depending on how Daedalus was searching for us, we had a good two-hour lead on them, more if they followed Archer.

Once we hit the outskirts of Ash Springs, we slowed to a walk, keeping off the sidewalks and away from the lampposts. The town was small—Petersburg small. Signs everywhere pointed to one of the many natural hot springs.

"I bet I smell like day-old funk." Kat stared longingly at a sign for one of the hot springs. "I'd love a bath right about now."

Both of us were covered in a fine layer of dust from the desert. "You do smell kind of ripe."

She shot me a dirty look. "Thanks."

Chuckling under my breath, I squeezed her hand. "You smell like a ripe blossom about to bloom."

"Oh, whatever. Now you're just being dumb."

I led her around a hedge shaped like…hell, I had no idea what it was supposed to be. An elephant crossed with a giraffe? "What things would you do for a bath?" I turned, lifting her over a fallen branch. "Nasty, bad things?"

"I have a feeling you're going to turn this into a perverted conversation."

"What? I would never do such a thing. You have such a twisted brain, Kitten. I'm aghast at your suggestion."

She shook her head. "I'm sorry that I've tainted your innocence and virtue."

I cracked a grin as we stopped at an intersection. Up ahead were several glowing signs for hotels. The streets were empty, and I wondered what time it was. Not a single motorist had gone by.

"I think I'd shank someone for a shower," Kat said as we crossed the street. "Including you."

I let out a surprised laugh. "You couldn't take me."

"Do not doubt my need to get this funk off me— Hey." She stopped, pointing down a side road. "Is that it?"

There was a sign in the distance. The *S* was a dim red, which made it look like THE PRINGS MOTEL. "I think so. Let's check it out."

Hurrying down the narrow side road and past dark storefronts, we hit the parking lot. It was definitely off the beaten track and…

"Oh boy," Kat said, slipping her hand free. "I think this is one of those motels that charge by the hour, and people come to overdose in them."

She had a point. It was ranch-style, one level, and shaped like a *U* with the lobby in the middle and a wooden deck wrapping around the entrances to the motel rooms. Lighting was dim in and around the building, and the parking lot had a few cars in it—the kind of cars that were a day away from hitting the junkyard.

"Well, now we know what kind of places Archer likes to visit," I said, eyes narrowing on the yellow light seeping out onto the wooden planks in front of the lobby.

"He hasn't been to many places." She shifted from one foot to the other. "He hasn't even eaten at Olive Garden, so I doubt he's a connoisseur of hotels."

"No Olive Garden?"

She shook her head.

"Man, we've got to get that boy some endless breadsticks and salad. Travesty," I murmured. "You talked a lot to him?"

"He was the only one who really was…nice to me. Well, in his own way. He's not really a warm and fuzzy guy." She paused, tilting her head back as she gazed at the star-strewn sky. "We didn't talk a lot, but he was always there with me. I never thought he'd be the one to help us in the beginning. I guess first impressions really don't mean jack."

"I guess not." A sudden wariness had etched across her face as she lowered her chin. I could see the weight of everything settling on her. Almost the same look I'd seen on Beth's face the morning I left, before she'd freaked out.

I didn't know what to say as we headed across the parking lot. There really were no words that fit how far Kat's life had been derailed. Nothing I could say would make it better, and trying to seemed to undervalue everything she'd gone through. Like telling someone who'd lost a loved one that the deceased was in a better place. No one wanted to hear that. It didn't change anything, make the grief go away, or shine any light on why it happened.

Sometimes words were cheap. They could be powerful, but in those rare occasions like now, words meant nothing.

We stopped under a faint lamp along the side of the hotel that faced several benches and picnic tables. Soot covered Kat's face. Dried blood dotted her cheeks. My stomach lurched. "You were bleeding?"

She shook her head, casting her eyes back to the sky. "It's not mine. It was a soldier's. I…shot him."

What little relief I felt was overshadowed by what she'd had to do and would still have to do if push came to shove. I handed her the gun.

"Okay. All right." I cupped her cheeks. "Stay here. I'm going to take a different form and get the keys. If anything looks fishy, you shoot first and ask questions later. Okay? Don't use the Source unless you have to. They can track that stuff."

She nodded. I noticed that her hands were fidgety. Adrenaline was still pumping through her, keeping her on her feet. She'd need a sugar overdose real soon. "I'm not going anywhere," she said.

"Good." I kissed her, wanting to linger so as not to leave her out there alone. But there was no way I could take her into the lobby like this. Sketchy people checking in or not, she was bound to draw attention. "I'll be right back."

"I know."

I still didn't move. My eyes searched her weary ones, and my heart rate kicked up. Kissing her once more, I forced myself to let go and then turned, heading back around to the front. I called up the image of one the guards and took his form. Memory supplied jeans and a T-shirt. All of it was a facade, like a mirror throwing off a reflection. Except the image I reflected was fake, and if you looked too long and too hard, you started to see cracks in the disguise.

A bell gave a jovial little *ding* as I entered the lobby. The air smelled of clove-scented cigars. There was a gift shop to the right, several old chairs positioned in front of vending machines, and to the left was the check-in desk.

An older man waited behind the counter. His eyes were bug-like behind thick glasses. He was rocking plaid suspenders. Awesome attire.

"Howdy," said the man. "Need a room?"

I approached the counter. "Yes. Got any available?"

"Sure do. Looking for a few hours or the night?"

I almost laughed because of what Kat had said outside. "For the night, maybe two."

"Well, we'll start out with just one night and go from there." He turned to the register. "That will be seventy-nine. We only take cash here. Nothing for you to sign and no ID required."

No big surprise there. I dug into my pocket and opened up the wad of cash. Holy shit, what was Archer doing carrying several hundred dollars with him all the time? Then again, it wasn't like he'd be easy to mug.

I handed over a hundred. "Mind if I take a look at the shop?"

"Go ahead. I ain't got much to do." He nodded at the TV on the counter. "Reception is always spotty around here in the middle of the night. The same with the TV in your room—room fourteen, by the way."

Nodding, I took my change and the key to the room and headed over to the gift area. There was a stack of unisex shirts with the words ROUTE 375: EXTRATERRESTRIAL HIGHWAY emblazoned in a bold green across the front. I grabbed a large one for myself and a small for Kat. There was a pair of jogging pants that would be a little big on her but would do. I picked a pair for myself and then turned, scanning for food.

My eyes landed on a stuffed green doll with an oval head and large black eyes. I picked it up, frowning. Why in the world did humans think aliens looked like a whacked-out Gumby?

The motel manager chuckled. "If you're into the alien stuff, then you're in the right place."

I grinned.

"You know you're about eighty or so miles from Area 51. We get a lot of visitors here on their way to do some UFO watching." His glasses had slid down his nose. "Of course, they don't get into Area 51, but people like to get as close as possible."

I put the doll back and turned toward the food aisle. "You believe in aliens?"

"I've lived here my whole life, son, and I've seen some crazy unexplainable things in the sky. Either it's aliens or the government, and I'm not a big fan of the idea of it being either."

"Me neither," I replied, grabbing up as much sugar as I could find. I added a THEY R AMONG US tote bag, one of those crappy pay-as-you-go phones, and a few other things that caught my attention. Before I headed back to the counter, I wheeled around and grabbed the stupid alien doll.

As I checked out, I kept an eye on the parking lot. Nothing had moved, but I was itching to get back to Kat.

"There's an icebox outside if you need it." He handed over the bag. "And if you need another night, just come on by."

"Thank you." I turned, spying a clock above the counter. It was a little after eleven. Sure felt a hell of a lot later than that. And it was damn strange that the town was so dead this early in the night.

Back outside, I pulled the key out of my pocket and waited until I was around the corner before I slipped back into the Daemon she was familiar with.

Kat was waiting where I'd left her, leaning against the wall, which put her back in the shadows. Smart girl. She turned, smoothing her hands through her hair. "How'd it go?"

"Great." I reached inside the bag. "Got you something."

She tilted her head to the side as I stopped in front of her. "A portable bath?"

"Better." I pulled out the alien doll. "Made me think of you."

A short, hoarse laugh bubbled out of her as she took the doll, and my chest did a funny spasm. I couldn't remember the last time I heard her laugh or anything that remotely sounded like one. "It looks just like you," she said. "I'm going to name it DB."

"Perfect choice." I dropped my arm over her shoulders. "Come on, we're on the right side for our room. Your shower awaits."

She held DB close to her chest, sighing. "I cannot wait."

The room wasn't as bad as I thought it would be. Recently cleaned, and the smells of Lysol and fresh linen were decidedly welcomed scents. Bed was a double, sheets turned down. A bureau across from the bed featured a TV that looked like it would have reception problems any time of the day. A small desk butted up to it.

I sat the goodies on the table and checked out the bathroom. There were towels, soaps, and the essentials, which was good because my dumb ass forgot about that. I returned to the room, finding Kat standing there, still clutching DB. It was ridiculous and weird and a thousand other things how cute I thought she looked, covered in dirt, sweat, and blood.

"You okay with me taking the first shower?" she asked. "Because I was joking. I wouldn't shank you."

I laughed outright. "Yeah, get in the shower before I throw your dirty behind in there."

She wrinkled her nose at me and then placed DB on the bed so the alien doll looked like it was about to watch some bad TV. She then sat the gun on the nightstand. "I'll be quick."

"Take your time."

She hesitated a moment, looking like she wanted to say something, and then changed her mind. With one last long look at me, she turned and disappeared into the bathroom. The hiss of the shower was so immediate it brought a smile to my face.

Heading to the bag, I dug out the disposable phone and opened the package. It was already preloaded with a hundred minutes. I wanted to call my sister and brother, but doing so this soon was too much of a risk. I set it aside and moved to the window. It faced the road and parking lot, which was perfect.

Peering out from behind the thick burgundy curtains, I wondered how long it would take for Archer to find us or if he even would. Might make me a cold-hearted bastard, but the outcome of Archer didn't matter to me. It wasn't that I didn't appreciate what he'd done for us and what he'd risked, but there wasn't enough room in me to worry about others. We were out. And we were never going back. I'd take out an army, burn down an entire city, and throw the world into chaos if I had to in order to keep Kat out of that place.

Chapter 20

Katy

The near-scalding, steady stream of water had washed away the grime and whatever else was stuck to my skin. I turned a few times and finally stopped, pressing shaky hands to my face. I'd already used the tiny bottle of shampoo—twice—and I needed to get out of there, but being in the stall with rust stains near the drain and uneven pressure was so different from the bathrooms in the compound that I didn't want to leave. It was like being in a bubble, safe from reality.

Water coursed over my body, cascading off the jagged scars along my back, pooling around my feet. Lowering my hands, I looked down. The water wasn't draining fast, causing it to gather in the bottom of the tub. The water had a pink tint to it.

I swallowed hard and turned off the faucets. Stepping out of the tub and into the steam-filled bathroom, I grabbed a towel and wrapped it around me, securing it at the top. I did my best to get the excess water out of my hair, going about it methodically. Wrap. Squeeze. Wrap. Squeeze. When that was done, I realized I had no other reason to hide in the bathroom.

And that was what I was doing. Hiding. I didn't know why, except it felt like my insides were bruised and frayed, too exposed. We were out—we were free for now. That alone was reason to celebrate, but we were far from in the clear. There was the unknown fate of Archer, where we would go from here, and an entire life I'd left behind in Petersburg—my mom, my school, my books…

I needed to leave the bathroom before Daemon thought I passed out or something.

Clutching the top of the towel, I went into the room. Daemon was at the window, his back straight like a sentry. He turned at the waist, his gaze moving from the top of my head to my feet. The light was on beside the bed, and it was dim, but when he looked at me like that, it felt like a spotlight had been turned on me. My toes curled into the carpet.

"Feel better?" he asked, not moving from the window.

I nodded. "Much better. There may be some hot water left."

One side of his lips curved up. "Know what date it is?" I shook my head, and he gestured at the desk. "There's one of the day calendars on it, the kind where you tear off the pages each day. If it's up to date, it's August eighteenth."

"My God," I whispered, deeply unsettled. "I've been gone… we've been gone for practically four months."

He said nothing.

"I knew it had been awhile, but time was so strange there. I just didn't think it was that long. Four months…"

"Feels like forever ago, huh?"

"Yes, it does." I inched closer to the bed. "Four months. Mom probably thinks I'm dead."

He turned back to the window, his shoulders tensed. Several moments passed before he spoke. "I got you some clean clothes. They're in the bag. I think you'll appreciate the shirt."

"Thank you."

"It's no biggie, Kitten."

I bit down on my lip. "Daemon…?" He turned to me, his eyes unnaturally bright. Two beautiful green eyes. "Thank you for everything. I wouldn't be out of there if it—"

He was suddenly in front of me, clasping my cheeks. I sucked in a startled breath as he lowered his forehead to mine. "You do not need to thank me for any of this. You would've never been in this situation if it weren't for me. And you don't need to thank me for something I wanted and needed to do."

"This wasn't your fault," I told him, meaning it. "You know that, right?"

He pressed a kiss to my forehead. "I'm going to clean up. There's food in the bag, too, if you're hungry. If not, you should try to get some rest."

"Daemon—"

"I know, Kitten. I know." He dropped his hands and gave me that cocky smile of his. "If anyone shows up while I'm in the shower, even Archer, you don't let him in, okay?"

"I doubt a door would stop him."

"That's what the gun is for. I don't think he's going to screw us, but I'd rather be safe than sorry."

He had a good point, but as I watched him grab a pair of sweats and then disappear into the fogged-over bathroom, I loathed the idea of picking up that gun again. I would if I had to. I just hoped I'd never have to again, which was silly because, more than likely, the violence of my recent everyday life was nowhere near over.

Picking up the bag, I brought it over to the bed. I sat down and started rummaging through it as the water kicked on in the bathroom. I looked up, my gaze falling to the closed door. A warm flush crept over my cheeks. Daemon was in the shower. Completely naked. I was in a towel. We were alone, for the first time in four months, in a shady motel room.

My stomach dipped.

The flush heated up, and I groaned in exasperation.

What was I doing even thinking about that kind of stuff right now? Over the course of the last couple of months, I'd heard Daemon in the shower a million times over. This wasn't a romantic getaway at the Ritz, unless running for your lives counted as foreplay.

Shaking my head, I refocused on the bag. Inside I found a wide selection of sugary goodness, which caused me to blink back tears because I knew he'd bought that for me. God, he was considerate when I didn't even know he was trying, when it mattered.

I pulled out the bottles of soda and got up, placing them with the chips and sugar on the desk. The tote bag brought a smile to my face. The shirt made the smile stretch in a way that felt unfamiliar, like it would crack my skin.

I glanced at the alien doll. "DB…"

Going back to the bed, I found flip-flops in the bag. Perfect. I never wanted to see those bloody shoes again. I reached the bottom of the bag, and my fingers brushed over a square box. I pulled out the last item.

Heat swept my face, and my eyes popped out. "Oh…oh, wow."

The water shut off, and a second later Daemon came out with the sweats hanging low on his hips, and his skin was dewy, glistening. My eyes were fixated on his stomach and the drops of water running over the dips, disappearing under the band of the sweats. I was still only in a towel.

And I was holding a box of condoms in my hand.

My face was red as a ladybug.

One dark eyebrow went up.

My gaze fell to the box and then went back to him. "Confident, aren't you?"

"I'd like to call it being prepared for any occasion." He sauntered over to the bed in a way only Daemon could without looking like a complete douche. "Although, I am disappointed they don't have little alien faces on them like everything else."

I choked on my next breath. "What kind of motel sells condoms?"

"My favorite kind of motel?" He took the box from my boneless fingers. "You've spent this entire time looking at this instead of eating something, haven't you?"

A laugh burst from me—a real, normal laugh.

Daemon's eyes widened, and the hue flared. The box fell from his fingers, landing with a soft *thud* against the carpet. "Do that again," he said, his voice gruff.

The sound sent a shiver down my spine. "Do what?"

"Laugh." He bent over me, the tips of his fingers grazing my cheeks. "I want to hear you laugh again."

I wanted to laugh again for him, but all the humor had dried up under the raw intensity of his stare. Emotion swelled inside me like a balloon tethered by a fine string. I opened my mouth, but I didn't know what to say. Muscles tensed throughout my body. My belly felt like a nest of butterflies was about to take flight. I raised a hand, placing it on his cheek. The slight stubble tickled my palm and caused my heart to jump. I slid my hand over the curve of his jaw and then down the cords of his neck to his shoulder. He jerked under my touch, and his chest rose sharply.

"Kat." He breathed my name; he took it into himself, said it like it was some kind of prayer.

I couldn't look away, and for a moment I was frozen, then I stretched up, placing my mouth against his. The slight touch sent a shock through my system. I moved my lips, familiarizing myself with the feel of him. Strange, but it was like we were kissing for the first time. My pulse was pounding, and my thoughts were in a heady, dizzy swirl.

He slipped a hand through my hair, his fingers curling along the back of my skull. The kiss deepened until his taste was everywhere, and there was nothing but us—only us. The rest of the world fell away. None of our problems vanished, but they were put on hold as my mouth opened for him. We kissed like we were famished for each other, and we were. Those kisses intoxicated me, and his fingers moved over my jaw and down my throat, delicately tracing a path. But my hands were greedy and rushed as they slipped over his chest, and I followed the lines of his hard stomach. The way my touch affected him was marveling to me. He made a throaty sound, and I melted.

He eased me back, positioning his body over mine and supporting his weight on one arm, but only our mouths touched in the sweetest torture. We'd been intimate before, twice, but right now it felt like the first time. Excited nervousness hummed through me while my blood heated up.

Daemon lifted his head. Between the narrowed slits of his eyes, his pupils were like polished diamonds following the movement of his hand. My insides tightened as his fingers moved dangerously close to the edge of the towel. Each slow pass along the fabric had my pulse pounding. My gaze traced over his broad cheekbones and then got hung up on the perfection of his lips.

His hand stilled around the knot I had made in the towel, his eyes flicking up to mine. "We don't have to," he said.

"I know."

"I really didn't buy the condoms thinking that we'd do this tonight."

I slipped into a grin. "So…you weren't overly confident?"

"I'm always overly confident." He swooped down, kissing me softly. "But I don't know if this is too much right now. I don't want—"

I silenced him by slipping my hands to the band of his pants, hooking my fingers under it. "You're perfect. I want this—with you. It's not too much."

A breath shuddered through him. "God, I was hoping you'd say that. Does that make me a terrible person?"

A little laugh came out. "No. It just makes you a dude."

"Oh? Is that it?" He captured my mouth again, then pulled back with a slight nip. "Just makes me a dude?"

"Yes." I gasped. My back arched as he moved his hand down my front and then back up to the knot. "Okay. You're more than just a dude."

He chuckled deep in his throat. "Thought so."

His breath was warm against my swollen lips, scorching hot as it trailed down my neck. He pressed a kiss to where my pulse pounded in my throat. I closed my eyes, happily swept away in the rush of sensations. I needed this—we needed this. A moment of normalcy, of just him and me, together like we were supposed to be.

He kissed me as his fingers worked the knot loose, distracting me as he parted the towel. Goose bumps followed the cool air rushing over my body. He murmured something in that lyrical language of his, a language I wished I could understand because his words sounded beautiful.

As he lifted up, his gaze chased away the tiny bumps, searing me from the inside out. The edges of his body blurred into a faint whitish light. "You're beautiful."

I thought about my back.

"Every part," he said, as if he read my mind.

Maybe he had, because when I tugged him closer by the band of his pants, he obliged, fitting his body to mine. Bare chest to bare chest. I tangled my hands in his hair as I wrapped a leg around his hips.

He took a sharp breath. "You drive me insane."

"Feeling's mutual," I rasped out, tilting my hips up against his.

The muscles in his arms bulged as he made a sound deep in his throat. The set to his jaw was hard, the lines of his mouth tense as he slipped a hand between us. Those clever fingers went from soothing to breath-stealing in a second, and I felt the coiling deep—

A bright yellow light suddenly flooded the room, shattering the moment.

Daemon was off me so quickly, he stirred the hair around my temples as he shot toward the window and peeled back a small section of the curtain. I scrambled up, smacking the mattress until I found the towel, covering myself as I darted off the bed, grabbing the pistol.

Terror climbed up my throat. Had they found us already? I twisted to where he stood, as I still clutched the towel around me. My hand shook so badly the pistol rattled.

Daemon let out a long breath. "It's just headlights—some ass with his high beams on pulling out of the parking lot." Letting the curtain fall back into place, he turned. "That's all."

My hand tightened around the gun. "Headlights?"

His gaze dropped to what I held. "Yeah, that's all, Annie Oakley."

The gun felt glued to my hand. My heart was still pumping fast with residual terror, and that horror was slow to drain from my veins. It hit me then, in startling clarity, that this was what our lives had been reduced to. Flying into defense and panic mode every time headlights came through a window or someone knocked on our door or a stranger approached us.

This was it.

My first reaction to headlights would be to grab a gun, to get ready to shoot—to shoot to kill if necessary.

"Kat…?"

I shook my head. A fire crawled through my stomach, up my throat. Tears burned my eyes. So many thoughts raced through my mind. Pressure clamped down on my chest, tightening around my lungs with icy fingers. A shudder rolled down my spine. Four months of tears I didn't let fall built inside me.

Daemon was in front of me in an instant, gently and carefully peeling my fingers away from the gun. He placed it on the bedside table. "Hey," he said, cupping my cheeks with both his hands. "Hey, it's okay. Everything is okay. No one is here but us. We're okay."

I *knew* that, but it was more than headlights in the night. It was *everything*—an accumulation of four months of no control over any aspect of my life or my body. *Everything* piled up on me—the tangy fear that never eased, the dread I had woken up with every day, the exams, and the stress tests. The pain of the scalpel and the horror of watching the mutated humans die. It all cut through me. The harrowing escape where I shot people—real, live people who had families and lives of their own—and I knew I'd killed at least one of them. His blood had been splattered all across my face.

And then there was Blake…

"Talk to me," Daemon pleaded. His emerald eyes were full of concern. "Come on, Kitten, tell me what's going on."

Turning my head, I closed my eyes. I wanted to be strong. I'd told myself over and over again that I had to be strong, but I couldn't get past *everything*.

"Hey," he said softly. "Look at me."

I kept my eyes squeezed shut, knowing that if I looked at him, the balloon that had been so full and tethered so delicately would burst. I was wrecked inside, and I didn't want him to see that.

But then he turned my face to his and dropped a kiss on the lids of my closed eyes and said, "It's okay. Whatever you're feeling right now is okay. I got you, Kat. I'm here for you, only you. It's *okay*."

That balloon burst, and I lost it.

• • •

Daemon

My heart cracked as the first tear rolled down her cheek and broke with a hoarse sob, making its way out of her lips.

I pulled her against me, wrapping my arms around her as she shook with the force of her grief, her pain. I didn't know what to do. She wasn't talking. There was no room around the tears for that.

"It's okay," I kept telling her. "Let it out. Just let it out." And I felt stupid for saying that. The words were so lacking.

Her tears streamed down my chest; each one cut like a knife. Helpless, I picked her up and brought her to the bed. I gathered her close, yanking up the blanket that seemed too coarse for her skin and wrapping it around her.

She burrowed into me, her fingers clutching the strands of hair at the nape of my neck. The tears…they kept coming, and my heart was shattering at the raw sound of each of her breaths. Never in my life had I felt more useless. I wanted to fix this, to make her better, but I didn't know how.

She had been so strong through all of this, and if I had thought for one instant that she hadn't been deeply affected, then I was an idiot. I *had* known. I'd just hoped—no, I'd *prayed*—that the scars and wounds would just be physical. Because I could fix them—I could heal them. I couldn't fix what bled and festered underneath, but I would try. I would do anything to take this pain away from her.

I don't know how much time passed before she settled down, until the tears seemed to dry up and her ragged breathing evened out, and she'd exhausted herself into sleep. Minutes? Hours? I didn't know.

I got her under the covers, and I stretched out beside her, tucking her warm body close. She didn't stir once through the whole thing. With her cheek against my chest, I kept running my hands through her hair, hoping that the motion could reach her in her sleep and would soothe some of her troubles. I knew she liked it when I played with her hair. It seemed like such an insignificant thing, but it was all I had at that moment.

At some point, I drifted off to sleep. I hadn't wanted to, but the last six or so hours had taken their toll. I had to have slept for a couple of hours, because when I opened my eyes, daylight streamed in through the gap in the curtains, but it only felt like minutes.

And Kat wasn't beside me.

I blinked quickly, rising up on my elbows. She was sitting on the edge of the bed, dressed in the shirt and pants I'd found last night. Her hair fell down the middle of her back; the waves shifted as she turned toward me, bringing a leg up on the bed.

"I didn't wake you, did I?"

"No." I cleared my throat, glancing around the room, slightly disoriented. "How long have you been awake?"

She shrugged. "Not too long. It's a little past ten in the morning."

"Wow. That late?" I rubbed my brow with the heel of my hand as I sat up.

She looked away, studying the strap on her flip-flops. Her cheeks were red. "Sorry about last night. I didn't mean to cry all over you."

"Hey." I scooted over, sliding an arm around her waist, and tugged her closer. "I needed the second shower. It was better than the first."

She laughed hoarsely. "That was a huge mood killer, right?"

"Nothing kills my mood when it comes to you, Kitten." I brushed her hair back, tucking it behind her ear. "How are you feeling now?"

"Better," she said, lifting her gaze. Her eyes were red and swollen. "I think…I think I needed to do that."

"Want to talk about it?"

She wetted her lips nervously as she fidgeted with the ends of her hair. I was happy to see the opal bracelet still on her slim wrist. "I… A lot happened."

I held my breath, not daring to move, because I knew it took a lot for her to get the words out sometimes. She internalized a ton of crap, kept it in. Finally, she gave a wobbly little smile.

"I was so scared," she whispered, and my chest spasmed. "When I saw the headlights? I thought it was them, and I just freaked out, you know? I've been in that place for four months. I know that's nothing compared to Dawson and Beth, but…I don't know how they did it."

I exhaled slowly. I didn't know how they did it, either, how Dawson and Beth weren't more messed up than they already were. I kept my mouth shut as I ran my hand up her back and then down, up again.

Her gaze focused on the bathroom door, and she was quiet for what felt like forever. Then, very slowly, the words tumbled out of her. The onyx sprays. The *thorough* exams. The stress tests with the hybrids and how she'd refused to participate, and what that had meant for her until they had paired her up with Blake. How he'd goaded her into fighting him and tapping into the Source. The guilt that she carried for his death was evident in her voice. She told me everything, and through it all, I had to check myself about a million times. Rage like I'd never known coated my insides.

"I'm sorry," she said, shaking her head. "I'm rambling. It's just that…I needed to get it out."

"Don't apologize, Kat." I wanted to punch a hole in the wall. Instead I slid over so I was sitting beside her, thigh to thigh. "You know what happened with Blake isn't your fault, right?"

She twisted a section of hair around two fingers. "I killed him, Daemon."

"But you were defending yourself."

"No." She let go of the hair and looked at me. Her eyes were glassy. "I wasn't defending myself, not really. He goaded me, and I lost control."

"Kat, you have to look at the entire situation. You were getting beat up…" Saying that out loud made me want to go back to the compound and burn it down. "You were going through *a lot* of stress. And Blake…whatever his reasons were for doing what he did, he repeatedly put you and so many other people in danger."

"You think he had it coming?"

A real sadistic part of me wanted to say yes, because yeah, some days I thought that. "I don't know, but what I do know is that he went into the room to goad you into fighting him. You did. I know you didn't want to kill him or anyone else, but it happened. You're not a bad person. You're not a monster."

Her brows pinched, and she opened her mouth.

"And no, you're not like Blake. So don't even go there. You could never be like him. You're good inside, Kitten. You bring out the best in people—even me." I nudged her with my arm, and she cracked a grin. "That alone should earn you the Nobel Peace Prize."

She laughed softly, and then she rose onto her knees. Wrapping her arms around my shoulders, she leaned down and placed the softest kiss, the kind I'd treasure forever, against my lips.

"What was that for?" I circled my arms around her waist.

"A thank-you," she said, resting her forehead against mine. "Most guys would've probably left in the middle of the night and run far away from the hysterics."

"I'm not most guys." I tugged her over so she was sitting in my lap. "Haven't you figured that out yet?"

She dropped her hands to my shoulders. "I'm a little slow sometimes."

I laughed, and she responded with a smile. "Good thing I don't like you for your brains."

Her mouth dropped open, and she smacked me on the arm. "That's so ignorant."

"What?" I wiggled my brows suggestively. "I'm just being honest."

"Shut up." She brushed her lips against mine.

I nipped at her lower lip, and a rosy flush appeared on her cheeks. "Hmm, you know how I like it when you get all mouthy with me."

"You're mental."

My hands flattened against the small of her back, and I pulled her close. "I have something really corny to say. Get ready for it."

She traced the line of my jaw. "I'm ready."

"I'm mental for you."

She busted into laughter. "Oh my God, that *is* corny."

"Told you." I caught her chin and brought her lips to mine. "I love the sound of your laugh. Is that too corny?"

"No." She kissed me. "Not at all."

"Good." I slid my hands up her waist, the tips of my fingers stopping below her chest. "Because I've got— " A sensation crawled through my veins, spreading all over my body.

Kat stilled, sucking in a sharp breath. "What is it?"

I gripped her hips and deposited her on the bed beside me. Swiping the gun off the table, I handed it to her, and she took it with wide eyes. "There's a Luxen here."

Chapter 21

Katy

I stood quickly, palming the gun. "Are you sure?" I winced. "Okay. That was a stupid question."

"I don't—"

A knock rattled the motel door, jarring me to the point that I almost dropped the pistol. Daemon shot me a concerned look, and I flushed. I really needed to pull it together. Taking a deep breath, I nodded.

He prowled to the door silently, with the grace of a lethal predator, and there I was, stumbling around like a colt. Inching closer, I told myself I was ready to use this gun. Using the Source, which was just as dangerous, would be too risky. Shooting a gun would draw attention, but hopefully only the local kind.

Daemon leaned in, peering out the peephole. "What the hell?"

"What?" My heart skipped a beat.

He looked over his shoulder at me. "It's Paris—the Luxen who was with Luc."

It took me a moment to remember who he was—the really pretty blond Luxen who had been with Luc at his club. "He's a friendly?"

"We'll see." Daemon squared his shoulders and cracked the door open. I couldn't see anything beyond his bare back, which, if I had to be stuck staring at something, at least it was that. "Surprised to see you all the way out here," he said.

"Should you be?" came the response.

"You tell me. Why are you here? And why shouldn't I blast you into next week?"

My palm was sweaty around the gun. Daemon really wouldn't blast Paris. Wait. Yes he would, risky or not.

"Because that would draw way too much attention," Paris replied in his smooth voice. "And besides, I'm not alone."

Daemon must have seen someone else, because his shoulders relaxed a fraction of an inch, and he stepped aside. "Well, come in."

Paris stepped through the door, his strides long and sure. He took one look at me holding the gun. "Nice shirt."

I glanced down, forgetting I was wearing the extraterrestrial highway shirt. "Thanks."

Then Archer popped in, looking fresh and clean. Not at all like someone who'd spent the night running around the desert. Suspicion bloomed like a noxious weed. He looked at Daemon. "Were we interrupting?"

Daemon's eyes narrowed as he closed the door. "What's going on?"

Archer reached into his jeans and pulled out a glass case. He handed it over to Daemon. "Here is the LH-11. I thought I'd let you do the honors." He looked at me. "Are you going to shoot me, Katy?"

"Maybe," I mumbled, but I lowered the gun and sat on the edge of the bed. "Where have you been?"

Archer frowned as Paris milled about, casting a distasteful sneer at the room. "Well, I did have a busy night keeping half the military off your tracks. Then when I was heading back to meet you, I ran into our friend here."

"I wouldn't consider him a friend," Daemon said as he came to stand beside where I sat.

Paris placed a hand against his chest. "You wound me."

Daemon rolled his eyes, and then in a lower voice, he said. "You can put the gun down, Kitten."

"Oh." I flushed. Stretching over, I placed it on the table. Then I addressed Archer. "We owe you a thank-you for…for everything." I waited for Daemon to chime in. When he didn't, I kicked his leg.

"Thank you," Daemon muttered.

Archer's mouth curved in amusement, and I think it was the first time I saw him really smile. I was blown away by how young it made him look. "You have no idea how gleeful that makes me feel to hear you say that, Daemon."

"I can imagine."

"Seriously," I cut in. "We do thank you. We would've never made it here if it wasn't for you."

He nodded. "It wasn't just for you two."

"Explain?" Daemon said.

Paris huffed as he hopped up on the desk. Thank God the thing didn't give out on him and wrinkle his pressed pants. "Do you guys really think that Archer enjoyed being Daedalus's perfect little example of how an origin should be?"

"I guess not." Daemon sat beside me. "And I guess Luc didn't, either."

Paris raised a slender shoulder. "And I guess you didn't enjoy being their perfect, little mutant-maker?"

"Oh, yeah, and Nancy was totally loving you." Archer folded his arms. "You were her all-star Luxen. How many humans did you mutate in the short period of time there? More than any other Luxen has."

Daemon stiffened. "That really has nothing to do with this. Why are you helping us, and why are you with Paris?"

"And where is Luc?" I piped in, figuring he couldn't be too far.

Paris smiled. "He's around."

"We don't have a lot of time for questions, but I can give you the short and dirty version," Archer said. "I owed Luc a favor, and Paris is right. *You* were right, Katy. Being in Daedalus means not having a life. They controlled every aspect. It doesn't matter how I came into creation." He spread his arms out, palms up. "What matters, always matters, is *living*."

"Why now?" Daemon asked, a hard edge of distrust to his tone.

"And that's the question of the year, huh?" Paris chimed in, grinning like he ingested some happy pills or something. "Why would Archer pick right now to risk everything—his life, what little life he had?"

Archer sent the other Luxen a dark look. "Thanks, Paris, for adding that. Escaping Daedalus is not easy. Besides Luc and a handful of others, no one has ever succeeded. Yeah, I could've run a hundred times over, but they would've found me. I also needed a diversion."

It hit me then. "You used us as a diversion."

He nodded. "Nancy and Sergeant Dasher are going to be more concerned about finding Daemon and you. I'm not going to be at the top of their priority list."

Some of the tension eked out of Daemon's frame. "Nancy had said that there were other origins out in the world pretending to be normal humans."

"There are some," Archer confirmed. "I doubt they'll be a problem right now. They have high-profile lives, so they won't come within ten miles of any of us."

There was still something I didn't understand. "Why didn't Luc just have you get him the LH-11? He could've hidden you."

Paris laughed softly. "Do you think there's a method to Luc's madness?"

"I hoped there would be," Daemon muttered, running a hand through his hair.

"Actually, there is a method. Besides the fact that I could play spy to keep Luc…and a few others up to date on what Daedalus was doing, I knew that they changed the LH-11 strain, and that's what Luc wanted, the new version—Prometheus. I was never around the new drug. No one was. Not until they brought you in," Archer said to Daemon. "It was sort of the perfect storm for everyone. But I don't know why Luc wants the drug."

"And I wouldn't ask him," Paris said ominously.

I shivered at his tone, but then I thought of what Archer had told me. "What about the Luxen—the ones Sergeant Dasher claimed wanted to take over? Was that true?"

Archer slid a look at Daemon. "It's true, and your boy toy over here seems to know one of them."

Daemon's eyes narrowed. "Stay out of my head."

I turned to him. "What is he talking about?"

"It's just something Ethan White said. Remember him?" he asked, and I nodded. I'd met the Elder Luxen briefly. "When I left the colony to come looking for you, he said something about Earth not belonging to the humans forever, but I really didn't give it much thought, because come on… I'm sure there are Luxen out there who want to be in control, but it would never happen."

Archer didn't look convinced, and neither was I, but then the origin cocked his head to the side. "Speaking of the devil…"

A moment later, the hotel door opened. Daemon shot to his feet, eyes turning all white as I started for the gun, my heart leaping into my throat.

Luc strolled in, holding a plastic bag and a pink box. His hair was pulled back into a short ponytail, a big grin plastered across that angelic face. "Hey, guys!" he said cheerfully. "I brought doughnuts."

I blinked slowly as I settled back down. "Good God, you almost gave me a heart attack."

"I'm pretty sure I locked that door," Daemon growled.

Luc set the box of doughnuts down, and I eyed them like they held the answer to life. "And I'm pretty sure I let myself in. Hey, Katy!"

I jumped at my name. "Hey, Luc…"

"Look at what I got." He dug into his bag and pulled out an extraterrestrial highway shirt. "We can be soul twins now."

"That's…um, really nice."

Paris's lip curled. "Are you actually going to wear that shirt?"

"Yeah, I am. Every day of my life. I think it's ironic." Luc's amethyst gaze circled the room, landing back on me. "Now, I think you two have something for me?"

Daemon let out a low breath and picked up the glass case. He tossed it over to Luc, who snatched it out of the air. "There you go."

The kid popped open the small and narrow case, exhaling slowly. He closed it reverently and slid it into the back pocket of his jeans. "Thank you."

I had a feeling that, like Daemon, he didn't say thank you a lot. "So…what do we do from here?" I asked.

"Well…" Luc drawled out the word. "Shit's about to get real. Daedalus will spare no expense or life to get their grubby little hands on you, Daemon. They are going to tear this town apart. They already are. And they will use every means possible to drag you back in."

Daemon stiffened. "They're going to go after my family, aren't they?"

"Most likely," he replied. "Actually, you can count on that. Anyway!" Luc spun on Archer so fast that the older origin took a step back. "I got us some new wheels."

"Really," Archer replied.

"And it's roomy enough for the five of us." Luc turned back to Daemon and me with an impish grin that spelled no good. "I have a surprise for you guys. But first, I'd suggest putting on some clothes." He reached in his bag, pulled out a shirt, and tossed it at Daemon. It was a plain white T-shirt. "Me and Katy look adorkable in extraterrestrial highway shirts. You would just look stupid. You can thank me later."

I wondered how in the world Luc knew that Daemon also had one of those shirts.

"And eat some damn doughnuts. In either order will do."

Daemon scowled, while I was just happy to start eating doughnuts. I peeked inside the box. Glazed. My favorite.

"What kind of surprise?" Daemon asked, holding the shirt and making no attempt to put it on.

"Now if I told you, it wouldn't be a surprise. But we need to get on the road soon. So eat and pack up. We've got places to go."

Daemon exhaled through his nose and then glanced at me. I could tell he didn't take too kindly to being bossed around by Luc, but my mouth was full of glazy goodness, so I really didn't have anything to add at the moment.

Finally, he nodded. "All right, but if you—"

"I know. If I'm screwing with you guys, you're going to find a way to make my death slow and painful. Got it." Luc winked. "I consider myself warned."

"By the way," Archer said as Daemon leaned over my shoulder and started poking around the doughnuts. "Don't forget the box of condoms on the floor."

My focus shot to the floor. There they were, right where Daemon had dropped them last night. My face burned like holy hell, and I almost choked on the doughnut, the sound of Daemon's laughter ringing in my ears.

• • •

Daemon

I so didn't forget the condoms when I packed what little stuff we had into our alien tote. Kat still looked a little red in the face, and it took everything in me not to tease her mercilessly about it. I went easy on her because she looked so damn cute standing there in that stupid T-shirt and those cheap plastic flip-flops, clutching the alien doll to her chest.

I dropped my arm over her shoulders as we headed out into the bright glare of the August desert sun.

Archer brushed past us, his gaze falling to what I carried. "Nice bag."

"Shut up," I replied.

He snorted.

We rounded the corner of the motel, and I got my first look at our ride. "Whoa! That's your wheels?"

Luc threw his new T-shirt over his shoulder as he patted the rear bumper of a black Hummer. "It suits me, I like to think."

Kat shifted the doll to her other arm as she took in the monster. "Did you drive this small village crusher all the way from West Virginia?"

He laughed. "No. I borrowed this."

Yeah, I had a feeling that Luc's "borrowing" was the same way I had "borrowed" Matthew's car. Heading around the driver's side, I opened the back door for Kat. "Think you can climb up in this thing all by yourself?"

She shot me a look over her shoulder, and I grinned. Shaking her head, she grabbed the bar and hoisted herself up. Of course, being the helpful guy that I am, I assisted with a well-placed push.

Kat's head whipped around, her cheeks flushed. "You're such a dog sometimes."

I chuckled as I hopped in beside her. "Remember what I said about petting me."

"Yeah, I remember."

"Keep that in mind for later." I reached around her, grabbing the seat belt before she could.

She sighed as she lifted her arms out of the way. "You know, I am totally capable of buckling myself in."

"How cute," Archer said from the other open door. He climbed in on the other side of Kat.

"There's a reason why I'm doing this." I ignored him, sliding the waist strap over her lap. She sucked in a soft gasp as my hands slid along her lower stomach. I gave her a wicked grin as I buckled her in. "Understand now?"

"Like I said: such a dog," she murmured back, but her eyes had turned a soft heather gray.

Leaning over, I pressed my lips to her temple and then lifted my arm. There was enough give in the seat belt for her to snuggle up against my side. "So, is this car my surprise? I can get down with that."

From the front passenger seat, Luc laughed. "Hell no. I think I might keep this one."

"Just sit back and enjoy the ride," Paris said, starting the Hummer. "Actually, it's a pretty boring ride. Besides the funny alien signs on the highway and maybe a cow or two, there's nothing to look at."

"Fun." As I readjusted my legs, I glanced at Archer. He was tapping his fingers over his denim-clad knees, eyes narrowed on the back of the seat. I didn't really trust any of them in this car, not 100 percent. They could be leading us right back to Area 51.

Archer turned his head to me. *We're not going to betray you or Katy.*

My eyes narrowed. *For the last time, get out of my head.*

It's hard not to. You have such a big head. One side of his lips curved up as he returned to staring at the seat in front of him. *Besides, how could I bring you back? You saw what I did to get us out of there.*

He had a point. *Could just be a setup, like it was with Blake. He did the same thing.*

I'm not Blake. I want to get away from them just as badly as you do.

I didn't respond to that. Turning my gaze to the window, I watched the small houses and the signs for the hot springs blur and then finally fade into the flat open highway of nothing but small brush and tan soil. It wasn't until I saw the sign that I relaxed a little.

"Las Vegas? Are we're going to gamble and take in a Flamingo show?"

Luc shook his head. "Not unless that's your thing."

Not knowing where we were going or why didn't settle well with me. I kept on guard, my eyes peeled to the road, looking for any suspicious vehicles that got a little too close. About seven miles into the almost two-hour trip, Kat dozed off. I grabbed the doll before it hit the floorboards and held onto it. I was relieved that she was getting more rest. She needed it.

Every time we came near a police car, I would tense, ready for them to pull us over for a multitude of reasons, varying from a stolen car to taking out military personnel. But no one stopped us. Not a damn thing happened the entire drive, except for Luc and Paris arguing over the radio like an old married couple. I couldn't figure the two out. Then again, I couldn't figure out myself.

I thought about the craziest shit on that drive to Vegas. And I mean some really far-out-there stuff, and I don't know if it had to do with the fact that there were two people in the car who could potentially be peeking inside my head that made me think of things I really didn't want other people to be privy to.

It all started when I looked away from the window and my attention fell to my leg. Kat's left hand was curled up against my thigh. For several minutes, I couldn't look away. What was it about the left hand? It was just a hand, and Kat had a really great hand and all, but it wasn't that.

It was what typically went on the left hand, on the ring finger.

God, thinking about rings and the left hand made me want to get out of this vehicle and do about a hundred laps, but being married to Kat—*married?* My brain tripped up over that word, but it wouldn't be terrible. Nah, it would be far from that. It would be sort of…perfect.

Spending the rest of my life with Kat was something I planned on. There was no question or doubt when it came to that. I saw her—*only* her—in my future. Making a decision like that didn't send me into a cold sweat. Maybe it was because my kind mated young, usually right out of high school, and our version of marriage was really no different than what the humans did.

But we were young. Wet behind the ears, or at least that's what Matthew would say.

Why in the hell was I even thinking about that right now, when our lives were a complete mess? Maybe it was because when everything was chaotic and tomorrow might not come, it made you think about these things? Made you want to seal the deal, so to speak? I hated thinking it, but there might not be a couple of years down the road to get married.

Shaking the thoughts out of my head, I tightened my arm around Kat and focused on the road. When the skyscrapers started to come into view, I gently roused her. "Hey, sleepyhead, take a look."

She lifted her head from my shoulder and rubbed her eyes. Blinking a couple of times, she bent a little and stared out the front window. Her eyes widened. "Wow…I've never been to Vegas before."

Luc twisted in his seat, grinning. "It's better to see at night, with all the buildings lit up on the Strip."

Eagerness filled her gaze, but she settled back, shoulders slumping. As much as I would love to take her out, there would be no sightseeing for us. It would be too risky.

I leaned over, pressing my lips to her ear, and said, "Next time. I promise."

She turned slightly, eyes closing. "I'll hold you to that."

Kissing her cheek, I ignored the speculative look Archer gave me. As we entered Vegas, Kat was straining over me to see everything. The palm trees lining the Strip were probably familiar to her, but the pirate ship in front of Treasure Island wasn't something you saw every day.

It took forever to get through the packed traffic, and normally that would have had me clawing at my eyeballs with impatience, but it wasn't too bad. Not with Kat practically bouncing halfway in my lap, pointing out well-known hotspots like the Bellagio, Caesar's Palace, and the Eiffel Tower at Paris.

I was sort of in heaven.

Unfortunately, this version of heaven had an audience. Dammit.

As we reached the outskirts of Vegas, I started getting weary of this whole surprise bullshit, especially when Paris turned off the main avenue, following another road around a country club and huge golf course. We kept heading farther down the road, farther away from the teeming city. There was nothing out there but a few sprawling mansions, and then a twenty-foot security wall came out of nowhere, a glittering sandstone structure.

I leaned forward, dropping my hand on the back of Paris's seat. "Is that quartzite in the stone?"

"You better believe it."

Kat glanced at me, her eyes widening with realization as Paris slowed in front of a wrought-iron gate that had tiny specks of the quartz in it. I'd never seen anything like it.

An intercom popped on and Paris said, "Knock. Knock."

Static and then a woman's voice said, "Who's there?"

Kat raised a brow at me, and I shrugged.

"The interrupting cow," Paris said, glancing at Luc, who shook his head.

From the intercom, "The inter—?"

"Moooooo!" Paris said, snickering.

Kat giggled.

Archer rolled his eyes and shook his head.

There was an audible huff from the intercom. "That was stupid. The gate is opening. Give it a sec."

"That was pretty lame," I said.

Paris chuckled. "I saw it on the Internet. Made me laugh. I got more. Want to hear them?"

"No." My rebuttal was joined by Archer's. Something we agreed on. Huh. Go figure.

"Too bad." Paris eased forward as the gates split, spreading wide. "That wasn't even my best one."

"It was pretty good," Kat said, grinning when I shot her a look. "It made me laugh."

"You're easy to impress," I told her.

She went to smack my arm, but I caught her hand. Threading my fingers through hers, I winked. She shook her head. "You do not impress me."

I would've believed her if she and I both didn't know better.

It took me a few seconds to realize the road also had large quantities of quartz embedded into the asphalt. The first house we came upon, a modest structure, looked like someone puked quartz all over it—on the roof, the shutters, the front door.

Holy crap.

Since there were no natural formations of quartz nearby, they had brought it in, protecting the Luxen community.

"You didn't know about this?" Surprise colored Luc's voice.

"No. I mean, never seemed impossible, using the quartz like this, but it had to cost a pretty penny, and I didn't even know there was a community out here."

"Interesting," Luc murmured, his jaw setting in a hard line.

Paris glanced at him, and I didn't understand the look they exchanged.

"Neither does Daedalus," Archer said. "It's right under their noses. Perfect hiding spot."

"This is insane." I shook my head as we passed more houses decked out in quartz, each home getting larger. "How did I not know about this? Do you know someone in here, Luc?"

He shook his head. "Not really. I have some…friends in Arizona, but we need to make a pit stop here first. Let it die down for a few days so the highway won't be such a danger traveling."

"So we're going to Arizona next?" Kat asked, glancing between Luc and me.

Luc shrugged. "It's an offer on the table. That's where Archer is heading to hide out for a while, but it's up to you guys. You can take my offer of hospitality or shove it up my rear."

Kat frowned.

"Makes no difference to me," he added.

She shook her head a little. "I don't get why you all would risk so much to keep helping us."

Good question.

Luc looked over his shoulder. "We have the same enemy, and we're stronger in numbers. Just like in the horror movies."

I started picking up on other Luxen who had to be in the houses or behind the tall walls circling most of the backyards. I really couldn't believe this—an entire community supposedly unseen by Daedalus and protected from Arum by man-made quartz deposits.

Huh. Mind blown.

We'd finally reached another wall and the gate opened before us. The house, if you could call the monstrous thing a house, loomed ahead like a mirage.

"This is where we're going?" Kat asked. A look of awe crossed her expression. "It's a palace."

That brought a smile to my face.

The place really was absurd. Had to be way more than seven thousand square feet, maybe more, rising three stories, with a sky dome over the middle section and a wing flanking each side. Like the rest of the houses, it was white sandstone with quartz embedded deep into the structure. It, too, had a tall wall blocking whatever existed behind the home.

Paris followed the driveway, stopping halfway through the circle in front of the wide steps. In the middle of the circle was a marble statue. Of a dolphin. Weird.

"All right, kids, we're here!" Luc threw open the passenger door and bounded up the steps. On the porch, he turned back to the Hummer. "I'm not getting any younger here."

Taking a deep breath, I grabbed Kat's hand. "You ready?"

"Yes." She gave me a little smile. "I want to see what it looks like inside."

I laughed. "Absurd opulence is what I'm betting on."

"Same here," Archer muttered, stepping out.

We climbed down and walked around the Hummer. She took the tote this time, sticking the alien doll in it so its head popped out of the top. Giving her hand a squeeze, I headed up the steps while I prepared myself for God knows what. The way Luc was smiling had me wary. He looked like he—

The feeling that swept down my spine was warming and familiar but totally impossible. So was the startling jump in energy that caused me to drop Kat's hand. No way.

I took a step back from the door.

Kat turned, concern pinching her face. "What is it? What's going on?"

Words failed me as I stared at the door. All I could do was shake my head once. Part of me was elated, while the other half was horrified by what I was sensing—and I hoped it was my imagination.

Moving to my side, Kat placed her hands on my upper arm. "What's—?"

The red-painted door opened, and, as a figure stepped out of the shadowy recesses, my suspicions were confirmed.

"We came all this way to rush in and save your ass, but then you end up saving your own ass before we could do anything." Dee popped her hands on her hips, and her chin was tipped up stubbornly. "Way to steal our thunder and glory, Daemon."

Luc clapped his hands together. "Surprise!"

CHAPTER 22

KATY

Daemon was absolutely dumbfounded into silence. So was I. The only two people who weren't gawking at Dee were Luc and Paris. Even Archer had the open-mouth thing going on, but I think that had less to do with what their appearance meant to Daemon than it did with how beautiful she was.

And Dee was out of this world, extraordinarily beautiful. With her glossy black curls cascading around her exotic face and with those emerald eyes, she was stunning. A more delicate, feminine version of Daemon and Dawson. She stopped humans, aliens, hybrids, and apparently origins in their tracks.

Archer looked like he just saw baby Jesus in a manager or something.

Dee dashed out the door, tears streaming down her rosy cheeks. I stepped back in the nick of time. She launched herself at Daemon from several feet away. He caught her as she wrapped her arms around his neck.

"Jesus," he said, his words muffled by all of her hair. "What are you doing here?"

"What do you think?" she responded, voice thick. "We had to do something. You just beat us to it as usual, you punk."

I clasped my hands over my chest, close to tears, as another form appeared in the doorway and drifted out. Sucking in a soft breath, I couldn't believe how…how different Dawson looked. Filled out and his hair trimmed up, with the gaunt pull to his face gone and the dark shadows under his eyes erased, he was the spitting image of his brother.

Daemon lifted his head, as if he sensed the arrival. His mouth worked, but there weren't any words. None of us could've expected to see them here. Like me, Daemon probably figured he might never see his siblings again.

Dawson crossed the porch and dropped his arms around his sister and brother. Their three heads were bent together. Daemon had one hand fisted around the back of Dee's shirt and the other around Dawson's.

"It's true," Dawson said, grinning. "What the hell, brother? Always got to one-up me, huh?"

Daemon grabbed the back of his brother's neck and pressed his forehead against his. "You idiot," he said, letting out a choked laugh. "You should know better. I've always got things covered."

"Yeah, and wait—I'm pissed at you!" Dee pulled back and hit Daemon in the chest hard. "You could've gotten yourself killed doing what you did! You jerk-face, douchebag, imbecile." She hit him again.

Archer winced and muttered, "Damn, that girl…that girl can hit."

"Hey!" Laughing, Daemon grabbed her hand. "Knock it off. I obviously didn't get myself killed."

"I worried, you ass!" Dee pushed her curls out of her face and inhaled deeply. "But I forgive you, because you're in one piece and apparently no worse for wear, and you're here, but if you ever do anything that—"

"Okay," Dawson said, dropping an arm around his sister's neck, spinning her. "I think he gets the point. We've *all* got the point."

Dee broke free as her eyes skipped over Paris and Luc. She didn't pay them much attention, but her gaze bounced over Archer, then went right back before moving on. I had stayed out of the reunion, remaining by one of the pillars. I didn't think Dee even noticed me until that moment.

In the blink of an eye, she practically knocked me over. I'd forgotten what her hugs were like. For someone who had a ballet dancer's body, she was ridiculously strong. And her hugs…well, it had been so long since I'd been on the receiving end of one of her bear squeezes.

I was slow to respond, more taken off guard than anything else, but then I dropped the tote and threw my arms around her. Tears welled up, and I squeezed my eyes shut. The part of my being that had felt achy over what happened with Dee warmed, and that warmth spilled over.

"I'm so sorry," she said, tears clogging her voice. "I'm so, so sorry."

"For what?"

She still hadn't let go, and I didn't mind. "For everything—for not seeing your side of things, for being so caught up in my grief and anger that I totally abandoned you. For never telling you that I missed you before…"

Before it was too late was what she was going to say.

Blinking back tears, I smiled against her shoulder. "You have nothing to apologize for, Dee. I mean it. None of that…" Well, it did matter. Adam's death mattered. "It's okay now."

She held me tighter and whispered, "Is it? Because I've been so worried about you and Daemon and what could've…"

My body roiled into nervous knots, and I willed the sudden rise of dread to go away. It wasn't welcome here, not in this happy moment. "It's okay."

"I've missed you."

A few tears snuck out. "I've missed you, too."

"Okay. Okay. I think you're starting to cut off her air supply." Dawson tugged on Dee's arm. "And I think Daemon is starting to get jealous."

"*Pfft.* It's my turn with Katy," she replied, but she let go.

And then Dawson replaced his sister. He hugged me, nothing as fierce as Dee's but still powerful. "Thank you," he said quietly, and I knew those two words encompassed so much. "I hope you know how thankful I am for everything you've done."

Unsure if I could speak, I nodded.

"Okay. Now I *am* getting jealous," Daemon said, and Paris laughed.

Dawson gave me a quick squeeze. "I'm forever in your debt."

I wanted to tell him that wasn't necessary. Helping him get Bethany was something I'd do all over again, even knowing that Blake had set us up. After being in Daedalus's grips, now more than ever I understood how important it had been to get her out. The only thing I would've changed was where I was standing in that damn tunnel in Mount Weather.

He stepped aside as his brother swooped in, picking up the tote and circling his arm around my waist. Dawson cocked his head to the side. "What is up with the alien doll?"

"Daemon thought it would remind me of him," I told Dawson.

"Tell him what you named it," Daemon said, and then he dropped a kiss atop my head.

My heart jumped, and my cheeks flushed. "I named it DB."

Dee peered at the alien toy over Dawson's shoulder. "It kind of does look like you, Daemon."

"Ha. Ha." I tugged the doll out of the bag and held it close. For some reason, I loved the stupid thing.

"Everyone want to head in?" Luc rocked back on the heels of his Converse sneakers. "I'm starving."

Dee spun around so that she was on my other side as we headed in. She stole a peek at Archer, who walked in behind us. If I noticed that, so did Daemon. And whatever Dee was thinking right now, most likely Archer was eavesdropping in on.

I so needed to give her a heads-up on that.

Plus the fact that Archer was, well, he was really different from all of us.

The temperature was a good thirty degrees cooler inside the brightly lit foyer, even with the glass sky dome allowing the sunlight inside. Quartz was embedded in the tile floor, making everything so *sparkly*. There were large, leafy plants positioned at the corners, which made my fingers itchy to dig into soil.

Sinking my fingers into soil…wow, how long had it been since I'd done that? The day we'd left for Mount Weather? Too long.

"You doing okay?"

"Huh?" I glanced up at Daemon, and I realized that I must've stopped walking, because everyone else was already in the hall beyond the foyer. "Yeah, I was just thinking about gardens."

An emotion crossed his face. Before I could decipher what it was, he looked away. I reached over and tugged on the hem of his shirt. "How about you? Seeing Dawson and Dee?"

He thrust his fingers through his hair. "I don't know what to think." He kept his voice low. "I'm happy to see them, but…dammit."

I nodded in understanding. "You don't want them anywhere near this?"

"No. Not at all."

I wanted to somehow lessen his concern, but I knew there was nothing I could say that would do so. I stretched up and kissed his cheek. That was the best I had.

He grinned down at me once I settled back on my feet. He opened his mouth to say something, but Dee popped back into the foyer.

Expression exasperated, she put her hands on her hips. "All right, you two, come in a little farther. There are people here in the great room who would like to say hi. Whatever a 'great room' is I really have no idea, but it is pretty great."

God, I missed her so much.

Daemon lifted his head, smiling at his sister. "Yeah, I think I know who's waiting."

The people waiting to say hello were none other than Matthew, plus Ash and Andrew Thompson. I shouldn't have been surprised to see them. All of them—Matthew, the Thompsons—were like a family. They converged on Daemon at once, and they swallowed him, Dawson and Dee included.

I hung back again, because this was his reunion—a well-deserved one. And the room was rather distracting. Oriental carpet. More statues of dolphins. Quartz-trimmed furniture. A couch big enough for the Duggar family.

Luc plopped down on a chaise longue and started texting away on his cell phone. Paris hung near him, like a grinning shadow. Archer was like me, on the outskirts, probably unsure of what to do as Dee started crying again.

Even Ash was crying.

I expected to feel the hot wave of jealousy when Daemon hugged her, but I didn't. Other than the fact Ash still managed to make crying look glamorous, I was so over that useless emotion. If there was one thing I knew and understood in this world, it was that Daemon loved me.

Matthew stepped forward, grabbing Daemon's shoulders. "It's good…it's good to see you."

"You, too." Daemon clasped his arms. "Sorry about your car."

I wondered what happened to Matthew's car, but that question was lost in the lump that was slithering up my throat. Watching them embrace each other, I was reminded of how important Matthew was to all of them. He'd been the only father any of them remembered.

"It's hard, isn't it?" Archer asked quietly.

Looking at him, I frowned. "Are you in my head again?"

"No. Your emotions are all over your face."

"Oh." I blew out a breath as I glanced back at the huddle. "I miss my mom, and I don't know…" I shook my head, not wanting to finish.

When the group broke apart, Matthew was the first to approach me. The hug was a bit stiff, but I appreciated it. Ash and Andrew both appeared in front of me, and I was immediately wary of the two. They had never been big fans of mine.

Ash's vibrant blue eyes were red-rimmed when she gazed at me, no doubt taking one look at my outfit and writing me off as a giant fashion fail. "I can't say I'm overly thrilled to see you, but I'm happy you're alive, or whatever."

I choked on my laugh. "Uh, thanks?"

Andrew scratched his chin, face scrunched. "Yeah, I second that statement."

I nodded, having no idea what to say. I raised my hands and gave a little shrug. "Well, I'm happy to see you guys, too."

Ash laughed, the sound throaty. "No you're not, but it's cool. Seriously, our rampant dislike of you really isn't at the top of the priority list right now."

Archer blew out a low whistle and studiously looked away, which gained Ash's catlike interest. As beautiful as she was, I doubted most could resist her.

I was saved from more awkward hellos by the newest entrance. The woman was around Matthew's age, early thirties, tall and slender, wearing a strapless white sundress that swished around her ankles. She was model beautiful with long blond hair.

Obviously an alien.

She smiled warmly as she clasped her hands together. Brown bamboo bangles on her wrists thudded off one another. "I'm glad to see everyone made it here. My name is Lyla Marie. Welcome to my home."

I murmured a hello as Daemon crossed the room and shook the Luxen's hand. He was surprisingly much better at this than I was. Who knew? But seeing everyone here, being surrounded by people I once thought I'd never see again, was a little on the overwhelming side. I was happy, and I was confused, and this terrible coating of foreboding was like sweat on my skin.

Here we were, all of us, a couple of hundred miles from Area 51.

Trying to push those thoughts out of my head as Daemon introduced Archer, I sat on the edge of the couch, holding DB in my lap. Dee sat beside me, her cheeks flushed with emotion. I knew she was going to start crying again.

Dawson made his way over to Lyla's side. "Is Bethany lying down?"

Bethany? My ears perked up. Of course she'd be here with Dawson. In the wave of faces, I just hadn't thought of her. Was she sick?

Lyla patted Dawson on the back. "She's okay. Just needs to rest a little bit. It was a lot of traveling."

He nodded but didn't look relieved as he turned to Daemon. "I'll be right back. I just want to check on her."

"Go," Daemon said as he sat on the other side of me. Leaning against the cushion, he draped his arm along the back of the couch. "So…how is all of this possible? How did you guys know to come here?"

"Your lovely sister and brother showed up at my club and threatened to burn it down if I didn't tell them where you were," Luc said, glancing up from his phone. "True story."

Dee wiggled under Daemon's glare. "What? We knew you'd go there and that he'd probably know where you were."

"Wait," Daemon said, leaning around me to look at Dee. "Did you graduate? You better have graduated, Dee. I'm freaking serious."

"Hey! Look who's talking, Mr. I Have No High School Degree. Yes. I did graduate. Dawson did, too. Bethany…didn't go back."

That made sense. No way could they explain Bethany's presence.

"We graduated, too, you know." Ash paused, picking at her purple fingernail polish. "Just want to throw that out there."

Running a hand through his blond hair, Andrew made a face at his sister but said nothing. Archer looked like he was fighting a grin—either that or he was grimacing at the crystal dolphin beside him.

"And what about this?" Daemon asked, gesturing at the house.

Lyla leaned against the arm of the couch. "Well, I've known Matthew since we were teenagers. We've kept in touch over the years, so when he called and asked if I knew of any places to stay, I extended him an invite."

Daemon dropped his arms between his knees as his gaze met Matthew's. "You never mentioned anything like this."

There wasn't any accusation in Daemon's tone, mostly confusion. Matthew sighed. "It's not something I felt comfortable telling anyone, nor did I think I'd ever have to. It just never came up."

Daemon didn't say anything for a moment; he seemed to ingest that and then rubbed both hands down his face. "You guys really shouldn't be here."

Beside me, Dee groaned. "I so knew you were going to start in with this. Yes. Being here is dangerous, we get that. But we weren't going to let this happen to you and Katy. What the hell would that have said about us?"

"You don't think before you act?" Daemon suggested gamely.

I smacked his knee. "I think what he's trying to say is that he doesn't want you guys to be in danger."

Andrew huffed. "We can handle anything they throw at us."

"Actually, no you can't." Luc swung his feet onto the floor and sat up, slipping his phone into his pocket. "But here's the thing. They were already in danger, Daemon. Deep down, you acknowledge that. Daedalus would've gone right after them. Make no mistake about that. Nancy would've shown up at their door."

Daemon's muscles locked up in his arm. "I get that, but this is like going from the frying pan into the damn volcano."

"Not really," Dawson said from the doorway. He carried two black billfolds in his hand as he walked them over to Daemon and me. He handed one to each of us. "We stay here for a day or so. Figure out our next move and where everyone is going to go, and then we all disappear. That's what's in your hands. Say hello to your new identities."

CHAPTER 23

KATY

Reading my new name for a third time, I still couldn't believe it. Something about this name was familiar. "Anna Whitt?"

Dee bounced a little. "I picked the names."

Things started to click into place. "What's yours, Daemon?"

He flipped his billfold open and snickered. "Kaidan Rowe. Hmm. That has a nice ring to it."

My mouth dropped open as I twisted toward Dee. "You picked names from a book!"

She giggled. "I thought you'd like that. Besides, *Sweet Evil* is one of my favorites, and you made me read it, so…"

I couldn't help it. I laughed as I stared down at my picture ID. It was an identical copy of my real driver's license, except it was a different state and address. Underneath it was my actual ID—Katy Swartz—and a few other sheets of folded paper.

Gosh, I missed my books. I wanted to hug them, love them, squeeze them.

"I found that in your bedroom," Dee explained, tapping a

finger off it. "I snuck in and got you some clothes and this before we left."

"Thank you," I said, sliding my new ID over my old one. Staring at both was going to give me an identity crisis.

"So, wait, my new name is from one of those books?" Daemon frowned. He also had his real ID, but there was a bank card underneath, set to Kaidan's name. "I'm afraid to even ask what it's about. I better not be named after any kind of magician or something lame like that."

"No. It's about angels, demons, and nephilim, and…" I stalled, acutely aware that everyone was staring at me like I'd grown a third eye. "Kaidan's like the embodiment of lust."

His eyes sparkled in interest. "Well, now that couldn't be any more fitting." He elbowed me, and I rolled my eyes. "Huh? Perfect, right?"

"Ew," Dee said.

"Anyway," Dawson said, sitting down on the arm of the couch, "I had your accounts switched over to the new names. You'll also find high school transcripts, so even though both of you are dropouts"—he flashed a grin—"no one will be the wiser. We're all rocking new identities."

"How did you guys take care of all this?" I asked, completely out of the loop when it came to making IDs and faking records.

Luc smirked. "Among my various and extensive talents, making fake IDs and forging documents is one of them."

I stared at the kid, wondering if there was anything he couldn't do.

"Nope." Luc winked at me.

My eyes narrowed.

Daemon thumbed through his papers. "Guys, really, thank you. This is a start." He looked up, his jade eyes bright. "This is something."

I nodded, trying not to focus on everything that I was losing by starting over. Like my mom. Somehow, I'd have to find a way to see her. "Yes."

We stayed in the room for a little while, mainly catching up. No one talked about plans, because I really didn't think anyone knew exactly where to go from there. Lyla gave me a tour of her beautiful home when I asked to use the restroom, which, by the way, was the size of a bedroom and had interior, glass walls.

The house had more rooms downstairs than any living person could find use for. And it seemed like Lyla didn't have a significant other, so it was just her in this sprawling home. Dee tagged along, wrapping an arm around mine as Lyla led me through an open kitchen and sunroom.

"You're going to love this," Dee said. "Just wait."

Lyla tossed a smile over her tan shoulder. "I think Dee's spent the last week out here, trying to come up with a way to free you guys, but…we really didn't have a plan that Matthew and I could allow them to carry out that didn't end with them being captured."

Filled with curiosity, I let them lead me outside, back into what I expected to be breath-stealing temperatures, but I ended up stepping into an oasis.

"Oh my God…" I breathed.

Dee rocked back on her heels. "Told you that you were going to love this. Beautiful, isn't it?"

All I could do was nod. Numerous medium-size palms lined a quartz-embedded privacy wall, creating the perfect shaded area. The space was rectangular, with a large patio with a grill, fire pit, and various lounge chairs. Brightly colored flowers lined the paver walkway, as did bushes I'd seen in the desert but couldn't name. The scent of jasmine and sage was strong in the air. Toward the end of the property was a pool with a natural stone deck.

It was the kind of garden you saw on TV.

"When Dee told me that you loved to garden, I knew we'd have something in common." Lyla ran her fingers along a red and yellow croton. "I think your love of gardening has rubbed off on Dee. She's been helping me."

"It helped." Dee shrugged. "You know, not to think about so many things."

That's what I'd loved about gardening. It was the great mind-emptier. After investigating everything from the mulch to the neutral-colored pebbles, I followed Dee upstairs to the second floor. Daemon was with Dawson, Matthew, and the Thompson siblings. He needed to spend time with them. Besides, hanging out with Dee was bringing me a world of warm fuzzies.

One of the bedroom doors was closed, and I figured that was where Beth was. "How is Beth doing?" I asked.

Dee slowed down, falling in step with me. Her voice was low. "She's okay, I guess. She doesn't talk much."

"Is she…?" Wow. How did I ask this question without sounding insensitive?

"Sane?" suggested Dee, but she did so without scorn. "Some days are better than others, but she's been really tired lately, sleeping a lot."

I stepped around a giant urn packed with snake plants. "Well, she can't be coming down with something. We don't get sick."

"I know." Dee stopped at a bedroom at the end of the hall. "I just think the traveling has her stressed out. She wanted to help, don't get me wrong, but she's scared."

"She has a right to be." I brushed a few strands of hair out of my face and focused on the room. The bed was big enough for five people and had a mountain of pillows stacked against the headboard. "So this is our bedroom?"

"Huh?" Dee was staring at me, and then she shook her head. "Sorry. Yes. For you and my brother." A giggle escaped. "Wow. A year ago, Katy…"

A smile tugged at my lips. "I would've rather stabbed myself repeatedly in the eye with a spork than sleep in the same *house* as Daemon."

"A spork?" Dee laughed as she went over to the closet. "That's serious."

"It is." I sat on the bed and immediately fell in love with the firmness. "Sporks are only used in the most dire situations."

Tugging her hair up into a ponytail, she stepped inside. I could see a few of my outfits in there. "I grabbed a couple of everything—jeans, shirts, dresses, underoos."

"Thank you. I mean it. This," I said, gesturing at myself, "is all I have. It will be nice to change into something that's mine after…" I trailed off, not seeing the point in going there. Scanning the room for a distraction, I spotted another door. "Do we have our own bathroom?"

"Yep. Every room does. This house is sick." She blinked out in front of the closet and reappeared on the bed beside me. "It makes it kind of hard to leave this place."

I'd only been here a few hours, and I wanted to adopt the house. "So, where are you going after this? With us?"

She shrugged. "I honestly don't know. I'm not thinking about it yet, because I don't know how possible it's going to be for all of us to stay together. Going home is out of the question for a ton of reasons." She paused, looking at me. "Everyone at school was so… different after you and Daemon disappeared. With all the police and the journalists back again, people really started to get paranoid. Lesa was beside herself, especially after what happened to Carissa. It's good she has her boyfriend. She thinks Dawson and I left town to visit family. Kind of true."

Worrying the hem of my shirt, I steeled myself. "Can I ask you a question?"

"Sure. Anything."

"My mom—how is she?"

Dee took a moment to respond. "You want the truth, or do you want me to make you feel better?"

"It's bad, isn't it?" Tears welled up in my eyes so fast I had to look away.

"You know the answer to that." She found my hand and squeezed. "Your mom is upset. She took a lot of time off work—her jobs were okay with that. Very understanding from what I heard. She doesn't believe you and Daemon ran away. That's what the police finally decided when they could find no evidence of why you, Daemon, and Blake disappeared, but I also think some of the officers were in on it. They jumped to the runaway conclusion way too fast."

I shook my head. "Why doesn't that surprise me? Daedalus has people everywhere."

"Your mom found the laptop Daemon bought you. I had to tell her that he got it for you. Anyway, she knew you'd never run away without a laptop."

I gave a short laugh. "That sounds about right."

She squeezed my hand again. "Your mom is doing okay, though, all things considered. She's really strong, Katy."

"I know." I looked at her then. "But she doesn't deserve this. I can't stand the idea of her not knowing what happened to me."

She nodded. "I've spent a lot of time with her, just hanging out and helping with the house until we left. I even kept your garden weeded. I thought that could somehow make up for everything we dragged you into."

"Thank you." I moved so I was facing her. "I mean that. Thank you for spending time with her and helping her out, but you guys didn't drag me into anything. Okay? None of this is your fault or Daemon's."

Her eyes glistened, and she said in a small voice, "You really mean that?"

"Of course!" Shock rippled through me. "Dee, you guys didn't do anything wrong. This is all on Daedalus. That's who I blame. They are responsible. No one else."

"I've just been so upset. I'm happy to know that you don't feel that way. Ash said you probably hated me—hated us."

"Ash is a douche."

Dee laughed outright. "She can be sometimes."

I sighed. "I just wish there was something we could do other than just run."

"Yeah, me, too." Her knee bounced as she let go of my hand and tugged her ponytail down. "Can I ask you a question?"

"Sure."

She bit down on her lower lip. "How bad was it?"

I tensed. The one question I didn't want to be asked, but Dee waited, her expression so earnest that I had to say something. "Some days were better than others."

"I can imagine," she said softly. "Beth talked about it once. She said they would hurt her."

Thinking about my back, I pressed my lips together. "They do that. They did and said a lot of things."

She paled and several moments passed. "While we were heading here, Luc said that you…that Blake is dead. Is that true?"

I sucked in a sharp breath. Archer must've told him. "Blake's dead." I stood, tugging my hair back. "This isn't something I want to talk about—not any of the stuff that happened there. I'm sorry. I know you're just concerned. But it's not something I want to think about. It screws with my head."

"Okay. But if you ever do, you know I'm here for you, right?" I nodded, and Dee fixed a bright smile across her face. "So let's move on to better stuff. Like that fine-looking specimen of a man who came in with you—the one with the military cut?"

"Archer?"

"Yes. He's hot. And I'd spell that H-A-W-T."

I busted out laughing, and once I did I couldn't stop. Tears tracked down my face while she watched, perplexed. "What?" she demanded.

"I'm sorry." I wiped at my face with my fingers and plopped back down beside her. "It's just that I'm positive Daemon would stroke out if he heard that."

She scowled. "Daemon would stroke out if I showed interest in any kind."

"Well, Archer is different," I started slowly.

"Why? Because he's older? He can't be that much older, and besides, he's obviously a good guy. He risked his life to help you guys. But there is something different that I'm picking up on from him. Probably it's the whole military vibe."

I figured it was time to drop the bomb. "Archer isn't human, Dee."

Her frown deepened. "So he's a hybrid? Makes sense."

"Uh, no. He's, well, he's something different. He's what they call an origin—he's a kid of a Luxen and a hybrid."

After that sunk in, she shrugged. "So? I'm an alien. I'm not judgmental."

I smiled at that, glad she was showing interest in a guy after Adam. "Well, there's one more thing. I'd be careful of what you think around him."

"Why?"

"The origins have some freaky abilities," I explained, watching her eyes widen into saucers. "He can read your mind without you even knowing."

Dee's face went from pale to bright cherry. "Oh God."

"What?"

She smacked her hands over her face. "Well, the whole time we were downstairs, I was *so* picturing him naked."

• • •

After changing into an old terry-cloth tube dress that passed the show-no-scars test, I joined Dee and everyone downstairs. A massive dinner of extravagant levels followed, consisting of juicy fruits I didn't even know existed, tangy and sweet meats, and a salad that filled the biggest bowl I'd ever seen. I ate more than I'd thought humanly possible, even some of the grilled meat off Daemon's plate. Bethany had joined us, and she had hugged me the moment we crossed paths. Other than looking utterly worn out, she seemed fine, and her appetite rivaled my own.

Daemon nudged his plate over to me with his finger. "You're going to eat Lyla out of house and home."

Shrugging, I picked up another cube from his shish kebab and popped it into my mouth. "It's been so long since I had food that wasn't bland and served on a plastic tray."

He winced, and I immediately regretted saying that. "I—"

"Eat as much as you want," he said, glancing away. A muscle began to pulse in his jaw.

Then he piled more skewers on my plate, plus a handful of grapes and roasted pork loin, so much food that if I ate all of it, they'd have to roll me out of there. My gaze flicked away, meeting Dawson's. He looked…he just looked sad.

I reached under the table and placed my hand on Daemon's knee, giving it a squeeze. His head swiveled toward me, a deep brown curl falling across his forehead. I smiled for him, and it seemed to go a long way, because he relaxed once more.

And I ate as much food as I could stomach, knowing that it did something for Daemon. What it did exactly, I wasn't sure, but by the end of the dinner, he was being his usual charming and douchey self.

Our group moved outside after dinner. Daemon stretched out his happy ass on one of the white-cushioned lounge chairs, and I sat by his legs. The talk was light, what everyone needed. Luc and Paris joined us, as did Archer. Even Ash and Andrew weren't their normal antisocial selves.

Well, they really didn't talk to me, but they chimed in whenever Daemon or Dawson or Matthew made a comment. I didn't say much, mainly because I was busy paying attention to Bethany and Dawson.

They were just too adorable.

Sharing a chair, Beth sat in Dawson's lap, her cheek nestled under his chin. He continuously moved his hand up and down her back. Every so often, he'd murmur something in her ear, and she'd smile or laugh quietly.

When I wasn't watching them, I was keeping track of Dee.

Throughout the evening, she crept closer…and closer to where Archer sat chatting with Lyla. I was counting the minutes until Daemon noticed.

It took twenty.

"Dee," he called out. "Why don't you go get me a drink?"

His sister froze halfway between the patio table and the fire pit. Her luminous eyes narrowed. "What?"

"I'm thirsty. I think you should be a nice sister and get a drink for your poor brother."

Twisting at my waist, I shot Daemon a dirty look. He raised his brows at me and folded his hands behind his head. I turned back to Dee. "Don't you dare get him a drink."

"Wasn't planning on it," she replied. "He's got two legs."

Daemon wasn't deterred. "Then why don't you come over here and spend time with me?"

I rolled my eyes.

"I don't think there's room for me on that lounge." She folded her arms. "And as I much as I love you two, I don't want to get *that* close."

By that point, Daemon had successfully captured everyone's attention. "I'll make room for my sister," he cajoled.

"Uh huh." She spun around and stalked over to the patio. Pulling out a chair, she plopped down next to Archer and shoved out her hand. "I don't think we've been officially introduced."

Archer glanced down at her slender hand, then at Daemon for the tiniest second, and then he took her hand. "We haven't."

Six feet and a lot of inches of alien stiffened behind me. Oh dear.

"I'm Dee Black. I'm the sister of the douchebag known as Daemon." She smiled brightly. "But you probably already know that."

"That he's a douchebag or that he's your brother?" Archer asked innocently. "The answer is yes to both."

I choked on my laugh.

Heat rolled off Daemon. "Am I also the brother who's going to kick your ass if you don't let go of my sister's hand? The answer is yes to that, too."

Dawson snickered from his chair.

I found myself smiling. Some things never changed. The overprotective side of Daemon was still an overbearing ass.

"Ignore him," Dee said. "He has poor social skills."

"I can vouch for that," I threw out.

Daemon knocked his foot off my hip, and I glanced back at him. He winked and said in a low voice, "*That* is so not happening."

Archer still hadn't let go of Dee's hand as he talked with her, and I wondered if he was doing that to goad Daemon or if he just wanted to hold her hand. Daemon opened his mouth to say something jerkish.

I grabbed his ankle. "Leave them alone."

"No can do."

Sliding my fingers under the hem of his jeans, I met his stare. "Please?"

His eyes narrowed into incandescent green slits.

"Pretty please?"

"Is there sugar on top?"

"Maybe."

"There has to be, and there better be a lot of sugar." He sat up fluidly and moved so that his knees were on either side of my hips. He wrapped his arms around my waist, resting his chin on my shoulder. I turned my cheek toward his. A shiver skated over my skin as his lips brushed my chin. "I needs lots of sugar," he added. "What say you?"

"Leave them alone and maybe," I replied, more than a little breathless at the prospect.

"Hmm…" He tugged me back into the *V* of his legs. "You drive a hard bargain."

Something really dirty popped into my head, and I flushed.

Daemon leaned back, head tilting to the side. "What are you thinking, Kitten?"

"Nothing," I said, biting my lip.

He didn't look convinced. "Are you having impure thoughts about *me*? Gasp."

"*Impure* thoughts?" I giggled. "I wouldn't go that far."

Daemon's lips brushed the lobe of my ear, and another shiver made its way down my spine. "I'd go that far and then some."

Shaking my head, I realized Daemon was thoroughly distracted from who Dee was talking to. She owed me. Not that being in Daemon's arms and feeling the length of him was a chore or anything. Not when his fingers started toying with the hem of my dress, the back of his hand lazily brushing my thighs.

Dawson and Beth were the first ones to call it a night. They shuffled past us, Beth sending me a smile and a soft "good night." Matthew and Lyla were next, though they seemed to go in different directions. I couldn't let myself entertain any other idea there. That would just be gross, because Matthew *had* been my teacher.

Night broke and everyone else headed inside, including Archer and Dee. As they entered the sunroom, Daemon craned his neck so far I thought his head would fall off, which was pointless because they both were going upstairs.

I decided to keep that observation to myself lest he go tearing after them.

Only Daemon and I remained in the courtyard, staring up at the star-ridden sky. As soon as we were alone, I crawled into his lap, tucking my head under his chin. Every so often he placed a kiss against my forehead, my cheek…my nose, and every time he did, he erased another minute of the time spent with Daedalus. His kisses really did have the power to change lives. Not that I'd admit that. His ego was ginormous as it was.

We weren't talking, because I think there was so much to say and, at the same time, there was nothing to be said. We were out of Area 51, and for that very second we were safe, but our future was unknown. Daedalus was searching for us, and we couldn't stay there forever. It was too close to Area 51, and with this kind of sizeable population there were too many prying eyes from people who would begin to ask questions. Luc had the LH-11, and we had no idea what it was truly capable of or why Luc wanted something so volatile. There were the hybrids and Luxen back at the facility and those kids…those freaky kids.

I had no idea what was going to happen from here on out, and even thinking about it scared the ever-loving crap out of me. Tomorrow wasn't guaranteed. Neither were the next couple of hours. My breath caught with that realization, and I stiffened. The next minute was unknown to us, and it might not even come.

Daemon's arms tightened around me. "What are you thinking, Kitten?"

I considered lying, but at that moment, I didn't want to be strong. I didn't want to pretend like we had everything under control, because we didn't. "I'm scared."

He tugged me back against his chest and pressed his cheek against mine. The stubble tickled and, in spite of everything, I grinned. "You'd be insane not to be scared."

I closed my eyes, sliding my cheek against his. I was probably going to end up with carpet burn, but it would be worth it. "Are you scared?"

Daemon chuckled softly. "Me, seriously? No."

"You're too awesome for that?"

He kissed the sensitive spot under my ear, sending a wake of shivers through me. "You're learning. I'm proud of you."

I laughed.

Daemon stilled, like he seemed to do whenever I laughed, and then he squeezed me until I squeaked. "Sorry," he murmured, rubbing his nose against my neck as he loosened his hold. "I lied."

"About what? You being proud of me?" I teased.

"No. I'm always in awe of you, Kitten."

My heart did a little trippy-trip dance as I opened my eyes.

He let out a shuddering breath. "I was terrified the whole time they had you and I didn't know where you were. I was scared out of my mind that I would never see you again or get to hold you. And when I did see you? I was afraid I'd never hear you laugh again or see your beautiful smile. So, yeah, I lied. I was terrified. I'm still lying."

"Daemon…"

"I'm scared shitless that I'll never be able to make this up to you. That I'll never be able to give you back your life and—"

"Stop," I whispered, blinking back tears.

"I've taken everything from you—your mom, your blog, *your life*. So much so that you found *enjoyment* in eating something just because it wasn't on a plastic tray. And your back…" His jaw locked down, and he gave his head a little shake. "And I have no idea how I'm going to fix all of that, but I will. I will keep you safe. I will make sure that we have a future to hold on to and look forward to." He took a breath at the same time I did. "I promise you."

"Daemon, this isn't—"

"I'm sorry," he said, voice cracking. "This—all of this—is my fault. If I—"

"Don't say that." I turned in his lap, my dress riding up as I placed my hands on either side of his face. I stared into his brilliant eyes. "This isn't your fault, Daemon. None of this is."

"Really?" he said in a low voice. "I think the whole mutating-you thing was my fault."

"It was either that or let me die. So you saved my life. You didn't ruin it."

He shook his head, sending the short, dark waves across his forehead. "I should've kept you away since the beginning. I should've kept you safe so you never ended up getting hurt in the first place."

My heart ached at his words. "Listen to me, Daemon. This isn't your fault. I wouldn't change a damn thing. Okay? Yes, things have sucked, but I'd go through it all again if I had to. There are things I would want to change, but not you—never you. I love you. That's never going to change."

His lips parted on a sharp inhale. "Say it again."

I smoothed the pad of my finger over his lower lip. "I love you."

He nipped at my finger. "The other words, too."

Leaning down, I pressed a kiss to the tip of his nose. "I love you. That's never going to change."

He slid his hands up my back, one stopping just below my shoulder blade and the other cupping the nape of my neck as his eyes searched mine. "I want you to be happy, Kitten."

"I am happy," I said, tracing my fingers over the curve of his cheek. "*You* make me happy."

His chin lowered, and he pressed his lips to the tips of each of my fingers. Under and all around me, his muscles tensed, and then he placed his mouth to my ear and whispered in a deep voice, "I want to make you *really* happy."

My heart fluttered. "Really happy?"

He dropped his hands to my outer thighs, his long fingers slipping under the material. "Exceedingly, insanely happy."

I was breathless. "There you go again with the adverbs."

His hands inched up, causing heat to flood my body. "You love it when I whip out the adverbs."

"Maybe."

He trailed his lips in a hot line down my throat. "Let me make you exceedingly, insanely happy, Kat."

"Now?" My voice came out an embarrassing squawk.

"Now," he growled.

I thought about all the people inside the house, but then his lips were on mine, and it felt like forever since he'd kissed me. His hand moved into my hair as the kiss deepened, our breaths mingling. He dropped his arm around my waist, and then he was standing, and my legs were wrapped around his hips.

"I love you, Kitten." Another deep, scorching kiss lit up my insides. "And I'm going to show you just how much I love you."

Chapter 24

Daemon

My arms tightened around her as I waited for her answer. Not that I really believed she'd turn me down. It wasn't about that. I wanted to make sure she was ready after everything. Last time, she hadn't been ready, and it hadn't just been the headlights. If she wasn't, it'd be okay. Holding her all night would be just as amazing.

But I'd need a cold and really long shower.

Because having her in my lap, with the softest part of her pressed against the hardest part of me, was testing my self-control and had me turned on like no one in and beyond this world could.

Kat lifted her chin, her eyes locking with mine. Everything I needed to see, needed to believe in was in her eyes. "Yes."

I wasted no time after hearing that one little word. Doing this, being with her in every way that I could, wouldn't replace all the terrible things that had happened, but it was a start.

"Hold on," I told her, and then I captured her breathy response with a kiss.

She circled her arms around my neck as I gripped her hips. As I stood, her legs clamped down on me, and I bit back a groan. Surprised by the fact that I was even attempting to make it to a bed, I never took my mouth off hers. Kissing her. Drinking her in. It wasn't enough, could never be enough.

I carried her into the house and through the many useless rooms that would never, ever end, it seemed. She giggled against my mouth when I bumped into something that probably cost a small fortune. I found the stairs, climbed them without breaking both our necks, and found the bedroom I'd deposited our stuff in earlier.

Kat reached out, slapping at the air until she found the edge of the door and closed it behind us, just as I caught her lower lip with my teeth. A little nip, and the sound she made boiled my blood. I was going to combust before anything got started.

I turned us toward the bed, lifting my mouth from her warm lips. I wanted to strip the sheets and comforter and find richer, suppler coverings that were worthy of Kat.

She pressed a hot little kiss against my pounding pulse.

Screw finding better sheets.

I placed her down on the bed, moving slower than my body demanded. She sent me a tiny smile, and my heart turned over in my chest as I knelt on my knees before her. Our eyes locked.

My pulse pounded fast, feeling it in every part of my body. "I don't deserve you." The words came out before I could stop them. They were the truth. Kat deserved the world and then some.

Leaning forward, she placed her hand on my cheek, and I felt the touch through every cell in my body. "You deserve everything," she said.

I turned my head, kissing her palm. So many words came to the tip of my tongue, but when she stood and reached down, hooking her fingers under the hem of her dress, my heart stopped, and the words died in the silence between us.

Kat lifted the dress over her head and dropped it onto the floor beside me.

I couldn't move. I couldn't even get my lungs to function. Thinking became almost impossible as I stared up at her. She consumed me. Wearing nothing but a thin scrap of cloth, her hair tumbling down her shoulders and over her breasts, she stood there, looking like some kind of goddess.

"You…you are so beautiful." I stood slowly, my eyes following the slight flush down her neck. I grinned. "You're really beautiful when you blush."

She ducked her head, but I caught her chin, forcing her eyes back to mine. "Seriously," I told her. "Absolutely beautiful."

The tender, almost shy smile appeared again. "Flattery will totally get you everywhere right now."

I chuckled. "Good to know, because I'm planning on going everywhere—and taking the scenic route."

That flush deepened, but she grabbed at my shirt. I beat her to it. Tugging it over my head, I let it fall wherever her dress landed. For a moment, we stood there, separated by only a few inches. Neither of us spoke. A current of electricity filled the air, raising the hair along my arms. The pupils of Kat's eyes started to dilate.

Sliding a hand around the nape of her neck, I gently pulled her toward me. Then we were chest to chest, and the shudder that rolled through her short-circuited my senses. Her lips parted the moment they touched mine; her fingers found the button on my jeans, and my fingers discovered the delicate string resting on her hips.

I guided her to the bed, and her hair fanned out around her like a dark halo. Her eyes were heavily hooded as she watched me, but I could see the dim white glow radiating from them.

Her stare burned me from the inside. I wanted to worship her. I needed to. Every inch. Starting at the tips of her toes, I worked my way up. Slowly. Some areas held my attention a lot longer. Like the graceful arch of her foot and the sensitive skin behind her knees. The curves of her thighs enticed me, and the valleys above beckoned me.

The way her back arched, her rapid breaths, soft sounds, and how her fingers dug into my skin rattled my world. When finally I climbed my way up to her, I placed my hands on either side of her head.

Staring down at Kat, I fell for her all over again. Lost my heart when she smiled. Found a whole new purpose when she reached between us and touched me. I broke away long enough to grab protection. And the moment there was nothing between us, there was no more waiting, any intentions of selflessness vanished. My hands were greedy. I was greedy, and my hands were everywhere, my lips following their path. Our bodies moved together like there had been no time separating us. And as I stared down at her, my gaze traveling over her flushed cheeks and swollen lips, I knew right then that there'd never be a more beautiful, more perfect moment in my life than this.

I was drunk on her taste, on her touch. There was only the sound of our pounding hearts, until she called out my name, and I broke apart. The room was awash in flickering white light; I wasn't sure if it was coming from her or me, and I didn't care.

For the longest time, I couldn't move. Hell, I didn't want to move. Not with her hands sliding down my back, her breathing ragged in my ears. But my weight had to be crushing her even if she wasn't complaining.

Lifting up, I rolled onto my side. My hand trailed over her rib cage, across her hip, and she turned in to me, wiggling so close that once again there wasn't an inch between us.

"That was perfect," she murmured sleepily.

I still wasn't capable of speech. God only knew what would come out of my mouth at that moment, so I placed a kiss against her damp forehead. She let out a contented sigh, and then she dozed off in my arms. I had been wrong before.

There was not a more perfect, more beautiful moment than *this*. And I wanted a lifetime of them.

• • •

KATY

In the morning, our legs and arms were tangled together, and the sheet twisted around my hips. It took some ninja-stealth moves to wiggle free from Daemon. Stretching my arms above my head, I expelled a happy sigh. My body was one big pleasant ache.

"Mmm, that's sexy."

My eyes snapped open. Startled and exposed, I grabbed for the sheet, but Daemon's hand shot out, catching mine. Fire swept across my face as my gaze collided with his forest-green one.

"What?" he murmured lazily. "You're modest now? Don't really see the point."

Heat swept down my throat, and my skin prickled. Daemon kind of made sense. Modesty hadn't been anywhere last night, but still. Early morning sunlight streamed in from the window. I tugged the sheet from his grip and covered myself.

He pouted, and it was ridiculous that he could do it and still manage to look sexy.

"I'm trying to keep the mystery alive," I told him.

He chuckled, and the deep sound rolled through me. Shifting closer, he kissed the tip of my nose. "Mystery is overrated. I want to get to know every freckle and every curve on a personal level."

"I think you did that last night."

"Nah." He shook his head. "That was just a meet and greet. I want to know their hopes and dreams."

I laughed. "That's ridiculous."

"It's the truth." He rolled then, throwing the sheet off him and swinging his feet to the floor.

My eyes widened.

Naked as the day he was born, he stood fluidly, totally uncaring that every inch of him was displayed. He raised his arms high above his head as he stretched. His back bowed, muscles popped and rippled. The indents by his hips tensed, drawing my attention for far too long to be decent.

Finally, I forced my gaze up. Our eyes met. "You know, there's this thing called pants. You should try it out."

He cast me a cheeky grin as he turned. "You'd be devastated. Just think, you get to see this every day from here on out."

My heart did a trippy dance. "Your naked ass? Gee. Sign me up for that."

He laughed again and then disappeared into the bathroom. Feeling way too warm, I closed my eyes. Every day? Like, forever? That had my tummy fluttering in all kinds of pleasant loops that had nothing to do with his current state of undress. Waking up next to Daemon, going to sleep beside him?

I opened my eyes when I heard the door reopen. He was rubbing his eyes, and I was staring at him again, like really staring at him in completely inappropriate places. It was like knowing you shouldn't look at something, so your eyes automatically just want to go there.

He lowered his arm. "I think you're drooling a little."

"What? I am not." But I might have been. So I tugged the sheet up over my face. "A gentleman would never point out something so unseemly."

"I'm not a gentleman." He shot forward, snatching the sheet from me. I held on, the playful struggle not lasting very long. "There's no hiding. I caught you."

"You suck."

"At least I don't drool on myself." He tossed the sheet to the other side of the massive bed. His slow perusal caused my toes to curl. "Okay. I think *I* might be drooling right now."

My face was going to burn off before breakfast. "Stop it."

"I can't help it." He planted a hand on the other side of my hips and leaned in, brushing his fingers over my chin. "Got the drool."

Laughing, I pushed at his rock-solid chest. "You have an overinflated sense of self-worth."

"Uh huh." He pressed down until our bodies were flush and his thigh was between mine. He supported his weight on his arms as he bent his head, brushing his lips against mine. "Kiss?"

I gripped his upper arms and gave him a quick peck. "There you go."

He lifted his head, scowling. "That was the kind of kiss you give your grandma."

"What? You want a better one?" Craning my neck, I put a little more *oomph* behind the kiss. "How about that?"

"Sucked."

"That's not very nice."

"Try it again," he said, eyes narrowing into lazy slits.

My breath hitched in my throat. "I don't know if you deserve a better kiss after telling me the last one sucked."

He did something truly remarkable with his hips, causing me to gasp. "Yeah," he said smugly. "I deserve another kiss."

Yes—yes he did. I kissed him again but settled back before the kiss could turn into something deeper. Daemon's scowl went up a notch, and I grinned. "That's all you deserve."

"I strongly disagree with that." The tips of his fingers drifted down my arm and across my rib cage. The featherlight touch continued over my stomach and farther south. The whole time his gaze was held to mine. "Try again."

When I didn't move, he did something clever with his fingers that caused my heart to pound against my ribs. I lifted my head, feeling dizzy and light. Brushing my mouth against his, I kissed him again, paying special attention to his lower lip. As I started to pull away, he wrapped his hand around the back of my neck.

"No." His voice was low. "That was barely better. Maybe I just need to show you."

I shivered at the heat in his stare. My entire body tightened. "Maybe you do."

And he did—oh God, did he ever. Last night had been sweet and slow and mind-blowingly perfect, but this was something entirely different and just as heart-stopping. There was a razor edge of desperation to each kiss, to each touch. A rawness had built between us, increasing with every breath we took. Daemon moved over me and then inside me, turning the slow fire into a tempest that burned out of control. My hands grasped at him as the tension inside me unfurled, and the edges of his body blurred as whatever restraint he had snapped.

Neither of us moved for what felt like ages. Our hips still pressed tightly together. My arms locked around his neck. One of his hands lay against my cheek, the other curved around my waist. Even when he rolled onto his side, he brought me with him. He didn't have much of a choice. I wasn't letting him go. I didn't want to. I wanted to press stop on everything and stay there, right there with him. Because I knew the moment we left this bed, left this room, an unknown reality waited. Serious stuff needed to be decided. Decisions that none of us could go back on had to be made.

But I thought about the every-morning thing—the forever. No matter what we faced, we would face it together. That made me ready.

"What are you thinking about, Kitten?" he asked, brushing the hair off my cheek.

I opened my eyes and smiled. "I was just thinking about the things we need to decide on."

"Me, too." He kissed me. "But I think we need to be showered and changed before we go down that road."

I laughed. "True."

"Have I told you that I love the sound of your laugh? Doesn't matter. I'm going to tell you again. I love the sound of your laugh."

"And I love you." I pressed my lips to his and then sat up, taking the sheet with me. "I call dibs on the shower."

Daemon rose up on his elbow. "We can always do it together."

"Yeah, we'd end up needing a shower after taking a shower." Wrapping the sheet around me, I scooted off the bed. "I'll be back."

He winked. "I'll be waiting."

• • •

DAEMON

If I'd had any doubts about Kat being the perfect female before, all doubts would've been cleared up right then. She took a shower in less than five minutes. Remarkable. I hadn't even thought that was humanly possible. Dee's idea of a quick shower was fifteen minutes.

And then she came out, a towel secured under her arms, as she dabbed at her soaked hair. When she looked over at the bed, a pretty flush crawled across her cheeks.

Guess I could've put some clothes on, but then I'd miss that blush of hers.

Throwing my legs off the bed, I strolled over. As I passed her, I tweaked her pink cheek. Her face flamed even brighter, and I laughed as she muttered something very unladylike under her breath.

The bathroom was nice and steamy. As I stood under the showerhead, letting the water beat down on my face, I thought about last night, about this morning. My thoughts spun further back, to the first time I'd seen Kat walking out her front door, heading over to my house to ask directions. Even if I hadn't wanted to admit it in that moment, she had sunk her claws into me, and I didn't want them out.

At that point, my brain pretty much unloaded a bunch of crap on me. Bringing up memories I'd almost forgotten—of Kat arguing with me over the flower bed and refusing to go to the lake with me the day Dee had hid my keys. Like I had needed my keys to go somewhere.

Even then I'd been looking for a reason to spend time with her. There were so many moments. Like when she went ninja on the Arum after homecoming. She had risked her life for me, even when I'd been nothing but a giant tool to her. And Halloween night? She would've died for Dee and me.

I would've died for her.

Where would we go from there? Not just where would we end up living or any of that crap, but both of us had and would sacrifice just about anything for each other. There was a next step involved. I thought about the car ride there, when I'd been staring at her left hand.

My heart did a funny thing in my chest, something between a panicked squeeze and an excited jump. I dipped my head back under the stream. Something was building in my chest, piling up until there was no denying what I wanted. My hands curled into fists against the tile.

Shit.

Was I really thinking this? Yes. Did I really want this? Hell yes. Was it probably the craziest thing I'd ever considered? Most definitely. Was it going to stop me? Nah. Did I feel like I was going to pass out? Only a little.

I'd been in the shower for more than fifteen minutes.

I was such a girl.

That panicked/excited feeling was increasing as I turned to the faucets, shutting the water off. My hand trembled a little, and my eyes narrowed.

I should really think about this.

Then again, who was I kidding? When I set my mind to something, I did it. And my mind was set. No pussyfooting around it. No point in waiting. It was right. It *felt* right. And that's what mattered—the only thing that mattered.

I was in love with her. I would always be.

Wrapping a towel around my hips, I entered the bedroom. Kat sat on the bed, cross-legged in jeans and wearing her MY BLOG IS BETTER THAN YOUR VLOG shirt. Yep, that pretty much sealed the deal for me.

"So I was thinking," I said, my mouth moving before my brain really caught up with it. "There're eighty-six thousand, four hundred seconds in a day, right? There're one thousand, four hundred and forty minutes in a day."

Her brow knitted. "Okay. I'll take your word for it."

"I'm right." I tapped my finger against my head. "A lot of useless knowledge up here. Anyway, are you following me? There're one hundred and sixty-eight hours in a week. Around eighty-seven hundred and then some hours in a year, and you know what?"

She smiled. "What?"

"I want to spend every second, every minute, every hour with you." Part of me couldn't believe something that cheesy had come out of my mouth, but it was also so beautifully true. "I want a year's worth of seconds and minutes with you. I want a decade's worth of hours, so many that I can't add them up."

Her chest rose sharply as she stared at me, eyes widening.

I took one more step and then went down on one knee in front of her, in a towel. Probably should have put some pants on. "Do you want that?" I asked.

Kat's eyes met mine, and the answer was immediate. "Yes. I want that. You know I want that."

"Good." My lips curved up. "So let's get married."

Chapter 25

Katy

Time stopped. My heart skipped a beat and then took several leaps. My stomach felt like I was hurdling mountains. I stared at him so long that one single dark brow rose.

"Kitten…?" He tipped his head to the side. Strands of wet hair fell across his forehead. "Are you breathing?"

Was I? I wasn't sure. All I could do was stare at him. He couldn't have said what I thought he had. *Let's get married*. The statement, because I was pretty sure it wasn't a question, came so far out of left field that I was stunned.

A lopsided grin appeared on his face. "Okay. Your silence is stretching out further than I'd thought it would."

I blinked. "Sorry. It's just…what did you ask me?"

He chuckled deeply and reached over, threading his fingers through mine. "I said: let's get married."

Sucking in another deep breath, I squeezed his hand as my heart did another flip. "Are you serious?"

"Serious as I'll ever be," he replied.

"Did you hit your head in the bathroom? Because you were in there a long time."

Daemon barked out a laugh. "No. Should I be offended by that question?"

I flushed. "No. It's just…you want to marry me? Like, really get married?"

"Is there more than one kind of marriage, Kitten?" His lips were tilting up again. "It wouldn't be legal, because we'd have to use our new IDs, so in a way, it wouldn't be real, but it would be real to me—to *us*. I want to do this. Right now. I don't have a ring, but I promise I'll get you one worthy of you when things…things die down. We're in Vegas. No better place. I want to marry you, Kat. Today."

"Today?" My voice came out a squeak. I thought I might faint.

"Yes. Today."

"But we're…" We were young, but really, was there such a thing as too young for us? I was eighteen, months shy from turning nineteen. I had always pictured being at least in my mid-twenties before I tied the knot, but our future was so unknown to us. And it wasn't the common world that people faced every day, not knowing how short their lives may very well be. We were on the sucky statistic side of things not working in our favor. If we didn't manage to make it into hiding and were captured again, I doubted Daedalus would be so keen on allowing us to be together. That is, if we survived any of this. We didn't have the guarantee of years to figure out our relationship.

"But what?" he asked softly.

I wasn't sure we needed those years to determine if we wanted to be together. I knew right that second that I wanted to spend the rest of my life with Daemon, but it wasn't that simple. Something else could be driving this decision of his.

He squeezed my hand. "Kat?"

My heart was going crazy fast. I felt like I was on top of a roller coaster. "Are you wanting to do this because tomorrow may never come? Is that why you want to marry me? Because there might not be a later to do this?"

He leaned back. "Can I say that doesn't play some role in wanting to do this now? No. It does. But it's not the sole reason or even the major reason why I want to marry you. It's more like the catalyst."

"The catalyst," I whispered.

He nodded. "I'm going to do everything in my power to make sure nothing bad happens. I will do anything to make sure we have the time for *everything* that we want, but I'm not stupid enough to disregard the fact that something may happen that I can't control. And, dammit, I don't want to look back and see that I didn't seize the chance to make you mine, to really prove that I want to spend the rest of my life with you. That I lost that opportunity."

Air hitched around the sudden lump in my throat. Tears burned my eyes.

"I want to marry you because I'm *in love* with you, Kat. I will *always* be in love with you. That's not going to change today or two weeks from now. I will be just as in love with you in twenty years as I am today." He let go of my hand and rose slightly, cupping my cheek. "That's why I want to marry you."

The tears welled up, and a few snuck out. He caught each one with his thumb. "Are the tears a good or a bad thing?"

"It's just…that was such a beautiful thing to say." I wiped at my face, feeling like an overemotional fool on the verge of having a stroke. "So you really want to get married today?"

"Yes, Kat, I really want to get married."

"In a towel?"

His head tipped back, and he let out a deep laugh. "Maybe I'll put some clothes on."

My thoughts raced. "But where?"

"There are tons of places in Vegas."

"Is it safe to go out there?"

He nodded. "I think so, if we're quick about this."

A quickie marriage in Vegas? I almost laughed because we would be just one in a million who came to Vegas and got married. Some of the numbness faded with the acknowledgment of how…common it was to do this.

To get married.

My heart did a backflip.

"If you're not ready, that's okay. We don't need to do this," he said, his eyes meeting mine. "I'm not going to be upset if you don't feel it's the right time, but I am going to ask one more time. You don't even have to say no. Just don't say anything. Okay?" He took a little breath. "Will you make me the luckiest bastard on Earth and marry me, Katy Swartz?"

My breath shuddered. Tension rolled through my entire body. I'd imagined a proposal being very different than this. It never involved a towel, and I'd have a long engagement, plan a wedding, and have family and friends witness the moment, but…

But I was in love with Daemon. And like he'd said, I'd be in love with him tomorrow and twenty years from now. That was never going to change. The emotions were complex, but the answer was simple.

I took a breath, and it felt like the first breath I'd ever taken. "Yes."

He stared at me in wonder. "Yes?"

I nodded vigorously, like a seal. "Yes. I will marry you. Today. Tomorrow. Whenever."

In the blink of an eye, he was standing, and I was captured in his strong embrace. His arms were tight around me, my feet several inches off the floor, and his mouth was on mine. That kiss was more a stake of claim than any marriage certificate could be.

I came up for air, clutching his shoulders. He'd started to glow a beautiful soft white as he stared back at me with a look of awe in his expression. I smiled. "Well, let's get this show on the road."

• • •

Daemon

I wouldn't let Kat change her shirt. I had a fondness for it. After all, it was the first shirt I'd seen her in, and I thought it was fitting.

Feeling like I might have just climbed Mount Everest in a second, I quickly changed into a pair of jeans and a shirt. Okay. Maybe not quickly. I kept getting distracted with Kat's lips, because those lips had said yes, which made them suddenly something I couldn't stop touching.

They were swollen by the time we made it downstairs. Still early, only Lyla was up. I had no qualms about asking her to borrow a car, because I didn't want Kat to hoof it into Vegas. Lyla easily gave up her keys to a Jag, which I traded in for a Volkswagen I saw in the garage, along with two more cars she owned. My fingers itched to get behind the wheel of a Jag, but that would draw way too much attention.

I honestly didn't think we'd run into any problems. The last place Daedalus would be looking for us would be at a place we could get married, but I took the same appearance of the guy I'd used in the motel, and we found a floppy sun hat and glasses for Katy.

"I look like a fake celebrity," she said, staring at herself in the side mirror. She twisted toward me. "And you're kind of hot."

I snorted. "I'm not sure if I should be bothered by that."

She giggled. "You know, Dee is going to kill us."

We'd decided not to tell anyone. Mainly because Matthew would probably object, Dee would freak out, and, honestly, we wanted to do this alone. It was our moment. Our little slice of pie that we weren't sharing.

"She'll get over it," I said, knowing that was doubtful. Dee would probably kill me for not being able to take part. Coasting the VW out of the driveway and down the access road, I reached over and patted

Kat's thigh. "Serious moment, okay? When all of this crap is settled, if you want the big wedding and all that jazz, I'll make it work. You just need to tell me."

She took off her oversize sunglasses. "Big weddings cost a lot of money."

"And I have a lot of money stashed away. Enough to make sure we have nothing to worry about until we figure out what we're doing, so more than enough to cover a wedding."

She shook her head. "I don't want the big wedding. I just want you."

I almost stopped the VW right there and crawled all over her. "Just keep it in mind for later if you change your mind." I wanted to give her everything—the ring that weighed her finger down and the wedding to end all weddings. Neither was feasible right now—and, I had to admit, I was turned on by the fact she didn't seem to care about either of those things.

Okay. I was almost always turned on by her, but that was beside the point.

"You know where I want to get married? Married. Wow. I can't believe I just said that. Anyway," Kat said, her eyes lighting up under the brim of her hat. "I want to do the little church—the one everyone goes to Vegas to get married at."

It took me a moment. "You mean The Little White Wedding Chapel? The one in *The Hangover*?"

Kat laughed. "It's sad that's how you know the church, but yes. I think there are a couple of them in Vegas. And it should be perfect. I doubt they require much but the fee and an ID."

I shot her a grin. "If that's what you want, you got it."

It didn't take us long to get into Vegas and to stop at one of the tourist vendors. Kat hopped out and grabbed a handful of brochures. One of them was about the chapel. Apparently impromptu weddings were a big theme. Duh.

We had to get a marriage license.

She frowned. "I don't want to do it under our fake names."

"Neither do I." I pulled up in front of the courthouse, letting the engine run. "But it's too risky to use our real names. Besides, we'll need the marriage license under our useable ID. You and I will always know the difference."

She nodded and grabbed the door handle, but her fingers slipped off. "You're right. Well, let's do this."

"Hey." I stopped her. "You're sure, right? You want this?"

She faced me. "I'm positive. I want this. I'm just nervous." Leaning in, she tipped her head to the side and kissed me. The edge of her hat brushed my cheek. "I love you. This…this feels right."

Air punched from my lungs. "It does."

Sixty dollars later, we had a marriage license in hand, and we were en route to the chapel on the Boulevard. Since our fake IDs were under the images of our real selves, I'd have to change back over once we pulled into the parking lot.

The whole drive, I kept an eye out for anyone suspicious. The problem with that was that everyone looked suspicious to me at the moment. Even as early as it was, the streets were teeming with tourists and people heading to work. I knew there could be implants anywhere, but I doubted there'd be one dressed as Elvis or hidden in a chapel.

Kat squeezed my arm when the sign for the chapel came into view. The heart on the side was a nice, gaudy touch. "The Little White Wedding Chapel isn't so little," she said as I turned into the parking lot.

I parked the car, and as I pulled the keys out of the ignition, I slid back into the form Kat was accustomed to.

An amused smile lit her face. "Better."

"I thought the other guy was hot?"

"Not as hot as you." She patted my knee, then pulled back. "I've got the license."

Turning to the window, I almost couldn't believe that we were here. Not that I was having second thoughts or anything, but I couldn't believe we were actually doing this, that in an hour or so, we'd be man and wife.

Or Luxen and hybrid.

We hurried inside and met with the "wedding planner." Handing over our license, IDs, and the fee, we got the ball rolling. The bleach-blonde behind the counter tried selling us every package they had, including the ones where we could rent a tux and gown.

Kat shook her head. She'd taken off the hat and sunglasses. "We just need someone to marry us. That's all."

The blonde flashed an ultra-white smile as she leaned against the counter. "You two lovebirds in a hurry?"

I dropped an arm over Kat's shoulders. "You could say that."

"If you just want something quick, no bells and whistles or a witness, then we have Minister Lincoln. He's not included in the fee, so we do ask for a donation."

"Sounds good." I bent down, brushing my lips along Kat's temple. "You want anything else? If so, we'll do it. Whatever it is."

Kat shook her head. "I just want you. That's all we need."

I smiled and glanced at the blonde. "Well, there you go."

The woman stood. "You two are adorable. Follow me."

Kat bumped me with her hip as we trailed behind the blonde entering the "Tunnel of Love"—and boy did I have a ton of nasty comments building up in me about the name of that. I'd save them for later.

Minister Lincoln was an older man who looked more like a grandfather than some guy who married people on a whim in Vegas. We chatted with him for a few minutes, and then we had to wait for another twenty while he finished up a few things. The delays were starting to make me paranoid, and I expected an army to storm the chapel any second. I needed a distraction.

I pulled Kat onto my lap and circled my arms around her waist. While we waited, I told her about the ceremonies my kind did, which were very much like a human wedding with the exception of rings.

"Is there anything you do in its place?" she asked.

Tucking her hair back behind her ear, I smiled a little. "You'll think it's gross."

"I want to know."

My hand lingered along the curve of her neck. "It's kind of like a blood oath. We're in our true form." I kept my voice low, just in case anyone was listening, though I was sure stranger things were heard in the Tunnel of Love. "Our fingers are pricked and pressed together. That's about it."

She lightly stroked my hand. "That's not too gross. I was expecting you to say something like you have to run around naked or consummate the relationship in front of everyone."

I dropped my head to her shoulder and laughed. "You have such a dirty mind, Kitten. That's why I love you."

"That's all?" She wiggled down so that her cheek was beside mine.

My grip tightened. "You know better than that."

"Can we do it—what your kind does—later?" she asked, tapping her finger on my chest. "When things die down?"

"If that's what you want."

"It is. I think that would make it more real, you know?"

"Miss Whitt? Mr. Rowe?" The blonde appeared at the opened doors. I was sure the tan chick had a name but couldn't recall it for the life of me. "We're ready when you are."

Hoisting Kat to her feet, I took her hand. The chapel portion was actually pretty nice. Enough room if you wanted people to be there. White roses were everywhere—on the ends of the pews, bouquets of them in the corners and hanging from the ceiling and placed upon the pedestals at the front. Minister Lincoln stood between the pedestals, holding a bible in his hand. He smiled when he saw us.

Our steps made no sound on the red carpet. Actually, we could've been stomping our feet and I wouldn't have heard it over the pounding of my heart. We stopped in front of the minister. He said something. I nodded. God only knew what it was. We were told to face each other, and we did, our hands joined.

Minister Lincoln kept talking, but it was like Charlie Brown's teacher, because I didn't understand a single word of it. My gaze was locked on Kat's face, my attention focused on the feel of her hands in mine and the warmth of her body next to me. At some point I heard the important words.

"I now pronounce you husband and wife. You may kiss the bride."

I think my heart exploded. Kat was staring up at me, her gray eyes wide and misty. For a moment, I couldn't move. Like I was frozen for a precious few seconds, and then I was moving, cupping her cheeks and tilting her head back. I kissed her. I'd kissed her at least a thousand times before this, but this one—oh, yeah—this one was different. The touch and taste of her reached down into me and branded my soul.

"I love you," I said, kissing her. "I love you so very much."

She gripped my sides. "And I love you."

Before I knew it, I was smiling, and then I was laughing like an idiot, but I didn't care. I pulled her into my arms, cradling her head against my chest. Our hearts were racing, beating in tandem—*we* were in tandem. And in that moment, it seemed like everything we'd been through, everything we'd lost and had to give up, was worth it. This was what mattered—would always matter the most.

CHAPTER 26

KATY

Feeling like one of those cartoon characters that daintily raised a leg when she was kissed by Prince Charming, I was dizzy with happiness and absolutely swept off my feet in a way I never believed possible. It was just a piece of paper I clenched in my hand. A certificate of marriage between two names that weren't even real.

But it meant the world.

It meant everything.

I couldn't stop smiling, nor could I get the emotional lump out of my throat. Since we'd exchanged vows, I'd been in a constant state of almost crying. Daemon probably thought I was insane.

On the way out, the blonde from the front stopped us. She handed me a photo. "On me," she said, smiling. "You two are a beautiful couple. It would be a shame if you didn't have something to capture the moment."

Daemon peered over my shoulder. The photo was of our kiss—our first kiss as a married couple. "Good Lord," I said, feeling my cheeks burn. "I'm pretty sure we're eating each other's faces."

He laughed.

The blonde smiled as she stepped aside. "I think that's the kind of passion that lasts a lifetime. You're lucky."

"I know." And in that instant, I did know how lucky I was, all things considered. I looked up at my...*my husband*. Deep down, I knew the marriage wasn't legal, but it felt real to me. My eyes wanted to start with the waterworks again. "I do know how lucky I am."

Daemon rewarded me with a scorching kiss that lifted me clear off the floor. Any other time I would've been embarrassed by that, since we were in public, but I didn't care. Not at all.

We totally cornballed it up on the way back to the house, holding hands and making googly eyes. It took us a couple of minutes to get out of the car. The moment he turned off the engine, we were all over each other. Greedy—we both were so greedy. The kissing wasn't enough. I crawled over the gearshift, straddling his lap. My hands were under his shirt, against the ridges of his stomach. He slid his hands up my back, tracing the line of my spine until his fingers tangled in my hair.

I was breathing heavily when he pulled back, pressing his head against the seat. "Okay," he said. "If we don't stop, we're going to do something very naughty in this car."

I giggled. "That's one hell of a way to pay her back for letting us borrow it."

"No doubt." He reached over and opened the driver's door. Cool air washed over us. "You better get going before I change my mind."

I wasn't sure if I wanted him to change his mind, but I forced myself to climb out of the car. Daemon was right behind me, his hands on my hips as we entered the house through the door that led into a small pantry.

Matthew was in front of us the moment we stepped into the kitchen, blue eyes flashing with anger. "Where in the hell have you two been?"

"Out," replied Daemon. He stepped around, blocking most of Matthew.

"Out?" Matthew sounded flabbergasted.

I peeked around Daemon, holding the license close to my chest. "I wanted to see a few things."

Matthew's mouth dropped open.

"I really don't think that was a good idea," Archer said, appearing in the open archway. "To go sightseeing when you have half the government gunning for your ass."

Daemon stiffened. "It's all good. No one saw us. Now if you would excuse us…"

Archer's eyes narrowed. "I can't believe you two…"

The whole time he was talking, I was singing "Don't Cha" in my head, desperately trying not to think about the marriage, but one of us must've failed, because Archer's mouth snapped shut, and he looked floored. Like someone just explained to him that you can have an endless salad bowl at Olive Garden.

Please don't say anything. Please. I kept thinking the words over and over, hoping he was peeping in my head at the moment.

Matthew glanced back at Archer, brows furrowed. "You okay, bud?"

Shaking his head, Archer pivoted on his heel and muttered, "Whatever."

"I know you're butt sore about this, Matthew. We're sorry. We'll never do it again." Daemon reached back, finding my hand. He started forward. "And you can yell at us all you want in about…five or so hours."

Matthew folded his arms. "What are you up to?"

Sliding past him, Daemon cast him a cheeky grin. "It's not what. More like who." I smacked his back, which was ignored. "So can your epic lecture hold off for a little while?"

Matthew really wasn't given a chance to say any more. We breezed out of the kitchen and through a purposeless room with lots of statues and a table in the middle. Dee's and Ash's voices echoed from another room.

"We'd better hurry," Daemon said, "or we'll never get away."

Though I was eager to spend some quality time with Dee, I knew why we were hurrying. Halfway up the stairs, Daemon turned and wrapped his arm under my knees, picking me up.

Biting back on the giggles, I looped my arms around his neck. "That's not necessary."

"Totally is," he said, and then made like an alien. Within seconds, he was placing my feet on the floor of the bedroom and closing the door behind us.

Clothing didn't stay on very long. Things were fast and tumultuous at first. He spun around, backing me up until I hit the door, his large body crowding mine. There was something different about what was happening. It seemed truer in its nature, as if that funny piece of paper that was now lying on the floor changed everything, and maybe it did. My legs were wrapped around his hips, and everything moved at a fevered pitch. I told him that I loved him. I showed him that I loved him. And he did the same. We finally made it to the bed, and things were sweet and tender then.

Hours passed, probably a little more than the five that Daemon had promised Matthew. No one had interrupted us, which was surprising. I was mighty comfortable in his arms, my cheek resting against his chest. I know it might sound stupid, but I loved listening to his heartbeat.

Daemon played with my hair, twisting strands around his fingers while we talked about anything and everything that had nothing to do with the immediate future and everything to do with the one we hoped for—the one where we were in college, we had jobs.

We had a life.

It was good, like cleansing the soul in a way.

Then my stomach grumbled like Godzilla.

Daemon chuckled. "Okay. We've got to get some food in there before you start gnawing on me."

"Too late," I said, nipping at his lower lip. He made that sexy sound in his throat, the kind that led to things that would take up another couple of hours. I forced myself to put some distance between us. "We need to go downstairs."

"So you can eat?" He sat up, running a hand through his hair. He looked adorably disheveled.

"Yeah, but we also need to find out what everyone is doing." Reality was a bit sobering. "We need to figure out what *we're* doing."

"I know." He bent over the edge of the bed and picked up my shirt. He tossed it to me. "But there better be food involved."

Thank God there was. Dee was in the kitchen making a late lunch—or was it an early dinner?—consisting of cold cuts. Daemon headed off toward the sound of his brother's voice, and I sidled up to Dee.

"Can I help?" I asked, rocking back.

She glanced at me. "I'm almost done. What kind do you want? Ham? Turkey?"

"Ham, pretty please." I grinned. "Daemon probably wants ham, too. And I can make them if you haven't."

"Daemon wants anything he can consume." She reached up, grabbing a paper plate. I thought it was kind of funny that this house even had paper plates in it. As she slapped two ham sandwiches on it, a burst of loud, male laughter caused her to glance over her shoulder. She looked relieved.

"What?" I asked, glancing back to the hall Daemon had disappeared down.

"I don't know." A small smile appeared. "I'm just surprised. Archer is in that room. I figured there'd be yelling instead of laughter."

"Daemon is just...you know, a bit overprotective when it comes to you."

His sister laughed. "A bit?"

"Okay. A lot. It's not against Archer. He's actually a really good guy. He helped me—helped us—while we were with Daedalus, but he's older, he's different, and he—"

"Has a penis?" Dee supplied. "Because I think that's Daemon's main problem."

Giggling, I grabbed two cans of soda. "Yeah, you're probably right. So have you been talking to him?"

She shrugged. "Not much. He's not very talkative."

"He's a guy of few words." I leaned my hip against the counter. "And he hasn't been exposed to a lot. So he's probably just taking all of this in."

She gave a little shake of her head. "It's just insane and horrible what they're doing to people. And there's more, right? I wish there was something we could do."

I thought about the hybrids I'd seen and the origins we let loose. Could some of them have escaped? Setting the cans aside, I sighed. "There's so much wrong with so much."

"That is true."

There was another explosion of laughter that I recognized as Daemon's. I was smiling like a goofball before I even realized it.

"Look at you. Aren't you chipper today." Dee elbowed me. "What's going on?"

I shrugged. "Just a really good day. I'll have to tell you about it soon."

She handed me a cold cut. "If it's what you two have been doing in that room upstairs all afternoon, I don't even want to know."

I laughed. "I'm not talking about that."

"Thank God." Ash slinked between us, grabbing the jar of mayo. "Because no one wants to hear about that."

Unless it involved Ash's past with Daemon, then she was all kinds of talkative, but whatever. I smiled at her, which earned me a strange look.

Ash grabbed a spoon, scooped up some mayo, and popped it in her mouth. My stomach turned. "The fact that you're so damn skinny and you eat mayo by the spoonful is universally messed up."

She winked a catlike eye. "Be jealous."

The funny thing was, I wasn't.

"Then again, maybe I'm the one who should be jealous, *Kitten*."

Dee smacked Ash's arm. "Don't start."

She grinned as she tossed the spoon in the sink. "I didn't say I wanted to be his Kitten, but if I did, well…this story may have a different ending."

A couple of months ago, she would've gotten a rise out of me. Now I just smiled.

She stared at me a moment, and then her blue eyes rolled. "Whatever."

I watched her leave the kitchen. "I think I'm growing on her," I said to Dee.

She giggled as she put the last sandwich on the platter. There were more than a dozen. "Actually, I think the biggest problem is that Ash *wants* to dislike you."

"She does a good job at it."

"But I don't think that's how she really feels." Dee picked up the platter, cocking her head to the side. "She really did care for Daemon. I don't think it was ever love, but I think she always believed that they'd be together. That's a lot to get over."

I sort of felt guilty. "I know."

"But she will. Besides, she'll find someone who can tolerate her bitchiness, and all will be right in the world."

"And you?"

She giggled and winked. "I just want everything to be right in the world for *one* night—if you know what I mean."

I choked on my laugh. "Good God, do not let Daemon or Dawson hear that."

"No kidding."

Everyone was in the rec room—bodies draped over couches, settees, and lounges. The biggest TV I'd ever seen hung on the wall, damn near the size of a theater screen.

Daemon patted the spot beside him on the couch, and I sat down, handing him his plate and soda. "Thank you."

"Your sister made them. I just carried ours."

Dee placed the platter on the coffee table and glanced over to where Archer sat with Luc and Paris. Then she took two sandwiches and retreated to the burgundy settee. Two pink spots bloomed on her cheeks, and I hoped she was having nice, clean thoughts.

One glance at Archer, who was now staring at Dee, had me assuming that she wasn't.

On the other side of me, Dawson leaned forward and grabbed two of the subs, one for him and the other for Beth. The girl was bundled up in a quilt, looking half asleep. Our eyes met, and a tentative smile brightened her face.

"How are you feeling?" I asked.

"Great." She picked at the bread, pulling off little brown patches. "I'm just tired."

Again, I wondered what could possibly be wrong with her, because something was. She didn't look just tired; she looked absolutely exhausted.

"It's been a lot of traveling," Dawson elaborated. "It's kind of worn me out, too."

He didn't look worn out. If anything, he looked like he was bursting at the seams. His green eyes were particularly bright, especially every time he looked at Beth.

Which was all the time.

"Eat," he said quietly to her. "You need to eat at least two of these."

She laughed softly. "I don't know about two."

We stayed there for a while, long after the food was gone, and I think everyone was delaying the inevitable—the big talk. So much so that Matthew left the room, telling us he'd be back in a few moments.

Daemon leaned forward, dropping his hands to his knees. "Time to get down to business."

"True dat," Luc said. "We need to get on the road soon. Tomorrow would be best."

"I think that's assumed," Andrew said. "But where exactly on the road are we heading to?"

Luc opened his mouth, but Archer held up a hand, silencing him. "Hold that thought."

The younger origin's eyes narrowed, but then he sat back, his jaw clenched. Archer stood and strode out of the room, hands closing into fists.

"What's going on?" Daemon asked.

Unease snaked down my spine. I glanced over at Dawson, who also was suddenly on alert. "Luc," I said, feeling my heart trip up.

Luc stood, his chest rising sharply. One second he was standing in front of the settee and the next he was across the room, a hand around Lyla's throat. "How long?" he demanded.

"Holy shit." Andrew jumped to his feet, moving in front of his sister and Dee.

"How long?" Luc demanded again, his fingers tightening on her throat.

Blood drained from the female Luxen's face. "I-I don't know what you m-mean."

Daemon stood slowly and stepped forward. His brother was behind him. "What's going on?"

Luc ignored him, lifting the frightened Luxen off the floor. "I'm going to give you five seconds to answer the question. One. Four—"

"I didn't have a choice," she gasped out, clutching the boy's wrist.

My blood chilled.

Understanding rippled across the room, followed by horror. I moved closer to Beth, who was struggling to unwrap herself from the blanket.

"Wrong answer," Luc said, voice low as he dropped Lyla. "You always have a choice. It's the one thing that no one can strip from us."

Luc moved so quickly that I doubted even Daemon could fully track what he did. His arm shot out. White swirled down his arm, exploding from his hand. A wave of heat and power flowed through the room, blowing the hair back from my face.

The energy smacked into Lyla's chest, throwing her backward into the oil painting of the Vegas Strip. A look of shock crossed her face, and then there was nothing. Her eyes were blank as she slid down the wall, her legs tucking under her.

Oh my God… I stepped back, clamping my hand over my mouth.

There was a hole in Lyla's chest. Smoke wafted out of it.

A second later, she blurred like bad reception, and then she was in her true form, the luminous glow fading until it revealed the translucent skin and network of dull veins.

"Care to explain why you just killed our host?" Daemon asked in a dangerously even voice.

Archer reappeared in the wide opening of the room, one hand clamped on the back of Matthew's neck and a crushed phone in the other. Blood trickled out from Matthew's nose, a deeper red with a blue tint to it.

Daemon and Dawson shot forward. "What the hell?" Daemon's voice thundered through the house. "You have two seconds to answer that question before I tear this room apart with your ass."

"Your friend here was making a phone call." Archer's tone was flat, so calm that a shudder worked its way through my muscles. "Tell them, Matthew, tell them who you were calling."

There was no response from Matthew. He just stared at Daemon and Dawson.

Archer's grip tightened, jerking Matthew's head back. "The bastard was on the phone with Daedalus. He screwed us. Bad."

Chapter 27

Katy

Daemon stepped back, actually physically recoiling from the accusation. "No." His voice was hoarse. "No way."

"I'm sorry," Matthew said. "I couldn't let this happen."

"Let what happen?" Dee said. Her face was pale as her hands clenched at her sides.

Matthew didn't take his eyes off Daemon. His voice, his entire being pleaded with Daemon to understand the unthinkable. "I can't keep losing you all—you're my family, and Adam is dead. He's dead because of what Daedalus wants. You have to understand. It's the last thing I wanted to go through again."

A cold sensation raced through my veins. "Again?"

Matthew's vibrant blue eyes slid toward me, and it was like the shutters were off. For the first time, I saw the distrust and the loathing in his stare. So potent and powerful, it reached across the room and latched onto me. "*This* is why we don't mix with humans. Accidents happen, and it's in our nature to save the ones we love. That's why we don't love humans. It leads to this! The moment one of us gets involved with a human, Daedalus is only a few steps behind."

"Oh my God." Dee clasped her hands over her mouth.

Paris *tsk*ed softly. "That is a terrible reason to betray those you consider family."

"You wouldn't understand!" Matthew struggled free from Archer's grip. "If I have to sacrifice one to save everyone else, I will. I *have* done it. It has been for the best."

I was dumbfounded. Struck absolutely stupid for a few seconds, but then I thought of that night Daemon and I had gone to Matthew after we saw the Arum go into the house with Nancy—the same night Matthew had confirmed that if Beth was alive, Dawson had to be.

There had been so much that Matthew had known that we never questioned. And the fact that he knew about this place and never mentioned it before? Horror rose in me as I stared at him.

Luc cocked his head to the side. "What did they offer you? Everyone would go free if you turned over just one of them? An equal exchange. A life for a handful of others?"

I was going to be sick.

"They wanted Daemon and Kat," he said, his gaze sliding back to Daemon. "They promised that everyone else would walk away from this."

"Are you insane?" shrieked Dee. "How is that helping anyone?"

"It will!" Matthew roared. "Why do you think they left Daemon and you alone? You two knew about Dawson's relationship and that Bethany knew the truth about us. All of you were at risk. I had to do something."

"No." Beth's quiet voice shook the room. "My uncle was the one who turned us—"

"Your uncle confirmed what was suspected," Matthew spat. "When they came to me about you two, they gave me an option. If

I told the truth about the extent of your relationship and what you knew, everyone else would be left alone."

"You son of a bitch." The edges of Daemon's body started to blur. "You turned over Dawson to them? My brother?" Venom dripped from his words.

Matthew shook his head. "You know what they do to Luxen who break the rules. They are never heard from again. They threatened to take you all in." He spun toward Ash and Andrew. "Even you. I had no choice."

Energy crackled through the room.

"Yeah, they end up in Daedalus," Archer said, his hands flexing. "Right to the same place you just sent Daemon and Katy."

"You told them about Beth and me?" Dawson's voice broke halfway through.

Matthew nodded his head again. "I'm sorry, but you exposed everyone to them."

Daemon looked stricken, as if he'd been sucker punched, but the sudden heat rising in the room wasn't coming from him. It was from Dawson. A fine current of energy rolled out from him.

"It's the same now." Matthew pressed his hands together, as if he were about to pray. "All they want is Daemon and Katy. Everyone else, including you and Beth, will walk away from this. I had to do it. I have to protect—"

Dawson reacted so quickly that if anyone in the room wanted to stop him, he or she didn't have a chance. Rearing back, he sent a blast of pure, unstable energy straight into Matthew. The bolt slammed into Matthew's chest, spinning him around.

I knew Matthew was dead before he hit the ground.

I knew it was Dee who screamed.

I knew it was Daemon who grabbed my arm and pulled me from the room.

I knew it was Archer's voice that rose above the chaos, joining Daemon's in issuing orders.

And I knew we had to get out of there. Fast.

But I never expected that Matthew would do something like this, or that Dawson would kill him without so much as blinking an eye.

"Stay with me, Kitten." Daemon's deep voice glided over my skin. We were passing the kitchen. "I need you to—"

"I'm fine," I cut in, watching Luc spin around to pull a thunderstruck Ash into the foyer. "They're coming. Now."

"You can bet your little behind on that," Archer said, reaching behind him. He pulled out a gun.

"I don't like you talking about Kat's behind, but besides that, where are we going?" Daemon asked, his grip on my hand tightening. "What's the plan? Run out of here like we're insane?"

"Sounds about right," Andrew said. "Unless we all want to get carted away."

"No." Luc kept a careful eye on Dawson and Beth. The Luxen was still sprouting some major rage face. "We head out of town, toward Arizona. I got a place those assholes won't find. But we have to get out of the city."

Daemon glanced at his brother. "Sound good to you?" When Dawson nodded, Daemon let go of my hand and stepped up to his brother, clasping him on the shoulder. "You did what you had to do."

Dawson placed a hand over Daemon's. "I'd do it again."

"All right, family bonding time aside, anyone who gets into one of these cars outside is in it for the long haul," Paris said, shaking a set of car keys. "If you even think you're not ready to put your life on the line for everyone here, then you stay behind. If you screw us out there, I will end you." He flashed a rather charming smile. "And I will probably enjoy it."

Daemon cut him a dark look but said, "I second that."

"I'm already in it this far," Andrew said, shrugging. "Might as well go all the way."

Everyone looked at Ash.

"What?" she said, tucking short strands of hair behind her ears. "Look. If I didn't want to take part in this craziness, I would've stayed home, but I'm here."

She had a point, but I wanted to ask why she or Andrew would risk everything when they weren't fans of Beth or me. Then it hit me. It wasn't about us. It was about Daemon and Dawson—it was about family.

I could get behind that.

We hurried toward the front door, but at the last second, I grabbed Daemon's arm. "Wait a minute! I need to go upstairs."

Archer whirled around. "Whatever it is, we can leave it. It's not important."

"Daemon..." My fingers dug in. I assumed everyone else had their IDs. I didn't know, but we *needed* our papers. We had to have them.

"Shit." He got what I was talking about. "Go ahead outside. I'll be faster."

Nodding, I darted around him and rejoined Archer. "Really?" he growled in a low voice. "Those *papers* are that important."

"Yes." We didn't have rings. We didn't have a certificate under our real names and, yeah, it wasn't *real*, but we had that license, our fake IDs, and right now those things meant everything. They were our future.

Dawson already had Beth loaded in the backseat of an SUV. Ash and Andrew were climbing in with them.

"Go with them," I told Archer, knowing he'd keep them safe. "We'll go with Paris and Luc."

Archer didn't hesitate. He intercepted Dawson and got behind the wheel. "You want me driving in case stuff goes down. Trust me."

Dawson didn't look convinced, and in that moment he was an exact replica of his brother, but he did something Daemon pretty much never did. He didn't argue. Just got in the passenger side and shut up.

A second later, Daemon appeared behind me. "They're in my back pocket."

"Thank you."

We climbed into the Hummer, Paris behind the wheel and Luc in the front. Luc twisted around as we slammed the doors shut. "Sorry about Matthew," he said to Daemon. "I know you were close. He was family. That sucked. But people do sucky things when they're desperate."

"And dumb," Paris muttered under his breath.

Daemon nodded as he settled back against the seat. He glanced at me and lifted the arm closest to me. I didn't hesitate. Heart aching something fierce, I scooted over and pressed against his side. His arm came around me, his fingers digging into my arm.

"I'm sorry," I whispered to him. "I'm so sorry."

"Shh," he murmured. "You have nothing to be sorry for."

There was a lot to be sorry for. Things I couldn't really even wrap my head around as we peeled out of the driveway. And the other things, like the fact that Daedalus was most likely en route right now? Yeah, I couldn't think about that. Panic was already simmering inside, wanting to sink its claws in me. I'd be useless freaking out.

The gate up ahead wasn't opening. Daemon held on tight as Paris didn't break. He plowed through the metal gate.

"Good thing we're in a Hummer," Luc said.

Daemon reached for the seat belt. "You really should be wearing this."

"What about you?" I let him buckle me in the middle seat.

"I'm harder to kill."

"Actually..." Luc drawled the word out. "I'm probably the hardest thing to kill."

"Special snowflake syndrome strikes again," Daemon muttered.

Luc snorted as Paris hit breakneck speed on the narrow road,

Archer close behind us. "Did Daedalus ever show you their neatest weapon?"

"They showed us a lot of things," I said, lurching sideways as Paris hit a curve.

"How about that special gun of theirs?" Luc put a foot up on the dashboard, and I hoped the airbag didn't deploy anytime soon. "The one that can take out a Luxen with one shot—the PEP? Pure Energy Projectile."

"What?" My stomach dipped as I glanced back and forth between Luc and Daemon. "What kind of weapon is that?"

"It's some kind of energy pulse that disrupts light waves—high tech. Kind of like onyx, but much worse." Daemon's brows lowered. "I didn't see it, but Nancy told me about it."

"It's an electromagnetic weapon," Luc explained. "And it's very dangerous to anything around it. If they break it out, they aren't messing around. The damn thing will disrupt signals and can even hurt humans since the brains, lungs, and heart are all controlled by low-voltage electricity. The Pulse Energy Projectile isn't fatal for humans in a low frequency, but it is catastrophic to our kind at any frequency."

Ice drenched me. "One shot?"

"One shot," Luc repeated gravely. "You two probably have nothing to worry about, since they want you alive, but you need to realize that if they bring out the big guns, people are going to die."

I froze, unable to drag in a breath. More people would die. "We can't let that happen." I twisted toward Daemon, going as far as the seat belt let me. "We can't let people die because—"

"I know." Daemon's jaw set with determination. "We can't go back, either. We just have to get out of here before we need to worry about anything like that."

My heart pounded in my chest as I glanced at Luc. He didn't look so convinced. I knew Daemon was trying to reassure me. I appreciated that, but guilt piled on top of the terror. If anyone died…

"Don't," Daemon said quietly. "I know what you're thinking. Don't."

"How can I not think about that?"

Daemon didn't have an answer. The creeping terror was like an endless hole, growing in size as we neared the teeming city at dusk. The red and blue neon lights of the billboards and flashing lights were harsh instead of welcoming.

Traffic had ground to a halt south of the Boulevard, an endless stream of vehicles that was more parking lot than road.

"Well, shoot." Paris smacked his hands on the steering wheel. "This is inconvenient."

"Inconvenient? Understatement of the year." Daemon gripped the back of his seat. "We need to get out of traffic. We're sitting ducks here."

Paris snorted. "Unless you have a hovercraft in your back pocket, I don't see how I'm supposed to get us out of here. There are side roads we can take, but they're farther down this road."

With shaky fingers, I unbuckled the seat belt and scooted forward until my knees pressed against the center console. A quick glance back confirmed that Archer was there. "Why isn't the traffic moving at all? Look." I pointed. The line of cars heading out of the city stretched all the way from the Caesar's Palace sign and down. "It's *completely* stopped."

"There's no need to panic yet," Paris said. A cheerful smile crossed his face. "It's probably just an accident or a naked person running through traffic. It happens. We're in Vegas, after all."

Someone outside laid on a horn. "Or the more likely scenario is that they have the traffic blocked at the interstate exit. I'm just saying," I said.

"I think he's trying to look on the bright and stupid side of things, Kitten. Who are we to bring a dose of reality into the mix?"

Running my sweaty palms over my thighs, I started to respond when a hushed sound caught my attention. Leaning back, I peered out the passenger window. "Oh, crap."

A black helicopter flew over the city, incredibly low. It looked like the whirling blades would clip a building at any second. It could be any helicopter, but I had a sinking feeling that it was Daedalus.

"I'm going to check this out," Luc said, reaching for the door. "Stay here. I'll be right back."

Luc was out of the Hummer and slinking around cars before any of us could respond. Irritation flashed across Daemon's face. "Do you think that was smart?"

Paris laughed. "No. But Luc does what Luc wants. He'll be back. He's good like that."

A soft knock on the back window caused me to jump out of my skin. It was only Dawson.

Daemon rolled the window down. "We got problems."

"Figured. Traffic not moving at all? Not good." Dawson leaned in. As always, seeing them together was a little disconcerting at first. "Luc up there?"

"Yeah," I said, pressing my hands between my knees.

Someone behind Dawson, in the other lane, whistled. He ignored it.

Luc returned. As he climbed into the Hummer, he tugged his loose hair into a stubby ponytail. "Guys, I have bad news and I have good news. What do you want first?"

Daemon's knuckles turned white from where he was gripping the seat. I knew he was about two seconds from smacking one of the guys up front. "I don't know. How about you start with the good?"

"Well, there is a barricade up the road about a mile in. That gives us some time to think of something."

My words came out hoarse. "That's the *good* news? What in the hell is the bad news?"

Luc grimaced. "The bad news is they got, like, a SWAT team

moving up the line of cars, checking each one, so the time to make a decision is sort of limited."

I stared at him.

Daemon made a masterpiece out of F bombs. He pushed back from the seat, rocking the car. A muscle flexed in his jaw. "This is not how we're going to go down."

"I would like to think it's not," Luc replied. He looked out the front window, shaking his head slowly. "But even I'm thinking the best case is to ditch the cars and run."

"Run where?" Dawson asked, eyes narrowing. "There's nothing but desert on either side of Vegas, and Beth— " He pushed off the car, thrusting his fingers through his hair. "Beth can't run for miles. We need another plan."

"You got one?" Paris quipped. "Because we're all ears."

"I can't." Dawson dropped his hand to the window. "If you guys want to run, I understand, but Beth and I will have to hole up somewhere here. You leave— "

"We're not splitting up," Daemon cut in, his voice sharp with anger. "Not again. We all stay together, no matter what. I have to think of something. There has to be something..." He trailed off.

My heart skipped. "What?"

Daemon blinked slowly, and then he laughed. I frowned. "I have an idea," he said.

"Waiting." Luc snapped his fingers.

Daemon's eyes narrowed on the kid. "You snap your fingers at me and I'll— "

"Daemon!" I shouted. "Focus. What's your idea?"

He turned to me. "It's risky, and it's completely insane."

"Okay." I pulled my hands free. "Sounds like something you'd come up with."

Daemon smirked, and then his gaze focused on Luc. "It's something you said before. About their strength being in the fact that no one knows about them—no one knows about *us*. We change that, we get the upper hand. They're going to be too busy doing damage control to look for us."

My brain hardly digested that. "Are you suggesting that we expose ourselves?"

"Yes. We go out there, and we make the hugest scene possible. Get the humans wound up. Create a big enough scene to cause a diversion."

"Like at Area 51? Except this time…" This would be epic and completely uncontrollable.

Dawson smacked his hands down on the side of the Hummer, earning an outraged look from Luc. "Then let's do it."

"Wait," Paris said.

Ignoring him, Daemon reached for the door handle. There was a series of clicks, and Daemon got nowhere. He turned a stunned look on Paris. "Did you just hit the childproof locks on me?"

"I did." Paris threw his hands up. "You need to think about this first."

"We don't need to think about anything," Dawson said. "It's a good enough plan. We cause enough chaos, we should be able to slip out."

Luc leaned over his seat, on his knees. His amethyst eyes fixed on the brothers. "Once we do this, there's no going back. Daedalus will be even more pissed and gunning for us."

"But it will give us time to get away," Daemon argued. His pupils were starting to glow. "Or do you have a problem with cutting them off at the knees?"

"A problem?" Luc laughed. "I think it's brilliant. Honestly, I'd love to see the looks on their faces when there are Luxen walking around on the evening news."

"Then what's the problem?" Dawson demanded, giving a quick glance to the line of cars ahead. There wasn't any movement yet.

Luc smacked the back of the seat. "You all just need to be sure about what you're planning to unleash. It's not just Daedalus, but the entire Luxen community that is going to be upset. Me? I'm all about causing a rebellion—and this will be a rebellion."

"There are others," Paris added quickly. "They will use this for their own benefit, Daemon. They will take advantage of the chaos."

I swallowed hard, thinking of that nasty percentage of Luxen Dasher had mentioned. "We're stuck between a mountain and a volcano about to explode."

Daemon's eyes met mine. I already knew what he'd decided. When it came down to his family and the rest of the world, he would choose his family. He put his hand on the handle. "Open the door."

"You sure?" Luc said solemnly.

"Just make sure there aren't any humans hurt," I said.

A wide, wild smile broke out across Luc's face. "Well then, it's time to introduce the world to a little bit of extraterrestrial awesomeness."

CHAPTER 28

DAEMON

This had to be one of the craziest stunts I'd ever pulled. Not only was I throwing everything in the face of Daedalus and the DOD, I was breaking every rule the Luxen lived by. This decision didn't affect just me, it affected everyone. Something this massive should make me hesitate at least a little bit. Make me rethink things, come up with another route.

But there wasn't time. Matthew…Matthew had betrayed us, and now we were here on the verge of being caught.

Like I said before, I'd burn down the world to keep Kat safe. The same went for my family. This would just be a different kind of fire.

People were already watching us, trying to figure out why we were abandoning our cars as we walked back toward where Archer waited behind the wheel. I knew the fact that Dawson and I were walking together was driving a lot of the attention.

"I already know." Archer killed the engine. "I think it's crazy, but it could work."

"What is crazy?" Dee asked from the front seat, which was duly noted. She must've been chomping at the bit to get her butt up there the moment Dawson got out.

"We're basically trapped in this line of cars," I told her, leaning in the window. "They have the road blocked up ahead, and there's a group of soldiers searching vehicles."

Beth sucked in a sharp breath. "Dawson?"

"It's okay." He was immediately at the back door, opening it. "Come here."

She slipped out of the SUV and planted herself to his side.

"We're going to cause a little bit of trouble to distract them," I said, eyes narrowing on the two. Something was definitely up, more than the overprotectiveness that might run in the family, but I didn't have time for that. "Hopefully we can get the roads cleared at the same time and get the hell out of here."

"Call me cynical, but how are we going to get this clusterfuck cleared and get out without being stopped?" Andrew asked.

"Because it's not a little bit of trouble we're going to cause," Archer explained, opening the door and forcing me to take a step back. "We're going to light up the Vegas strip like they've never seen before."

Dee's eyes went wide. "We're going to show our true selves?"

"Yep."

Ash leaned forward. "Are you insane?"

"Quite possibly," I answered as I knocked a strand of hair out of my eyes.

Archer folded his arms. "Need I remind everyone that by getting in that car back at the house, you agreed that you'd be down for just about anything? This would be the part of 'anything' Paris had been talking about."

"Hey, you have no arguments from me." Andrew grinned, hopping out. "So we're exposing ourselves?"

Kat made a face, and I almost laughed. Andrew did seem way too excited about this.

He stopped at the front of the SUV. "You have no idea how badly I've wanted to freak out a few humans."

"I'm not sure if I should be offended by that or not," Kat mumbled.

He winked, and I felt a rumble move up my chest. "You're not too human anymore," Andrew pointed out and then grinned at me. "When do we do this?"

We were minutes away from nightfall. "Now. But—pay attention—we don't split up too far. We keep everyone in eyesight. Either I or…" The next words took a lot for me to say. Physically hurt my soul. "Or Archer will let everyone know when it's safe to get out of the city. If our wheels are gone—"

"God I hope not," Luc whined.

I shot him a look. "If our wheels are gone, we'll get the next best thing. Don't worry about it. Okay?"

There were a few nods. Ash still looked like we'd lost our damn minds, but Dawson tugged her out of the SUV. "I need you to do something big for me, okay? A huge favor," he said.

Ash nodded seriously. "What?"

"I need you to stay with Beth. Keep her out of the way and safe if anything starts to go wrong. Can you do that for me? She's my life. If anything happens to her, it happens to me. You understand?"

"Of course I can," Ash said, taking a deep breath. "I can keep her out of trouble while you guys run around glowing like a bunch of fireflies."

Beth scowled. "I can help, Dawson. I'm not—"

"I know you can help, baby." He placed his hands on her cheeks. "I don't think you're weak, but I need you to be careful."

She looked like she was about to argue, and I was starting to get antsy *and* feel bad for my brother. God knew I'd spent way too much time arguing with Kat about not running in front of a firing squad. Speaking of which…

"Don't even say it," Kat said without looking at me.

I chuckled. "You know me too well, Kitten."

Beth relented and was handed off to Ash. Thank God, because people were starting to follow our trend, getting out of their cars and milling around. Some guy opened a can of beer and plopped down on the hood of his car, watching dusk deepen into a dark blue. I could go for a beer right about now.

"Ready?" I said to Andrew.

Andrew cracked his neck. "This is going to be awesome."

"Please be careful," Ash pleaded.

He nodded. "I'm cool." Then he swaggered past where I stood. "Cause a scene? Got it."

Turning around, I felt the need to hold my breath. There was no going back. Out of the corner of my eye, I saw Ash usher Beth through the backed-up lane and to the median. They stopped under a cluster of palm trees.

"Stay close to me," I told Kat.

She nodded as she watched Andrew easily navigating the cars. "Not going anywhere." Pausing, she bit down on her lower lip. "I almost can't believe you guys are going to do this."

"Me neither."

Kat looked at me, and then she laughed. "Are you having second thoughts?"

I grinned wryly. "A little late for that."

And it was. Andrew stepped up on the sidewalk, heading toward a ginormous pirate ship. Dozens of people were behind him. Many of them had cameras hanging from around their necks. Perfect.

"What do you think he's going to do?" Kat asked, still nibbling on her lower lip.

I had to give it to her. She was trying so hard to be brave, but I could see her hands shaking and the way she kept glancing up toward the bend, where Daedalus would surely be making their way toward us. She was strong, and I was constantly in awe of her.

"How do you say it?" I said, drawing her attention. "He's going to go all Lite-Brite on us."

Her eyes lit up. "This should be fun."

Andrew hopped up on the retaining wall of the pool the boat was rigged over. I tensed as several of the humans turned to him. It seemed like time froze for a full minute, and then, with that shit-eating grin on his face, Andrew spread out his arms.

The edges of his body blurred.

I heard Kat's sharp inhale.

No one noticed the minute difference at first, but then the haze shifted over Andrew's white shirt and down the rest of his body.

A low murmur rose from the crowd.

Then Andrew faded out. Gone. Poof.

Shouts of surprise were a crescendo, a symphony of excited squeals and sounds of confusion. Motorists gawked from inside their cars. People stopped mid-step on the crowded sidewalk, creating a domino effect.

Andrew reappeared in his true form. Nearly six and a half feet, his body shone brighter than any star in the sky or light on the Strip. A pure white light with edges tinged in blue. His light was like a beacon, forcing everyone and anyone on the street to look at him.

Silence.

Man, it was so quiet you could hear a grasshopper karate chop a fly.

And then thunderous applause drowned out my expletive. Andrew was up there, standing in front of a damn pirate ship, glowing like someone shoved a nuclear weapon up his ass, and people were cheering?

Paris chuckled as he stepped up beside me. "Guess they've seen weirder stuff on the streets of Vegas."

Huh. He had a good point.

Soft flashes of light from cameras flickered all through the crowd. Andrew, who apparently was a showman at heart, bowed and then straightened. He did a little jig.

I rolled my eyes. Seriously?

"Wow," Kat said, her arms falling to her sides. "He didn't just do that."

"Time for me to join the fun," Paris said, striding forward. He made it to the car in the next lane, a red BMW driven by a middle-age man, and then slipped into his true form.

The man jumped out of his car, shuffling backward. "What the…?" he said, staring at Paris. "What the hell is going on?"

In his true form, Paris drifted among the cars, heading toward the crowd gathered in front of the pirate ship and Andrew. He stopped just short, and his light pulsed once, bright and intense. A wave of heat blew off him, forcing several of the gawkers to take a hurried step back.

Dee hopped up on one of the cars several feet back and stood tall and straight, the slight breeze picking up her long hair, tossing it around her face. Within seconds, she was in her true form.

The couple in the car darted out and rushed to the sidewalk, where they spun around and stared openmouthed at Dee.

Dawson was next. He stayed near Beth and Ash, on the other side of the congested road. When he took his true form, several people let out startled shrieks.

"I mean it, Kitten, stay close to me."

She nodded again.

Off in the distance, I could hear the helicopter. No doubt it was circling back to make another run at the Boulevard. It was about to get all kinds of real.

Unease grew among the humans, becoming as thick as the heat-clogged air. It seeped into me, making me itchy as I let my human form slip away.

Like someone pressed a universal pause button, the humans around us seemed frozen. Their hands clenched on cameras and cell phones. The awe in their expressions changing from surprise to confusion, and then fear slowly crept in. Many were exchanging glances. Some were starting to move away from Andrew, but they couldn't get far on the congested sidewalks.

We need to turn this up a notch. Dawson's voice filtered through my thoughts. *See the Treasure Island sign? I'm going to take it out.*

Make sure no one is hurt, I said.

Dawson floated a step back. Raising an arm, he looked like he was reaching up into the sky to grab a star. Energy crackled in the air, charging it with static. The Source flared, wrapping down his arm like a snake. The burst of light shot from his palm, shooting high into the sky and racing across the four lanes. It arched over the pirate ship, striking the white bulkhead.

Light exploded in a flash, turning night into day for a brief second. The energy rolled across the sign and then shot down, flaring out the eye sockets of the giant skull under the sign in a shower of sparks.

Andrew had spied the Venetian tower and all the pretty golden lights at the top. He turned to me. Twisting at the waist, I summoned the Source. It really was like taking a nice deep breath after being underwater for several minutes. Light arced from my hand, smacking into the tower, taking out the lights in a shower of fireworks.

That's about when people realized that this wasn't some kind of show, an optical illusion or something to stand around and point at. They might not have understood what they were seeing, but whatever instinct humans possessed that triggered that flight response kicked in.

It became all about survival—about getting away from the big, bad unknown—while trying to snap pictures of the spectacle at the same time.

Got to love the near-innate human response to capture everything on film.

People scurried like ants, running in every direction, abandoning their cars in their rush. They streamed out of the streets, a flood of different shapes and sizes, pushing into one another, falling over their own feet. Some guy knocked into Kat, forcing her away from the SUV. For an instant, I lost sight of her in the pandemonium.

I rushed forward, parting humans like the Red Sea. Their excited screams were already an annoying buzz in my ears.

Kat!

Her answer was both in my head and out loud. "I'm here!"

She stumbled around a woman who had frozen in front of me. The look of shock on the lady's pale face roused a bit of guilt in me, but then Kat was in front of me, her eyes wide.

"I think we got a lot of people's attention," she said, dragging in air.

You think? I touched her arm, overly glad at the welcoming spark that traveled from her skin to mine.

Luc appeared beside us, along with Archer. "We should move some of the cars out of the way?"

Good idea. Keep Kat with you.

I centered my attention on the line of cars in front of us. Four lanes. All packed with vehicles ranging from ones on their last leg to luxury cars I was really sad about scratching.

Archer joined me. "I'll help."

He took one lane while I focused on the one in front of the Hummer. The ability to repel things away from us was easier than pulling it toward us. It was the release of energy, like a shockwave.

Stretching my arms out, I watched the car before me start to shake, its rims rattling and gears grinding. Then it shifted to the side. One after another, cars were sliding out of the way like an invisible giant had swiped its arm across the road. I went as far as I could see, then pulled back, knowing that Daedalus already had to be aware of what was going on.

Turning back to where Andrew stood, I saw him shooting off blasts of energy like there was no tomorrow. Hidden behind an empty tourist bus was a teenage guy, filming it all on his phone.

A bit of restlessness trickled through my veins. This would be all over YouTube in seconds. Off in the distance, I could hear sirens. With the way traffic was backed up behind us, I doubted they'd be here soon.

"Look!" Kat shouted and pointed to the sky.

Overhead, a helicopter circled the scene, shining floodlights over where Andrew stood. It wasn't the military. A KTNV 13 News emblem was emblazoned on the side. Damn. They'd gotten here before the police.

"This will be live," Kat said, stepping back. Her eyes were wide. "They'll be filming live—it'll be *everywhere*."

I don't know why it didn't sink in until that moment. Not like I didn't fully grasp what this would mean, but seeing the news copter circling the Boulevard struck home. The images were fed into the newsrooms, and from there it would be signaled out to the entire nation within *seconds*. The government could take down a few videos here and there, even a hundred of them, but this?

They couldn't stop *this*.

Right now people were most likely sitting in front of their TVs, watching this unfold and having no idea what they were really seeing, but knowing that what they were viewing was something serious.

"Something epic," Luc threw out, meaning he was being a peeping bastard. "You did it, man. They can't lock this down. The world will know humans aren't the only life-form chilling on this planet."

Yeah, it was going to be…epic.

My gaze crawled along the road. There were still a lot of people fixated on what Andrew and Dawson were doing. Both were zipping back and forth across the road, practically skipping over the cars behind us like an alien game of Frogger.

That was what people all across the world were seeing.

There was no way that could be explained away. Daedalus was going to freak.

"That's what you wanted, right?" Archer frowned as a man darted across the street. "Go public. You got—"

A dark helicopter flew in from between two large hotels—a large black bird. It didn't take a genius to realize *that* was a military copter. It flew overhead but didn't shine any lights down like the news copter was doing, tracking the movements of Dawson and Andrew.

It circled around Treasure Island, disappearing behind the wide hotel. The feeling of unease magnified. Reaching out, I wrapped my fingers around Kat's wrist and at the same time yelled for my brother.

He stopped on top of a red BMW, crouched in his true form. When he picked up what I was feeling, he shot off the car, grabbing Dee from the car behind him and bringing her down to road level.

Not a second too soon, either.

The black bird circled back around, rising high in the sky as it flew sideways, as if it were lining itself up…

"I have a real bad feeling about this," Luc said, walking backward. "Archer. You don't think—"

I saw it first—the tiny spark from the bottom of the military bird. It was nothing. Just a minimal flare of light and shouldn't have turned my insides cold or stopped me dead in my tracks. What came out of the copter moved too fast for human eyes to track. The stream of white smoke against the dark blue sky told me all I needed to know.

Whirling around, I pulled a stunned Kat against my chest and brought us both down to the warm pavement, curving my body over hers.

A loud *crack* caused her to jerk in my arms, and I tightened my hold.

Horror settled in my gut like stones. Anger was an acid in my veins. The news copter spun erratically as smoke billowed out of the tail. It whirled across the sky, its floodlights dipping and rising over the pirate ship and beyond. The copter kept spinning, falling out of the sky, heading straight for Treasure Island.

The explosion rocked the cars. Kat screamed as she twisted in my arms, trying to look up. But I didn't want her to see it. I held her down, pressing her face against my chest. I knew my touch was hot and had to be nearly unbearable this long, but I didn't want her to see this.

Oh my God… Someone's thoughts mirrored my own. Dawson? Dee? Archer? Luc? One of the Thompsons? I didn't know.

Flames shot out of the center of the hotel, an orange glow that quickly crawled up the trembling structure. Plumes of thick smoke rose, darkening the sky.

Archer was frozen beside the Hummer. "They did it. Holy… They shot it down—the military *shot* them down."

CHAPTER 29

DAEMON

Panic erupted, the kind of which I'd never witnessed before. People streamed out of the hotel—the ones who'd been able to escape—and spilled into the pavilion and the streets.

Still in my true form, I pulled Kat off the street. She was saying something, but her words were lost in the screams. Christ. I never expected this—I never thought they'd go after humans, but I had underestimated the extent to which they'd go to keep us secret.

"But it's too late," Luc said, grabbing the arm of a woman who'd tripped and went down on her hands and knees. He pulled her up. The side of her face was a mess of raw tissue and burns. "There's no stopping what has already been seen. And look."

I twisted around, bringing Kat with me. She'd been staring at the woman's mangled face for too long. The man who'd been in the car Dee had jumped on was still filming everything—us—on his phone.

Shielding Kat, I turned back to Luc. He had his hand on the woman's forehead, and she stood as still as a statue. He was healing her.

"Go," Luc ordered when he finished. The woman stared back at him. She was in some kind of costume—leather bra and skirt. *"Go."*

She scrambled off.

Archer swung around. "They're coming."

They were.

Men dressed in SWAT gear edged along the sides of the street—not Vegas SWAT. Daedalus—military. And their guns were big.

PEP.

They shot first—a flare of red light aiming straight for Andrew.

Andrew avoided the hit, flying off the retaining wall and rearing back. A bolt of energy streaked out from him, slamming into the ground before the advancing men. The pavement cracked and rolled, knocking several of them off their feet. Guns fired. Red light flashed into the sky.

There were more—men in camo behind those in black.

"Shit," Archer groaned. "This is about to get bad."

Thanks for the update, Captain Dickhead. Shoving Kat behind me, I slammed my foot down, sending a fissure through the road. Raising my arms, I let the Source roll through me.

Placing my hands on the bumper of a Mercedes in front of me, I sent a shock of electricity dancing over the exterior. I lifted it up, tossing it like a Frisbee toward the advancing soldiers, who scattered like cockroaches. It flew through the air, rolling and rolling until it smacked into a palm tree, taking it out.

Red light pulsed, flying over our heads and between Archer and me, narrowly missing Luc. I turned slowly. *Oh no, no you did not.*

Energy burst from me in a tumultuous wave, smacking into four of the five soldiers, throwing them back into the tourist bus.

Another blast went off to our right, and I spun, grabbing Kat as I saw Paris dart in front of me. He slammed into Luc, knocking him out of the path of the PEP.

Paris took a direct hit.

He jerked to a stop, his body spasming as his form shifted from human to Luxen, back and forth. Electricity crawled across his body, blowing out at his elbows and kneecaps. He went still, his light dulling until he crumbled to the ground. Shimmering blue liquid pooled underneath him.

Dead.

Luc let out an inhuman sound, and a bright glow swallowed him. He rose several feet into the air, static and little fingers of light crackling out from under his body. His light flared once, as bright as the sun at noon, and then there were screams. The smell of burned flesh permeated the air.

Shots rang out, zinging past my head and smacking into the cars. The cavalry had arrived, it appeared, with good old-fashioned guns.

Dawson zipped up to my side, his fingers brushing the back of a sedan. It was flung at the bus, pinning the soldiers.

Stay behind me, I warned when I felt Kat inching around me.

I can help.

You can die. So stay behind me.

Anger radiated from her, but she gritted her teeth and stayed back. There were bigger problems. The grinding of heavy tires drew our attention. Clearing the road had worked against us. A fleet of Humvees came out of the smoke, and a— *Is that a tank?*

"You have got to be kidding me," Kat said. "What do they plan on doing with that?"

Its gun moved toward where we all stood, glowing like damn Hit Me Now, Please and Thank You signs.

"Crap," Archer said.

Racing across the cars, Andrew slammed his fist into the hood of a truck. Flames erupted as he used the truck to Molotov the tank. Soldiers streamed out of the hull, scrambling away seconds before the thing blew. The M1 went up in the air like a firecracker, flinging across the Boulevard. Hitting the gardens in front of the Venetian, it rolled across the parking lot.

Heart pounding like a jackhammer, I willed the pieces of broken asphalt off the ground. I flung them toward the cops, forcing them back. Everything was happening fast. Soldiers were coming out of everywhere, and Luc was going after them, holding nothing back. Cops were coming down the Boulevard shooting at just about anything that breathed. People—innocent people—were hiding behind cars, screaming. Dee was trying to usher them off the road, out of harm's way, but they were all frozen in fear. After all, she was glowing like a damn disco ball.

Dee slipped into her human form in front of a man and woman clutching two children. "Get out of here!" she screamed. "Go! Go now!"

They hesitated a second, and then the couple picked up their kids and raced back toward the median where Ash still stood guard before Beth.

Red light streamed past my face, spinning me around. A bolt of white light arced, and I heard a body hit the ground behind me. I saw Kat before me, her pupils glowing. I turned slowly, finding a soldier on the ground, a PEP weapon by his lifeless hand.

"I can help," she said.

You saved my life. I turned back to her. *That is so hot.*

She shook her head and lifted her chin. "We need to get— Oh my God, Daemon. *Daemon*."

My heart tripped in response to the fear in her voice. I started toward her, and then I *felt* it. I felt it deep and in every part of my being. I saw Dawson stop. I saw Andrew spin back.

Over the neon signs for Caesar's Palace and the Bellagio hotel, dark clouds moved incredibly fast, blocking out the stars. But they weren't clouds…or a swarm of bats.

They were Arum.

• • •

Katy

Things went from bad to craptastic in a matter of seconds.

At no point from the second Daemon had announced his plan, up until the military took down the chopper full of innocent humans, had I believed that it would go down like this. All we'd wanted was to throw them off guard—to cause a little bit of chaos to make our escape.

We hadn't planned on starting a war.

Now Paris was dead and something worse than monsters under the bed was coming our way.

At no point did I doubt that the shadows racing across the sky were not here on accident. Yeah, there was a lot of Luxen mojo going on right now, but the likelihood of Arum just popping up and joining the fun? Not likely.

They were here because of Daedalus, because they worked with them.

The dark cloud broke apart, streaming across the sky like blotches of insidious oil. It dipped behind Caesar's Palace, disappearing for a second, and then exploded out of the side of the hotel. Shards of glass and debris flew into the air.

I opened my mouth to scream, but there was no sound.

An Arum came down the Boulevard, moving so fast I couldn't even say it took a second to get where it was going.

Flying over the back of the Hummer, it slammed into Andrew, lifting him several feet into the air. Ash's horror-filled scream ricocheted through me. The Arum took shape mid-flight, its skin black and shiny like obsidian. It threw Andrew like he was a rag doll and nothing more.

Another Arum shot down the strip, zipping in and around the

cars. It rose, catching Andrew, and the two of them nosedived into the Treasure Island pool.

Daemon leaped off the ground—a burst of bright light and then he was in the air—slamming into the other Arum, cutting him off from the pool. They collided, a mixture of darkness and light, rolling through the sky like a cannonball. Dawson raced forward, dodging the blasts of red light.

The Arum and Andrew resurfaced in the pool and, rearing back, the Arum slammed its hand into Andrew's chest. He jerked, his light flickering like a lightning bug.

I started forward, but arms circled my waist.

It wasn't a friendly hug.

Panic sliced through me as my feet were lifted off the ground just as I saw the Arum lift Andrew into the air. Another pulse of light, and then Andrew… Oh God…

Ash's scream confirmed what I suspected. I saw her switch into her true form and then back out again, like she couldn't control it. A wave of energy rolled across the lanes.

A second later I was on my back, the air knocked from my lungs, and I was staring up into a shielded face. My breath faltered, and for a moment I had no idea what to do. I was frozen, caught between disbelief and terror. Paris was dead. Andrew was dead.

The muzzle of a strange-looking gun was pointed right at my face.

"Don't even think about moving," the muffled voice said.

My brain stopped processing things at a normal level and speed. As I stared up, my own wide eyes reflected in the tactical helmet, the human part of me switched off. Rage boiled up in me, and it felt good. It wasn't fear or panic or grief. It was power.

The scream that had been building inside me, the kind of scream that left an imprint on its surroundings decades later, let loose. I don't know how I did it, but the soldier and his gun were no longer above me. All around me, vehicles rattled and slid forward, overturning.

Glass cracked and then exploded, pelting the road and me with tiny shards. The little nicks of pain were nothing.

Who knew where the soldier went? He was simply gone, and that was all that mattered.

I pushed myself up, looking around. Fire poured out of Treasure Island and Caesar's Palace. The Mirage was smoking. Windows were knocked out of cars. Bodies were lying in the street. I'd never seen such destruction before, not in real life. I searched for Daemon and my friends, finding him first. He was battling an Arum, and they were nothing more than a blur of black and white. Archer was wrestling with the Arum from the pool, and Dee was pulling Andrew's lifeless body from its depths. Water streamed off her face and clung to her hair. She got him over the retaining wall and wrapped her arms around him. The scene…it made every part of me hurt.

I turned to where Ash was still guarding Beth. She was in her human form and looked torn between doing what she promised Dawson and going to her brother. That was something I *could* do. I could keep Beth safe, and Ash could go where she needed to be.

The military chopper circled back around, halting my progress. Archer appeared out of nowhere. The Source radiated over him like a wave of light, and he threw out his arms. A bolt of pure white light hit the belly of the chopper, sending it spinning back toward one of the casinos.

The impact was deafening, and the resulting fireball lit up the night sky.

I turned back to where he had been standing, but he was gone, like a ninja. Jesus.

Digging my toes into the cracked pavement, I eyed the path to Beth and Ash. Luc had the soldiers occupied. Or what was left of them. There was this god-awful smell that turned my stomach, and I remembered what the origins could do. Apparently, evil little fire-starters could be added to their list of freakish descriptors. I pushed out, running around an overturned truck.

Beth's head swung in my direction. Her arms were wrapped around her waist protectively. She looked terrified. I made it around a downed palm tree and was so close.

And then I was off my feet, flying backward.

I hit the side of a van; the impact rocked my body and snapped my head back. Darts of pain shot down my spine. My sight clouded as I slid to the road. Criminy. That hurt. I blinked slowly, trying to clear my vision.

Groaning, I rolled onto my side and placed my hands on the split asphalt. My arm shook as I attempted to push myself up. My insides felt rattled and rearranged. I needed to get—

Darkness crept along the edge of my vision. There was a second before I realized it wasn't because I was on the verge of passing out. Goose bumps rose along my arms. Something cold pressed along me.

Arum.

I flattened my body and wiggled under the van, seeking a few extra seconds to regain my strength and bearings. The smell of oil and fumes clogged my throat. I squeezed my eyes shut as I slid over the road, ignoring how the asphalt abraded my skin. I made it out on the other side and crawled around a sedan, gripping the bumper to lift myself.

The van started to shake, and then it slid out of the way.

The Arum stood in his human form, pale and eerily beautiful, a cold and apathetic beauty that stole my breath and repelled me. A slow, unnerving smile twisted his lips, and it was like being hit with frigid air.

He didn't speak as he raised his arms.

Air stirred around me as I stumbled backward. Behind me, the palms shook and metal groaned. Wind roared, and at the last second I ducked. The trees were uprooted, spinning toward the Arum. The car slipped out of my grasp as if he were sucking it in. A tourist brochure rack spun in the air. Pieces of the road rose up, hovered for a second, and then flew to him. There was a sharp scream that pierced my ears.

A woman was flung past me, disappearing behind the Arum. Another crumpled body joined those on the ground.

He was like his own personal black hole, sucking up everything around and drawing it to him. I was no exception. No matter how hard I dug in, my feet dragged over the ground.

His icy fingers wrapped around my throat, and he lowered his head to mine. I couldn't remember seeing an Arum's eyes before. They were the palest shade of blue, like all the color had been leeched from them.

"What do we have here?" The Arum spoke out loud. He inhaled deeply, closing his eyes as if he could taste me. "A hybrid. Tasty."

I was so not down with being an intergalactic late-night snack.

I threw my arm back, pulling on the Source, but the Arum's free hand clamped down on my wrist, his grip punishing. My heart leaped in my throat as his cold cheek pressed against mine. His lips moved near my ear, sending a shudder of revulsion through me.

"This might hurt. A little," he said, and then he laughed harshly. "Okay. It might hurt a lot."

He was going to feed.

And that little part of my brain that still functioned thought this was a hell of a way to go out. After everything—Daedalus, the guns, the bullets, and everything else—I was going to be sucked dry.

Everything tightened inside me, a mixture of fear and rage, disgust and panic. It unraveled like a compressed Slinky, lashing out from the inside.

Energy roared through me, heightened my senses. I felt the Arum against me. I felt him align his mouth with mine, a scant few inches apart. I felt the breath he took, the deep shudder of power opening up inside him. And I felt the chilling, sucking pull that reached deep inside me, digging in with tiny hooks.

I placed my hand on the Arum's chest, and that rush of energy left me like a sucker punch. There was no space between it and the Arum, nothing to lessen the effect. The Source exploded from me and immediately went into the Arum. The flare of light from me to him was intense. Energy *imploded*, throwing us apart.

The stars did cartwheels.

I hit the pavement on my side and rolled onto my back. The Arum was suspended in the air, his arms and legs spread wide. His body trembled once, then twice. A spot of light over his chest, the mark the Source had left behind, raced across his body in tiny fissures of white cracks, encompassing his entire body.

He burst into a thousand little pieces.

Holy alien babies…

As I staggered to my feet and twisted at the waist, my eyes met that of a young man. He looked like someone who was on autopilot, seeing everything but not really understanding what he was witnessing. I kind of sympathized with the dude. I was sure I'd had that same WTF look on my face when I saw Daemon stop the truck and realized I wasn't dealing with something human.

I probably had that WTF look on my face right now.

My gaze dipped.

In his white-knuckled grip was a smartphone. Everything—he had captured *everything* on his cell phone. Namely my face. Such a stupid thing to worry about in that moment, especially considering everything else he must've captured, but I thought of this video being loaded on the Internet, going viral like those damn Hey Girl memes.

This wasn't how I'd wanted my mom to discover that I was alive. Maybe not alive *and* well, but definitely kicking around.

But it was really too late.

I started toward the guy to get the phone, but he snapped out of it and took off. I could've run after him, but there were bigger problems to deal with.

The stench of smoke and death was everywhere. I staggered back to where I knew I had seen everyone last, using the red tourist bus as a destination, aching on a cellular level as I took in the damage. The guns—those PEP weapons—weren't harmless if they didn't hit a Luxen or hybrid. Lampposts were broken in two or melted, about to collapse. Pockets of fire lit up the entire Strip.

There were bodies littering the road.

I shuffled around them, grimacing at the melted and burned clothes, the ragged holes and scorched skin. It seemed unnecessary that there'd be so many innocent deaths. The Luxen were glowing like walking lightbulbs, and even we hybrids were pretty obvious. It was like the military didn't care how many were taken out in friendly fire. Were they insane?

And I knew how the government would spin this—that it was our fault, that the Luxen were to blame, even though they had made the first strike, taking innocent lives.

Looking at all the bodies turned my stomach, but I kept picking my way through them until I felt the warmth skittering over the nape of my neck. Lifting my head, I saw Daemon in his human form fighting hand to hand with a soldier. My heart leaped when the soldier got a right hook in, but Daemon rebounded, taking him out with one punch.

He looked over, his gaze locking onto mine. His hair was damp, clinging to his forehead and temples. His eyes glowed like diamonds. Relief shot across his face, and he shook his head, the emotion in his eyes unbearable.

There was a flare of red farther down the Strip, reminding me of how incredibly dangerous the streets still were. I took another step forward, seeing Ash and Beth rounding an overturned Humvee. I was happy to see them still standing, even though tears were flowing freely from Ash's eyes. Her brother…

I sucked in a breath. So much—

"Kat!" roared Daemon.

Strong arms circled me from behind. The instinct to fight and struggle kicked in, but I was pulled back an instant before a red pulse shot past right where I'd been standing. The PEP zoomed by, heading straight for Beth. I heard Dawson's enraged shout, and time slowed down until it was a near crawl. The arms around me loosened enough. Archer's voice was yelling in my ear. Daemon was running, leaping cars.

Ash spun toward Beth, moving incredibly fast, as fast as a bullet. Her arms went around the girl and she twisted, shoving Beth out of the way.

The shot hit Ash in the back.

Light exploded up her spine, following the network of veins. Her head snapped back and her knees folded under her. She fell forward, lacking the grace that always seemed natural to her.

She didn't move.

I broke free from Archer's hold, reaching her side the moment Daemon did. He grasped her shoulders, turning her over. Shimmery blue liquid spilled out of her mouth as her head flopped back over Daemon's arm.

Somewhere, a man's scream was cut short by a sickening crunch.

"Ash," Daemon said, giving her a little shake. *"Ash."*

Her eyes were fixed on the endless sky above. Part of me already knew it, but my brain refused to accept it. Ash and I would never be friends. We probably would never be upgraded to frenemy status, either, but she was incredibly strong, stubborn, and I honestly thought she'd be like a cockroach, outliving nuclear fallout.

But that beautiful human form—those painfully stunning features—faded in the soft glow that quickly dulled. There was nothing of Ash in Daemon's arms, just a shell of translucent skin and narrow veins.

"No," I whispered, staring at Daemon.

His body shuddered.

"Dammit," Dawson said. His arms were around a softly crying Beth. "She…"

Beth gulped. "She saved my life."

Standing beside Dawson, Dee pressed her hands to her mouth. She said nothing, but it was all etched upon her face.

"Guys, we really need to…" Luc appeared behind Daemon, pausing with a severe frown. "Damn."

I lifted my head, having no idea what to say. And it would be pointless if I had. A car or something exploded somewhere.

"I've got a big SUV about a block down the road—all of us will fit in it," Luc started. "We've got to go while the road is clear. They'll send more soldiers, and I won't be able to take them out again. Neither will all of you. We're running out of steam."

"We can't leave them here," Daemon argued fiercely.

Archer chimed in. "We don't have a choice. We stay here a second longer and we join them—Kat joins them."

A muscle flexed in Daemon's jaw, and my heart ached for him. They'd grown up with the Thompsons, and I knew a part of Daemon did love Ash. Not the same way he loved me, but no less important.

"I don't want to leave Paris here," Luc said, catching Daemon's eyes. "He doesn't deserve to be left behind, but we have *no* choice."

Something must've connected in Daemon's head, because he laid Ash down gently and stood. I followed his lead. "Where's the car?" he asked, his voice hard.

Luc gestured down the road.

I reached out to Daemon, and he took my hand. There had been ten of us however many minutes ago. Now only seven raced across the dark road strewn with burned-out cars, bodies, and debris. I kept my legs moving, refusing to allow myself to really think about things.

Luc had found a Dodge Journey and a truck, but we only needed one of them now. That realization sent a pang of grief through me. Archer got in the driver's seat of the Journey and Luc in the front.

"Hurry," Luc urged. "There's still some traffic up ahead, but it's moving, and the blockade is gone. People are fleeing the city. We should get lost among them."

Dawson helped Beth into one side while Daemon and I went to the other. We climbed into the very back, and Dee joined Dawson and Beth in the middle row. The doors weren't even shut before Archer peeled off.

Numbness settled into my body as I twisted in the seat, staring out the back window as we raced around cars and narrowly avoided panicked people in the streets. We were leaving the city behind—leaving Paris, Andrew, and Ash behind.

I kept staring out the back window, watching Vegas burn.

Chapter 30

Katy

The ride was silent and tense. Besides the fact that all of us were looking over our shoulders, expecting the entire military to be on our tails, none of us knew what to say or if anything could be said.

Turning in Daemon's arms, I pressed my face into his chest and inhaled the rich, woodsy scent. The scent of death and destruction hadn't lingered on him, and I was grateful. If I closed my eyes and held my breath until I lost a few brain cells, I could almost imagine that we were just taking a ride in the desert.

He hadn't bothered with the buckling stuff. At some point, he had pulled me away from the back window and nestled me between his thighs. I didn't mind. More than anything, his embrace was grounding in the aftermath. And I think he needed it, too. I wished I could be inside his head, knowing what he was thinking right now.

I smoothed my thumb over the spot above his heart, mindlessly tracing odd shapes against his chest. I hoped guilt wasn't eating away at him. None of what happened—the deaths—had been his fault. I wanted to tell him that, but I didn't want to break the silence, either. It seemed that everyone in the car was mourning someone.

I hadn't been close with Andrew and Ash, and I hadn't known Paris that well, but their deaths hurt nonetheless. Each of them had died saving someone else, and most people would never know their names or what they'd sacrificed. But we would. Their loss would leave a mark on all of us for a long time coming, if not for eternity.

Daemon's hand smoothed up my back and threaded through my messy hair until his fingers brushed the back of my neck. He shifted slightly, and I felt his lips on my forehead. My grip on his shirt constricted along with my chest.

I stretched up, my lips brushing against his ear. "I love you so very much."

His body tensed and then relaxed. "Thank you."

Unsure of what he was thanking me for, I curled against him, listening to his heart beat steadily. Every part of me ached, and I was tired, but sleep seemed impossible. Two hours in, Luc had said that heading to Arizona would be too risky and too close to Vegas. I hadn't even noticed in which direction we were heading. There was another place he had—in one of the largest towns in Idaho, something called Coeur d'Alene. Another fifteen hours from where we were.

Dee had spoken up then, asking how he had so many properties when he was barely pushing fifteen. I thought that was a very good question.

"There's a lot of money in the kind of club I run, and favors don't come cheap," he said. "So I like to keep my options open, own a couple of hidey holes around the States. You never know when you'll need them."

Dee seemed to accept the answer. And really, what choice did we have?

We stopped once to get gas somewhere in northern Utah the following morning. Dawson and Daemon went in to pick up some drinks and food, but not before changing their appearances. The rest of us stayed behind the tinted windows while Archer filled the tank, keeping his head low under a baseball cap that had been in the car.

Too anxious to sit still, I leaned forward and checked on Bethany.

"She's sleeping," Dee said quietly. "I don't know how she can sleep. I don't think I'll ever sleep again."

"I'm sorry." I placed my hand on the back of her seat. "I really am. I know you were close to them, and I wish…I wish a lot of things were different."

"Me, too," she said, placing her hand over mine. She laid her cheek on the seat and blinked several times. Her eyes were misty. "None of this seems real. Or is it just me?"

"It's not just you." I squeezed her hand. "I keep thinking I'm going to wake up."

"And it'll be months ago, right before prom, huh?"

I nodded, but that kind of wishful thinking was a one-way ticket to Downersville. Daemon and Dawson returned, their arms full of bags.

When Archer was once again behind the wheel, they started doling out drinks and snacks. Daemon handed me a small green bag of Funyuns. My breath was going to be kicking. "Thank you."

"Just don't try to kiss me for a while," he said.

I smiled, and it felt weird to do so, but his eyes glimmered when I did, and I knew the no-kissing rule wasn't going to last very long. Not when he had that look in his eyes.

"Did you hear anything interesting in the convenience store?" I asked, curious.

Daemon and Dawson exchanged a quick glance. I couldn't decipher it, but I was immediately suspicious when Daemon shook his head. "Nothing important."

My eyes narrowed.

He arched a brow at me.

"Daemon..."

He sighed. "There was a TV on behind the counter, airing live from Vegas. It was muted, though, so I couldn't hear what they were saying."

"Nothing else?"

There was a pause. "A few people checking out were talking about aliens and how they always suspected that the government was covering it up. Something stupid about a UFO crashing in Roswell back in the fifties. I honestly stopped listening."

I relaxed a little. That was good news. At least there was no mention of lynch mobs hunting down aliens. We drove most of the day, but the more miles we put between Vegas and ourselves didn't really ease the tension. It would be a long time before any of us was truly comfortable.

The first things I noticed about northern Idaho were the tall fir trees and the majestic slope of the mountain range in the distance. The town near the large, deep blue lake was small in comparison to Vegas but bustling. We passed an entrance to a resort, and I tried to pay attention to the directions Luc was giving Archer, but I sucked at directions. He lost me at "turn right at the intersection."

Another fifteen minutes or so and we were at the edge of the national forest. And if I thought Petersburg was in the middle of nowhere, I obviously hadn't seen anything yet.

The Dodge bumped along a narrow dirt road crowded with firs and other trees that looked perfect for hanging Christmas decorations.

"I think we might get eaten by a bear," Daemon commented as he stared out the window.

"Well, that might happen, but you won't have to worry about too many Arum." Luc twisted in his seat and flashed a tired grin. "This place has natural quartzite deposits but no Luxen that I'm aware of."

Daemon nodded. "Good stuff."

"The Arum...do you think they just happened to show up?" Dee asked.

"Not at all," Archer replied, looking in the rearview mirror for a second. He smiled a little, I think for Beth. "Daedalus has some Arum on the back burner, called out when Luxen…step out of line. There was this issue in Colorado, right before they caught up with you guys outside of Mount Weather. Some lady in a wrong place, wrong time situation, and an Arum was brought in."

"You met him," Luc said, glancing back at Daemon. "You know, the Arum at my club you wanted to go all He-Man on? Yeah, he was called in by the DOD to take care of one of the problems."

I looked at Daemon, who was sporting a major frownie face. "He didn't look like he was taking care of the problem."

Luc's smile turned part mysterious, part sad. "Depends on how you look at taking care of things." He paused, turning back around. "That's what Paris would say."

I settled back in the crook of Daemon's arm, planning on asking him about that later. The vehicle slowed down on a bend, and parts of a log cabin peeked out from the firs—a very large, very expensive log cabin that was two floors and the size of two houses.

Luc's bar must have been doing amazingly well.

The vehicle coasted to a stop before a garage door. Luc hopped out and loped around the front of the car. Stopping in front of the doors, he flipped open a keypad and entered a code with quick, nimble fingers. The door opened smoothly.

"Come on in," he called, ducking under the door.

I couldn't wait to get out of the vehicle as it rolled into the garage. My butt was numb and my legs a little shaky when I put my feet on the cement. Getting the blood moving again, I walked out of the garage and into the sunlight. It was significantly cooler for August, probably in the low seventies. Or was it September? I had no idea what month it was, let alone the day.

But it was beautiful here. The only noise was the chirping of birds and the rustling of small woodland creatures. The sky was a nice shade of blue. Yeah, it was pretty here and reminded me of… home.

Daemon came up behind me, wrapping his arms around my waist. He leaned into me, resting his chin atop my head. "Don't run off like that."

"I didn't run off. I just walked out of the garage," I said, placing my hands on his strong forearms.

His head slid down, and the stubble on his cheek tickled me. "Too far for right now."

Any other time I would've read him the riot act, complete with the diva crown, but after everything, I understood the why behind it.

I turned in his arms, forcing mine under his and around his waist. "Is everyone already investigating the house?"

"Yep. Luc was talking about one of us going back into town later and getting some food, before it gets too late. Looks like we're all going to be holed up here for a while."

I squeezed him hard. "I don't want you to go."

"I know." He reached up and smoothed my hair back off my face. "But only Dawson and I can change the way we look. And I'm not letting him go by himself or letting Dee go."

Inhaling deeply, I squared my shoulders. I wanted to rant and rave. "Okay."

"Okay? You're not going to give me evil Kitten eyes?"

I shook my head, focused on his chest. Sudden emotion crawled up, getting stuck in my throat.

"Hell must've frozen over." His fingers splayed across my cheek. "Hey…"

Pressing forward, I rested my head against him, and my fingers dug into his sides. One arm slipped to my waist, and he held me close. "I'm sorry," I said, swallowing hard.

"A lot has happened, Kat. There is no need to apologize. We all are doing the best we can right now."

Lifting my head, I blinked back tears. "And you? Are you doing okay?"

He stared down at me, silent.

"You don't blame yourself for what happened back in Vegas, do you? It wasn't your fault. None of it."

Daemon was silent for a very long time. "It was my idea."

My heart turned over heavily. "But we all got behind it."

"Maybe there was something different we could've done." He looked away, throat constricting. A taut pull appeared at the corners of his mouth. "The whole way here I kept thinking it over. What other options did we have?"

"We didn't have any." I wanted to crawl inside him and somehow make it better.

"Are we sure of that?" His voice was quiet. "We didn't have a lot of time to think it through."

"We didn't have *any* time."

Daemon nodded slowly, eyes narrowed and focused on the tree line. "Ash and Andrew and Paris—they didn't deserve that. I know they agreed to it and knew the risks, but I can't believe that they are..."

I stretched up, cupping his cheeks. The aching spread though my chest, becoming a physical pain. "I'm so sorry, Daemon. I wish there was something more I could say. I know they were like your family. And I know they meant the world to you. Their deaths aren't your fault, though. Please don't think that. I couldn't—"

He silenced me with a kiss—a sweet, tender kiss that eclipsed all my words. "I need to tell you something," he said. "You might hate me afterward."

"What?" I pulled back, totally not expecting that comment. "I couldn't hate you."

He cocked his head to the side. "I gave you a lot of reasons to hate me in the beginning."

"Yeah, you did, but that was in the beginning. Not anymore."

"You haven't heard what I have to say."

"It doesn't matter." I sort of wanted to punch him in the face for even suggesting that.

"It does." He took a breath. "You know, when the shit started really going down back in Vegas, I had my doubts. When I saw Paris get taken out, then Andrew and Ash, I asked myself if I would've done this again, the same way, knowing the risks."

"Daemon…"

"The thing is, I knew the risks when I got out of the car. I *knew* people could die and that didn't stop me. And when I looked up and saw you standing there, alive and okay, I knew I would do it all over again." His bright emerald eyes settled on me. "I would do it, Kat. How incredibly selfish is that? How messed up? I think that makes me pretty worthy of your distaste."

"No," I said, and then I said it again. "I get what you're saying, Daemon. It doesn't make me hate you."

His jaw clamped down. "It should."

"Look, I don't know what to say. Is it a hundred percent right? Probably not. But I understand it. I understood why Matthew turned Dawson and Bethany over and then tried to turn us over. We'll all do crazy shit to protect the ones we love. It may not be right, but…but it is what it is."

He stared down at me.

"And you can't beat yourself up over this. Not when you told me I couldn't beat myself up over what happened with Adam because of the decisions *I* made." My breath was shaky. I wanted to erase the pain in his eyes, the hurt. "I couldn't hate you. Ever. I love you no matter what. And it doesn't matter what happens in the future or what happened before this." Tears burned my eyes. "I will always love you. And we are in this together. That's never going to change. Do you understand?"

When he said nothing, my heart skipped. "Daemon?"

He moved so fast that he startled me. He kissed me again. It wasn't sweet and tender like the last one. It was fierce, intense, and powerful—a thank-you and a promise rolled into one. That kiss broke me down and then rebuilt me. His kiss…well, it made me.

He made me.

And because of that, I knew it went both ways. He made me. And I made him.

• • •

Daemon

The trip into town with Dawson had been surprisingly uneventful. We were in and out of the market quickly. There was no avoiding the newspapers with pictures of glowing figures splashed all across them or overhearing the conversations while in line. Some of it was just plain crazy, but tension cloaked the people in the store, in a small town nestled against a lake, a world away from Vegas.

From what we could gather, the government hadn't made any official announcement with the exception of declaring a state of emergency for Nevada and labeling the "horrific actions" an act of terrorism.

Things were going to get bad. Not just from the human standpoint but from the Luxen. Many of them had no problems living in secrecy. We'd blown that right through the roof. And then there were those who would take advantage of the chaos, like Luc had said. I couldn't help but think about Ethan White, and his warning.

It was late once we got back to the cabin, and Kat and Dee fixed spaghetti. It was mostly Kat cooking, since Dee tried to heat up everything with her hands, which usually had disastrous results. Beth had helped with the garlic bread, and it was good seeing her up and moving around. I almost couldn't remember what she'd been like before Daedalus. I did know she was a lot more talkative then.

And she had smiled more.

I helped Kat clean up afterward. She washed the dishes, and I dried them. The kitchen was outfitted with a dishwasher, something Luc had felt the need to point out, but I think the tedious task was calming. Neither of us spoke. There was something intimate about this, our elbows and hands brushing.

Somehow Kat got a cluster of frothy white bubbles on her nose. I wiped it off, and she grinned, and, damn, her smiles were like basking in the sun. They made me feel and think a lot of things, including some majorly cheesy stuff I would probably never say out loud.

She could barely keep her eyes open by the time we finished. I ushered her into the living room, and she plopped down on the couch. "Where are you going?" she asked.

"I'm going to finish up in the kitchen." I dropped an old patchwork quilt over her. "Get some rest. I'll be right back."

Heading through the rec room, I could hear Archer and Dee talking in one of the rooms. I was halfway there before I stopped myself. Closing my eyes, I cursed under my breath. Dee needed someone to talk to. I just wish it wasn't *him*.

I stood there in the dark hallway, staring at the gaudy wood paneling for God knew how long before I forced myself back into the kitchen.

Dee would not be taking him to Olive Garden. That was where I drew the line.

Grabbing the wet dishcloth, I slopped it on the table and cleaned up Luc's mess. The kid's eating habits and spaghetti didn't go together well. Finishing up, I glanced at the clock. It was almost midnight.

"You lied to Kat."

I turned at the sound of my brother's voice, already knowing what he was talking about. "You would've done the same thing."

"True, but she's going to find out sooner or later."

Picking up a bottle of water off the counter, I chose my next words carefully. "The last thing I want her to know right now is that her face is plastered all over national news. Instead of being concerned about what that means for her, she's going to worry about her mother and… there's nothing we can do about that right now."

Dawson leaned against the counter and folded his arms. He stared at me, and I stared back. Knowing what that look meant, the lowered brows and determined set of his jaw, I sighed. "What?" I demanded.

"I know what you're thinking."

I tapped my fingers on the water bottle "Do you?"

"It's why you're in here playing Suzy Homemaker. You're wondering what you've started."

I didn't answer for a long moment. "Yeah, I'm wondering that."

"It wasn't just you. It was all of us. We *all* did this." Dawson paused, staring out the window over the sink into the dark void that surrounded the cabin. "I would do it again."

"Would you? Knowing that Ash and Andrew would die?" Saying their names was a hot slice of pain.

He ran a hand through his hair. "I don't think you want me to answer that question."

I nodded. We'd answer that question the same way. What did that say about us?

Dawson exhaled heavily. "That's some shit, though. God, they were like family. It's not going to be the same without them. They didn't deserve to die like that."

I rubbed my jaw. "And Matthew…"

"Screw Matthew," he spat, eyes narrowing.

Setting the bottle aside, I watched my brother. "We sort of did the same thing, bro. We risked people's lives to keep Dee and the girls safe."

He shook his head. "That's different."

"Is it?"

Dawson didn't immediately respond. "Well, then screw us."

I let out a dry laugh. "Yeah, screw us."

His lips twitched as he looked at me. "Man, what the hell are we going to do?"

I opened my mouth, but I laughed again. "Who the hell knows? I guess we have to wait and see what the fallout will be. I need to figure out how to make Kat look like the innocent victim in this. She can't hide forever."

"None of us can," he said solemnly. Then he added, "I would pay good money to know what the Elders are thinking right now."

"Easy. They probably want our heads."

He shrugged, and a couple of moments passed before he spoke again. Whatever he was about to say, I knew he was unsure of it. His mouth worked on it for a while. "I know this isn't the best time to tell you this. Hell, I'm not sure there is a right moment for this, but it seems like after what happened to Ash and Andrew, I should just keep my mouth shut."

My muscles tensed. "Just spit it out, Dawson."

"Okay. Fine. I do need to tell you because, well, I think someone other than us needs to know." The tips of his cheekbones flushed, and I really had no idea where this conversation was going. "Especially as things start to progress and—"

"Dawson."

He took a deep breath and said two words that blew my mind. "Beth's pregnant."

My mouth opened, but there were no words. Truly no words at all.

Everything came out of Dawson in a rush. "Yeah, so she's pregnant. That's why she's been tired a lot and I didn't want her doing anything when we were in Vegas. It was too risky. And the traveling had really worn her out, but...but yeah, we're having a baby."

I stared at him. "Holy..."

"I know." His face cracked into a smile.

"Shit," I finished. Then I shook my head. "I mean—congratulations."

"Thank you." He shifted his weight.

I almost asked how Beth got pregnant but stopped myself before I asked that stupid question. "Wow. You're…you're having a baby?"

"Yeah."

I gripped the edges of the counter. I was struck stupid, and all I could think about were those kids in Daedalus—the origins. The children of a male Luxen and female hybrid, so rare that if Daedalus learned of this…

I couldn't finish the thought.

Dawson let out a shaky breath. "Okay. Say something else."

"Uh, how…how far along is she?" Is that what people asked under normal circumstances?

His shoulders relaxed. "She's around three months."

Damn. They must've had one hell of a reunion.

"You're mad, aren't you?" he asked.

"What? No. I'm not mad. I just don't know what to say." And I kept thinking that in six months we were going to have a baby that could fry brain cells with a single thought if it didn't get its binky. "I just wasn't expecting this."

"Neither was I, or Beth. We didn't plan this. It just sort of… happened." His chest rose sharply. "It wasn't like I thought having a baby at this age was a smart thing, but it happened, and we're going to do our best. I…I already love him more than I've loved anything."

"Him?"

Dawson's smile was part awkward, part joyous. "The baby could be a girl, but I've been calling it a 'he.' Drives Beth crazy."

I forced a smile. He didn't seem to know about the origins. Was it possible that Beth didn't know, either? If so, they had no idea what they were about to bring into this world. I started to say something but cut myself off. Now wasn't the time.

"I know things are going to be hard," he went on. "We can't go to a normal doctor. I know that, and it scares the shit out of me."

"Hey." I pushed forward, clamping a hand on his shoulder. "It'll be okay. Beth and the…and the baby will be okay. We'll figure this out."

Dawson's smile of relief was evident.

I had no idea how we were going to figure this out, but women had been having babies since the beginning of time without doctors. Couldn't be that hard, right? I sort of wanted to punch myself in the face after that, though.

Childbirth scared the crap out of me.

We talked for a little while longer, and I promised to keep things quiet. They weren't ready to share the news with everyone, and I could understand that. Kat and I hadn't told anyone that we were sort of married.

Marriage.

Babies.

Aliens in Vegas.

The freaking world was coming to an end.

Still feeling a little shell-shocked, I headed into the living room. I stopped in front of the couch where Kat was curled up against the arm, the quilt bunched up under her chin. She was asleep.

Lowering myself, I carefully picked her up and placed her in my lap, her legs spread out between mine. She stirred, rolled onto her side, but remained asleep.

I stared out the window into the darkness for hours.

Now more than anything we had to do something. Not just run and hide. That was going to be damn near impossible as it was. The world knew about us now. Things would only get more dangerous from here on out.

And in a few months, we'd have a baby to worry about—a baby that could wreak all kinds of havoc.

We had to do something. We had to make a stand, change the future, or there'd be no future for any of us.

I smoothed my hand up Kat's spine, curving my fingers around the nape of her neck. Tipping my chin down, I pressed my lips to her forehead. She murmured my name sleepily, and my chest clenched with the degree of emotion I felt for her. I leaned back on the couch and stared through the window into the darkness.

The uncertainty of tomorrow loomed like a storm cloud, but there was one thing I was fairly confident of, something more ominous than the unknown waiting for all of us.

We would be hunted by the humans and the Luxen.

And if they thought exposing the truth to the world was the most extreme thing I could do to protect those I loved, they hadn't seen anything yet.

They had no idea what I was truly capable of.

Chapter 31

Katy

I'd been vaguely aware of Daemon coming to the couch and wrapping himself around me, but that wasn't what woke me several hours later. At some point during the night, his arms had tensed around me in a near chokehold.

And he was in his true form.

As beautiful as that was, it was also very hot and blinding.

Struggling to loosen his grip, I twisted in his embrace, squinting against the harsh glare. "Daemon, wake up. You're—"

He jerked awake, sitting up so fast I almost fell onto the floor. The light dimmed, and he was back in his human form, a bewildered expression on his face. "That hasn't happened since I was a kid—changing into my true form without realizing it."

I stroked his arm. "Stress?"

He shook his head, his gaze settling over my shoulder. His expression tensed. "I don't know. It…"

Footsteps pounded upstairs and within seconds, the whole crew was downstairs looking just as out of it as Daemon did. Untangling myself from his embrace, I shoved the quilt off and stood. "Something's going on, isn't it?"

Dee moved toward the window and pulled the thin curtain back. "I don't know, but I feel…"

"I woke up thinking someone was calling my name." Dawson wrapped an arm around Beth's shoulders. "And I was glowing."

"Same here," Daemon said, standing.

Luc ran a hand through his messy hair. In his pajamas, he finally looked his age. "I feel itchy."

"So do I," Archer commented quietly. He rubbed the side of his jaw, squinting into the darkness outside the cabin window.

I looked at Beth, and she shrugged. It seemed we were the only two who weren't feeling whatever it was that had the Luxen and origins in a tizzy.

All of a sudden, they stiffened—all of them except Beth and me. One by one, Daemon, Dawson, and Dee switched to their Luxen forms for a brief second and then resumed their human facades. It was so quick, so immediate, that it was like the sun was in the room for a moment or two.

"Something is happening," Luc said, spinning around. He headed for the front door. "Something big is happening."

He was out the door and everyone followed. I stepped out into the cool night air, sticking close to Daemon as he walked onto the gravel pathway in front of the porch and then into the grass. The cool blades were soft under my bare feet.

A strange fissure worked its way down my spine and then out through my nerve endings. A sense of awareness tightened the muscles in my neck as Luc walked farther across the patch of cleared land. The edges of the forest appeared dark and endless, wholly uninhabitable in the darkest hours of night.

"I feel something," Beth said, her voice barely above a whisper. She glanced at me. "Do you?"

I nodded, unsure of exactly what I was feeling, but Daemon stiffened beside me, and then I felt his heart rate kicking up in his chest, jarring mine.

"No," he whispered.

A small burst of light lit up the sky far off in the distance. Air hitched in my throat as I watched that tiny speck of light travel down, a bright, smoky tail trailing behind it. The light disappeared as it zoomed behind the Rocky Mountains. Another appeared in the sky. Then another, over and over again, and they fell as far as the eye could see, like stars shooting down to Earth. The sky was lit with them, thousands and thousands of bursts of light as they entered our atmosphere and rained down. So many of them that I couldn't keep track of just how many there were, until their streaming tails blended together, until night turned into day.

Luc let out a strangled, hoarse laugh. "Oh shit. ET so phoned home, kids."

"And he's brought friends," Archer said, taking a step back as several of the speeding lights came close, disappearing among the tall elms and firs.

Daemon reached down, threading his fingers through mine. My heart jumped as they continued to fall before us. Tiny explosions rocked the trees, shook the ground. Light pulsed, lighting up the forest floor every couple of seconds until an intense light flared for several seconds and then faded out.

Then there was nothing. Silence fell around us. There were no crickets, no birds, no scurrying of small animals. There was nothing but our respective short breaths and my own pounding heart thundering in my veins.

A speck of light appeared farther back among the elms. One by one, they appeared, an endless succession of lights coming into existence. So many that I knew there had to be hundreds here just in the forest surrounding us.

"Should we be running right now?" I asked.

Daemon's hand tightened on mine, and he pulled me against his side. His arms wrapped around my body, holding me close, and when he spoke, his voice was hoarse. "There's no point, Kitten."

My heart stuttered a beat as pressure clamped down on my chest.

"We wouldn't outrun them," Archer said, his hands closing into fists. "Not all of them."

I could only stare as a bone-deep understanding settled in me. They neared the edge of the woods, taking shape. Like Daemon and every Luxen I'd seen, their forms were human-shaped and their arms and legs well defined. They were tall, each and every one of them. Their lights cast shimmery shadows as they stopped a few feet outside of the edge of the woods. One continued forward, its light brighter than the sun during summer, tinged in a deep, vibrant crimson, just like Daemon when he was in his true form.

Sergeant Dasher and Daedalus may have lied about a lot of things, but this—oh God—this had been the truth. They had come, just as Dasher had warned, and there had to be hundreds here, and hundreds of thousands elsewhere.

The light flared red again from the one in front. A pulse of energy rolled across the clearing, raising the tiny hairs along my body. I trembled, unsure of what was happening, but then something did.

Dee was the first to lose hold of her human form and then Dawson. I wasn't sure if it was confusion, fear, or something otherworldly, something in them that responded to the proximity of so many of their kind, but a heartbeat later, Daemon's arms shuddered around me, and he slipped into his true form as well.

His arms fell away from me, and it was suddenly unbearably cold without his warmth. I saw Dawson do the same and move toward his sister. The three of them stepped forward, separated from us.

"Daemon," I called out, but he didn't hear me.

He didn't respond.

Suddenly Archer was beside me and Luc was near Beth. We were backing up, but I didn't feel my feet moving or my muscles working. My eyes were trained on Daemon until the others of his kind swallowed his light.

Fear coated the inside of my mouth and turned the blood into slush in my veins. In that instant I couldn't help but think of what Dasher had said about what would happen when the Luxen came—and whether Daemon would stand with his own kind or with mine.

I wasn't sure Daemon even had a choice.

I wasn't sure I did, either.

Acknowledgments

I have to give my family and friends major props for putting up with my nonstop writing and for being so understandable.

There are many people I'd like to thank who were an integral part in the creation of the Lux series and *Origin*. Major kudos to the team at Entangled: Karen Grove, Liz Pelletier, and Heather Riccio. Daryl Dixon from *The Walking Dead* also was a big help. Not sure why, but I think he and his cut-off shirt look good in my acknowledgments. Thank you to Kevan Lyon, the agent of awesome, for knowing when to go to bat for me and when to pat me on the head. Much appreciation to Stacey Morgan for listening to me ramble on about what Daemon and Kat are doing and insisting that there be more kissing. And cowbell. And country music. The last two things did not make it into the books. Cannot forget Marie Romero for helping shape *Origin* into something readable! I'm pretty sure I'd be nowhere without *Honey Boo Boo* and *Supernanny*. Another thing I'm not sure why, but why not? Thank you to Lesa Kidwiler for doing things I probably shouldn't ask her to do. Wink. Wink. Nudge. Nudge. Thank you to Wendy Higgins for allowing me to borrow from her wonderful books.

I also want to thank some people who have always been huge supporters of my writing and the Lux series: Stacey O'Neale, Valerie from Stuck in Books, the YA Sisterhood, Good Choice Reading, Mundie Moms, Vee Nguyen, the Luxen Army chicks, Amanda from Canada (because that's how I know you), Kayleigh from England (because that's how I know you), Laura Kaye and Sophia Jordan (two awesome ladies I can talk to forever), Gaby, Books Complete Me ladies, Book Addict, Momo, and I am forgetting a ton of other people, so please don't stone me, but it's sort of late as I'm writing this, and my brain stops functioning around this time, and all I can think about is when is *The Walking Dead* coming back on?

The biggest and most important thank-you is to you—the person reading this right now. If it weren't for you, Daemon Black wouldn't be much of anything. You are the reason why I write these books, and I can never say thank you enough.

Read on for a sneak peek at Renee Collins's magical and romantic *RELIC*

Available in stores and online now!

After a raging fire consumes her town and kills her parents, Maggie Davis is on her own to protect her younger sister and survive best she can in the Colorado town of Burning Mesa. In Maggie's world, the bones of long-extinct magical creatures such as dragons and sirens are mined and traded for their residual magical elements, and harnessing these relics' powers allows the user to wield fire, turn invisible, or heal even the worst of injuries.

Working in a local saloon, Maggie befriends the spirited showgirl Adelaide and falls for the roguish cowboy Landon. But when she proves to have a particular skill at harnessing the relics' powers, Maggie is whisked away to the glamorous hacienda of Álvar Castilla, the wealthy young relic baron who runs Burning Mesa. Though his intentions aren't always clear, Álvar trains Maggie in the world of relic magic. But when the mysterious fires reappear in their neighboring towns, Maggie must discover who is channeling relic magic for evil before it's too late.

Relic is a thrilling adventure set in a wholly unique world, and a spell-binding story of love, trust, and the power of good.

Chapter One

We were home alone the night that Haydenville burned. Mama and Papa had gone to a political meeting and left me in charge. I was sixteen, old enough to keep an eye on my younger brother and sister. Or so my folks figured. They had no way of knowing how I would be tested.

The evening started off so calm. Crickets were singing in the sagebrush, and the oppressive heat of daytime had been swept away by a velvety breeze, which drifted in through the open windows. Ella was playing with Sassy's new litter of kittens up in the loft, and Jeb sat by the fire, polishing the brand-new gun he'd gotten for his fourteenth birthday the week before. I was scraping a broom over the floor of our little one-room house, trying my best to banish the red-orange sand that seemed our constant companion. But my mind soon drifted from my chores.

I stood in the doorway, in the warm twilight, gazing at the vast desert beyond. It stretched endlessly in either direction, with nothing but sage and rocks and the occasional rabbitbrush to break the monotony. The dark smudge of Haydenville sat on the horizon, a small spit of a town, not much more interesting than the cactus. It always made me feel lonesome to stare out at the stillness around us.

As I leaned my head against the doorframe and watched the first star pierce through the indigo sky, a reckless wish burned in my heart. I gazed up and let myself envision a sleek dragon diving out of the scrape of clouds, a creature long extinct, returned to breathe life back into this barren place. I pictured the ancient animal curling around the moon and soaring over the red-rock cliffs beyond our house. But as it swept downward, a strange glow on the horizon caught my attention.

I straightened, squinting in the direction of the wavering light. It was a wide line of orange spreading across the dark landscape in the distance, painting the night sky a deep amber. The breeze that drifted past my cheek carried the distinct scent of smoke. This was no figment of my imagination. This was fire.

And it was coming from Haydenville.

The broom slid out of my fingers and clattered to the floor.

"Maggie?"

I met my brother's gaze, and his brow furrowed. "What is it?" he asked, tightening his grip on the rifle as he stood. "A rock devil?"

"Fire." I pointed, my heart beating fast. "In the town."

Jeb raced to my side and gripped the doorframe. "God Almighty," he breathed. "The whole street's burning." Then he gave me a sharp look. "Mama and Papa."

"I'm sure they're okay," I said, more confidently than I felt. "They would have seen the fire before it spread. They're probably on their way back right now."

Jeb squinted at the horizon, now rippling in the heat. "Someone *is* coming. A whole bunch of people…"

A row of separate flames undulated in the twilight. Torches. They moved across the desert toward us with a speed that could only mean they were carried on horseback.

"Maybe *most* people in the town got out," I said, but my voice faded away.

Jeb stared hard at the fast-moving torches. "I don't think so, Maggie."

We looked at each other, and the same thought came to us.

"Ella," I whispered.

I scrambled up the loft ladder, struggling to stay calm. I had to keep it together until Mama and Papa got home. I just wished they'd hurry.

Ella was lying on her back, holding a squirming kitten over her chest. "Look at this little orange one, Mags," she said. "Isn't she the sweetest thing you…"

As her large brown eyes fixed on me, the smile dropped from her face. "What's wrong?"

She was only seven, but she had a real knack for reading people's faces.

"You need to come down," I said, reaching for the kitten.

Ella pulled it out of my grasp. "Hey! I was holding her."

"You can have her back in a minute. Right now, we need to talk."

She held her pet close, scowling at me. I clenched my jaw. Sometimes that girl tried my patience like none other. "You come right now, or Mama's gonna hear about this." I grabbed the kitten and set it on the mattress.

"I want Jeb," she said, sitting up angrily.

Jeb was her favorite. Ever since she could walk, she'd followed him like a shadow. I wrapped my hand around her wrist. "You can talk to him when you come down. Now move it."

We climbed down the ladder steps swiftly. Jeb was standing in the doorway, watching the fire, his rifle poised. Ella ran up to him, hugging his pant leg. He stroked her hair absently but kept his gaze on the flames. I came up behind him, looking at the burning desert beyond us. Staring back at me was the undeniable reality: Mama and Papa weren't going to reach home before those torches did. Our safety now rested in my hands alone.

"We gotta get out of here," I said under my breath to Jeb.

"And go where?"

"To the hiding spot, just like we always talked about."

Jeb grimaced. "We don't need to do that. I can protect us here."

"Don't be a fool. You barely know how to use that gun."

"I do, too!"

"It doesn't matter. Mama and Papa put *me* in charge, and I'm sayin' we go to the hiding place."

Ella pulled on Jeb's arm. "What's goin' on?"

He hoisted her up against his hip. "It's nothing you need to worry about, baby girl."

It surprised me how calmly he spoke the lie. My anxiety was surely written all over my face.

I turned away from them, trying to mask my fear as busyness. "Help your brother grab some coats and blankets," I said. My gaze fell to the floor beneath Mama's and Papa's bed. "And some water…"

I bent down and lifted up the quilt. After feeling around a moment, I located the loose floorboard and, beneath it, the small jewelry box. My heart quickened as I set the box on my lap. Our family's single relic lay inside on dark velvet. Kraken.

At first glance, it was little more than an almond-sized piece of bone, oval cut, which was one of the more popular styles. It had been polished a clouded blue-green color. Only exceedingly rare types were diamond clear. Papa had it set in a silver necklace, another common choice for relic wearing. My breath trembled as I lifted it into my palm. I'd dreamed of the day I would be allowed to use it for the first time. This remnant of the ancient world, live with magic.

"What are you taking that for?" Jeb asked, looking over my shoulder. "It's too small. That thing doesn't have enough magic to ward off a vampire scorpion, let alone whoever's coming."

"You got any better ideas?"

It was true that the relic wouldn't help much if those people with the torches meant to cause trouble. Kraken bone fossils possessed only water magic, and a pebble-sized piece like we had could barely contract or expand water as needed. Papa had spent our savings on it to help keep our animals and ourselves alive, should we ever have another drought like the one that had nearly killed us three years before.

I knew Jeb, like me, was wishing right now that Papa had bought a dragon claw or phoenix piece, or any of the other fire relics I'd read about. Not that we could ever even dream of affording such rare, potent ones, but still, I wished it. So many nights, I'd lie in my bed, turning the worn pages of Papa's relic almanac by candlelight. The more I learned about all the fierce and wonderful relics out there, the more keenly I felt that the day might come when we'd need something better.

And now, we were face-to-face with that day.

I clutched the kraken piece to my chest. "It's all we have."

Ella pulled the fabric of my worn calico skirt. "Someone's gotta tell me what's happening."

"Everything's going to be fine. Looks like there was some trouble in the town, that's all. We need to head to our hiding spot and wait for Mama and Papa."

"The hiding place?" Her expression went from shock to resolute fear. "No. I'm not goin'. There's rock devils up there!"

Every settler knew to stay away from the red-rock cliffs that cast their huge shadow over our little town. The rock devils, horse-sized lizards with endless teeth and claws like hunting knives, lived in the shadowed nooks and caves. Though not magical like their ancient relative, the dragon, rock devils were the most dangerous creature to haunt our desert lands. And with rattlers, vampire scorpions, and ghost coyotes behind every sagebrush, that was really saying something. But that was exactly why Papa said we should hide in the cliffs in case of trouble. Because no one would dare come after us.

"We don't have a choice," I told Ella. "We gotta go."

She ran into Jeb's arms. He held her and looked at me, his jaw clenched. I gave him my firmest look, and he sighed. "Fine. But I'm bringing my gun."

The three of us rushed into the warm night. The minute we were out, though, Ella slammed her little heels into the ground.

"The kittens!" She gasped. "We forgot Sassy and the kittens!"

Jeb gripped Ella's hand to keep her from running back. "They'll be fine. They'll get out in time."

But we all knew the kittens couldn't make it down the loft ladder on their own.

"I won't leave them!" Ella cried, tears springing to her eyes.

I rubbed my forehead. There was barely time to save ourselves, let alone the animals. But how could we leave them to die?

"You two go on ahead," I said.

"Maggie..."

"Go! I'll catch up."

Jeb hesitated, but then nodded once. Holding Ella's hand, he ran for the cliffs as I dove back into our house. Sassy hissed at the edge of the loft, surely sensing the danger.

"It's all right," I said, climbing up the ladder. "We'll get you out."

The kittens mewed loudly as I scooped them up into my apron. But when we got outside, I realized all I could do was release them and hope for the best.

"Run, Sassy girl," I said as they scampered into the darkness. "Get on out of here with those babies."

I had to get *myself* out of there. The burning line of torches on the horizon looked closer than ever, and it filled me with a wild, shaking panic. I turned to run, but then my gaze fell on Dusty, our horse, peacefully padding his hooves in the sand of the corral. He was a good horse, hard working and gentle with children. I couldn't leave him, either.

It wasn't until I reached the gate that I remembered the lock. Put there to keep horse thieves away. Papa always carried the key with him.

"No..."

I gripped the fence, but the realization struck that it stood too high for Dusty to jump, even if I did climb it. I shook the wooden planks, then threw myself against them. They hardly budged. I slammed into the fence once more, to no avail. I could hear Jeb calling my name in the distance; the raw fear in his voice only sharpened my own. I looked to the shadowy cliffs, to the approaching fire, and then back to Dusty. Choking down a lump in my throat, I patted his glossy neck and prayed he'd somehow make it out all right.

I ran hard all the way to the cliffs, sagebrush and scrub scraping against my legs. Jeb and Ella were waiting outside the mouth of the little cave. When they spotted me, they rushed up, and we hugged. "It's okay," I said. "We made it. We're gonna be okay."

I flopped to the ground of our hiding spot. We called it a cave, but it was little more than a crawl space. If anyone *did* come looking for us, we'd be done for.

Ella climbed into Jeb's lap, trembling. With his free hand, he gripped his gun, his eyes fixed in the direction of our house. "I should try to get help," he said, shaking his head.

"No," I said sharply. "We're staying right here until Mama and Papa find us."

But *would* they find us? Were they all right? Try as I might, I couldn't shake the thought of a raid we'd heard of not two weeks before. A tiny town called Buena—just a general store, bank, and livery—burned to the ground. No one survived. People blamed the Apaches—everyone knew they were ready to go to war over the relic mining in the hills and mountains. Likely that had been the first attack of many. I still hadn't made up my mind whether to believe the stories or not, but suddenly they didn't seem so far-fetched.

I stared at Ella and prayed inwardly for my parents. In this light, Ella and Jeb looked so much like Papa; they shared the same golden hair and big brown eyes. Even the same freckles on their noses and cheeks. Everyone said I was the spitting image of Mama, with my black hair, amber eyes, and a touch of copper to my skin. Josiah, our brother two years younger than Jeb, had looked a lot like Mama, too, when he was alive. The Good Lord took him when he was ten. Pneumonia.

In the distance, the sharp, panicked whinny of a horse cut through the air, and my spine straightened. Jeb's as well. We both recognized the sound.

Dusty.

Listening with my breath clenched in my throat, I could make out the low, rumbling sounds of men's voices. Then the repeated shatter of glass. Ella shot up.

"Our house!" Her voice sounded small and pained. I squeezed her hand.

Through the distance, Dusty's whinny came again. Louder. More panicked. Then the blast of gunshots.

And the whinnying stopped.

Jeb and I were on our feet. I couldn't breathe for the tension in my chest. "Why are they doing this?"

His eyes were distant with horror. "Mama…"

I grabbed his hand. I wanted to tell him that Mama and Papa were probably laying low somewhere or gathering a group of men to surround those attackers and put them to justice. But the words felt like sand in my mouth. All I could do was hold onto his hand as hard as possible.

An acrid wave of smoke blew against us, stinging my throat. In the distance, the glow of our burning home lit the sky. As I looked harder, I realized that the flames were moving, traveling over the rabbitbrush and sage that dotted the landscape. Heading this way.

They took the dry shrubs at terrifying speed, faster than any normal fire should. Men's voices rumbled on the air, so close that the hairs on my arms stood on end.

"They're coming," I whispered.

Jeb's brow lowered. "We gotta make a run for it."

The thought froze my very bones, but he was right. We couldn't stay in the cave. Either the fire or those men would reach this place in a matter of seconds. With a shaky nod to Jeb, I knelt down by Ella.

"We're gonna leave the hiding place now, okay, honey?"

Ella ran into Jeb's arms, breaking down into tears. "I want Mama," she sobbed.

He picked her up, stroking her hair. "Don't cry, baby girl. We'll be okay. I promise we'll be okay."

"Jeb's right," I said. "We'll be fine. But listen, we have to be real quiet. We all have to run as quiet as a little pack of deer."

She kept her face buried in Jeb's shoulder, so I kissed her head.

"Right," I said. "Let's go."

We tore out into the flickering darkness. The heat of the blaze immediately pressed against us as smoke filled our lungs, and we all started coughing. My eyes blurred from the fumes, but I kept running. I could hear Ella's sobs behind me, muffled as she pressed her head into Jeb's neck. I ran and ran, but part of me knew I had no idea where we were going. We could be headed right toward the mob.

Ahead, a huge rock formation blocked our path, and to the other side, a wall of fire. Coughing into my arm, I spun around, searching for a way out. There was only one. A tiny ravine to the left might provide just enough space for a person to squeeze through. With the billowing smoke, I couldn't see too far down that path, but there didn't seem to be any other choice.

"Down there," I called to Jeb over the roar of flames and crackle of burning trees.

He examined the ravine, hesitating for a moment, but then nodded. Together, we climbed down into the little canyon of red-rock.

And I immediately saw what a terrible mistake it was.

Fire. Huge yellow tongues of it crawled toward us from the other end. A twisted, dead bristlecone pine blazed right in our path; the blast of heat made me stagger back. But when I turned to climb out of the ravine, I could see that the other flames had closed in, sealing off the entrance. We were surrounded. Trapped like animals.

Jeb and I stared at each other, ashen.

And then I remembered the relic. A flicker of hope lit within me, and I pulled the silver chain off.

"The water," I called to Jeb.

I knew we only had whatever drops were left in the canteen Jeb had grabbed on the way out of the house—but it still might do the trick.

With trembling hands, I twisted open the lid and held the kraken piece over the water. As much as I loved reading about relics, I'd only used one once before—my grandfather's kraken relic. He had taught me how close contact with the body was required to activate the magic, and that the more you concentrated, the more powerful the reaction was, but it was a skill most people had to practice to get good at.

I exhaled slowly. My fingers felt stiff and clammy with sweat.

My head was pounding. I'd read that water magic supposedly had a calming effect on the user. Maybe I was just too worked up to feel it? I closed my eyes and forced a deep breath. *Come on. Expand. Please.*

I opened one eye to check. The water hadn't budged.

"Nothing's happening," Ella said, her voice high with panic.

"I told you it wasn't strong enough," Jeb said.

"Hush," I snapped. "I'm trying."

I swallowed a dry gulp and took a breath to calm down. *"Please,"* I whispered fiercely.

But the water in the canteen stayed at the exact level as before. I scraped a hand through my hair with a growl. "Why isn't this working?"

A horrible thought started to pound through me. *What if it's not working because it isn't real?* Forgeries were a serious problem in these parts, where the average family could hardly afford a single relic chip. Desperate miners and farmers were often swindled by a slick peddler with an irresistible price.

I stared at the beautiful relic in my hand. Beautiful, and useless as a piece of glass. I felt as though I'd been stabbed in the heart.

"Maggie..." Jeb's brown eyes were deep and sorrowful, even as they mirrored the approaching wall of flames.

Reading the emotion on his face, Ella hooked her little arms around his neck, and I knew she understood. I threw my arms around both of them and held on tight, stricken by my inability to save them. Stricken that I would never see another sunset on the desert. Never have my first kiss. Never be able to hug Mama and Papa good-bye.

A voice penetrated the crackling roar of fire. The sound of it shattered me.

They'd found us.

When I looked up above the ravine, I saw a dark face illuminated in the flames. It was a young man with black hair and black eyes. He was Apache. A warrior about my age—maybe a few years older.

A swell of terror rose up in me. But then, looking harder into those midnight-black eyes, a realization cracked through the fear, and memories flooded in.

I knew this boy.

Ages ago, when I was an awkward and gangly girl of nine, I'd gone to a year of schooling at the St. Ignacio Mission outside Burning Mesa. The friars taught any who came to read and write. But I didn't quite fit in there. Mama said it was because I asked too many silly questions. There was one boy who took kindly to me, though. Another misfit. An Apache boy with the darkest eyes I'd ever seen. He'd come to St. Ignacio to learn English. We both stuck out like weeds together.

We were friends until the day I made the mistake of telling Mama all about him. She refused to explain why, but after that, I never stepped foot in St. Ignacio again.

And now, there he stood before me. He looked the same in many ways but grown up in others. He was a warrior now. I could tell from the red band of cloth he wore tied over his forehead.

"Maggie Davis," he called, and he held out his hand.

I didn't move, stunned. He remembered my name?

"You stay away!" Jeb had his rifle aimed.

I pushed the barrel of the gun down. "Stop!" I cried. "I know him. He won't hurt us."

Jeb stared at me like I'd gone mad. "You know him?"

"You have to trust me, Jeb. There's no time to argue."

Fire choked the little ravine with startling speed. The Apache looked at the growing flames and held out his hand with more urgency. "You must come. I will help you."

I stood, and Jeb grabbed my arm. "No!"

"It'll be all right," I said, pressing my hand over his. "I promise."

I looked back at the Apache. I could see in his eyes that he wouldn't hurt us. I nodded once. He lay on his stomach on the rock face and reached his arms down.

"First the child," he said. "Hurry."

The flames pressed in. The entire ravine would be burning within a matter of minutes.

As I lifted Ella up into the warrior's hands, a smoldering branch of the nearby bristlecone pine snapped off and fell to the ground. Sparks scattered, spreading over the dry desert grasses spotting the ground. The grasses caught flame instantly. Fire joined with fire, spreading like floodwater. The heat rushed over us like a wave, stinging our eyes and singeing our throats. I turned to Jeb.

And I knew he could see it, too. There would only be time to lift one more person out before the fire engulfed the ravine completely. If even that.

As the angry yellow flames rushed toward us, roaring and crackling over the dry ground, we pressed our backs to the cliff wall.

"God Almighty," Jeb whispered.

I squeezed his hand, speechless with horror.

The Apache reached down again, and his eyes flashed with dismay.

"Hurry!" he cried.

"Can you lift us both at once?" I asked desperately. But then I felt Jeb's hand on my shoulder. He was looking up at the warrior, exchanging silent words. Then he looked back to me.

"Take care of Ella," he said softly.

"Don't you dare, Jeb."

The heat was blinding, oppressive. I could barely breathe or see in the onslaught of thick gray smoke, but I caught Jeb giving the Apache a nod.

"No!" I shouted, coughing, shaking my head violently.

Jeb grabbed my hand. He pressed a firm kiss to it, then yanked my fist up to the Apache.

"Jeb! No!"

The warrior's strong grip wrapped around my wrist, and he pulled me up with startling speed. I tried to kick, but he didn't release me. I stretched my free hand to Jeb, screaming. "No! No!"

Above me, Ella reached over the edge of the rock, shouting Jeb's name.

The flames below clawed at my shoes and bare ankles. They caught onto my skirt and seared my skin. Through the ruthless smoke below, I could just make out a final, mournful flash of Jeb's brown eyes. And then the Apache gave a big heave, pulling me over the ledge.

I crumbled to the high ground with an anguished cry. The Apache rushed to stamp out my burning skirt, but I wished he wouldn't. In that moment, I felt like dying right there on the hot sand.

But then I noticed Ella, still reaching for the flames, screaming for Jeb with raw anguish. I fell to her side. She resisted my embrace with all of her might, crying and sobbing for Jeb. I held her tight until she collapsed, her little body shaking with sobs, and I knew that even if I truly did want to die, I couldn't. And I couldn't break down, either, not here, not yet. For Ella, I had to be strong.

"It is not safe yet," the Apache said, crouching beside me, his voice gentle but tense. "We cannot stay here."

I felt the heat of the fire behind us. Tongues of flame curled up from the edge of the ravine. Thinking of Jeb down there hurt me more than any burn could have. A scream boiled in my throat, desperate to escape. It took all of my strength to keep myself together.

The Apache took my hand. "We must run."

He pulled us through a narrow path of red-rock. Smoke from the advancing inferno followed, relentless and cruel. The heat hung heavy on the air. When the rock widened, I spotted a black horse tied to a low pine.

Ella and I were too dazed with grief and fear to protest as the Apache lifted us onto the beast's back. He jumped on behind me, gave the animal one gentle kick, and we tore off across the wide desert.

The horse's hooves pounded fiercely against the moon-bleached sand, and the wind beat in our ears. We didn't speak. Finally, after what felt like hours, a settlement surfaced on the dark horizon. A wide adobe wall spread out before us as we drew closer. Behind it, a church dozed beneath the branches of shade trees and a large willow. I recognized the exposed bell tower and the run-down, crumbling wall. It was St. Ignacio.

We rode up the gates, and the warrior called for the horse to slow. The trauma had finally overwhelmed Ella, and she'd collapsed into sleep against me in spite of the long, pounding journey. Seeing this, the warrior hopped down from the horse. He gently lifted Ella, then reached for me with his free arm.

In the pale moonlight he looked tall and strong as an ox. His long black hair hung over his shoulders and blew gently in the wind like dark feathers. He wore thick pants, a vest over his bare chest. My face warmed to my ears as he lifted me effortlessly from the horse.

Stepping onto solid ground, my saddle-sore legs wobbled, but I kept my composure. I quickly smoothed down my wind-blasted hair and wrinkled clothes. I probably looked as bedraggled as I felt.

Seeing a patch of singed fabric on my dress, the memories came flooding back in a river of fire. Mama. Papa. And Jeb. Oh, Jeb.

I scanned the dark, night-bathed surroundings of the mission. The quiet whistle of wind over the desert filled me with a consuming emptiness I couldn't escape.

Just then, I felt a hand on my arm. The warrior held Ella out to me, and I took her into my arms. The sight of her face, so sweet and utterly peaceful in sleep, only twisted the knife of sorrow deeper in my throat.

"You can stay here," the Apache said. "The fathers will protect you for a time."

"Thank you," I said softly. "For everything." Suddenly, words felt like little rocks in my mouth, but I forced myself on. "I…remember your face but not your name."

"Yahnuiyo," he said. "Yahn."

I didn't dare meet his gaze. "It's so strange to see you again. And under these circumstances…"

He turned his face in the direction of Haydenville. "My people did not burn your home," he said, somehow answering the very question I hadn't dared to ask. "Or your village."

"Then who did?" I asked quietly.

Yahn's gaze was firm on me. "May we never have to find out."

I flexed my grip over Ella. Something in his tone made me want her as close as possible.

"Leave if you can," he said. "Go far from these desert lands. Take your sister."

His words sent a shiver over me. Perhaps sensing this, he softened. "I am sorry," he said. "For the loss of your brother. I regret deeply that I could not save him." The sincerity in his voice stung my heart like a hot needle.

He sighed and took up his horse's reins. "Farewell."

"You're leaving us?"

"The fathers will take care of you. They are good men."

He mounted his horse. I took a halting step forward. "Will I ever see you again?" The words had tumbled out before I could stop them. I immediately snapped my gaze away, but then looked back.

"Perhaps, Maggie Davis. Perhaps."

The Catholic friars opened their gates warily, eyeing us in the faint candlelight. When I explained what had happened, they exchanged grim frowns. People had been uneasy enough after hearing about Buena. To find out that it had happened again sent a chill through the air. Some didn't want us to be allowed entrance, afraid the Apaches would follow to finish the job.

But the Father Superior stepped up from the shadows and spoke one phrase. "Suffer the little children to come unto me."

It was all he needed to say. The friars opened the gates.

When they had settled Ella and me into their spare quarters in the nuns' wing, I pulled Ella into my arms on the lumpy, straw-filled mattress. The room was barren, cold, and deathly quiet. So quiet, we had no choice but to face everything that had happened, everything we'd lost.

I was now all Ella had in the world. How could I possibly take care of her? How could I be her mama and papa when I was practically a kid myself? Lying there with my sister, I'd never felt so small or helpless. I didn't want her to see my tears, but then I noticed that she was crying softly. She looked up into my eyes, trembling.

"Jeb," she said, her voice hoarse and weak with sorrow.

The sound of his name on her lips broke me. I took her into my arms, unable to stop the flood of grief. Clinging to each other on the little bed, Ella and I wept well into the night.

Get tangled up in our Entangled Teen titles…

Hover *by Melissa West*

On Earth, Ari Alexander was taught to never peek, but if she hopes to survive life on her new planet, Log, her eyes must never shut. Because Zeus will do anything to save the Ancients from their dying planet, and he has a plan. On Loge, nothing is as it seems…and no one can be trusted.

Blurred *by Tara Fuller*

Cash's problems only leave him alone when he's with Anaya, Heaven's beautiful reaper. But Anya's dead, and Cash's soul resides in an expired body, making him a shadow walker, able to move between worlds. As the lines between life and death blur, Anaya and Cash find themselves falling helplessly over the edge...

Naturals *by Tiffany Truitt*

Ripped away from those she loves most, Tess is heartbroken as her small band of travelers reaches the Isolationist camp in the mysterious and barren Middlelands. Desperate to be reunited with James, the forbidden chosen one who stole her heart, she wants nothing to do with the rough Isolationists, who are without allegiance in the war between the Westerners and Easterners. But having their protection, especially for someone as powerful as Tess, may come at a cost.

Get tangled up in our Entangled Teen titles...

The Liberator *by Victoria Scott*

When Dante is given his first mission as a liberator to save the soul of seventeen-year-old Aspen, he knows he's got this. But Aspen reminds him of the rebellious life he used to live and is making it difficult to resist sinful temptations. Though Dante is committed to living clean for his girlfriend Charlie, this dude's been a playboy for far too long... and old demons die hard. Dante will have to go somewhere he never thought he'd return to in order to accomplish the impossible: save the girl he's been assigned to, and keep the girl he loves.

Everlast *by Andria Buchanan*

When Allie has the chance to work with her friends and some of the popular kids on an English project, she jumps at the chance to be noticed. And her plan would have worked out just fine...if they hadn't been sucked into a magical realm through a dusty old book of fairy tales in the middle of the library. Now, Allie and her classmates are stuck in Nerissette, a world where karma rules and your social status is determined by what you deserve. Which makes a misfit like Allie the Crown Princess, and her archrival the scullery maid.

Dear Cassie *by Lisa Burstein*

You'd think getting sent to a rehabilitation camp after being arrested on prom night would be the worst thing that happened to Cassie Wick. You'd be wrong. Chronicled in Cassie's diary over the course of her 30-day rehab, Cassie's story is one of hope, redemption, and the power of love.